DEAD SAND

A LEWIS COLE MYSTERY

BRENDAN DuBOIS

THE NEW ENGLAND
STEAMSHIP COMPANY
OF MASSACHUSETTS

POCKET BOOKS
New York   London   Toronto   Sydney   Tokyo   Singapore

POCKET BOOKS, a division of Simon & Schuster Inc.
1230 Avenue of the Americas, New York, NY 10020

Copyright © 1994 by Brendan DuBois

Published by arrangement with Otto Penzler Books

All rights reserved, including the right to reproduce
this book or portions thereof in any form whatsoever.
For information address Otto Penzler Books/Macmillan
Publishing Company, a division of Macmillan, Inc.,
866 Third Avenue, New York, NY 10022

ISBN: 0-671-89998-8

First Pocket Books printing March 1995

10 9 8 7 6 5 4 3 2 1

POCKET and colophon are registered trademarks of
Simon & Schuster Inc.

Cover art by Marc Burckhardt

Printed in the U.S.A.

This is for my parents, Arthur and Mary DuBois

Cover art by Marc Hirschfeldt

Printed in the U.S.A.

The author wishes to thank Mona Pinette, Jed Mattes, William Wrenn, and the members of his family and the Cadaver Club for their advice, assistance, support, and friendship.

roads leading into Tyler Beach, and took out three state police

I'M NOT MUCH OF AN EXPERT ON HIGHWAY safety, but I would guess that the bright red Toyota Celica was going at least double the 25-mile-per-hour speed limit that evening when it left Cable Road and struck the utility pole and the stone wall. The pole was splintered and bent, and gray stones from the wall had been cast into someone's front yard. The car was now twisted and steaming, cast off like a crumpled-up beer can, the doors having been scissored open by firefighters from the uptown station of the Tyler Fire Department. The teenage boy and girl in the car had been taken away in two fire department ambulances not five minutes ago, and I had sat there on the stone wall, not moving, watching the firefighters at work.

It was the first warm weekend in June after a cold and recession-darkened spring, and the crowds with their money, towels, and suntan lotion were streaming into Tyler and onto its beaches from Massachusetts and Maine, Quebec and Montreal, bringing with them a sense of frenzy, of knowing that the summer was open to them after so many cruel and cold months, and determined to squeeze every bit of fun out of the next twelve weeks.

Sometimes their search for fun landed them in town-owned vehicles, like ambulances or police cars.

I sat on an undisturbed section of the stone wall, my brown topsiders resting in the tall grass, my tan reporter's notebook in my hands. At the side of Cable Road two men in a Public Service of New Hampshire line truck were getting ready for their work, and a green-and-white police cruiser from the Tyler Police Department was at the sharp curve of Cable Road, the strobes of its lights casting pillars of blue across the houses on the road. People from the homes were standing at the side of the road and in their yards in silence, sometimes murmuring to each other, as if embarrassed at being there. Two of the uniforms were taking pictures and getting tape measurements and Detective Diane Woods was talking to two of the fire-fighters. A red pumper truck was farther down the road, its engine making a loud rumbling that seemed to make my teeth ache.

Hanging from a clip attached to the collar of my red polo shirt—distinctive because it didn't have any reptiles or mammals stitched over its chest—was a thin plastic card. It said PRESS IDENTIFICATION in capital letters and was issued by the New Hampshire Department of Safety, and in two sections it said: THIS WILL IDENTIFY *LEWIS COLE* AS A STAFF MEMBER OF *Shoreline*. In other sections the ID said I was six feet tall, with blue eyes and dark brown hair, and the listed date of birth gave me an age of thirty-five. The photo is as good as one can expect, since it came from the same people in the state who issue drivers' licenses.

To get the press ID, I had to provide a letter to the Department of Safety from my editor at *Shoreline* and provide the basic bio, and report to a National Guard armory in Porter some weeks later to get my photo taken. That's it. Tonight I had it on my chest because it was summer and, although I knew all of the full-time members of the Tyler Police Department, I didn't know all of the part-timers. The part-timers—called special police officers—are hired for a three-month period to fill out the department at the time when Tyler and Tyler Beach are among the most populous spots in the Northeast. I wanted to avoid trouble with any new cop, and avoiding trouble is something I've always tried to do, with some success.

Diane Woods came walking over to me, a thin smile on her tanned face. Diane was wearing her summer uniform of black running shoes, blue jeans, and a buttoned short-sleeve shirt. The shirt was blue with thin white stripes, and was not tucked in, the better to hide her badge—clipped to her belt—and her revolver—a Ruger .357, snug in a waist holster. She had short but thick light brown hair, cut in a wedge shape that an Olympic ice-skater some years ago had made popular. Diane thought it was the latest fashion, which was probably true for this state. She stands three inches shorter than me and when she smiles, it can warm the heart of a Colombian hit man, but when she frowns, it's as if her skin is stretched over the bones of her skull. She has a short scar on her chin, from a time when she was a uniform and a drunk struck her head in the booking room at the Tyler police station. Besides leaving her with a scar, the incident also left her with a distaste for drunks and a hatred of having her back exposed, either out on the streets or in her office.

She came up to me and said, "Seen enough?"

I shrugged. "Nothing I can use, you know that. They going to make it?"

She turned and looked at the car. The front tire was flat and for a silly moment I almost said, What a pain, to have to change that tire.

"I hope so, Lewis," she said. "I certainly hope so."

"You want them to live because they should live, or because it'd mean less work for you if it's not a fatal?"

Diane's light smile flickered. "You can sometimes be a bastard, Lewis Cole."

"Sometimes," I agreed. "Ready to ride?"

"Yeah. Let's see if we can do some real cop work tonight."

I got up and followed her to her unmarked cruiser, a dark blue Crown Victoria with blackwall tires and a whip antenna at the trunk, which was the best unmarked cruiser the Tyler selectmen could afford, and which was also instantly identifiable to those people in Tyler who had an interest in things illegal. As I went past the Toyota I glanced in to see what was left behind. The windshield had been shattered, scattering fingernail-sized chunks of glass throughout the interior, and there was crusty blood along both front seats, and a woman's black high-heeled shoe, stuck between the brake and clutch pedal.

Among other things I write for a monthly magazine. I don't write for a newspaper. I was with Diane this night to tickle my mind for an upcoming column, and this accident wasn't going to do it. I kept on walking.

From Cable Road we made a left onto Route 51, which is a straight shot to the east and to Tyler Beach. Though the Crown Vic had air-conditioning, I had my window down: cold air from air conditioners gives me a headache and I like the smell of the ocean and the salt marsh. Traffic was fairly steady for the one-mile ride to the beach, and the night sky was clear, but the streetlights and the glow from the beach faded out all but the brightest stars. Before us and about a mile away was a long stretch of low lights, marking the cottages and hotels, bars and motels, and the famous and popular Strip of Tyler Beach, featured in newspapers and magazines that pay their writers better than mine. Rearing up near us was the water tower for the beach, painted white with TYLER in large black letters. Off to the north and beyond the marsh were the dimmer lights of North Beach and to the south, two miles away by

Tyler Harbor and other flatlands of the marsh, were the white-and-orange lights of the Falconer nuclear power plant.

Route 51 is two-lane and narrow and has one of the highest traffic accident rates in the state. There have been studies and letters to the editors and campaigns to the Department of Transportation to have the road widened, but it will never happen, unless the governor himself is killed in an accident or the Republicans succeed in dismantling the entire Environmental Protection Agency. The road is bounded on both sides by federally protected marshland, and there will never be any additional construction allowed on the marshland here or anywhere in this state. Period.

That reminded me of something and I said to Diane, "You hear anything new about the Body in the Marsh case?"

She made a face and said, one hand casually on the steering wheel, "You know, Lewis, that's a case I could really sink my teeth into. Remains of a woman found in the marsh. Mysterious death. Unknown cause. Wrapped in canvas. Instead of a good case like that, I might have to investigate a fatal 'cause two bonehead teenagers decided to get drunk on wine coolers."

When we got to Tyler Beach, we took a right onto Ashburn Avenue, which goes one-way south, to Tyler Harbor and to Falconer. The traffic at this hour was even heavier, almost bumper-to-bumper. Most of the cars and pickup trucks were playing rock music, and people were crowded along the sidewalks. So many people, so many places to go. It made me feel like I was missing something important, something I would always remember from this summer.

"Jealous of the North Tyler cops?" I asked.

"Insanely."

A little over a week ago, a developer in North Tyler—next town over—was doing some illegal trench work in one of the marshes between the town and the ocean, when his backhoe dug up the remains of a woman, wrapped in canvas. No ID or anything. The marsh had preserved the body fairly well and the best guesses from the M.E.'s office was that she had been buried there for at least thirty to forty years; besides the initial flurry of articles in the Tyler *Chronicle* by Paula Quinn, there had been no more information released by the North Tyler cops.

I was going to say something else when the radio chattered to Diane and she made a sharp turn and I felt the small of my back press into the seat as she accelerated the Crown Vic. The night air was quite warm and I was sure I was sweating. Something was up.

Within two minutes we were on Dogleg Avenue, a short street that jutted off at an angle from Ashburn and headed to the harbor before petering out in a dirt parking lot. What's known as the main beach at Tyler is mostly bound in between Atlantic Avenue (also known as Route 1-A), which runs parallel to Tyler Beach and the ocean. Between Atlantic Avenue and Ashburn is a confusing collection of cottages, motels, grocery stores, miniature golf courses, and stores that sell everything from Frisbees to black-and-red T-shirts that say TYLER BEACH, EVERY SUMMER. Rising up over all of this was the Tyler Beach Palace, a two-story wooden structure that contains dozens of shops, arcades, and a stage for rock concerts, where most of the bands that play are either on their way up or out.

At this part of Tyler Beach, most of the streets connecting the parallel avenues of Atlantic and Ashburn are lettered, going from A Street to T Street. Think of a long ladder with the rungs being the lettered streets and that gives you a pretty good idea of the layout. The joke among the old-timers at Tyler Beach is that the town is lucky the genius who named the streets didn't number them, or there'd be a street called "To Keep Counting, Take Your Shoes Off" between 10th and 11th.

Dogleg was shaped like an animal's leg, crooked and bent. It was lined on both sides by one- and two-story cottages, and cars with Massachusetts and New York license plates were parked on the cracked asphalt sidewalks. Diane pulled the cruiser over at a yellow cottage that had a number 12 painted on the front steps. Less than two minutes ago the call had come to her from Tyler dispatch: Report of a body at 12 Dogleg Avenue. No other information. The caller was possibly male and had hung up.

I got out of the Crown Vic and joined Diane in front of the cottage. There were men and women and only a few children visible along the street, sitting on cars or on folding chairs in front of the cottages, most of which had no heat and soiled furniture and 1950s-era appliances and usually rented for several hundred dollars a week. Some deal. From up and down the narrow street I saw a furtive motion of hands and the clinking of glass as beer and wine bottles were hidden away. Tyler has a tough open-container ordinance, to cut down on such vacation attractions as public drunkenness, vomiting, and urination, but Diane had more important things on her mind. There was loud rock music from one of the cottages, the lyrics saying something like, "Bang your head, kill your parents."

"See any lights?" she asked, carrying a portable radio in one hand and a long black flashlight in the other.

"Not a one."

She sighed. "Jesus, I hate this shit."

The cottage was one story and had a small porch, and if it contained anything larger than a family of two, they'd be elbowing each other just getting from one room to the next. The yellow paint was peeling and I saw something that gave me a little twinge: in this hot weather, every window was closed, and every shade was drawn. I pointed that out to Diane, and she said, "Looks worse and worse. Let's take a look."

We walked up to the porch and flies buzzed around us from three or four bursting green bags of trash piled in one corner. The door was locked and Diane knocked a few times with the long flashlight, saying, "Tyler Police, anyone home?"

There was no sound. From up the street I heard some more

rock music and I looked at the people in the cars and chairs, the men mostly shirtless and with beer guts, the women in shorts and smoking cigarettes, and here they were, with one of the most beautiful beaches in the Northeast a walk away, and you'd think they were in the parking lot of Sullivan Stadium in Massachusetts, waiting for the hapless Patriots to play.

"You looking for backup?" I asked.

She shifted the radio in her hand and gave me a curt smile. "Why, Lewis? I've got you here."

"Glad to make you feel better."

"Appreciate that."

Diane knocked again, harder, and nearly yelled, "Tyler Police, anyone home?" and, in a softer voice, "I hate barging in—depending what we find, some scuzz defense lawyer may call this an illegal entry."

I looked around us and said, "Diane, I think I hear someone in there, calling for help. And I'd be a witness to that."

She seemed startled and said, "What—oh. I understand. Thanks, Lewis. Come to think of it, I thought I heard something, too. Here. Hold this."

Diane handed over her flashlight and in a moment reached under her shirt and pulled out her Ruger .357, and I felt tingly again and wished that instead of a flashlight, I was carrying one of my own pieces, a 9-mm Beretta or my .32 Browning. But on ride-alongs Diane is adamant that I don't carry a weapon because of some department procedure and insurance regulations. Diane also tells me that she doesn't trust automatics, and I've told her that I don't trust weapons that are only good for stirring drinks after six shots, but since she can beat me shooting at the police range without breathing hard, I always let it slide.

With one sharp motion she shattered a pane in the door and reached in past the flapping curtain and opened it wide. The door creaked and the thick smell assaulted me, and I said, "Diane, this definitely does not look good."

She took a few steps, saying "Shit, shit" over and over again in a whisper, and I stood with her, switching the flashlight on, and things became very bright and very awful.

Something moved before us and Diane brought up her piece in a quick motion, saying, "Who's there?" and then she took a deep breath and let her hands drop to her side. I stood with her and tried to breathe through my mouth, not wanting to think of what bacteria and odors were settling on my tongue.

The young woman before us was dressed in a man's white T-shirt that went to mid-thigh. Her flesh was swollen against the soiled fabric of the shirt and I saw that her toes and fingernails were painted red. Her eyes were closed. I was thankful for that. Her hair was long and blond. At her feet, fallen over to the side, was a wood three-legged stool. There were dark stains on the floor and along her legs.

Her head was canted sharply to one side, as if tilted to hear some far-off whisper. The flesh around her neck was also swollen, so I could only make out the rope as it went up past her head to the open rafters of the cottage's ceiling.

She moved again, twisting from side to side, as a breeze came through the open door. Diane backed away, the glass crunching underneath her feet, and I was with her in a moment, standing on the porch, both of us blinking our eyes quite hard.

Diane looked at me with no expression and said, "What a goddamn waste." She picked up her portable radio and started making her calls for a backup unit, an ambulance, and the medical examiner's office.

I stood on the porch, still breathing through my mouth. My four-wheel-drive Range Rover was parked at the Tyler police station, a five-minute walk away. It was late and I was tired and needed a drink.

As I mentioned before, among other things I write for a monthly magazine. I don't write for a newspaper. This really wasn't something for *Shoreline* magazine.

But it was something for me. I stayed.

2

ON SATURDAY MORNING I WAS RIDING MY TEN-
speed along the seawall at the north end
of Tyler Beach, known for some unknown reason as North
Beach. There are no stores or restaurants or fried-dough booths
on North Beach, just the concrete seawall to the east and about
a hundred feet's worth of Atlantic Avenue and beach homes
and condos with such names as SeaView and Tide Pond to the
west, and, beyond that, the flat emptiness of the salt marsh. I
headed south, to Weymouth's Point, which has some of the
more exclusive homes in Tyler and mostly unexclusive people.
Beyond Weymouth's Point is the main beach at Tyler, where
I had been until at least two this morning.

The morning was cool, with an ocean fog that made it impossible to see more than thirty feet or so of the ocean, which
roared softly against the rocks and empty beach. The sea gulls
were quiet this morning, racing in and out of the fog like plaster
models on wires, making not a sound. Some of the cars driving
by, their tires humming softly on the slightly wet road, had
their headlights on and their wiper blades going at slow speeds,
smearing away the fog's moisture.

I stopped and leaned my bicycle against the concrete wall, looking out to the fog and the ocean. I had on a pair of cutoff dungarees, a blue-and-white UNH T-shirt, and a pair of Nikes that had seen better miles. I had the sidewalk to myself. Another car drove by and was followed by a woman on a bicycle, wearing red-and-green tights and with a radio headset against her ears. I smiled at her and she made no motion, no change of expression, as she whispered by. She probably didn't like the battered black Schwinn I was riding or my clothes. Not fancy enough, I guess.

The sun began to glimmer through the clouds. The fog would burn off soon. I thought about last night, about what might have happened to force a young girl onto a stool to kill herself by slow strangulation. Something about it bothered me, something that made me look behind me at odd moments. I waited and I thought and I wondered what it would all look like, once the fog had burned off.

The night before, about a minute after Diane had spoken into her portable radio, she came back from the trunk of her Crown Vic with a thick roll of yellow crime-scene tape (POLICE LINE—DO NOT CROSS), and I helped her block off the cottage. As we unwound the tape she said, "You touch anything in the cottage when we were there?"

"Nope." I tied one end of the tape around a utility pole. "And you?"

"Not a goddamn thing."

"Except for the doorknob."

Diane said, "Shit. Yeah, the doorknob. But I only undid the lock, Lewis. Didn't touch the entire knob."

"Suspicious?" By then we were going down a narrow dirt driveway that separated the yellow cottage from its green neighbor. The grass looked brown and stunted, and I was sure not much light ever got between the two cottages.

"Always suspicious," she said. "Always. We got an untimely

death here, no matter what else happens. And I want to keep everything tight before we decide just how untimely it is."

Within a few minutes Dogleg Avenue became even more crowded, and I snapped my press ID back on and leaned against the trunk of Diane's Crown Vic. Two more Tyler cruisers showed up, along with a black Saab that belonged to the county medical examiner. A news photographer—paunchy, bearded, with a Banana Republic vest and camera bag—stood outside the taped barrier, taking photos. He nodded at me and I returned the gesture. I knew he worked free-lance for the Tyler *Chronicle,* but I had forgotten his name. I wondered what was keeping the paper's reporter, Paula Quinn, and I saw the photographer pull out a reporter's notepad and talk to Diane. He was probably stringing the story as well.

Diane came over to me and said, "You don't have to stay, you know."

"I want to."

She looked at me oddly. "This for *Shoreline* or something else?"

"My curiosity, what else."

Diane made to say something but a light blue Lincoln Town Car pulled up and she muttered, "Shit," as a heavyset man in his early fifties got out of the car. He had on dark pink polyester pants, white shoes, white belt, and a snug black polo shirt that gave him a round, polished look. He was tanned, and his thin white hair was combed back, held up in a slight pompadour with hairspray. His face was a weird mix of firmness and fleshiness, and he looked like a retired pimp on vacation. He was Jack Fowler, owner of Fowler Motel, the Fowler House restaurant, a few grocery stores, and a laundromat, and prominent in the local Chamber of Commerce. His family was fairly well represented in the town governments and police departments in this part of Wentworth County. He was also the chairman of the Tyler board of selectmen—the two men and single woman who were the town's part-time government. I think

Jefferson said people pretty much get the government they deserve. I wasn't too sure if the people of Tyler deserved this.

He came right over to Diane and I caught a whiff of his clearance-sale cologne, and I caught him asking something about the poor girl, and Diane said, "No, not a thing, Jack," and I resumed looking at the crowd. I wondered if anyone there knew her, knew who she was and what had happened to her, and I was awfully glad at that moment that I didn't work for a newspaper, because an editor would probably make me work the crowd. I don't mind talking to people who are grieving—it's something I've done before. I just mind being told to do it. So instead of talking I resumed waiting.

Diane walked away with Jack a few feet, and I knew she was talking to him through clenched teeth. The Tyler Police Department has only one full-time detective to handle major crimes, and I was looking at her pretty jean-encased butt as she walked to the cottage. Jack Fowler was the main reason for the department's lack of detectives, because he had his We're Really Overtaxed and Can't Afford Big-City Police Luxuries speech down pat for every March's town meeting. Jack Fowler stood next to Diane, looking grave and serious, and then he smiled after the *Chronicle*'s photographer had taken his picture.

Two firefighters came out of the cottage, carrying the folded gurney with a blanket-enclosed shape on it, tightly belted in, and I thought for a moment that the smell had come back to my tongue. There was a sigh from the vacationers and beach-goers behind the barrier, and their camera flashes joined those of the *Chronicle*'s photographer. Some vacation shots, I supposed, to go between those of Dad and Mom at the beach and Sis and Buddy eating their first lobster.

They put her into the rear of the ambulance and slammed the door. The firefighters in their dark blue uniforms looked sweaty and tired, and I knew they had just come back from Exonia Hospital after bringing in either the driver or passenger from the Toyota Celica. Thinking of what had happened earlier, I wasn't sure that the young girl from the cottage would be alone in the hospital's morgue that night.

In a while Jack Fowler eased his bulk back into the Lincoln Town Car and left, and when Diane came out from the cottage again, I asked her if I could go back inside.

"Your curiosity again?"

"You got it."

She looked over at the photographer. "He might be pissed if he doesn't get invited."

"Then invite him later. I go in and come out and go home and leave you alone. How does that sound?"

The past hour had dirtied up her hair and her hands were sweaty from having worn latex gloves. "Sure. Why the hell not. Just be careful not to touch a thing."

She went inside the cottage with me and spoke for a moment to the two uniforms—wearing black-zippered jumpsuits—who were taking photographs and drawing diagrams on clipboards. I knew them both by sight and they nodded and went back to work. The lights were now on, making everything seem much smaller than when I was there earlier, carrying the flashlight. The stool was still on its side and there were stains on the wooden floor. The rope was still hanging from a beam in the rafters, dangling free. It had been cut in the middle to allow the firefighters to load the girl's body onto the gurney, and to keep the knotted piece around her neck for the autopsy. What a job. Against the wall was a black vinyl couch with a red-checked blanket tossed over one side. There were rips in the black vinyl, with white stuffing hanging out. There was a dusty television set, a Sony boombox, and a scattering of cassette tapes on the floor. All of the windows were closed. All of the shades were drawn. So embarrassed at what she was doing, she drew the shades beforehand?

Before the couch was a lobster trap made up to be a coffee table, with a slab of plywood over it. On the plywood were a mess of magazines for young women, *Savvy* and *Seventeen*, and some advertising circulars. There was also a buff envelope, with an address: Lynn Germano, 12 Dogleg Avenue, Tyler, N.H. I could just make out the postmark: Lawrence, Massachusetts.

Off to the right was a kitchenette area, with a Formica table and two metal chairs—why anyone would have designed something so uncomfortable to eat on was beyond me—and a minifridge and hot plate.

I went past the two uniforms and through an open door, into her bedroom. There was a single bed, with a pile of pale sheets and a solitary wool blanket. The closet was an open space in the wall filled with dresses and blouses hanging from wooden hangers, and there was a mirrored bureau, with makeup and hairbrushes scattered about. There were four high school photos stuck into the side of the mirror: three girls and a boy. All were smiling, all looked confident, all looked like they would live forever. Another door led into a bathroom, with sink, toilet, and a metal shower stall that looked slimy, and another shelf filled with hair spray, mousse, shampoo, and the usual other bathroom items.

Back in the bedroom, a wooden ladder led up to the rafters. There was a black curtain there, pulled back, and two suitcases and a duffel bag. Storage area. I looked back into the living room and saw the two uniforms, dusting away at the mini-fridge. I climbed up the ladder and peered into the storage area. Part of the area was cleared away, and there was an electrical extension cord, leading away and into a wall. I climbed back down and stood still for a moment, trying to remember what it was like when I was in high school, wondering about what little pressures of grades and friendships had whispered to me, of going over the edge, of doing something crazy, like stealing the family car and driving off to California. I thought about what might have pushed her. I wondered if it was an event, or a person. I remembered again the closed eyes, the swollen body, the faint *creak-creak* of the rope rubbing against the rafter as she shifted in the breeze, and I went outside, feeling hot and greasy.

Diane was leaning against the trunk of her Crown Vic, writing on a metal clipboard. She was nibbling on her lower lip and some of her fine, short brown hair hung forward.

"Her name be Lynn Germano?" I asked.

"That's what we're working with, but you never know." She looked up at me and flipped her hair back. "Do me a favor, Lewis. I don't know if this is something personal for you or for *Shoreline*, but don't start tracing the name quite yet. Let me do that."

"It's yours," I said. Most of the crowd had drifted back to their own porches and seats. With the body gone, the show was over. It was now time to get back to drinking, smoking, and yelling at each other, and other wonderful beach pastimes.

"Any note?"

She was back writing. "Nope. No note." She put the pen down on the pad and rubbed at the back of her neck. "Next day or so will be rough, Lewis. Gotta find out who she is, trace her movements the last twenty-four hours, find out what could have depressed her so much that she killed herself."

"And find out who your mystery caller was."

"Ah, the mystery caller," Diane repeated softly. "Maybe a boyfriend. Maybe someone who was breaking into the house and panicked. Or someone who was walking by and peeked through an open shade and saw her dangling there. Love to find out who that caller was, Lewis."

I tasted the air and it was the taste of salt and exhaust. I no longer tasted what was inside the cottage, and I was glad for small favors.

"Time?" I asked.

"Almost one in the morning. You heading out?"

"Yeah, I can walk to the station from here. You be in touch?"

She smiled and touched my hand briefly. "As always, Lewis."

I walked up Dogleg Avenue, smelling the pungent odor of someone brave enough to smoke a green leafy matter in the presence of so many cops, and then walked along Ashburn Avenue. A Camaro drove by, people inside yelling in my direction for no apparent reason, and in a couple of minutes I retrieved my dark green Range Rover from the lot behind the Tyler police station, a squat, one-story cinderblock building. I tossed the PRESS PARKING sign under my seat and in a matter of seconds was heading north on Atlantic Avenue. Traffic was thinning out, with most of the drivers around then leaving because they were bored or they had someone male/female to spend time with, or some other excuse. My excuse was that I was tired, and nothing else.

From over the darkness of the ocean I saw the star Vega, and its hard brilliance stayed with me on the short drive home.

I pushed myself off the concrete seawall and resumed bicycling to the south, then took a left up onto Weymouth Road, which looped through the outcropping of land called Weymouth's Point. Homes on this part of Tyler Beach sell for $300,000—minimum—and my destination that morning was the most exclusive home of them all. The road was steep and shaped like a U, and at the base of the U at the top of the hill was a chest-high stone wall and an open wooden gate. The nearest homes on either side of the wall were at least a hundred feet away. Beyond the gate was a two-story house, late Victorian, with an attached garage. Both house and garage were painted white, and parked in the garage was a dark blue Volvo. I drove my bike onto the gravel driveway and leaned it against the front porch.

A woman was sitting on the porch in a white wicker chair, and she took off her glasses as I went up the three stairs. Alice Crenshaw. Alice had never told me her age, though I guessed her to be in her mid-fifties. She had on sandals, knee-length black shorts, and a sleeveless red blouse with three buttons at the throat. Her skin was tanned and fairly firm, and she loved to boast that she had not one varicose vein. Even on an early Saturday morning she was carefully made up, with painted toenails and fingernails, and red lipstick. The flesh about her face sagged only a bit, though there were fine wrinkles about her eyes and lips. Her eyes were a moist blue, and her hair was light blond, permed into a shape that I jokingly teased Alice was her own personal crash helmet.

I also once teased her about her meticulous appearance and in an uncommon bout of seriousness, she had said, "When you get to a certain age, Lewis, appearances count. Sometimes they're the only things that count."

On her lap was the *Boston Globe*, and at her elbow was a wicker stool, with a used ashtray and empty glass. We touched hands briefly and she said, "Thirsty, Lewis?"

"Always, you know that."

She smiled at me. "Probably too early in the morning for someone like you to drink, but I can get you an orange juice, with no kick."

"That would be fine."

I followed her into her living room and to a wide kitchen, with windows that looked over a bluff of land that was the very edge of Weymouth's Point. The home had been in Alice's family since the turn of the century—the Gilliam family—and she had been raised there, growing up as the only child of a doctor who was prominent in Tyler in the 1940s and 1950s. Dr. Gilliam had done well for himself and his family, for even that many years ago real estate was expensive on Weymouth's Point.

She poured two glasses of orange juice and we went out to a rear porch from the kitchen, and she sat in another wicker chair while I sat on the porch railing. From there the ocean's sounds were much louder, and the fog had finally burned off. Out on the swells of the ocean the Isles of Shoals were visible, as well as a red-and-black tanker, heading to Porter and the

Piscassic River. Tiny colored buoys belonging to lobster fishermen that worked out of Tyler Harbor and Wallis Harbor—farther north—bobbed in the ocean's swells. Up along the north was the concrete seawall I had just bicycled past, and the land curved out again to the east, forming a tree-covered point: Samson Point, site of the Samson State Wildlife Preserve, and former site of the Samson Point Coast Artillery Station. Just before the point of land was a tiny cove, where the shingled roof of a small home was barely visible. My home, purchased after much pain and expense.

At my elbow on the porch was a U.S. Navy quartermaster's spyglass, mounted on a swivel set into the railing, which had belonged to the late John Crenshaw, Alice's husband and navy veteran. The spyglass had been the cause of the introduction between Alice and myself. A year ago, biking past her house on a summer afternoon, I had seen her standing at the gate, and she had called out: "You must be the man with the telescope. Why don't you ever wave back?"

That had made me stop. On the small deck off my bedroom on the second floor, I often brought out my 4½-inch reflecting telescope, but only at night. I really didn't have much use for such a telescope in the daytime. Thinking about that, I had rested a foot on the ground and replied, "I've been looking up at the night sky. I usually don't peek into people's homes."

She had laughed and said, "You should try it. Adds a little something to the day."

She had offered me a glass of water and I had gone out to her rear porch and sure enough, I could see my house from there, and that disturbed me a bit, that my hard-won privacy was being violated, but once I got to know Alice, it had been all right. She used her spyglass to keep track of the vessels and what was going on at the Isles of Shoals and the beaches, for the porch on her house had wonderful views of North Beach and the main beach to the south. Alice knew Tyler and its people and its history better than almost anyone else I knew.

She was on a half-dozen town boards, including the Historical Society, and she would talk for hours about the history of Tyler and its beaches and the wonderful things her father had done, and I would listen, never bored, always pleased to be in her company.

This morning she told me of a sailboat she had seen, flailing against the waves, the sails flapping and the boat almost broaching, obviously skippered by someone who didn't know one end of a sailboat from another, and I must have been staring too intently at the sea, for she stopped short and said, "You're not listening, are you?"

I then noticed that my glass was empty. "Of course I am, Alice."

She wrinkled her nose at me. "Don't lie to your elders, Lewis. I just said that when the boat got under way again, there was a couple copulating on the forward deck, and all you said was, 'Unh-hunh.' What's the matter? Something on your mind, or have you lost your interest in the two-backed beast?"

She got me there, so I told her of last night, and of seeing the body of a young woman, bloated and stained, swinging by a rope, alone in a dreary cottage, and how no matter how hard I showered when I got home, that the scent and smell remained with me for the rest of the night.

Alice shook her head and said, "Jesus, the young'uns we're raising today."

She put down her glass and crossed her legs and looked out to the Atlantic and said, "You know, when John died, I felt like one of those Egyptian mummies, the ones you see down in Boston at the art museum. Felt like all of my insides had been ripped out and dumped in those big clay jars, and that there was nothing but this big black emptiness inside me. For weeks all I wanted to do was to end it quick and join him. But I didn't. You know why? I knew he'd be pissed at me, that's why. Pissed that I couldn't have gone on without him. So I did go on without him, just to show him up."

She shook her head again and said, "What must have happened to that poor girl. They know the name yet?"

I was going to say something but I remembered my promise to Diane and said, "No, they don't. And don't be so hard on the younger generation, Alice. They face a lot of pressures none of us had to when we were growing up."

"Bah." She picked up her empty glass, remembered it was empty, and returned it to the table. "Look out on yonder ocean, Lewis. 'Bout three hundred and fifty years ago, less than a hundred Englishmen came over on two leaky boats and bumbled their way into Tyler Harbor. There was nothing here but trees, swamps, wolves, and Algonquin Indians who weren't too happy to see them. You want to talk about pressures. You tell me why there were no recorded suicides those first years of settlement."

"I'd rather not," I said, getting up from the porch railing and passing my glass over to her. "I might end up continuing this history lecture."

"Something you wouldn't appreciate, you Indiana boy."

"You forget. I'm native-born, about fifteen miles north of here, in Dover. Blame it on my parents for moving me out when I was five."

"Maybe I will. And when are you going to tell me what brought you back to New Hampshire?"

I smiled. "Never. You know that. Gotta go, Alice."

"You young goat," she said. "Here, give me a kiss before you leave."

I bent down and kissed her firmly on her lips, tasting her lipstick and tobacco, and she murmured, touching my face with her weathered hand, "Ah, if only you were twenty years older, Lewis."

"Still wouldn't work," I said, smiling.

"And why?" she said, in mock anger.

"Because you smoke, Alice, that's why."

As I walked through her living room to the front porch, she was still laughing.

The ride back to my home was slower, for the morning sun was quite bright and cars and trucks were pulling into the slant-angled parking spaces just adjacent to the seawall. The North Beach was more popular for families; the younger crowd—who raised more hell—tended to stay at the main beach, where there were shops, stores, video games, and bars. There was nothing at North Beach save for the beach and the condos and motels across Atlantic Avenue and the flatness of the marsh. I had to dodge children and parents lugging coolers and umbrellas and folded beach chairs as I bicycled north.

After about a mile the sands of North Beach disappeared into a collection of rock ledges and boulders, and the road rose up some and curved to the right. I bicycled in an easy fashion, for I was not one for racing either myself or anybody else. Traffic was heavier and I was conscious of the tons of metal speeding by me, with only feet to spare, and I was thankful when I saw the Lafayette House up ahead, for it meant I was almost home and no longer had to gamble that a driver working on his first six-pack of the day would miss me.

The Lafayette House is near the border of Tyler and North Tyler, and supposedly the Marquis de Lafayette stopped there for a quick drink in 1825 during his famed tour of the United States. Most of the original tavern is gone, of course, and the current Lafayette House was built in 1902 in the old, rambling Victorian hotel style. Its customers were mostly middle-aged people who still thought there was something glamorous about paying hundreds of dollars a week for staying at a beach. Across Atlantic Avenue was a small parking lot that said PRIVATE PARKING FOR LAFAYETTE HOUSE ONLY and I turned into the lot and went to the lot's north end, passing the parked Mercedeses, BMWs, and Porsches. There was a low stone wall and a place where some of the rocks had fallen free. There was a path open to a walker, bicyclist, or someone who owned a four-wheel-drive vehicle.

I followed the path as it went down and to the right, past my own No Trespassing signs, and my house came into view. It's a weatherbeaten cottage, two stories tall, with a dirt crawl space for a cellar and a tiny oil-furnace room. There is no lawn, just rocky soil with some green tufts of grass that poke up every summer and which I leave alone. The thin soil rises up to a steep rocky ledge that hides my home from Atlantic Avenue. To the right of my house was a sagging shed that served as a garage, and my Range Rover was parked inside. I dropped off the bicycle in the garage and went up the three stone steps to my front door, unlocked it, and went inside.

It's unusual for people to visit me here, but when they do I always enjoy their reaction as they first step into my house. They usually are surprised at the roominess and furnishings. The outside is unimpressive, and I've kept it that way, both because of historical accuracy and because of sheer laziness. The best I can guess about my house is that it was built nearly a hundred and fifty years ago and served first as a home for the supervisor of a lifeboat station that was operating at Samson's Point sometime in the middle part of the nineteenth century. When the government took over the station and built the Samson Point Coast Artillery Station, my home was junior officers' quarters. Somehow, over the years, it ended up still being owned by the U.S. government, but now it belongs to me.

That took a lot of effort and work, but there are always times when I think it was worth it.

Entering the front door there's the landing for the switchback stairs, which go up to the second floor. To the left is a wide living room, and to the right is a kitchen and dining area, which remains spotless because it's hardly ever used. There's a couch and two chairs, a stereo and G.E. television with VCR unit, and there are three bookshelves, crammed with hardcover and paperbacks, mostly history, some fiction, and a couple of biographies and astronomy texts. Framed on one wall is an old photograph of the White Fleet, the U.S. fleet that Teddy Roosevelt sent around the world in 1907 to prove that the United States was a great power to be dealt with. There's also a framed picture of the space shuttle *Discovery* taking off, and I'm sure it's a coincidence that the ships and the shuttle are both colored white. The hardwood floors are covered by Oriental rugs I purchased at estate auctions in small towns up north, and there are a couple of floor lamps. I went through the living room, past the cold and empty fireplace, and checked the green light of the answering machine and saw that it was glowing steady. No calls.

I drew open the floor-to-ceiling curtains, undid the locks to the sliding glass doors, took out the wooden rod that I had jammed into the runners, and stepped outside to the deck to catch some of the morning air before showering. The ocean was at low tide but the tide was running in, and out on the water the Isles of Shoals—nine tiny islands several miles out —looked close enough to swim to. There weren't many boats out there, and I wondered if Alice Crenshaw was disappointed. She'd have to go back to looking at the early morning sunbathers, and I would be hearing a lecture the next time I saw her about the bathing suit fashions of today's young'uns.

The deck is wide and has two wooden chairs and an outdoor grill that is about as clean as my kitchen. Below was a small cove—my own private cove, no matter what the state says. Even though the beaches along the state's eighteen miles are all public, it's hard to get to these hundred feet or so. To the south—where I could just make out Alice Crenshaw's home at the edge of Weymouth's Point—there is a mass of boulders and fissures, ravines and raw rocks, which ocean waves pounded at constantly. Only the most physical and agile bother to climb over those rocks, and with wide sandy beaches just

down the road, not many people do. And my illegal No Trespassing signs near the rocks also help.

To the north is the wooded expanse of Samson's Point, part
of the Samson State Wildlife Preserve. Most of the preserve is
open to hikers and picnickers, but the southern end—just abut-
ting my property—has been closed off because of toxic chemicals found in some of the decaying buildings that were once
part of the Samson Point Coast Artillery Station. Throughout
the preserve are underground bunkers and gun chambers, and
the day-trippers and hikers are content to spend their time there
instead of coming south and bothering me. It was an arrangement I liked.

Off somewhere I heard the sound of a helicopter. The noise
made me shiver and I went back inside and then upstairs. At
the head of the stairs is my bathroom and to the left is a small
study with desk, chair, filing cabinet, and my Apple Macintosh
Plus—with modem—which I use to write my column for *Shoreline* magazine and other things. A door to the right leads to my
bedroom.

After showering I dried myself and checked my skin, as I
always do. There are faded scars along my left side just above
my kidney, on my back near the coccyx, and on my left knee.
Every time someone sees me like this it's cause for a comment
like, "Jesus, what kind of fights have you been in?" And always, I say, "You should have seen what happened to the
other people involved." I never smile when I say that, and I
always change the subject.

In my bedroom I put on a fresh pair of light blue gym shorts
and another UNH T-shirt. My bed is an old four-poster oak
antique, and I have a matching set of oak bureaus to go with
it. In one corner, sitting on a black tripod, is my reflecting
telescope, and in another corner is another bookshelf. Once
Paula Quinn, the *Chronicle* reporter, asked me how many books
I owned, and I said I had lost track after two thousand.

Another sliding door leads out to a smaller deck on the south end of the house. Just another typical summer residence, I thought, as I dried my short hair with a towel. Except, of course, for the 12-gauge Remington pump action with extended magazine that I keep under the bed, the 8-mm FN assault rifle in the closet, the 9-mm Beretta in my study, the .357 Smith & Wesson revolver I keep in the kitchen, and the .32 Browning automatic in the downstairs closet.

Not that I'm paranoid. I just like protection.

I went downstairs and in the living room the light on my answering machine was blinking. The phone must have rung when I was in the shower. I played back the message. It was from Diane Woods, the sole detective of the Tyler Police Department, telling me something that I had already guessed: Lynn Germano had been murdered.

3

THE EIGHTEEN-MILE-LONG ROCKY SEACOAST
of New Hampshire begins after Salisbury,
Massachusetts, and ends just before Kittery, Maine. It lies entirely within Wentworth County and is anchored on both ends
by the power of uranium: the 1,150-megawatt nuclear re-
actor of Falconer Unit 1 at the southern end of the coast, producing electricity and headlines for one million New England
homes, and the naval shipyard in Porter at the northern end,
where sleek Los Angeles–class attack submarines glide into the
Piscassic River for refueling and refitting after their never-
reported-in-any-newspaper missions.

The nuclear power station at Falconer has attracted thousands of demonstrators in its short history. In researching
through years of newspaper clippings, I've not found one story
about any demonstrators at the naval shipyard in Porter. I guess
certain types of uranium attract certain types of publicity.

Route 1-A—also known as Atlantic Avenue—begins at a set
of traffic lights at the Salisbury-Falconer line. In February the
light is set on blinking yellow and the wind off the ocean blows
snow and fine sand across the cracked asphalt, past the closed

27

motels and shuttered clam huts, and the cars drive by fast, as if not daring to stop in such an empty place. In July the light is back to its normal timing, and traffic is often backed up for miles, as tattooed men from Lawrence, young women with teased hair from Lowell, and sweating families from towns and cities along the north shore of Massachusetts stream into Falconer and to Tyler Beach, crossing over the Felch Memorial Bridge, which spans the channel into Tyler Harbor.

Atlantic Avenue travels through the wide sands and the Strip at Tyler Beach, past Weymouth's Point and Samson Point, to the Samson State Wildlife Preserve. From that park, Atlantic Avenue winds its way through the wide marshlands and up and down rocky points of land, past the hotels, homes, and beaches of North Tyler, to the mansions with soft lights and long driveways in Wallis, and past Wallis Harbor. Through the crowded nineteenth-century elegance of Foss Island and the brick sprawl of Porter, one of the largest cities in New Hampshire—once known for its whorehouses during the navy days and now known for its shops that sell Italian T-shirts for $30—Atlantic Avenue ends halfway across the Piscassic River, on the Memorial Bridge going into Maine.

And out on the ocean, quietly watching it all, are the nine rocky islands of the Isles of Shoals.

On Sunday afternoon I parked my Range Rover at the State Park just adjacent to Tyler Harbor and was standing on the Felch Memorial Bridge, a bunch of early summer flowers in my hands. I had purchased them at Tyler Point Grocery and had removed the plastic wrapper and rubber band at the store before making the short walk to the bridge. Behind me was the wide harbor, mostly empty this afternoon of the lobster boats, bottom draggers, and charter boats that bring seasick tourists out for a few hours of fishing, warm beer, and vomiting. The marshland stretched out nearly to the horizon, to Route 1 and the center of the town of Tyler proper, and there were "islands" of trees and shrubs across the marsh. Near the harbor was a mass of stores, boating supply houses, and the marina support buildings, and several condominium developments, one of which housed Diane Woods of the Tyler Police Department.

Before me was the harbor's channel and the two long stone breakwaters that bordered it, leading out to the rolling waves of the Atlantic. Powerboats hammered out to the ocean, with tanned men wearing gold chains around their necks, beers in their hands, pushing the boats to high speeds. I waited for a moment of reasonable silence before I tossed the flowers into the water. They scattered on the short drop to the water, and their bright colors only lasted a minute or two before the cold Atlantic swallowed them up. But they had lasted long enough. Something tugged at me again as I thought of Carl Socha, Trent Baker, Cissy Manning, and the others, the forgotten others of my section, lost so many centuries ago. And the damnable George Walker. I looked again for the flowers but they were gone. Not much, but a ceremony nonetheless. I think they would have liked it. I hoped they did. I try to do a ceremony similar to this one every few weeks or so.

Then I walked back to my Range Rover.

The town of Tyler has always had a dual personality and rivalry between the uptown and the beach. The "uptown" is a typical New England town, with woods and some farmland and light industry, and the white-steepled churches around a small town common. The banks, the library, the town offices, and an uptown fire station are all within walking distance of each other. Route 1 runs straight through the middle of the town, and Tyler is a five-minute exit from the eight lanes of Interstate 95, which cuts through New Hampshire on its journey from Massachusetts to Maine.

Yet only ten minutes away from this typical and sober New Hampshire town are the sands of Tyler Beach, along with the Strip and the arcades, fried-dough stands, dance clubs, night-clubs with "best hooters" contests, and charming boutiques that sell roach clips, bongs, and Captain Condom T-shirts.

The relationship between the town and the beach has always been an uncomfortable one: The town has always complained that its taxes go toward big-ticket items—like the police budget—which mostly benefit the beach, and the beach always says that without the money they bring in, Tyler would have some of the highest property taxes in the state.

The fight goes on and will probably go on for years. It's sort of like the old Irish landlady who has a hooker for a tenant upstairs: She hates what's going on and hates sweeping up the broken beer and whiskey bottles every Sunday morning, but by God, she loves the high rent money that goes into her pocket every month.

Over the years there have been some compromises. The town is governed by three elected selectmen, but the beach has limited self-rule through the Tyler Beach village precinct. My friend Paula Quinn of the *Chronicle* hates to cover the village precinct meetings. "Jesus, Lewis," she complained to me one day. "It's like attending a Future Capitalists of America meeting. All they bitch and moan about is taxes and how best to drag tourists into the beach so they can better fleece them."

The Tyler police station is a result of one of those compromises, and, as in many compromises worked out in anger, it has never really satisfied anyone. On Ashburn Avenue, right next to the beach fire station, the police station is a one-story cinderblock structure that's too hot in the summer and too cold in the winter. The townies complain it's too big—all that wasted space in the fall and winter—while the beach people point out that it's too small—not enough cell space in the summer, when the hundreds of arrests each weekend provide the bulk of money in fines each year for the town and the state.

In the police station, the detective bureau is a small room in the rear, adjacent to the police locker room and the booking room, and that is where I found Diane Woods that Sunday afternoon.

There are two desks there, one for Diane and one for the other full-time detective that she's always promised every budget year, and who never shows up when the budget gets cut. The cinder blocks are painted a faint green and the room is jammed with dented black filing cabinets and cardboard filing cartons. On one wall is a chart from the DEA, listing dozens of legal and illegal drugs and their side effects, and on another wall is a poster that shows a blonde in a tight, wet, black string bikini, holding a .44 Charter Arms revolver to her large cleavage. The caption under the poster says GUN CONTROL MEANS BEING ABLE TO HIT YOUR TARGET. Some uniforms had placed the poster up as a joke, but Diane had gone them one better by leaving it there. The two windows to the office—looking out over the police parking lot—are barred, and on one windowsill a marijuana plant is growing. Diane's desk was covered with files and papers, and a stone paperweight shaped like a skull held down some reports.

She leaned back in her swivel chair and propped her feet up on the desk when I came in. She had on tight jeans and a rugby-type sweatshirt, with the sleeves pulled back. Her shoes were off and her feet were brown and worn; she had an open file on her desk. Her voice was light but there was no cheer in her eyes. They were red-rimmed and cloudy, and I wondered how much sleep she had gotten since Friday night, the night when we walked into Lynn Germano's cottage.

I said, "What do you have?"

Diane grimaced and said, "What I have is the undying thanks that Jack Fowler was not elected to a position that can control our county M.E.'s budget, so at least Wentworth County is lucky that it has a medical examiner who knows which end of the scalpel is up. That's what I have. I also have the fact that one seventeen-year-old Lynn Germano of 16 Rye Lane in Lawrence, Massachusetts, up here for the summer and working as a waitress nights and weekends at the Palace Diner, was murdered."

"Strangulation, with the hanging to make it look like suicide."

"Exactly." She frowned and flipped through a couple of pages in the file. "A slick bastard, that's for sure. M.E. found some surface bruises on her hands and wrists that made him think that she had been bound, and when he started cutting, he found what he needed. When someone's strangled, Lewis, there's a fracture of a horseshoe-shaped bone at the throat, called the hyoid bone. But that will only happen with a manual strangulation, not a ligature, like a rope. Lynn was strangled and then hung to make it look like a suicide."

"Any evidence of sexual assault?"

"Yeah. Some vaginal bruising and during a swab the M.E. detected the chemical used in condom lubricant. So we don't know the bastard's blood type. Fingernail scrapings came up empty, and a neighborhood canvass turned up squat, Lewis. You know the types down there. Rent a cottage for a week or a month, you hardly know who's next door, never mind what's going on down the street. So many people moving in and out. No one saw a thing. And we still don't know who the hell our mysterious caller was, telling us about the body."

"Roommate?"

"Our Lynn lived alone."

"Oh. Then the killer might have been the mysterious caller."

Diane shrugged. "Or someone who doesn't want to get involved. It happens, even here."

The outside door to the booking room slammed open and I heard someone cursing. Each summer weekend the Tyler Police Department averages about two hundred arrests, mostly for drug and alcohol offenses. Concerned about the image this was bringing to the beach, the Chamber of Commerce took out advertisements in area newspapers, posted signs on all the roads leading into Tyler Beach, and took out radio spots, warning about the strict open-container laws in Tyler. When that media campaign was over, every summer weekend, the Tyler Police Department still averaged about two hundred arrests.

"Here's her picture, Lewis." She handed over a high school class photo, and I imagined a victims' gallery, with hundreds of similar pictures of young women, with the same long hair, bright smile and attractive face. So many victims. And for what? I didn't want to think of what that face looked like, in her last minutes with a stranger thrusting upon her and then twisting his hands around her throat, but I couldn't help it. It must have been awful.

I handed the photo back and said softly, "I'm thinking of doing a column on this one, Diane."

She took the photo and slowly lowered her feet to the floor. "You are, are you?"

"Yep."

Diane put the photo back into the folder and said, her voice low, "Any other police department or town, I'd tell you to stay the fuck away, Lewis. I want you to know that. But in this town . . . Lewis, I've got about twenty major felony cases I'm working on, from that arson last April that killed the old lady to two rapes last week. The state police's on board on this case and I'll be doing what I can, but, Jesus, there's only so much I can do. . . ."

"We've had this talk before."

She slapped down the folder on her desk. "Damn it, I know, and I didn't like this talk the first time. I just want to make sure there's no misunderstanding, right? Anything of interest you find, you come to me. The state or anybody else gets a handle on what's going on, I'm going to pretend I don't even know you, Lewis Cole. And if it means me saving my job here in Tyler by arresting you for interfering in an investigation, I will gladly do it."

I got up and said, "Thanks for the words of encouragement. And there'll be no misunderstanding."

"Good," and she opened the folder again and I left.

I went down a short corridor, past the empty chief's office and through the dispatch area where a short woman with long blond hair was writing something down in a wide notebook. She had on a short denim skirt and white sneakers with no socks, and a black polo shirt. A large tan leather handbag hung from her right shoulder. She turned and said, "Lewis! You been talking with Diane the dick?"

"That I have."

Paula Quinn, reporter for the Tyler *Chronicle* and second-best writer in Tyler, stuck her black pen behind an ear and said, "What's she telling you?"

"That the state police are working with her, and that she needs a good night's sleep."

Paula arched an eyebrow. "I'm sure she does. Listen, let's get something to eat. I'm going to try to talk to Diane but I'm sure she'll give me shit. The Whale's Song sound all right?"

I shuddered. "Make it the Harpoon."

"Good. See you in about ten."

The Harpoon Restaurant was a five-minute walk from the police station, and two blocks south from the Tyler Beach Palace on Atlantic Avenue, where the Palace Diner was, Lynn Germano's place of employment. It was a warm evening, one of the warmest so far this year, and there was a slight edge to the people eddying around me as I walked down Atlantic Avenue. It was Sunday evening and some of the people were looking for their last hour or two of fun before returning home and back to their jobs the next morning. Traffic was stop and go and the smell of the sea wavered and died in the traffic's exhaust.

At the Harpoon entrance I hesitated for a moment before going in. It's located in the basement of a 1950s-era hotel, the Colonial, but it tries to maintain the decor and style of a restaurant that had been at Tyler Beach for a hundred years.

Unfortunately for the Harpoon, in the late 1890s there had been a couple of grand hotels and some fishing shacks at Tyler Beach, and not much else. Still, it had its pretensions, and one was its dress code. I had on tan chinos, worn topsiders, a short-sleeved blue Oxford shirt and no socks. The Harpoon's dress code was an accurate reflection of the beach's economy. A good season meant jacket and tie required. A bad season meant that bare feet were acceptable.

The maître d' just frowned at me as he led me to a corner table, so I guessed it was too early to tell how the season was going. The lighting was subdued and there was walnut paneling on the sides of the restaurant, and—unusual for a beach restaurant—each table had a white tablecloth with matching napkins.

The restaurant has two levels, and loud laughter from the upper level made me turn my head. The upper level has a wooden ship's railing, and a man sitting at a table there with two women and two other men gave me a slight nod of the head. Felix Tinios. Tonight he was wearing a double-breasted dark blue suit and red tie with matching handkerchief, and his smile was wide and white. His skin was dark and his black hair was slicked back with some sort of mousse. The men were beefy and red-faced, and their lime green and lemon yellow polo shirts looked ready to burst from the cholesterol content of their bodies. The women had teased blond hairdos and they whispered together. From the way he was talking, Felix was working, but I could tell it wasn't heavy work. That was one of his favorite suits, and I knew Felix would hate to get blood on it. Someone else's blood, of course.

I knew that if I was going to work on the Lynn Germano story, I would eventually need to talk to Felix, and I had a slightly queasy feeling, like I was remembering a bloody hunk of road kill I had passed on my way into Tyler Beach.

Just as I was ordering dinner—bottle of Heineken, French onion soup au gratin, and six fresh jumbo shrimp—Paula

Quinn bustled in, slinging her black leather bag over the back of a chair.

She sat down and, taking both hands, she tossed her hair back with a shudder, saying, "Should have just walked out with you, Lewis. She didn't tell me shit. Damn woman. You'd think she'd give me a break, the circumstances and being another working woman and all, but the way she talks to me and gives me information, you'd think she pissed standing up."

"That's not the way Diane is."

"Hunh. Tell me about it." A waitress came by and she ordered a tonic water, salad, and a haddock dish. Paula is seven years my junior. Her face has a flawless complexion, but her chin is a tad too large and her nose is just shy of being a pug. She's also self-conscious about her ears, which she thinks stick out at an odd angle and which have an annoying tendency to poke through her long blond hair when she's trying to be serious.

We met soon after I started publishing in *Shoreline*, when she called me one night and said, "Lewis Cole, the name is Paula Quinn and I work for the *Chronicle*. You seem to be about the only other person in this town who can put three sentences together, and I'd like to buy you a drink." Being a reasonable person, I let her, and things have gone on from there.

Tonight she sighed and leaned back and said, "So. Why were you seeing Diane tonight?"

"The same reason as you. Information."

"What did she tell you?"

I smiled and said, "Same as you, Paula."

She stuck out her tongue. "Go ahead. Play your little game. Why are you so interested anyway?"

I said, "Thought I might do a column about Lynn Germano's death."

"Hunh. Column. What are you planning—something about a young girl coming to a beach town for fun and money and ending up getting murdered? Story of life and death in a small

New Hampshire beach town? Doesn't sound like you, Lewis."

"Doesn't matter if it sounds like me. If it sounds like *Shoreline*, that's all I care."

"I think you and *Shoreline* should do something about the Body in the Marsh case, Lewis. More up your alley. Deep mystery and history and the great wilderness, all wrapped up in one. Imagine that poor son-of-a-bitch developer—doing some illegal drainage work at night, thinks no one will notice, and his backhoe operator pulls up a woman's body wrapped in canvas. Ugh. Cops called it a dead sand case."

"Which is . . ."

"Dead sand. Body's been in there so long, open the mouth and sand falls out, and not much else."

"Anything new?"

"You working on a column right now?" she asked, tilting her head at me.

"Nope."

"Good." The waitress approached with a tray and Paula unsnapped her white linen napkin and said, "Cops in North Tyler said the mystery woman was wearing a ring. And that's all they'll say—won't tell me if it's a wedding band or an old secret decoder ring. Just a ring."

Paula likes to boast of her steady weight, and I'm sure it's because of her energy level. By the time I had unpeeled my third jumbo shrimp, she was wiping off her plate with a roll. As we talked and ate, I looked up at Felix Tinios, and wondered what streets he was traveling on tonight.

When the dishes had been taken away I said, "Looking for a little information, Paula. Maybe you can help me."

"Really?" she said, smiling, as if not believing a word I was saying.

"Sure. I could spend half the day tomorrow on the phone but you could probably tell me right now—who owns the Palace Diner?"

"Where Lynn Germano worked. Some coincidence." She

leaned back in her seat again, one of her ears poking through her hair. She had a satisfied smile on her face. "Funny you should ask, because I do know who owns the Palace Diner. Make a deal with you, Lewis. A trade. I tell you who owns the Palace Diner, and you tell me what you did before you came to Tyler."

I felt like sighing but I enjoyed the look on her face and said, "Deal."

Her smile grew wider and she said, "Oliver Mailloux. Owns the diner, some cottages and a motel, the St. Lawrence Seaway. Likes to cater to the French-Canadian market."

"What do you know about him?"

She shrugged. "Typical business owner. Moans about the weather and taxes. Always threatens to close down every winter, and every spring, he comes back."

The waitress dropped off the check and I reached out to it, but Paula slapped my hand. "Hey. Your half of the deal."

"Oh. All right. Paula, the first time you asked that question, what did I say?"

She made a show of rolling her light blue eyes. "You said you were a spy."

"Exactly. That's still the truth."

I reached for the check again and she murmured, "Bastard," as she grabbed it away. "This'll be paid for by the Tyler *Chronicle.*"

"I'm never one to argue with an expense check."

When I left I made it a point to see if Felix Tinios was still at his table, but he was gone. The high-haired women and beefy men were still there, but as he can do so well, Felix had slipped away without being noticed.

Paula and I walked back to the police station together, and halfway there she put her arm through mine. Since we've known each other she's sent up her share of signals, and I've returned them with my own: Thanks, but not right now. Too much going on. Still, I enjoyed the touch, and I didn't discourage her.

At the police station she turned to me and said, "You've got more going on than just a column, and don't bullshit me, Lewis."

I looked at her earnest face and I said, "No bullshit, Paula. Something more than a column will be going on."

She shook her head. "You be damn careful. Not many writers around here, and I don't want that to change."

"It won't."

I said good night, and for some reason, I stroked her cheek before I went to my Range Rover. Just for a moment. But I liked the feel of her skin.

After taking a shower and throwing on a pair of faded black gym shorts, I stood by myself on my second-floor deck, just outside of my bedroom. The night air was warm and there was a soft breeze coming from the east. The sky was clear, and off on the horizon, the flashing light of the solitary lighthouse at the Isles of Shoals blinked out its warning. There were also boats out there: fishermen getting in a few more hours of dragging their nets, sailors who didn't mind seeing the sun set behind their sails, and drunken partyers who were no doubt seeing the lights of Tyler Beach in a foggy and dreary haze.

The waves coming in made a soft crashing noise against the rocks and sand below me. I drank from a Jameson's and water and wondered again why Paula was interested in me, and why I was so hesitant in responding to her. And I thought about other things.

Off at Weymouth's Point I saw the light of Alice Crenshaw's home, and I wondered how she would be sleeping tonight. Out in Tyler this late evening I was sure there were many others who were having a troubled night. Tourists who were here to have a good time, but who somehow ran afoul of the drug laws and open-container ordinances and who were now spending a night in a cold and dirty cell with sixty or seventy other drunks. Runaways and the homeless—yes, we have some homeless at Tyler Beach—scurrying into hidey holes and deserted cottages, looking for at least one peaceful night. And men and women, waking up with strangers by their sides, wondering if they could slip away without making a fuss.

I took another sip from my drink. My home. My town. My state. Tonight there was a man—maybe in Tyler still—who had killed one Lynn Germano, and I hoped he was not sleeping well. I hoped for that very much, because I was going to ensure that the rest of his nights would also be troubling.

Off in the west, I made out the tiny fast-moving dot of a satellite, and I thought about who it belonged to. Us? The Russians? The Israelis, perhaps? And what was its purpose? Who was looking at whom?

I thought about that, and I also thought about Lynn Germano, who worked as a waitress but who could afford the rent on a prime beachfront cottage by herself.

It didn't make sense. But I would leave that for tomorrow.

4

MONDAY MORNING DAWNED HOT AND SUNNY
as I parked my Range Rover at the Tyler
police station. On good beach days parking is almost an im-
possibility at Tyler Beach unless one arrives an hour or so after
sunrise, since in all of Tyler Beach there is not one free space
for visitors. The parking spaces are either metered—twenty-
five cents for fifteen minutes, quarters only—or they are part
of a few large parking lots, which charge six dollars per car,
no matter if it's for ten minutes or ten hours. But I was able
to park free, thanks to my police parking pass, which allowed
me to stop at the police station any time of the week, whether
I was visiting the station or not.

This morning was one of those days when I wasn't going
into the station, and within a few hours of my arrival that
morning at the beach, I learned very quickly why Diane Woods
and her friends at the state police had made no progress in
their canvassing of Dogleg Avenue. I had arrived in the morning
for a reason, since most people would still be home sleeping
off their previous night's adventures. But I was surprised at the
chaos I found when I started knocking on doors at the homes

around Lynn Germano's cottage. The men and women who answered the doors had just moved in that morning. Or they were staying with a friend or a cousin in that cottage. Or they hadn't seen a thing. Or they didn't care. Or they were out getting hammered the evening of Lynn Germano's murder.

At each door I said the same thing. Who I was and what I was doing: a column for *Shoreline* magazine on the death of their teenage neighbor. With each opened door and to each bleary face, I made my well-rehearsed pitch and passed over my business card.

I'm quite proud of my card. It's light blue and the magazine's logo is centered in the middle, the letters of *Shoreline* curling like a wave to a lighthouse in one corner. The ink is dark red and embossed, and my name is below the logo, along with the word *Columnist* in italics. There's my post office box number and home telephone number in Tyler just below my name. I had them made up myself at Tyler Printing and Copying, and many times the little rectangle of cardboard had opened doors and memories of people within a hundred miles of my home. A funny thing about the business cards: It cost me all of ten dollars for five hundred, yet people trusted the cards, put their faith behind the person passing them out, and often told me everything I wanted to know without too much trouble. A scary thought. I wondered if Ted Bundy or his friends ever carried business cards during their busy and bloody lives.

My last visit of the day fairly summed up the entire morning. A sweaty young man answered the door to a cottage four houses away from Lynn Germano's. His breath was of stale beer and he was wearing only University of Lowell gym shorts. He looked like a football player, with slabs of muscle along his thighs and chest. His hair was blond and cut short, and he reminded me of those old photos of young Aryan German soldiers, shirtless and smiling, exercising in a Ukrainian wheat field on their way to tearing out the heart of Mother Russia.

He took my card in his thick fingers and turned it over, and after I gave him my spiel, he grunted and said, "Man, you're asking me about some chick who got croaked up the street? Shit"—and this member of the younger generation grinned at me—"I hardly know who I'm waking up with sometimes, you know?"

I knew. "Still in college?"

"Yep."

For lack of anything better to say, I asked, "What are you studying in school?"

He shrugged. "Business. What else. Look. Gotta go."

I blinked and stepped out onto the narrow street, and walked back to the police station. The sun seemed too bright and its rays seemed to bore right through my eyes and rattle around in my head. The young man's look and attitude stayed with me, and as I went back to my Range Rover, I started looking at the legion of parked cars on both sides of Ashburn Avenue and began identifying the countries the cars had come from. There were only a few from a country that had a red, white, and blue flag, and those were older and rusting.

"Business," I said aloud. "What else."

And I smiled when I got to my Range Rover. When I was shopping for a vehicle, the year I came into Tyler Beach, I had considered buying domestic. But I thought the British auto-worker needed a little bit more assistance that year, and living near the saltwater, I liked an aluminum body, so I went with the Range Rover. It was expensive and sometimes wasn't the best and the speed wasn't the greatest, but it had style, and sometimes that was good enough for what I did for a living.

After going to the post office and picking up my mail, I went home, showered, and checked my answering machine. There was a blinking green light and in playing the machine, I got a message and a dinner invitation for Tuesday night from Alice Crenshaw. I spent an hour or so in my upstairs office, tapping out a real column for the November issue of *Shoreline*. It certainly is a challenge, with sweat rolling down your back and wearing nothing but shorts, to write a column that will sound appropriate for winter, when the tourists and the fishermen are mostly at home, huddling near the heat and wishing for the summer to return. After a while, I gave it up. I was working on something else.

I spent a couple of hours on my ground-floor deck, reading the latest issue of *Smithsonian* and tossing some things around in my head, while just half-hearing the sounds of the waves against the rocks and the cry of the gulls near my cove. It's a habit, one I've never been able to break, and one that was useful during my previous life. I've always been able to read and have my thoughts racing through problems and solutions as I've flipped through magazines or books or reports, and once a woman I loved complained that she always came in second, behind the printed word, behind anything that was a sentence. As much as I hated to admit it, she was right, and even so, I would love to hear that complaint from her again.

As it grew darker I changed back into jeans and white shirt and headed back to Tyler Beach.

The Tyler Beach Palace is on a section of the beach called the Strip, a name that is probably used in dozens of beach resorts from the Atlantic to the Pacific. The Beach Palace was built in 1912 and has been added on to over the years, and has even made it through a couple of fires. It's two stories high and stretches over three blocks. On the top floor is a kiddie amusement park with rides and games, some shops, and the Palace Theater. Years ago the Palace Theater was the site of evening ballroom dancing, with orchestras coming from their East Coast tours, from the Glen Miller band to the Count Basie orchestra. Today it hosts rock bands and comedians who have a fixation with the one word that can serve as a noun, adjective, and verb. Some of the bands were quite good, and last year I went with Diane Woods to see Bruce Hornsby; it was odd to see a modern concert with speakers and electric guitars and who knows what, played in a place with wooden floors and tall rafters. About the only remnant of the Palace Theater's earlier and simpler life is the second weekend in August, when it hosts the Miss Tyler Beach Contest. Other than that, it features speaker feedback masquerading as music and comics with grasping voices and hands.

The ground floor of the Beach Palace is open to the beach, and its concrete sidewalk is crowded with tourists and out-of-towners walking up and down the Strip, looking at the stores and each other. Across Atlantic Avenue is a bandshell and state park buildings and the widest stretch of Tyler Beach and, just a ways up the road, the Maid of the Seas monument. Inside the Palace there is a warren of video and pinball arcades, T-shirt shops, souvenir stores, and the usual photo shop where a group can get their photographs taken with costumes, as 1920s flappers or 1880s outlaws. There were also the Whale's Song restaurant, an ice cream and frozen yogurt store, and the Palace Diner.

I sat in a two-person booth in the Palace Diner and ordered a cheeseburger and fries and a small Coke, trying to do my best to blend in. The Coke was adequate and the fries were cold, but the cheeseburger was quite good, thick and cooked medium, just the way I like it.

The diner was set up as a large square, with an open kitchen area and counter forming the center square, with outer squares of booths and tables. The noise from the arcades and the traffic out on the Strip was constant, and there were shouts and loud voices from some of the younger customers in the diner. As I ate I watched the waitresses. They were all high-school-aged, wearing white shorts and black T-shirts that said PALACE DINER in bright pink neon. They did their work but they seemed determined to have a good time as well, joking and gossiping with each other. I kept looking at all of their faces and actions, until I found the one I was looking for. The quiet one, the one who kept to herself and watched what was going on. While the other waitresses would group together and talk and laugh, she did her job with a slight smile and forced enthusiasm, as if wanting to be somewhere else. She was about five feet five inches, with curly black hair and a pudgy figure. Unlike the other waitresses, she hadn't teased her hair into a lion's mane, and her skin wasn't tanned or sunburned, and she wasn't loaded down with jangle jewelry. She stayed to herself as she worked, and as she came by, I spotted her nametag: Sarah L.

After I had gotten my check and left a ten-dollar bill to cover it, I picked up my Coke and took a seat in her section; she was quick to come over. I ordered a refill and I said, "What does the *L* stand for, Sarah?"

She looked up from her notepad and said, "Lockwood. Why do you want to know?"

I passed over my business card and she looked at both sides. I said, "I'm doing a story, Sarah Lockwood. About Lynn Germano. Can I talk to you?"

"About what? She wasn't really one of my friends."

"Just ten minutes. That's all."

She walked away and came back with my Coke and said, "Would you use my name?"

I was going to say, Of course I will, but I saw the hesitancy in her eyes and I said, "No. Only if you want me to, Sarah. I'm just looking for some background information, that's all."

There was a neon clock over the cash register and she said, "Shit, I don't know. . . . Look. I get a fifteen-minute break in a couple of minutes. We can talk then."

"Thanks," I said, and I watched her walk back to the counter and look at her order pad, her shoulders bowed over, alone.

We got out of the Palace Diner and walked a ways up Atlantic Avenue and sat on a park bench, looking over the beach and the ocean. The sun was almost setting behind us toward the marshes and the sands looked cold; the only people out there were kids running around and couples walking hand in hand.

She sat there, arms folded, and said, "You know, I hate the beach. I really do. It's hot and sweaty and sand gets up in your skin, and there's nothing to do except read and get sunburned and watch the boys do their mating thing."

"So why are you here?"

Sarah turned and said, "I ride my bike here from Falconer every day and save every dime and nickel I can, Mr. Cole. The diner may not be much but the job is as good as one can get here in this county, and it's going to pay my way to UNH this fall, and that place is going to get me into law school one of these days. Any more questions?"

"How well did you know Lynn Germano?"

She drew up her legs and wrapped her arms around her knees. "Not very well. She stayed away from most of the girls. You know, most of us are from around here, but Lynn was from Massachusetts. You don't often get the out-of-state girls up here, you know. They usually stay home and save money and find work near where they live. But we do get them, and usually they bundle up, two or three to a motel room. But Lynn stayed a lot to herself. Not that she was stuck up or anything. Well, not too much stuck up."

"The state police talk to you?"

"They talked to all of us."

"What did you tell them?"

"Exactly what I told you. That she was a good kid, Mr. Cole. She didn't deserve to get killed, and there wasn't anyone we could figure who'd want to hurt her."

Out on the sands a young boy was trying to fly a kite, but his little legs wouldn't let him run hard enough. I said, "Did she have any boyfriends?"

"Nope."

"Who was her closest friend among the waitresses?"

She rubbed her chin against her arms. "Hard to tell, Mr. Cole. She hung around with all of them, but none of them.

You know what I mean? It was like she had her own thing, her own agenda. Like she was too good for them. Or too different."

The boy with the kite was crying. "How did she get along with the owner?"

"Mr. Mailloux?" She shrugged and looked away from me. "All right, I guess. He doesn't come by that often, but he's an okay boss."

"Lynn like him?"

She grunted. "I don't know if anyone liked him, but yeah, I guess she got along with him all right. You know, besides this place and a motel, he owns some cottages on the beach, and he lets some of the girls live there on a discount."

"But you prefer to bike in and out every day, even at night?"

She kept her face turned away from me. "I prefer to sleep in my own bed, in my own home, Mr. Cole."

By now the boy was tearing up the kite with his hands, still crying. Sarah looked at her watch and said, "I'm going to be late, so I gotta run." She looked at me with her head cocked and said, "You're supposed to be a writer. Why didn't you take notes?"

"Cursed with a fine memory," I said. "Sarah, you've got my card. Call me if you think of anything else, anything you think I should know."

From the way she nodded her head and turned to leave, I had the feeling the card would end up in the first trash can she met on her way back to the Palace Diner. I watched the waves for a while and the lights, and tried to see the stars, but the light pollution was too bad and I gave up and walked back to my Range Rover.

At the police parking lot Diane Woods was sitting on the bumper of her dark green Volkswagen Rabbit, her arms folded, staring down at her feet. She wore her usual jeans and had on a wrinkled blue-and-white Colby sweatshirt. She looked up at me as I walked over to her.

"How goes the story?" she asked, her voice tired. A sea gull was perched on a telephone pole in the lot, looking over the expanse of buildings, and two green-and-white Tyler police cruisers were parked at the rear entrance to the station, which led into the booking room.

"It goes," I said, sitting next to her, on the car's hood. "You look wiped."

"Thanks for the compliment."

"It's the truth."

Diane stirred and scratched at her brown hair and said, "The Lynn Germano case isn't going anywhere, Lewis. About the only thing that's happened is that her body was buried yesterday. And the Chief is bugging me about a shitload of other cases and I'm out here, trying to get some fresh air, and I feel like I'm too tired to drive."

I said, "I'll take you, then."

She lifted her head up and smiled. "Where?"

"To my place. Where else?"

"Oh?"

I said, "I'm ten minutes away. Your place is easily fifteen. Those extra five minutes of sleep could be vital, Diane."

"And leave my Vee-dub here?"

"Yep."

Diane stood up and stretched, muscles and bones cracking. "Such a scandal, Mr. Cole. Such a scandal, when my fellow officers see my car still here, and see you dropping me off here tomorrow."

I took her arm and walked her to my Range Rover. "A little scandal may be just what you need."

About halfway home she fell asleep, head resting against the door, and she woke up only when I went through the reserved parking lot of the Lafayette House and down the bumpy trail to my house.

"Jesus," she said, rubbing at her eyes. "Here so soon."

"Sleep well?"

She yawned. "Stupid question, Lewis."

I pulled the Range Rover into the garage and we made the short walk to my house. Without the light pollution of Tyler Beach the stars were quite bright, and Diane stopped for a second before my door, craning her head back.

"Sweet God, I never get tired of looking at these stars, Lewis. At my condo there's too many streetlights and I'm lucky to see the moon at night. All these stars. They seem like they were put right here, for your house."

"Nice thought," I said.

She stood there, weaving. "So many stars, so many millions of miles away. Sometimes it makes you and everything you do seem so small and worthless, Lewis. All your work and efforts and ideas."

"You need some sleep, Diane. Too much philosophy can ruin a person's mind."

She yawned again. "There's the Big Dipper, Lewis. I'm embarrassed to say that's the only constellation I recognize."

I touched her elbow. "Here. I'll tell you something—you can impress your friends."

"Oh?"

I came closer, smelling her scent. "Look up at the handle, at the middle star. You see it?"

"Yep."

"Well, you see wrong, Diane," I said. "That's actually two stars, Mizar and Alcor. And if you have a very good telescope, you'll see that each of them is a double star—so instead of looking up at one star, you're looking at four."

She weaved again. "Is there a point?"

I tapped her on the shoulder. "Yeah, a cop point," I said. "It pays to look at things, real close. You'll be surprised at what you'll find."

I sensed her grin. "You'll be surprised to find me sleeping on your lawn if we don't hurry up and get inside."

When we got in she went upstairs and I listened to the sounds of water running as she showered. In the living room I got to work and by the time she came downstairs, wearing a red-and-white Boston Museum of Science T-shirt from my bedroom dresser and nothing else, the couch had been unfolded and I had the blankets and pillows ready.

She smiled as she came to me, rubbing her hair with a green towel, water still beading along her tanned thighs, her clothes and revolver in her other hand. "Lewis, thanks for the astronomy lesson, really. It was just that I needed to get inside. A lesson and a place to sleep. Such a host."

"Such a guest."

She rubbed at her hair and smiled, and that made me feel good. The dispirited woman I had seen in the Tyler police station lot wasn't the Diane Woods I knew.

"One of these nights, I'll get to sleep in your bed, Lewis Cole," she said, tossing the towel to the floor.

"Promises, promises," I said, kissing her on her nose. "Sleep well."

I went and locked the front door, and when I came back, she was on the couch, blankets over her, breathing slowly and softly. I trod upstairs quietly and stripped down and crawled into my own empty bed, pulling a sheet and a single wool blanket over me.

As I lay there, my eyes closed, I remembered other places and times. I remembered a group of people in uniform, smiling faces and a certain high desert, and the thrumming sound of a helicopter that eventually brought me from those sands to this sea.

So many lifetimes ago.

I listened for a while, wondering if Diane was dreaming, but there was nothing but the sound of the waves upon my beach.

5

IN THE EARLY MORNING ON TUESDAY I AWAKened to the sound of a shower running. I lay there silently, not moving under the single blanket and sheet. The strong sunlight from the rising sun was coming through my windows, making everything look store-bought new, which was one of the many side benefits of living on the ocean, and which sometimes made up for the sea gull droppings that littered the house and the deck, and the beach sand that blew and sometimes got into everything, including my sugar bowl. I waited, lightly dozing, listening for the shower to turn off, and then listening to see which way the footsteps would go: here, to my bedroom, or back downstairs. From some time back, soon after I had met Diane Woods, I already suspected what the answer was going to be, but one never knew. One always had to be open to other options, other changes, possible surprises. And so I waited.

Then came the sound of the footsteps, returning back downstairs. I closed my eyes and dozed a bit more, and then got up and showered.

* * *

I joined Diane out on the deck. She had made each of us a cup of tea—we both belong to the breakfast-sounds-nauseating-at-this-hour club. She ran her fingers through her still-wet hair as we sat in the deck chairs, mugs of tea in hand, our legs stretched out to the wooden railing.

She turned and smiled and said, "In a few minutes, I'm back in that stinking concrete place they call an office, and you get to stay here."

I said nothing and Diane looked around at the deck and the ocean, and the bright sun upon the early morning waves. There was a shape, moving out there on the horizon, and again I silently thanked myself for not having the desire or need to be a fisherman working out on those empty waters called an ocean.

Diane took a sip of her tea and said, "Times like these, I'm jealous of you, Lewis. You can just go upstairs and get right to work. No one over your back. Nobody screaming in the rear cells. No families calling you up, wondering why you're rousing junior. Nothing like that at all. Just bliss."

I smiled and raised my mug to her in a salute. "It's not always bliss, but you should try it sometimes, even though the temptation's always there to goof off and watch the morning talk shows. Child-abusing nuns who are closet Nazis, that sort of thing. To make it work right, you have to enjoy what you do, or else you'll start hating where you live. But I do admit, working out of your home is different."

Diane looked into her mug for a moment before saying, "Different, I guess, than what you did before, right?"

I sat silent, remembering. How to explain to her what it had been like? With the three different kinds of photo ID and the key card that let you into your work area. Rules that anything left on top of desks overnight would be shredded and burned by next morning. Signs on your telephone, reminding you that the lines were not secure for confidential conversations. The late-night and early-morning calls, demanding your presence, demanding your special knowledge in reading the printed word, in comprehending what was going on, and then writing and rewriting a report—sometimes hundreds of pages long— that you knew would be read only by a handful of sharp-fingered men nearing retirement. And reading the newspapers every morning, and seeing what was on the front page, thinking to yourself, that story's wrong, that story's wrong, and that one is only about half right, and feeling smug about it all.

How to explain what it had been like?

I finished my tea. "It was different, Diane. You're absolutely right."

She nodded and did not press any further. That type of technique made for a lousy cop but a good friend.

After dropping Diane off that morning at the Tyler police station—I had offered to let her off a block away but she would have none of that ("Scandals, remember?" she had said. "At least give me something to look forward to.")—I drove west on Route 51 and went into Tyler town for a few minutes. I bought a copy of the morning *Globe* and *Union Leader*, and at the Sweet Honey doughnut shop near the town common, I picked up two chocolate bran muffins and a large orange juice. I thought I was getting hungry.

Getting onto I-95 cost me two toll tokens and by the time I neared the Massachusetts border, I had finished the orange juice and had tossed one and a half chocolate bran muffins out on the side of the road, for the benefit of anything furred or feathered that could eat something like a chocolate bran muffin. My stomach wasn't into the work I was going to do that morning, and I wasn't in the mood for eating. I decided that the pangs in my lower region weren't from hunger.

Crossing over the Massachusetts line, I saw a sign welcoming me into the Commonwealth by the current Democrat who was governor, followed by a cheerful sign that warned me of Massachusetts's mandatory one-year jail sentence for unlawful possession of a firearm. Just before the Merrimack River, I took the exit onto I-495 and within a half-hour, I had taken one of the several exits into Lawrence. Like any city it had its downtown and uptown, its barrios or ghettos, and the upscale section where the lawns were always green and well cut. Lately, though, the downtown had been slashing and burning its way into the green sanctuaries, and like rich refugees everywhere, the people of the uptown had been pushing their way north.

Pulling over to the side, I glanced through my eastern Massachusetts map book and found the street I was looking for. It took me only a few more minutes to get there, but in those few minutes it was like passing into another world. Hispanic men and women stood in front of grocery stores and restaurants with Spanish names, looking at the strange vehicle with New Hampshire license plates. Graffiti had been sprayed on walls and abandoned cars, using crooked and angular characters that made no sense to me. Less than an hour from the white sands and even whiter population of Tyler Beach, I could have been in another hemisphere.

Rye Lane was a residential area of small homes with even smaller yards. It was the type of neighborhood where each postage-stamp-sized yard was separated from its neighbor by an unfriendly chain-link fence or shrubbery. I had a thought of walking down here at night and seeing no life, no activity, just the quiet, empty yards and long fences, the incessant blue glow of each home's inhabitants watching their tubes, watching nothing else.

Number sixteen was a light shade of yellow and nearly identical in shape and size to its neighbors. A late-model blue Buick was parked in the short cement driveway. I parked the Range Rover on the street and, not particularly enjoying what I was doing, I walked up the short walk and rang the doorbell. GERMANO was printed on a piece of paper in a little slot on the side of the door and covered with clear cellophane tape.

A woman in her late fifties answered, her face puffy and

pale, her eyes red-rimmed. Her gray hair was curly but flattened on one side, as if she had been sleeping, and there were creases along her face. She was wearing a pink corduroy housecoat and she looked up at me with a puzzled expression as I went into my usual spiel.

She said nothing and then I pulled out my card and passed it over to her, and she looked at it and gave it back to me.

"Mr. Cole, my husband and I just buried Lynn yesterday. I'm sure you'll understand."

She started closing the door and I said, "Mrs. Germano, it'll only take a—"

The door was closed. I raised my hand to the doorbell and let it drop, and then I took out a pen and scribbled a note on the back of my card: *Please, if you can, do call me.* I left it in the little slot, hiding the Germano name.

When I got back to my Range Rover I looked back and thought I saw the curtain at the front window move, but I wasn't sure. My card was there, alien in its little spot, and I thought of walking back and taking it away, but I was too embarrassed to go across that small yard again. I got in my Range Rover and headed north, back to where I felt at home.

The things I do, I thought. The things I do.

So much for the glamour of magazine writing.

Later that morning I spent a half-hour at the Tyler town hall, which is a five-minute walk from the town common. It's a two-story building with white clapboards, made up to look like a Unitarian church without the steeple. Inside are the town offices, from town clerk to tax collector, and the town records and assorted bric-a-brac that every small town has collected, including a dusty weathervane made to look like a grasshopper, which was in the basement, leaning up against an old safe that has a couple of hundred years' worth of town records hidden away. Next to the town hall is the uptown fire station, which was built during one of those great compromises between the town residents and the beach people, so that the town would have adequate fire coverage in the summer when traffic was so bad at the beach.

Tyler being Tyler, after the fire station was built, the selectmen cut back on the fire department budget, so the station remained empty most of the week.

Both the town hall and the fire department—along with the Gilliam Memorial Town Library—are on Marshwood Avenue. About a mile from the town hall is Cable Road, which connects Marshwood with Route 51, and where that Friday evening a few nights ago, I had seen two high school students pulled, bleeding and screaming, from their crumpled car.

I wondered how they were doing.

I spent my time that morning with Clyde Meeker, the tax assessor for Tyler and a retired accountant who used to commute into Boston every day to work at some enormous bank that had branches in Maine and Vermont and was now in such financial straits that polite men with New York accents and suits from London were busily tearing it apart and feeding its bloody pieces to a bankruptcy court.

Clyde told me once that after his retirement, he sold off his car, because "I got so goddamn tired of driving, all I wanted to do was walk, bike, or bum rides for the rest of my life." Even in this hot weather he was wearing a suit and tie, and his dyed black hair was impeccable.

This morning, like all mornings, Clyde was his usual helpful self. I told him what I was looking for and he gave me a grin and said, "Town records, my friend. Public information. You can root around in here all day. See if I care."

When I was done with my work at his office I went out into the small lobby, just as Jack Fowler, the selectmen chairman, came into the town hall. The last time I had seen him was that same Friday night, when he was outside the cottage at 12 Dogleg Avenue, talking to Diane and smiling at the photographer from the *Chronicle* after his picture had been taken.

He nodded at me and I gave him a half-smile as I tried to go past him through the outside door. Next to us on the brick wall was a large bulletin board, listing the monthly blood drive at the fire station, the American Legion's pancake breakfast, minutes of the planning board and zoning board meetings, and the agenda for next week's selectmen's meeting.

He held his hand up for a moment and said, "Hold on. You're that magazine writer, right? Cole. Live out in that old government cottage near Samson Point."

"That's right, Jack," I said, smiling and trying to think of a way to go by without seeming too rude.

I knew Jack slightly, having attended a handful of selectmen's meetings over the past few years, and last Christmas, I actually went to a party at his house up in the Towler Hill section of Tyler, on Hillside Road. He held it each year for the politicians in the town and county, and for reporters who covered town events, and I went as Paula Quinn's date. The party featured lukewarm punch and drinks in little plastic glasses, tortilla chips in white plastic bowls on paper tablecloths, and old eight-track cassettes playing Andy Williams Christmas tunes. Paula had left the house after exactly three minutes of conversation with Jack Fowler and eight minutes with the other two selectmen. "I may be a reporter," she had told me that December day, "but I'm no goddamn martyr." I thought of that as Jack nodded to me.

"Got a little piece of news for you, you being a writer," he said. Today he wore light pink polyester pants and a white short-sleeved shirt. His thin white hair was so slicked back it looked like a petroleum product.

"That so?"

"Yeah," he said, smiling, and he nodded at two elderly women standing in line at the town clerk's window. "Last night I was elected president of the Tyler Beach Chamber of Commerce. Think I could get a write-up in that magazine of yours?"

I thought of what I wanted to say, and what I should say,

and the latter won out. "I'll give it a try, Jack, but I can't promise anything. My editors are in Boston, and they're pretty tight on space."

"Thanks," he said, slapping me on the arm and strolling across the tile floor, heels clicking, leaving behind the scent of his aftershave, which smelled like a pine forest in the middle of a strawberry patch. I went outside to my Range Rover and thought ahead to the rest of the afternoon.

Just another day of lying.

Back at Tyler Beach, I lucked out and found a parking space only a few blocks from where I was headed. It was in a small town lot on Atlantic Avenue and was metered, and I had only two quarters, which would give me only thirty minutes of parking. As I walked along the sidewalk I came across a T-shirt store and a poster store. Both places had signs in their windows: NO CHANGE GIVEN FOR PARKING METERS. Since I didn't want to buy either a T-shirt or a poster showing off the latest cartoon cable television star in order to get more quarters, I kept walking.

Tuesday traffic was light that late in the morning, and there were only a few people walking along the sidewalk, none of them shopping. The sun was high but didn't feel intense, and there was a good breeze coming off the ocean. Near the beach was a parking area reserved only for motorcycles, and there was a group of leather-clad men there, talking and joking, slapping each other on the shoulders, and not looking at the ocean at all. I made a reasonable guess that they probably weren't discussing French philosophy, and decided not to cross the street to ask them and prove my theory.

Instead, I kept on walking, and when I reached Baker Street I went to the place that Oliver Mailloux called home.

From the tax assessor's office I had gone through real estate listings, and in talking with Clyde Meeker learned that Oliver Mailloux lived and worked in his hotel, the St. Lawrence Seaway. I also found out that besides the Palace Diner, he also owned about a half-dozen cottages.

The St. Lawrence Seaway was at the corner of Baker and the southbound side of Atlantic Avenue, and was three stories high with the usual hotel sliding windows. It was light gray and had a basement parking garage. I went into the lobby, past the sign that said FRENCH SPOKEN HERE—NOUS PARLONS FRANÇAIS ICI. The lobby was small, with only a couch, two chairs, and a check-in desk. The wallpaper was a pattern made of yellow and light green seashells, and on one wall was a rack of folders and brochures listing the marvelous things one could do in Tyler Beach and the State of New Hampshire. One of the summer attractions farther north, in the White Mountains, is Santa's Village, which is open only from June to October, not really the season one would normally think of for Santa. Still, it was one of the state's most popular tourist destinations. Go figure it.

A young woman, about high-school age, was behind the counter. Her nametag said Lucy and she had short-cropped blond hair and four earrings in one ear. Her nose and face were dusted with freckles and she wore a white polo shirt with the motel's name in blue letters and blue slacks, and it made me wonder who had the motel and restaurant polo shirt franchise at Tyler Beach. He or she must be doing very well.

After some talking on my part and phone whispers on her part, she put down her phone and said, "He'll see you, Mr. Cole. But only for a moment. Go through this hallway, go upstairs, and it's the office on the right."

"Thanks." As she began tidying up her counter I said, "Lucy?"

"Yeah?"

"Your boss. Oliver Mailloux. How do you like him?"

She quickly flicked her eyes back and forth, as if looking to see if anyone was watching, and then she looked down at the counter and said, "Just go down that hallway. Please."

So I did.

* * *

I went past the numbered and closed doors of the first-floor rooms and heard a woman yelling at another woman in French. The floor and stairs were carpeted with a sickly green material, and at the top of the second stairs was an open wooden door that had OFFICE on it in black-and-silver stick-on letters.

In the office there were two men. One was at the right, sprawled out in a captain's chair, while the other sat behind a cluttered desk that was covered with forms and receipts and had an adding machine on one corner, along with a brown ceramic ashtray full of squashed cigarette butts. There were filing cabinets on all sides, and hanging up on an open space on the white walls were two calendars: one was a large-sized *Sports Illustrated* swimsuit edition, and the other was something called *Best California Buns*. Both were open to the month of June.

The man in the chair looked up at me for a moment and then went back to cleaning his dirty fingernails with a short knife on a key ring. He wore a red tank top, cutoff dungaree shorts, and black Reebok sneakers with no socks, and his upper arms and thighs were solid and hairy. His hair was black and combed back in a thick mass and his face was light red and puffy, as if it had been slapped a lot when he was younger. He looked like the type of guy who liked his women tattooed.

Across the desk the other man looked up at me when I came in. He wore a short-sleeved white shirt and had three gold chains around his neck. His skin was dark and his face was slightly pockmarked, and his teeth were dim and uneven. His hair was gray-black and wet and parted on one side. I wondered if the two of them shared their lotion.

"Oliver Mailloux?" I said to the man behind the desk.

He nodded and I passed over my business card. "I'm a writer for *Shoreline* magazine," I said. "I'm working on a piece about the waitress who worked at your Palace Diner. I'd like to ask a couple of questions and then I won't take up any more of your time."

He looked at my card, and without waiting for an invitation, I sat down in the other free chair. The man cleaning his fingernails looked up for a moment and then went back to work.

Oliver tossed the card across his desk. "Never heard of your magazine, pal. But then again, I'm too busy working. Moved up here from Massachusetts a few years back to earn an honest living, and I'm still tryin'. You got a thousand and one things to worry about in a place like this, from the food to the towels. You know, the job is so hard, I gotta live right over this office. So—sorry again, pal, I've never heard of your magazine."

I said, "Guess I'll have to talk to our subscription department."

He smirked. "Derek, you ever hear of a magazine called *Shoreline?*"

The man he called Derek grunted something that sounded like no. Oliver smiled and I had an urge to put a hand on my wallet. Oliver looked like he balanced his checkbook every night to make sure no one was cheating him. He said, "That's Derek Cooney for you. Best hands-on manager I got, but he only reads magazines if it shows broads with big tits. Now. Why are you so interested in a girl that worked at my diner? News that slow? You trying to sell magazines, make a little money?"

I didn't pick up my business card. It sat on top of an invoice from a local Coca-Cola distributor.

"I get paid the same amount of money, no matter what kind of stories I write," I finally said. "This one interests me, that's all. Young girl comes to a resort beach and ends up getting murdered. Something unusual. Something that belongs in a story."

Oliver smiled again and leaned back in his chair, both hands against the back of his head. There were yellow sweat stains in the armpits of his white shirt.

"Let me tell you something, Mr. Cole," Oliver said. "It doesn't surprise me, this type of thing that happened last week. Not that I expected this particular girl to get killed, but some of these girls, they come up here looking for something more than spending money to buy some short skirts or tight jeans. No, they're up here looking for a good time. They're away from home for the first time, Mommy and Daddy aren't watching over them, and they're looking for that first drink of booze. Or toot of coke. Or their first lay. You remember your first lay? Pretty important day, right?"

"I've had others," I said.

"Maybe you have. So. These girls come up here and play around and get loose, and maybe they run into someone not so nice. Someone who has other ideas of what's fun. So they die. It happens."

"It ever happen before to one of your waitresses?"

"Nope."

"Did you know Lynn Germano that well?"

He rolled his eyes, held his hands out. "Mr. Cole, these girlies come in and out of my diner and my hotel, I can't keep track of 'em. You show me pictures of her and two other girlies, I couldn't tell the difference."

"Did you know where she lived?"

"No idea. Probably on the beach, I guess. Most of 'em do."

"Your other workers, did they get along with her? Do you know who her friends were?"

He glanced at Derek and leaned over on his desk and pointed a finger at me, one that was nicotine-stained, the fingernail bitten down.

"You look here, mister," Oliver said, finger still extended, his voice rising with every sentence. "I'll tell you this, and it's my last answer. I get these little chickies in here all the time. I give 'em a job and some working experience, and give 'em cut-rate rooms here, and how do they pay me back? Complaining. Quitting after a week or two 'cause they miss home.

Calling in sick 'cause they're on the rag or their boyfriend boffed them too hard and it hurts too much to stand up. Stealing food and silverware and sheets. All I know about this broad is that she's causing me a load of problems. Period. I gotta find someone to fill her schedule. I gotta talk to the cops. And I gotta talk to assholes like you. There.''

He sat back in his chair, face red, breathing hard but looking triumphant, like he had won a race. Derek was no longer cleaning his fingernails, but he still had his little knife in his beefy hand. I got up from my chair, knowing it wasn't going to get any better.

Oliver grinned. "Happy now? Got enough for a story?''

"Happy has nothing to do with it, but I have a rule when it comes to interviews.''

"Oh?''

"That's right. The rule is, I'm done with an interview when the interviewee begins to sound like a sea gull with rotten breath who's having a bad day.''

His smile disappeared and he said, "Better leave now, smart-ass. And stay the fuck out of my diner and my hotel. Leave, before I have Derek take you out.''

"Very original,'' I said, going out the door without turning my back to them. "You see that in a movie somewhere?''

As I went outside Lucy's face was red and she was busy moving a couple of sheets of paper from one end of the counter to the next, so I knew that Oliver's loud voice wasn't something unusual. I winked at her as I made for the door but I didn't feel particularly cheerful.

Even when I got outside into the sun and salt-air breeze from the ocean, I still felt greasy. I walked back up Atlantic Avenue and saw that the boys in leather had attracted a red Nissan sports car with Massachusetts license plates, and leaning out of both windows were two young women with teased blond hair and long fingernails, talking to the five or six men who had gathered around the car. No accounting for taste, and my mood didn't improve when I saw a parking ticket flapping in the breeze from my Range Rover's windshield wiper.

Still, it had been a productive morning. I had learned a lot, and I had also learned that Oliver Mailloux was a liar, since Lynn Germano had lived in 12 Dogleg Avenue, and earlier in the morning I had found out that 12 Dogleg Avenue was owned by one O. Mailloux of Baker Street.

That night I sat at a table for four at the Marshside Restaurant in North Tyler. It was located at the end of Morgan Avenue and had three things going for it: It was slightly remote, which meant that the average tourist never found it; it had the best Italian food on the seacoast; and it was built right next to the salt marsh and at night had a marvelous view of the long row of twinkling lights and signs that made up Tyler Beach.

I was on the outside veranda, which was screened from top to bottom, waiting for Alice Crenshaw to come back from the rest room. The dishes from our non-Heart Association-approved dinners had been cleared away and there was a cup of coffee for me and a small cup of cappuccino for her, and the check on the table between us. The marsh stretched out like a flat table, dark and quiet, with the lights of lonely fireflies flickering out in the distance. I've been told by Alice and other older residents of Tyler that the fireflies used to be so thick that it looked like a Las Vegas display out there at night. But with the march of the years and improved housing and pesticides, the fireflies had been darkened. Progress.

No doubt, one of these days, there'd be so much progress that they'd be able to send up fake fireflies, so no one could tell the difference.

Alice came back, touching the back of my neck for a moment. She wore a simple black dress with brown sandals and no stockings, and a string of pearls around her neck. Her hair was in its usual shape, but instead of the perfume of before I smelled tobacco.

"Rest-room break or cancer-stick break?"

She sat down and gave me a wan smile. "You can go to hell, and you know that."

Alice took a sip from her small cup and gazed over my shoulder, as if looking at someone, but that night we had the whole veranda to ourselves. She had been quiet for most of the night, not saying much. She had ordered her favorite veal dish ("and screw anyone who doesn't want me to eat veal," she would always say, but not tonight) and had only eaten half of it.

I took a swallow from my cup and said, "I'm not going to bother asking you if something is wrong. I just want to know if you're going to tell me."

Alice rested her chin in a hand and looked out across the marsh to the bright and low lights of Tyler Beach. "You're too damn sensitive, you know that?" she said. "My husband John, now, I have the blues about something and he wouldn't notice until I burnt his toast three days in a row. But not you, Lewis. You can tell."

She stopped for a moment, still looking out to the marsh. "Father could tell, too, Lewis. He could tell when something wrong was going on. He'd say, 'Honey child, as a doctor, it's my job to know.' And he was right, it was his job. Father was something else in this town, Lewis, a doctor who took care of you, no matter what the problem or how much money you made. House calls, if you can believe it. He was at home in those mansions up in North Tyler, just as much as he was at home in some of the backwoods shacks in Falconer. He never turned anyone away, and when he died, the town named a ballpark and a library after him, Lewis. A lot of people here still remember him. And now the doctors won't see you unless you got money, a health-group card, and time to sit around in their lousy offices all day."

I said, "Something else going on, Alice?"

"Shit, I don't know, Lewis," she said, looking back at me,

her face yellowish in the candlelight. "Sometimes the years just weigh down on you, like lead shoulder pads. I look out on those lights and wonder who's getting hurt and who's not getting loved and who's getting abandoned tonight. And you wonder about all the other nights, years and years back, and think of all the bad things that have happened out there. It just leaves a sour taste in my mouth."

"A lot of good things have happened out there, too," I said. "Your dad the doctor, for instance."

She shook her head. "The good things just flow right through you. The bad things stick around."

I waited, wondering if she would speak again, but instead, she finished her cappuccino and pulled out three twenty-dollar bills from her purse and left them on the check.

"Is that all?" I asked. "Anything else making you glum?"

She tried to smile, and then paused, as if she wanted to say something else.

Instead, she said, "Just the years, Lewis. Just the years." She looked down at the stained tablecloth. "Take me home, will you?"

I stood up and offered her my hand, and said, "Only if you don't try to drag me into your house," and with that usual saying on my part not producing the usual smile on her part, I walked out of the Marshside Restaurant with Alice Crenshaw at my side, suddenly afraid of what was happening to her.

6

LOOK THROUGH THE NEWSPAPER ADVERTISE-
ments and brochures and Chamber of Com-
merce mailings for the Granite State, and you will learn an
interesting fact about New Hampshire—it has no crime. None
whatsoever. The brochures and handouts mention the long
sandy beaches of Falconer and Tyler and Wallis, the cool blue
waters of the Lake District, the sharp-edged granite peaks of
the White Mountains, and the deep green forests of the North
Country. There are the historic sites and buildings—America's
first astronaut, Alan Shepherd, was born in Derry, and John
Paul Jones lived for a while in Porter when a ship of his was
being refitted—but there's no crime.

But Diane Woods knows better, and so do I, and so does
Felix Tinios, whom I was meeting that Wednesday afternoon.
And while the crime in New Hampshire doesn't approach the
numbers of our foul-mannered sister state to the south, it does
have an oddness about it. There may not be much crime, but
it does make the newspapers. Like the case up north, where a
husband and wife were involved in a spouse-swapping game.
Husband and wife number one divorced and husband number

two disappeared, while husband number one married wife number two. Years later, after the deathbed confession of husband number one's father, the bones of number two were dug up from number one's front yard. And I said to Diane, "Good God, how could he have lived with that woman, knowing her dead husband was buried just yards away?"

And Diane had said, "Never mind that. How could he have slept with her and produced a child, knowing that husband number two was rotting away in his front yard?"

There have been other cases as well. Like the former CIA agent from New Orleans who had climbed Mount Washington, the highest peak (6,288 feet) in the Northeast, and who died on the summit like a Buddhist monk from Vietnam in 1964, ablaze in a fireball. Except there was no fuel can or bottle next to the body to suggest that he had done it to himself.

There was also a case in Tyler a few years back, which Diane absolutely refuses to discuss with me to this day, where a retired Tyler police sergeant who had held a grudge against his neighbor for ten years walked over to the neighbor the night the Red Sox lost game six of the 1986 World Series and blew him away with a 12-gauge shotgun blast to the chest when the neighbor came to answer the door. When he was caught, months later, the retired sergeant had just shrugged and said of his neighbor: "He was a Yankees fan, and I knew he'd gloat."

After some beers and some discussions, Diane had told me one night, "Our lack of quantity in crime is made up by its quality," and I couldn't argue with that.

This Wednesday afternoon a light rain was falling; it was foggy in Tyler, and the ocean breeze was sharp and salty. I drove my Range Rover north on Atlantic Avenue, heading into North Tyler to Felix Tinios's house. Traffic was light, and with the cooler weather, most of the tourists were heading to the malls in Porter or to the four-screen movie house in uptown Tyler. In addition to my jeans and plaid flannel shirt, I wore a light green shell parka. Underneath the parka I wore a shoulder holster and my 9-mm Beretta. Not that I was concerned about Felix, but I was concerned about being with him if someone else a little less friendly than me came to visit at the same time.

Felix and his work are some more things that never make it into the brochures. Mention organized crime and you hear of Boston's North End and Providence in Rhode Island and maybe Portland in Maine, but you never hear of Wentworth County, New Hampshire. Which is no doubt the way they prefer it. There are small interests here, and small activities, and from what I've been able to gather and pry out of Diane, Felix does free-lance work, whether it be disciplining someone or keeping an eye on a summer estate in winter. While he has a minor record in Massachusetts, he is clean in New Hampshire and everywhere else in New England. In my discussions with him he is adamant about one thing: no drugs, or anything connected with drugs, and I wish I could believe him.

He lives on Rosemount Lane in North Tyler, a small road off Atlantic Avenue, just north of the small North Tyler beach, which boasts only a state-owned strip of sand, a couple of motels, and a general store. Rosemount Lane heads off to the right, to the east, and rises up to look out over the ocean. There are six houses on the road. Five of them are grouped near the intersection of Rosemount Lane and Atlantic Avenue. The sixth is a modern ranch-style house with sliding glass doors and open balconies that is on the highest point of Rosemount Lane. It belongs to Felix Tinios. The lawn is kept well and there is not a single shrub, bush, or tree on the property that can hide anyone.

I parked my Range Rover in the gravel driveway, next to his red convertible Mercedes Benz, knowing better than to block his car by parking behind it. Out of habit I checked the four tires of the Benz, and they looked fine. I walked up to the house, feet crunching on the gravel path, listening to the ocean waves hiss and moan against the rocks below me. The rainwater was cold against my face and I was almost shivering by the time I got to his house.

I knocked on the door and heard a muffled yell, then went inside. If my house is antiques and old books and wide wooden floors, then Felix Tinios's is framed Boston Museum of Fine Art prints, Scandinavian design furniture, and track lighting. He was standing in his kitchen at the counter, watching me as I came in, and he was eating a plate of pasta. Felix is proud of his gourmet cooking skills and I caught a whiff of sautéed garlic and fried tomatoes. He had on a sleeveless black T-shirt and gray sweatpants. His upper arms and chest were tanned and muscled, and his fine black hair was combed back. On the marble counter was a small television set. He was watching a tennis match, which he switched off as I came over.

"Manners," he said, wiping off his mouth with a light blue napkin. "Momma taught me a lot about who to trust and what to know and she also taught me about manners, about shutting off the television when you have a guest."

I sat across from him, on a high wooden stool. Behind me was a window that overlooked the ocean. Behind Felix were three kitchen cabinets. Gunmen can't hide in kitchen cabinets.

I said, "Then I'll be polite in return and let you know I'm carrying."

He nodded, picked up a glass of wine. "Knew it the moment you came in, Lewis. You should see yourself in the mirror sometime when you're carrying your piece. You have this strained look on your face, like you just had an enema. Or like the weight of your gun's dragging your chest down. You've got to lighten up, Lewis, or someday someone you're trying to fool ain't gonna be fooled. Get you something to drink?"

"Ice water," I said. "Coming here or talking to you has always been an educational experience, Felix."

"That so," he said, coming back from the refrigerator and giving me a glass mug with ice chips and water. "You haul out your twelve-gauge anytime recently?"

I think we both smiled at the memory as I drank the water. We had first met a couple of years back, when I was working a story similar to the one I was working on now, about Lynn Germano. Not that it was about a murdered high school girl working as a waitress—no, it was about a woman friend of Alice Crenshaw's who had been embezzled of her life savings. But the stories were similar in that neither would ever be published in *Shoreline*. After a few weeks of poking around and asking questions, Felix arrived at my elbow one day as I was having a beer at the Whale's Song. His message was simple. Someone was upset at my activities, and Felix was there to make sure that I stopped them. My message was equally simple, somewhat shorter, and exceptionally more vulgar. Felix left, I finished my beer, and when I went out to my Range Rover, I found that all four tires had been slit.

Getting the tires replaced took two days. Finding out who Felix was took another three. On the sixth day, I went to his house with my 12-gauge and returned the favor to the four tires of his Mercedes Benz. He came out. I stood there, the smoking shotgun in my arms at parade rest. He looked at me with a blank stare, smiled, and said, "You want to come in for a beer?"

And that was that. On the seventh day, we both rested, and he took me to an afternoon game at Fenway Park and dinner at Locke-Ober's in Boston and said, "You're about the only guy in this state who could have done that and gotten away with it."

We've been close acquaintances—not friends—ever since.

Felix took his plate and dropped it into his dishwasher and leaned against the counter, resting on his thick forearms, the wineglass still at his elbow.

"You said you were looking for something," he said. "Which might be what?"

"Some information. Looking into what you might have

heard about this Lynn Germano case, the waitress who was strangled and found hanging in her cottage.''

Felix picked up the glass and swirled around the wine, looking at the light amber fluid. "You asking me if I was involved in it?"

"No, but I will if you want me to. Were you involved with it?"

He smiled, showing off teeth that were the result of either very good genetics or very expensive dental work. "I don't think you'd believe any answer I'd give you, Lewis, so I'll give you this. That one was not professional. Not professional at all. You got too many potential witnesses, you're in an enclosed area, and you leave the body and a ton of evidence behind when you're done. That's not professional."

I said, "Professional would be an empty cottage and nothing else, except maybe a body wrapped in chains and weights and dumped off of Hampton Shoals. Right?"

Felix smiled again. "Exactly. That's professional. Leave nothing behind but empty rooms. People and her friends and the cops think she's run away, or got kidnapped, and soon her face's on milk cartons, while her real face's getting nibbled over by lobsters, and you can feel good about things, knowing that it was clean."

"And since you're a professional, Felix, you weren't involved," I said. I shifted my weight, feeling again the stiffness of the Beretta at my side. Damn Felix and his observations.

"That's right."

"So what do you hear?"

He shrugged and glanced at the television set, and I knew he wished I was away so he could turn it back on. "Hardly a peep, Lewis. Just that it must've been a grudge hit, or something that got somebody else mad."

"Not much."

He shrugged again. "I've seen worse."

"Really?"

He didn't look at me. "Let's leave it at that."

So I did, and I finished off the ice water. "One more thing," I asked. "What can you tell me about Oliver Mailloux, and a guy that works for him—name of Derek?"

Felix tapped the edge of his wineglass. "Yeah. Some pair. Oliver Mailloux and Derek Cooney. Couple of sleazeballs, Lewis, not worth knowing."

"Your business ever run into their business?"

He crinkled his nose, as if smelling some foul body odor. "No, not really. We had a somewhat heated discussion some years ago, and he knows well enough what areas to stay away from. But he's always scamming, always looking to twist a little here and there. Wouldn't surprise me if those two do a little pharmaceutical sales with their French-Canadian clientele. Or do a little cross-border work—hell, thousands of Canucks come through here every week. Wouldn't take much for Oliver to work up something where he's making some good bucks under the table off of that traffic."

"What's he up to now?"

"Don't know," Felix said, running a fingertip across the edge of his wineglass. "He's up to something, though. I heard that he's been boasting about doing something that'll be settling some scores and bringing in a lot of money. Says this is his last summer on the beach, and that he'll be going out West just as soon as the leaves turn."

I saw the look on his face as he glanced at the television, and I knew it was time to leave. Being in Felix's house always makes me nervous, because I know it's a target area for a number of people out there who skirt along the shadows and have long memories. Felix is pretty confident about his skills, but I lost confidence in mine some years ago.

As I got off the stool he said, "You working on this thing, then?"

"I'm doing a column about it, yeah."

He smirked. "Sure. Just be careful around Oliver and his

buddy Derek. That Derek isn't too bright but he's very literal —he'll do anything that Oliver tells him to do, whether it's kicking some frat boys out of a room or torching some magazine writer's home."

The ice water seemed to gel a bit in my belly at that. "Thanks for the tip."

"No problem." He smiled and leaned forward and lowered his voice. "Tell me, Lewis. About why you do it. And don't ask me why I do what I do, because the answer is easy: I make a lot of money. Period. But not you. Why do you do it, when you and I both know that your column isn't ever going to get published?"

I put my hands on the back of the stool. "It keeps me busy, and it gives me a sense of satisfaction. And in a way, I think it balances off some of the activities you're involved with, Felix. So I think that's a good trade."

If I had planned to insult him, it had failed. Felix smiled and stood up from the counter, rubbing at his biceps. "The people I deal with, Lewis, they deserve whatever's coming to them. The funny thing is, they don't realize that. They yammer on about bills to pay and an unhappy childhood and parents who used to beat them up, and I don't give a shit. I really don't. The day the criminal justice system adopts my philosophy, it'll be the day you can go for a midnight stroll in Central Park and come out in one piece."

"You think Lynn Germano deserved what happened to her?"

The same smile, the same shrug. "Maybe. You never know, Lewis. You never know. She might've deserved it, and right now you and the cops don't know."

"Thanks," I said, heading to the front door. "And let me know how the tennis match works out."

I was a stride away from the door when he called out, "One more thing, Lewis."

I turned and said, "What's that?"

"I know something else."

"Which might be what?"

His grin was wider. "That before you came to Tyler you were in a hospital in Nevada. And before that, you worked in Washington. At the Department of Defense."

For a moment I thought the waves outside were making the foundation of Felix's home shift, for it seemed like the floor was moving beneath my feet. I was glad I had drunk that ice water beforehand, or I was sure that my mouth would have dried into dust at that last comment.

"Pretty good work there, Felix," I said. "I'm impressed. How did you get that information?"

"Is it true?"

"I'm not going to say."

He crossed his thick arms across his chest. "Groups I do work with, Lewis, there's two levels. There's the level that gets in the news, about the garlic and spaghetti eaters and family members and messy hits. And there's the other level, which is quite busy, quite rich, and quite adept at keeping itself out of the news. Think of the budget in the DoD and how much money's spent there, and how much money there is to be made, and that gives you some idea of their influence. I made a few phone calls. That was it. And no matter how much prying went on, that's all I could gather about you."

"Why did you want to know?"

He gave me a joking frown. "Because I like you, Lewis. And I hate guessing about why you're so quiet about what you did before you came to Tyler. It makes me uneasy."

"So quit guessing," I said, and I left.

A minute or two later I was in my Range Rover, shivering slightly, wondering what was propelling Felix Tinios. And I remembered what he said about Oliver Mailloux and Derek Cooney, and I shivered some more. The thought came to me of driving down my driveway and seeing nothing there except a smoldering ruin, and it almost made me ill.

And another thought came to me. Felix said the murder of

Lynn Germano was unprofessional, so unprofessional that he couldn't have done it. Of course, a true professional could have made it look sloppily amateurish, to draw attention away from himself. A true professional like Felix Tinios.

I backed out of the driveway and headed back to Tyler Beach.

A while later I was standing at a metal railing at a sidewalk on Atlantic Avenue, looking over the wide and near-empty sands of Tyler Beach. I had added an Irish tweed hat to my clothing collection, since the rain had transformed itself into a steady mist and I was going to be outside for a while, and the wind off the ocean was a sharp one, biting at my hands and face. Traffic was quite light for a Wednesday in June and I had gotten a parking space on one of the side streets with ease, and that afternoon I even had the quarters to pay for it.

After buying a carton of coffee from the Surf Coffee Shop, I had trudged across the road and was now leaning against the railing, looking at the surf pound against the sands of Tyler Beach State Park. There were a few kids and some parents on the sands, walking slowly and bundled up from the raw weather, and no doubt wondering where in hell the sunshine and happy beaches that the brochures had promised were. The red wooden lifeguard stands were empty of tanned lifeguards in orange suits, and I wondered if they worked on their tans during cloudy days like this one. Even with the foul weather I felt something warm inside of me, looking at the wide sands and the harsh sound of the waves rolling in, seeing the white foam of the breakers pounding against the shore. This was a lovely place, despite all the touristy stuff, and too bad if people were staying inside this day and not enjoying what was here.

The Maid of the Seas monument—formally known as the New Hampshire Marine Memorial—was about fifty feet up on my left, built on a little outcropping of rock that jutted from the sidewalk. The monument, a reclining stone woman looking out to the ocean with a wreath in her hand, was built to commemorate the New Hampshire sailors and marines who had died on the world's oceans. Around the statue is a low concrete wall, with each of the dead men's names carved into it. There were a group of kids there, jawing and playing with skateboards. Off to my right was a two-story glass-and-concrete building that was the state park's headquarters, and an empty bandshell with rows of benches. Directly across the street was the Tyler Beach Palace and inside the Palace I could barely make out the neon lights of the Palace Diner.

The coffee was hot and soothing. I stood for a while, thinking that maybe Lynn Germano had come to this very spot to look over the sands and fantasize about the summer that lay ahead for her. Or maybe she had dreamed about a certain boyfriend, thought and feared for her future, and fretted over college catalogs, deciding which slots she would go into, which courses she would take.

Too late to know. It was beyond that. And I hadn't had much luck in getting a grasp of who she was and what had happened to her. Sarah Lockwood, her coworker at the Palace Diner, hadn't been much help, and the same was true of her neighbors, her boss, Oliver Mailloux, and her mother, who had closed a door in my face.

But there was someone else out there. Someone who had gone into her cottage that night and had sex with her and squeezed the life from her throat, and then had enough nerves and composure to stage a fake suicide.

I took another sip of the coffee. A couple of the kids had crawled up on the Maid of Seas and were rubbing their crotches against her stone head.

Lynn Germano. Here I was, rooting around for you, and I don't even know which college you were going to, what you had decided for your life. I didn't even know if you had planned that far ahead, or if you were too young and too sure of yourself to worry about decisions like that.

Some decisions. I had become a journalism major when I

was in college and had gone down some very strange roads before arriving here. And I thought again of what Felix Tinios had found out through his few phone calls. So strange, that he had gotten that far in his quest, and I knew that he had done just that, for Felix was not one for easy exaggeration. But I had been told that the records and names would be erased, would be put in deep storage, would be forgotten. Somebody down there wasn't doing their job, and that surprised me not one bit.

The sands of Tyler Beach looked cold and sodden, not at all like the desert sands I had been on so many years ago. In Nevada, of course, since Felix Tinios was right on target.

The names came back to me, the section I worked for: Carl Socha, Trent Baker, Cissy Manning, and the others. And the damnable George Walker. Carl had been my best friend and George had been our section leader, leading us around in circles in the desert for our annual qualifications that certain year. Everyone in the section knew we were lost, of course, and Carl and I had joked about it every day. But George was determined to bring us back at the end of the week-long exercise, lost or not. We all knew that the transponder he carried could have been switched on to trigger a search party, since we seemed to be doomed to spend a month in the desert. But George had been so determined, so stubborn.

It had been almost funny, even in the heat during the day and the cold at night, until the morning when the helicopters flew by.

Until those damn helicopters flew by.

I finished my coffee and crumpled up the container and tossed it into an overflowing KEEP TYLER BEACH CLEAN wastebasket and walked north. When I reached the Maid of the Seas statue I gave the youngsters my best smile and told them that if they didn't get their young asses away from there, I would call the cops. They went. I stayed, looking at the names carved in stone. None of them was familiar; there was a lot of room for others, but I knew my section would never be memorialized. Part of the deal, part of the deal that had gotten me here.

I sat on the low concrete wall and watched the waves roll in. After some minutes of deciding whether to call Paula Quinn or Diane Woods to have dinner with me, I gave up and decided to eat by myself.

On my way to my Range Rover, I made a phone call; after a handful of words from me, Mrs. Germano had hung up the phone in mid-sentence.

Some things weren't going to change.

A few hours later it was dark and the rain was pouring down now, not even pretending to be a mist. I drove my Range Rover down the trail from the Lafayette House's parking lot to my house and slammed on the brakes before I reached the garage.

The house was still there, undamaged, and I remembered Felix Tinios's warning about Derek Cooney and how he would do anything that Oliver Mailloux told him to do. The truth is, I had thought a lot about that conversation during my solitary dinner at the Lighthouse Restaurant, and I had eaten too fast and had skipped coffee and dessert.

I should have felt fine, looking at my house with a meal of sautéed haddock and two glasses of wine inside of me, but there was something wrong. Something had been added.

There was something on my front door.

In a moment my Beretta was in my left hand, and I scrabbled through the Range Rover's glove compartment, digging out my high-powered halogen flashlight. I stepped outside, the light shining through the streaming rain, and before I went to the front door I went through the garage and looked at everything. Nothing seemed to be disturbed.

I went back outside, into the rain, and walked around the house, shining the light into the darkened windows, trying to see if anyone was in there hiding or waiting. Along the ocean side of the house the waves were quite loud, pounding and booming, tossing up their spray, and I walked carefully on the jagged rocks, not wanting to fall into my little cove and be swept away. Off to the south were the lights of Weymouth's Point and I thought for a moment of the comfortable friends and families sitting there, talking and reading and watching television and making love, feeling safe and secure from the rain.

Back out front my face and hands were soaked, and rainwater was running down my neck, dodging my Irish tweed hat. The Beretta was heavy and cold in the rain. I walked up to the front door, shining the light closely, looking for fishlines or tripwires, but there was nothing.

Except for the square piece of white paper on the door, tacked on its four corners. The overhang had kept it fairly dry. Stapled to the bottom of the paper was a familiar business card, with the *Shoreline* magazine logo and my name. There was a typed message:

If you want to know more about the waitres death, come see me tomorroww at my boat, the Carla V., at five thirty am, in Tyler Harbor. Dock 4. No phone calls, and no cops.

Henry Desmond

Just above the name was a scribble. It was a familiar name, and I recalled a column I had done last year—for real—about the attempts of the Tyler fishermen to form their own cooperative. Henry Desmond. I remembered a man in his fifties, wearing dark green chinos and workshirt, with leathery skin and thin white hair and an eye that was somewhat damaged, which made him look like he was scowling all the time.

As I thought back to the last time I had seen Henry Desmond, I kept my flashlight on the piece of paper, reading and rereading the note, and I started forming questions in my mind, about Henry and what he knew about Lynn Germano, and what kind of relationship they had, and how he had gotten hold of my business card from my canvass of Lynn's neighborhood earlier this week.

But first I would ask Henry Desmond who the hell did he think he was, coming on my property.

The rain kept falling and I tucked my flashlight under my arm as I unlocked the door and went inside. I only took off my wet clothes after a half-hour search of the house, flashlight and Beretta still in my cold hands.

Nothing seemed to have been disturbed except me.

7

AT ABOUT 5:30 ON THURSDAY MORNING, I
was on Ashburn Avenue on Tyler Beach,
squeezing both hands on the Range Rover's steering wheel,
wondering how in the world I could be stuck in traffic at that
hour of the morning. A moment ago I had driven past the Tyler
police station and wasn't surprised to see the lot empty of Diane
Woods's Volkswagen. Even police detectives need their sleep.
From the police station to the turnoff that led to the Tyler
Harbor docks is a drive of about one hundred seconds, but man
and his works were conspiring against me that morning in the
form of the Felch Memorial Bridge, which spanned the harbor
and led Route 1-A into Falconer, and then to Salisbury.

The span over the harbor is a drawbridge, and this morning
it seemed to be stuck in the upright position. As I waited behind
the other cars, I remembered reading a story about the bridge
written by Paula Quinn in an April issue of the Tyler *Chronicle*.
In the story, the town engineer had predicted problems with
the bridge unless the state fixed the drawbridge drive mecha-
nism, and shivering slightly in the cool interior of my Range
Rover, I was ready to believe him and to believe any predictions

he might also have about the weekend's Tri-State Megabucks numbers.

At this hour the bars and fried-food stands along Ashburn Avenue were closed, and there were only a couple of convenience stores open, their lights bright white and garish in the faint morning light. Most of the cottages were darkened, the parties and the lovemaking and loud music long gone. A long-haired boy zipped by on a skateboard, wearing jeans that had been hacked off at the knee and a tie-dye T-shirt. He was sipping from a fruit juice box and weaving in and out of the stopped cars. Someone blew a horn and he tossed them the finger. Rush-hour communications at Tyler Beach.

So I waited. And I remembered.

It had been a cold February evening, and in the selectmen's meeting room at the town hall, a blue haze of cigarette smoke was still drifting across the humming fluorescent lights and the rows of wooden chairs were in disarray. Most of the people had left after the meeting's conclusion and I had gone over to talk to Henry Desmond, who was sitting by himself in the rear of the room on a folding wooden chair. His chinos were patched and stained, and he wore a quilted blue jacket with tattered cuffs and a faded Red Sox cap. His skin had the look of belonging to someone who wasn't familiar with and didn't care about sunscreen protection factors.

I sat next to him and said, "You must feel pretty good, Henry, about the fishermen's cooperative being approved."

His arms were folded against his chest and, with his damaged right eye, it looked like he was about ready to fall asleep. "Well, yeah, I guess," he said, "but it's one of those victories you feel sad about gettin'."

"Why's that?"

He nodded in the direction of the other side of the meeting room, where a couple of younger fishermen were laughing and talking to each other. "Look at 'em there, laughing and thinking everything's gonna be all right now that we got the co-op. They don't know squat. All we did tonight was to stretch out the pain."

I was jotting in my notebook as he talked, but I kept an eye on what he was doing, and he was looking at something very far off.

Henry sighed and rubbed at the stubble on his face and said, "It used to be that my dad, when he was a young'un and the family needed lobsters, they'd just go out at low tide near the town line with Tyler and North Tyler with a washtub and take whatever they needed. Nowadays, you gotta work twelve or fourteen hours to get the same catch you could get in three or four hours ten years ago. Hell, I remember when there only used to be eight or nine boats in both Falconer and Tyler harbors, and now there's damn near thirty, out tryin' for the same schools, the same stocks. And they don't listen to you, not at all. They don't care about what it was like years ago—they think these are the good days, if you can believe that, where you gotta work so hard for so little. And don't even get me talking about what we're dumpin' out there in the water every day, from oil tankers to septic tanks."

"I've always thought that lobstermen and fishermen never say when they have a good day, that they're afraid it's a curse," I said.

"Mebbe so," Henry said. "But it's turning out that there's no good news and no good days, and you can write that down. It's becoming a wet desert out there, with more and more boats from up and down this coast, chasing less and less fish. The co-op's just delaying the inevitable, maybe for another five years, maybe another ten. One of these days the whole industry—commercial and family—it's gonna collapse, and those seafood restaurants are gonna become gourmet restaurants, 'cause by then, no one's gonna be able to afford fish."

"Then why fight so hard to set up the co-op?"

He nodded again to the younger fishermen at the other end

of the room. ''Those boys need help now, Mr. Cole. They got their bills to pay and their kids to feed, and you can't tell 'em to be patient and try to conserve and try to save things for the future. They gotta worry about today, and I was just doin' what I could to help 'em out. They don't have nothing else to do with their lives. Nothing.''

I put my pen down and looked up at the other side of the room, and maybe it was the cigarette smoke, but I sensed that there was no smile behind the eyes of those laughing fishermen, supposedly pleased at the co-op they had just won.

They knew.

Up ahead some traffic moved and the bridge span slowly came down, and more car horns blew. I checked the time on the Range Rover's dashboard clock. Fifteen minutes late. Something seemed to gnaw at my stomach. I hate being late. Someone once told me that being late at my own funeral would make me upset and I said of course it would, because I'd be disappointing those friends and family who had gotten in early to get a good seat.

I've always remembered that thought.

Just before the Felch Bridge I turned off to the right to the Harbor Road, past other stores, restaurants, and charter fishing outfits that charge you a fistful of dollars a day for the privilege of being on a crowded boat, drinking warm beer and eating baloney-and-cheese sandwiches, trying to catch fish with a dozen other people. There was a gravel road that led down to the docks and I parked next to a NO PARKING sign by a series of Dumpsters. It seemed too early in the morning for parking regulations and their enforcers. The morning light was getting stronger and there was a good breeze.

Tyler Harbor is a jumble of docks, public and private, and two marinas, with the usual mess of boats in dry dock, condominiums under construction, and sea gulls scrabbling around, looking for something decaying and fly-ridden to eat.

There were a number of pickup trucks scattered around in the parking lots, and out on the waters of the harbor, boats were churning their way out to the Atlantic, both the smaller lobster boats and the larger trawlers, with their nets rolled up on their sterns like coils of rope. Across the harbor was a smaller inlet that marked Falconer Harbor, and beyond that were the marsh and low lights of Falconer and the bright lights and round, boxy shapes of the Falconer nuclear power plant, quietly producing power. No protestors in sight.

I knew I was late, and after grabbing a pair of binoculars from inside the Range Rover I walked down to the docks, and when I reached number four, I started across the worn wooden planks. To my right were the lights of Tyler, and farther up, I could make out the condominium complex where Diane Woods lived. Near the condo were some small moorings, where Diane kept her 24-foot sailboat, *Miranda,* at bay. This time of the morning, she was probably getting up, and I wondered who was there next to her in bed as she slipped out from underneath the sheets for an early morning shower.

Dock four stretched out about six lobster-boat lengths into the blue-gray waters of Tyler Harbor. I walked out to the edge of the dock and looked down at the water lapping against the large and barnacle-encrusted pilings. I wasn't too sure what the tide was. Diane and other sailors I knew could just look and sniff at the air and tell you if it was high tide or low, but I could tell it was low only when some mudflats around the harbor were exposed and one could practically walk across to Falconer.

I wasn't too sure what tide it was this morning, but I was sure of one thing. Dock four was empty. I had missed Henry Desmond.

From across the waters there were sounds of engines growling and another stern dragger rumbled out. No doubt some of the men I had seen that February evening were heading out to the Atlantic this morning. Did they feel any better, I wondered, now that the cooperative was set up? Was it any easier? I doubted it and I lifted up my binoculars and saw a lobster boat swinging around, an old man at the wheel. Most lobster boats have two-man crews, but a lot of the old-timers, like Henry, can only afford to work alone. The boat swung around some more and I saw the blue letters against the bow: *Carla V.*

I started waving my arms and the boat seemed to hesitate. I brought the glasses up again and saw the old man wave back. How pleasant. Two lonely people, early in the morning in a smelly New Hampshire harbor, waving at each other.

Damn. I was going to start waving again like an idiot but things happened very quickly over the next few seconds.

There was a bright flash of light and my mind, not really thinking that well, thought: The Falconer nuke plant? Then there was the loud boom that slapped at my ears and a warm breath of wind that knocked me on my back, and my binoculars fell from my hands and into the harbor waters, and I thought, damn, a two-hundred-dollar pair of binoculars, gone.

Time seemed to have dragged on for a bit, until I knew I was on my back, opening and closing my mouth and eyes, feeling pain at the base of my skull, and I slowly sat up, resting my arms against my knees. I shook my head, trying to make things feel clearer. I failed. Out on the harbor the initial plume of smoke was drifting away and two stern trawlers were making circles in the sluggish water, their diesels grumbling quite loudly, their men leaning over the gunwales, looking and shouting and pointing. Moored boats that had been near the *Carla V.* rocked to and fro from the force of the explosion. Sirens were sounding somewhere off behind me and I wondered if Diane Woods's overnight guest—if there was one—was now being shown the door as she ran out. My face and ears and head hurt, and I had splinters in my right hand, feeling like tiny razor cuts.

Out on the harbor, the *Carla V.* had turned turtle and its shattered hull was now burning. The plume of smoke was a weak, black one, straggling up into the cold morning air. There was other debris out there, also smoking in the now-oily waters. I didn't recognize the shape of a man in the water and I didn't want to.

I started pulling out the splinters from my right hand. It was all I could do, but it was damn hard work, as my hands were shaking so. If I had been on time instead of late . . . And I began to remember other plumes of smoke and dust and other things. And I wondered again why it was happening to me.

Though we didn't know it on that September morning years ago, it was going to be our last day in the desert. There were a dozen of us, all Department of Defense employees, wandering through the government-owned wastes of Nevada as part of a yearly training exercise, in the infinitesimal chance that we would actually be sent somewhere in a Mideast desert, far from our usual offices and cubicles at the five-sided palace. The only people I was familiar with that week so long ago were the members of my own section: Carl Socha, Trent Baker, and Cissy Manning. We had on tan-and-gray desert uniforms and carried packs and our water and freeze-dried MRE's—supposedly to stand for Meals, Ready to Eat, but after a couple of days, we all agreed it stood for Meals, Rejected by Everyone. It was an odd time, being in that desert that year, almost the last in a series of very odd times from my previous life, when I knew next to nothing about Tyler Beach.

It was supposed to be a training exercise to get us used to the desert, in case the DoD needed people who read and guessed for a living to be shipped over to Dhahran. Some training, and some exercise. The only exercise we got was wandering up hills and sand dunes, hopelessly lost, as our section leader, the damnable George Walker, led us deeper and deeper into the back country. We crossed a lot of range signs and U.S.

Government *No Trespassing* notices, but we ignored them all. We were the government.

And there was no training. Just the damn walking and the hot days and cold nights, and waiting for George to give it up and switch on the transponder, so the helicopters could come and take us home. About the only part of the grind that I enjoyed was seeing the stars every night, for never had I ever seen them so clear.

That September morning we had finished the sludge that was called breakfast, and we were taking a break before walking again. Carl Socha sat next to me, looking like a bedouin, with a scarf around his black face. He had two passions in his life: the New York Knicks and the Politburo of what remained of the Soviet Union. He could—and often did—bore me for hours with obscure bits of information about tall men who could throw a ball through a rim or squat men who could stay in one piece in a place that was now known for lynching its leaders. He was from Morningside Heights in New York City and loved to tease the other member of our section, Trent Baker, who had grown up on the Gold Coast of Long Island.

"Same state but a million miles away, right, Trent?" Carl would always ask. "How does it feel, growing up without working a day of your life?"

And Trent smiled sweetly and would shoot back in his cultured Gold Coast accent, "How could I have worked, my dear fellow, when you and your kind were taking all of the best jobs?"

Carl would snicker and say, "Yep. And the best women, too. All those upper-class nightmares are true, Trent, about the horny help, slobbering over your mothers and sisters. You go back and tell your folks that."

And Trent would only smile.

This morning, though, Carl took a swallow from his water bottle and said, "End of today, I swear to God, Lewis, that shithead George doesn't trip that transponder, I'm gonna rap his head and do it for him. I'm about out of water and I'm all out of patience."

"Sounds good to me," I said. "You do that, and I'll sit on his chest while you go through his pockets."

"Damn right." He screwed the top back on his bottle, stashed it in his pack, and then looked over our tired and dirty crew. "Cissy's looking over at you, Lewis. Been doin' it all morning. What's up?"

I tried to keep my voice light but I'm sure I failed. "I think she's thinking something over, and hasn't quite made up her mind yet."

"Yeah? And what's that?"

"Whether or not to move in with me."

Carl looked at me, his brown eyes unwavering. "Hey. Don't even joke about shit like that."

"It's no joke. I asked her day before we left."

"And what she'd say?"

"She said she'd think about it. I believe she's still thinking."

Carl shook his head. "Damn. 'Nother fine bachelor man gets himself hitched."

"Things are tough all around," I said. "And it's not a hitch. Just a trial run, to see if things can go anywhere."

"Man, with Cissy Manning, that's a place I wouldn't mind going to."

I got up and winked at him and brushed the sand off my desert fatigues and walked over to Cissy Manning, who was sitting with her pack at her side, tying back her red hair in a ponytail. Her face was grimy and her hands were roughened and her lips were chapped, but when she looked up at me and smiled with her light green eyes, it felt like she was sitting on my own chest, waiting to set off my own transponder.

Squatting down beside her, I said, "You better watch it. Carl's noticed that you've been making goo-goo eyes at me all morning."

She smiled, finished tying the ribbon, which—believe it or

not—was also desert tan. "He's wrong. I've just been thinking about what it's going to feel like, taking a shower again."

"Doing any other thinking?"

Cissy picked up a handful of sand and tossed it at me. "Damn you, Lewis, yes I have. And I need some answers."

Around us were other members of the group, including George Walker, who had a map and compass and who was still trying to figure out where we were, but I only noticed Cissy and the light freckles across her face and the little laugh lines, which were creased with dirt. Before we left for the desert she had shown me a slinky pair of black panties, and had said that she'd be wearing them throughout the trip, and that one thought had made many long minutes pass away.

"Go ahead," I said. "Start asking."

"You still going to hang around Carl if we do move in together?"

I shrugged. "But of course. Next."

She laughed and said, "Maybe I find him a bad influence on you."

"Maybe you do. Next question?"

"You know the rules. One of us will have to transfer out of the section, once we're sharing a roof. Which one?"

"Entirely negotiable," I said. "But if it's me, I want you to move into my place. I don't like your neighborhood. There. Satisfied?"

George started making announcements about moving out and we both stood up and she gave me a quick peck on the nose. "Quite," Cissy said. "And you'll have your answer at the next break, Mr. Lewis."

Of course, I would never hear it.

Within a few minutes we crossed over a ridge, I walking with Carl, he muttering under his breath about governmental incompetence, and I looked ahead, watching Cissy, seeing her pretty little butt swing underneath her tan camouflage clothes, and though I was busy drawing up the list of people I wanted to tell when she said yes, I still heard the yell from someone at the head of the column.

We bunched together, looking down at the impossible site below us. There, in the middle of the desert and government-owned lands, was a herd of sheep. Fenced in with a stockade and wire, peacefully eating some hay.

Sheep? In a pen? So far from any road?

Some people were huddled around George, who was looking over his map, looking for a farm. Carl said, "Damn fool's taken us off the government reservation," and I was going to say something back to Carl, when I noticed on one of the fence posts a video camera.

Then came the sounds of the helicopters.

And later I would think, God, if only some of us were more alert that morning, had remembered better, and had started running, we might have made it.

And I might have gotten my reply.

Within a number of minutes after the explosion on the *Carla V.*, police and fire units had arrived, and Diane Woods had met me on the empty dock. By then I had the splinters out of my right hand and had wrapped a handkerchief around it, and only a few splotches of rust-brown blood had seeped through. Diane's wedge-cut brown hair was still slightly wet and through it all, I still had the slightly smug feeling of one who had gotten up earlier than another. And that of course was mixed with the slightly hysterical feeling that if I had gotten to this dock on time, I would have been on the *Carla V.* as it was shattered this morning. My chest still hurt from trying not to think about it that much.

Diane had on a short leather jacket over a polo shirt, and her usual jeans and black Reeboks. She said, "You want to tell me again what the hell you were doing here at this hour of the morning?"

"Sure," I said, looking out over the harbor. The fire had

burned itself out and the overturned hull of the *Carla V.* was slowly moving in the harbor swells. A stern trawler had tied off a line to the blackened hull and an 18-foot aluminum boat that belonged to the Tyler Fire Department was slowly plowing through the waters, picking up blackened lumps of something that I didn't want to look at too closely.

"Got a note from Henry last night," I continued. "He said he had some information for me about the Lynn Germano case. Nothing else more than that. He told me to meet him here, and I did. But the Felch Bridge decided to have a gearbox attack, so I was late, and here I am."

"So here you are," she said, her arms folded. She looked out over the harbor and said, "This really sucks, Lewis. You get a note from someone saying they have information on a homicide in this town. Less than twelve hours later, this person's dead. Like I was taught in the academy, that's one hell of a fucking coincidence. You telling me that he didn't tell you anything more?"

"Nothing."

"And you weren't so curious about his note and what he might have known about Lynn Germano's murder that you didn't call him? And you didn't think of passing on this little piece of information to me, that there was a guy out there who said he knew something about the case?"

I said, "His note said no calls, either to him or to you."

"You always so dumb?"

I sighed and said, "You always this mean?"

Kicking at a chunk of gravel on the parking lot, she said, "Yeah, I'm always this pissed when things like this begin happening. I don't need the grief and I don't need the aggravation, and you of all people should know that. You being straight with me, Lewis?"

I held my bleeding hand against my chest and looked back out to the harbor. The fire department boat had halted in the water, and it looked like one of the firefighters was leaning over the side, busy being sick. "You needing to ask me that question tells me something, Diane."

She nodded. "Yeah. You're right. And let me tell you something, Lewis. I have to go to the state police and the assistant attorney general working with me on this mess and tell them what you've told me. Tell them that a witness—hell, maybe even a suspect in this case—got blown out of the water this morning. That although it might have been an LPG tank that let loose, right now it looks like explosives. And that my friend the magazine writer saw it all happen. And they'll probably want to talk to you. And I'll have to say some stuff about how I've known you ever since you moved here and how upstanding a guy you are. I just don't want something you're doing to come back and bite me on the ass. Got it?"

I said, "I'm working on a column, Diane. You know that, and you've trusted me before when I've done other columns. You want me to stop working, you let me know, and I'll tell you if I'll go along with that."

"Oh, fuck this," she said, and walked off to her Crown Vic. I looked back at the fire department boat. One of the firefighters still had his head hanging over the water. I walked to my Range Rover, past a useless fire department pumper and two marked cruisers from the Tyler Police Department. The windshield for my Range Rover was ticket free. A very small victory in a day full of defeats. Henry Desmond was dead, dead before he could tell me or anyone else what he might have known about Lynn Germano's death. Diane Woods was pissed at me. And the guy who had killed both Lynn and Henry—if it was the same person, which was a pretty good guess—was still out there. He was close. He was sticking around for some reason.

I drove home with one hand, keeping a close look on the rearview and sideview mirrors.

At home there were two messages on my answering machine. I let the little green light blink as I showered, and as the water ran, I had the bathroom door locked and my 9-mm Beretta on the bathroom counter. I shivered as the water ran down my back and legs, remembering again the hot blast that morning and that damn Nevada desert, so many miles and years away. I put a bandage on the largest cut on my hand and as I dried myself I looked down again at the scars along my left side, on my back, and on my left knee, and I wondered again why I didn't think of Nevada more often. Not that I was complaining.

I threw on a blue terry-cloth robe and padded downstairs, still carrying the Beretta, the weight making my hand shake. Of course it was the weight. I went to the answering machine and played back the messages. It was now 7:30 in the morning. One message was from Paula Quinn: "Lewis, this is Paula. What the hell happened down at the harbor this morning? I heard you were in the area. Give me a call." The other was from Alice Crenshaw. She sounded nervous: "Lewis, this is Alice Crenshaw. Please call me as soon as you can."

I called Alice and there was no answer. I tried Paula at her apartment in North Tyler and the phone rang and rang, so I tried her at the *Chronicle* office. She answered the phone by herself on the second ring.

"You're there pretty early," I said.

"Yeah, well, I get a lot of work done in the morning when no one else is here to bug me," Paula said. "Only problem is, sometimes when you answer the phone, you get some old geezer on the line who's complaining about his subscription or a classified ad. Tell me, Lewis, what happened at the harbor?"

I sat down on the floor, my back against my couch. "You know Henry Desmond?"

"Sure," she said. "I've talked to him, doing a couple of stories about the fish co-op. But it's been a while since I last saw him."

I adjusted my back and looked at my reddened and still bleeding hand. "Well," I said, "Henry Desmond was going out on his lobster boat this morning when it exploded. Henry got himself killed, and the Tyler cops—and I'm sure the state police and maybe even the coast guard—are looking into it."

"My word," she murmured. "Henry Desmond. Were you there, Lewis?"

I looked out the glass doors to the outside deck. The ocean was a gray-blue this morning. "No comment."

"Damn it, Lewis. All right. Off the record?"

I thought for a moment. "Okay. Off the record, I was at the harbor."

"Jesus," she said. "What were you doing there?"

"No comment."

"Lewis," she complained. "I told you, we're off the record."

"Paula, on or off, the answer's the same. No comment."

Before she hung up she said, "Sometimes you're a prick, Lewis Cole," and I told her that sometimes I agreed with her.

When I was done with the phone I unlocked the sliding glass doors to my deck and stepped outside, breathing deeply of the ocean air. My hands were no longer shaking, but I still had the Beretta with me, and I knew it would always be close at hand over the next several days. It's been said that men who carry guns have a need to feel important or larger than life, and that the gun is just a compensating phallic symbol for their own feelings of impotence.

Maybe. All I know is that I like to be armed when the wolves are out there, especially the two-legged, rabid beasts who can strike at any time, at any place. Below me were the cold and wide waters of the Atlantic, and I thought for a moment about the dead Henry Desmond and how particles and atoms of his were now being mixed in the saltwater, and even though it was a horrible death, whatever now existed of Henry Desmond was probably happy that he had been buried at sea.

I just didn't know. I also didn't know much about psychiatry, but I did know I liked having my Beretta at hand.

I also knew that I didn't want to join Henry Desmond. Or Lynn Germano.

8

SOME YEARS AGO I MOVED TO TYLER BEACH,
New Hampshire, soon after I was able to
leave Nevada on my own. I knew I would never return to Nevada, and there were a couple of other places on the map that were now forbidden territory, which I would never go to again. These places included Washington, D.C., the Maryland suburb that I had called home, and the Virginia suburb where someone special had lived. Another forbidden place was the state of Indiana, where I grew up and went to school and got what passed for my education. Those places were now in another life that I was trying to put behind me, as far behind as the forgotten memories of grade-school homework assignments.

In trying to think of a new place to live and breathe in peace, I remembered the first time I had seen the ocean, as a young child during those few years when my parents and I had lived in New Hampshire. I still remember the awe and excitement of seeing for the first time something so huge and fearless and blue lapping at my feet, and in that instant—living in a motel somewhere in Pennsylvania—I knew that Tyler Beach was my destination.

Phone calls were made and deals were struck, and eventually I got here and got a job at *Shoreline* magazine. I also eventually got to meet Detective Diane Woods of the Tyler Police Department. I had been in Tyler Beach for about a year, feeling myself out and spending long afternoons on the deck of my house with a lemonade and gin in my hand, just waiting and thinking, and trying to deal with that acidy guilt that seemed to fill me up at odd times. I had worked hard in cleaning my house and buying the antiques and books that filled it up, and though I worked myself to exhaustion every day, I would often wake up at 2:00 A.M., staring at the ceiling, listening to the whispers of the waves upon the coast, trying to sense the sounds of helicopters. I knew if I didn't do something about the guilt it would swallow me and one day I would go swimming out in the ocean and not come back. One day, I decided it was time.

It took a while, but in researching one of my first columns for *Shoreline* that I knew would never appear in the magazine, I was curious about a group of surfers who would show up at odd times on North Beach, between my house and Weymouth's Point. Surfers of all ages went there at different times of the week, and especially in the fall, when hurricane season spawned tremendous spinning storms that churned up the Atlantic seaboard, causing great swells along all the beaches. The surfers in New Hampshire are under no illusions: They know the waves along this part of the Atlantic are anemic compared to the monsters out in California and Hawaii, and they also know that surfing in thick black wetsuits to protect themselves from the cold water doesn't fulfill the sexy surfer image.

Yet they did it, because it was all they had, which is a motto that most live by. Which was fine. But I was also curious about a certain group of surfers who came almost every other day, no matter the shape of the waves or the tide, and who didn't go out onto the waves that much. With the help of a Nikon camera with 200-mm zoom lens, I got the usual and customary photos of this group, passing along small plastic packages in exchange for folded bills of money to spectators who just happened to wander by. I took down the license plate numbers, traced them, and found their residences, and after a month of research on this particular "column," I had some nice documentation that stretched all the way into Boston.

When I felt like I couldn't go any further with this particular project, I noticed that the burning feeling in my stomach had decreased so much that I could actually eat some food and keep it down for longer than a few minutes. I also noticed that I was able to sleep at night, and that the nightmares of flying helicopters and hooded creatures with labored breathing didn't return as often. One morning I woke up and almost started weeping, because I felt good. That was it. Nothing too out of the ordinary. Just that I felt good.

I then called the Tyler Police Department and asked to speak with a detective, and they gave me their only one, Diane Woods. I made an appointment to see her, knowing quite well what was going to happen. I would pass along the information and then she would chew me out, talking about interfering in a police matter. She would threaten me with arrest. She would tell me not to do anything like this again. And then she would kick me out. And I would go home and have another gin and lemonade, and watch the evening news out of Manchester a week later and see a piece about a major drug bust in Tyler Beach.

Well, I was partly right.

She listened to my spiel and looked at my collection, and then she said, "Let's go for a walk." We walked for a bit and then ended up at the Whale's Song and she had a club soda with a twist and I had a Coke with crushed ice, and she listened to me again and said, "Not that I don't trust my department, but it's easy to bug someone, and sometimes I have sensitive things to talk about. You know?"

Knowing where I had worked just over a year ago, I nodded.

"This is a hell of a town," she continued. "They like to think of themselves as a typical small New Hampshire village, with a pretty town common and white church steeples and a historical society that knows exactly where Reverend Bonus Tyler landed back in 1638. And that's partially true."

She stirred an ice cube with a finger. "That small town means they freak when it comes to budget time, and in another way, you can't blame them. There's no sales or income tax in this state, which means that the towns around here have to make do on property taxes and not much else. And the number of people who enjoy seeing their taxes get raised in this town can probably fit in my cruiser."

I said, "There's a point here you're trying to make."

She nodded. "So true, Lewis Cole," she said, still looking into her drink, as if embarrassed to look at me or anyone else in the restaurant. "The point is that I'm the only detective for this sunny little community, which is manageable in the wintertime, when we really are just a small town. Not too many felony cases and I can do a good job on what does show up. But in the summer, when you get a hundred thousand tourists streaming through here on a weekend, you start drowning. You start picking and choosing, concentrating on the cases that count, knowing you're missing a lot of stuff, like a certain group of nonsurfers that hang out on North Beach. You feel like quitting, but this is your town and you have a sense of responsibility. And in a way, though you hate admitting it, and you would never admit it on a courtroom stand, you like getting the odd pieces of help tossed your way."

"You're welcome," I said.

"Sure," she said. "But it's dangerous, Lewis. If you have the balls for it, fine. But anything goes down wrong, I don't know you, Mr. Cole. And I'll toss your ass in jail with a smile on my face, doing everything I can to protect my job."

I finished off my Coke and said, "I'm beginning to like you

already," and that was my first meeting with Detective Diane Woods of the Tyler Police Department.

After returning those two phone calls from Alice and Paula, I switched down the volume of the answering machine, and after making sure all the doors and windows in my home were locked, I went upstairs and lay down and stared at the ceiling for an hour without once closing my eyes, and then something happened, because the next thing I knew, I was waking up and it was five in the afternoon. I got dressed and saw no messages on the answering machine. When I called the Tyler Police Department, the dispatcher told me that Diane was not in the building, and in the fine tradition of dispatchers everywhere, she wouldn't tell me where she was.

I had an idea, though, and went through my Porter area phone book, which contains the listings for the Tyler area, and found an address on the beach. I also grabbed a manila file folder and I went out to my Range Rover, carrying my holstered Beretta in my other hand, and I stashed it under the front seat. As I drove up my bumpy driveway, I couldn't get the sight of that damn plume of smoke and the burning hull of the *Carla V.* out of my mind, and I hoped Diane was where I thought she was.

She was. Ten minutes later I pulled into a tiny street called Clipper Lane, just off Atlantic Avenue, about a hundred yards from the harbor. Diane's Crown Vic and a marked police cruiser were parked out in front of a weatherbeaten two-story cottage, with the name *Desmond* carved into a wooden sign hanging over the door. There was a small garage next to the cottage and an empty dirt driveway that looked like it would be overwhelmed by a Volkswagen Beetle. I parked in a No Parking—Loading Zone area, behind a fried-dough restaurant. I decided to leave the Beretta in the Range Rover—I didn't think I'd get into too much trouble with Diane and the other police firepower being around. As I walked up to the cottage, Diane came out, carrying a clipboard under her arm. She was still wearing a short leather jacket over a polo shirt, and her jeans and black Reeboks.

She stopped and made a show of rolling her eyes, and said, "Lewis, I'm really too busy for your nonsense this afternoon."

I was carrying the manila file folder and I said, "I know, Diane. But I have something for you. Something in trade. You give me five minutes in that house and I'll give you something that might be able to help you."

"Why should I give you five seconds?"

I said, "Because I was straight with you this morning. If I was trying to futz around with your case, I wouldn't have told you anything. I could have said that I was down at the harbor looking for a boat charter or bait or a good deal on a twenty-foot sailboat, but I didn't, Diane. I was straight with you."

She seemed to ponder that for a moment and I was thinking, well, if she didn't want to go with that, then I would just leave. It wasn't worth it. But I wanted to see some things firsthand, get a feel and taste of what was going on.

Diane shifted her clipboard. "All right. Just a couple of minutes. And I'm with you every second, and when we're done, we go over to the station. I got people there from the attorney general's office and the state police. We'll be wanting to get your statement."

"Deal," I said, and I followed her into the cottage.

Even with the window shades up, the place was dark. The same two uniforms in black-zippered jumpsuits who had been taking photographs and drawing diagrams on clipboards nearly a week ago at Lynn Germano's place were back in Henry Desmond's home, doing the same work. I just nodded at them as I wandered around. The two of them must have fascinating conversations with each other when they were off duty. The place was relatively clean but absolutely stacked with old books, magazines, and newspapers, and there were a couple of piles of clothes in one corner. I looked at some of the books. Most of them were that awful cheap coloring that marked Reader's Digest Condensed Books, and there were a lot of paperbacks with their covers torn off. There were even a couple of dusty light green high school yearbooks from 1952 and 1953. *The Tyler Warrior*. Hanging on the dirty white plaster walls were a couple of faded black-and-white photos of what looked like a family at the beach, and I thought I recognized a much younger Henry Desmond in a couple of them.

The kitchen was also small, with a metal table and two chairs that looked like something that might have been advertised in a 1958 issue of *Life* magazine. In the white porcelain sink was an empty coffee mug and cereal bowl, with a small puddle of milk in the bottom of the bowl. Henry Desmond's breakfast dishes. I felt a twinge of sadness, wondering if anyone would wash the dishes from this pathetic last meal.

Upstairs were a bathroom and a bedroom. The bed was made and was covered with a pink sheet with tassels. Pink? Henry must've stolen it from a motel in Massachusetts. On the walls were more photos of nameless people and some fishing boats, and a couple of framed certificates: Henry's high school diploma from Tyler High School, in 1953, and next to that, his honorable discharge certificate from the United States Navy, in 1957. Scattered across the floor of his bedroom were copies of *National Fishermen*, the Tyler *Chronicle*, and that magazine for manly men who don't date, *Penthouse*.

Diane had followed me all the while, not saying a word, and I went back downstairs and out on the front porch, feeling warm and dusty. There was no basement, and from where I stood I could look at the open garage and see some fishing gear. I wondered how many other men and women of Henry's age were living in similar cottages, alone in the stillness with their old books, living out the long days until the time quiet strangers would come into their silent homes, taking notes and filling out forms.

"Family members?" I asked as Diane joined me on the pavement. The road wasn't wide enough for a sidewalk.

Diane shrugged. "Couple of cousins, down in Gloucester. In fact, he was visiting them the past week and just got back to Tyler two days ago. Not much else."

"Did he know Lynn Germano? Any love letters in there from a high school waitress smitten with a lobster fisherman in his fifties?"

From up the street an old Cadillac with Massachusetts plates roared by, its muffler rotting away, and it slowed immediately when the driver spotted the marked cruiser.

"That's what we're checking, Lewis. Among other things." She was looking at me, tilting her head, as if each ounce of patience were dripping away.

Before she could say anything else I passed over the manila folder. "Here. Inside's the note I got, telling me to meet Henry at the dock this morning."

She opened the folder and I said, "Careful, now. It's only got my prints on it. Anything else you find, it belongs to someone else."

"Like Henry?" Diane asked, closing the folder and looking up at me.

"Maybe so, but I doubt it, Diane." I gestured to the cottage. "You and I've both been in there, Diane. Went on both floors, in every room. Did you see a typewriter? I didn't. But that note's typewritten. Somehow I don't get the feeling that Henry borrowed a neighbor's typewriter to write me that note. Maybe he did and maybe you'll find that neighbor when you guys do your canvass, but I don't think so."

Then I saw Diane's face change; the tight-lipped police detective who was somewhat angry at me and my existence turned into the Diane I could make smile with my Tom Snyder imitation.

She said, "Seems obvious then."

"Yep. The guy who blew up Henry Desmond and his boat

was looking to take a magazine writer along on the ride. Someone who didn't want to risk writing up a note, in case I knew Henry Desmond's handwriting.''

"Jesus, Lewis."

"Yeah. Right." I was feeling antsy, both in confirming what I had suspected, and in seeing the look on Diane's face. I said, "You still want to talk over at the station?"

She nodded and said, "Give me a minute or two with the boys inside, and I'll meet you there."

I walked back to my Range Rover, feeling my hands and feet itch. Over the years I've traded words with a lot of people and a couple of them have actually tried to do me bodily harm. But save for one accident, not one person has ever tried to kill me. They say that coming close to death makes one appreciate one's surroundings and breathe deeper of life. All I saw was the cracked asphalt of Clipper Avenue and a couple of sea gulls rooting around a ruptured green garbage bag, and the smell that afternoon was the constant salt and decaying trash odor of this part of Tyler Beach. I got into the Range Rover and in the short drive to the police station I kept the Beretta on the front seat, within easy reach.

I spent another two hours at Tyler Beach, with about ninety of those minutes at the Tyler police station, talking to two very large, well-dressed and polite men from the state police and the attorney general's office. In New Hampshire the state police and the attorney general's office take immediate control of a homicide investigation. In some instances—in the smaller towns—it means the local cops are demoted to fetching coffee and doughnuts and making boring canvasses. In other towns —such as Tyler, I'm sure—it means an uneasy triumvirate of officials trying to piece things together and work cooperatively without stepping on each other's toes. Sort of like the American-British-Soviet alliance during the last Big One.

During my talk with the state boys Diane was with me,

professional but polite, and in her friendly tone I could tell that she was telling the boys that I was "all right," so the tension level was quite low. They asked me about my background, about any relationship—imagined or real—I had with either Lynn Germano or Henry Desmond. They didn't seem to like my answers but they had no choice. It was all that I could offer them.

Though they didn't realize it, they did offer me something: When a couple of phones started ringing I stole a photocopy of Henry Desmond's driver's license, blown up in detail, and in my remaining half-hour at Tyler Beach, I went to the Palace Diner at the Tyler Beach Palace. None of the waitresses recognized Henry Desmond's photo, and no one could even recall Lynn Germano being seen in his company. Sarah Lockwood, the high school student from Falconer who had told me some information about Lynn Germano, was not working that day.

I left the diner after having yet another cheeseburger for dinner and an apple crisp and a cup of coffee for dessert. The apple crisp was delicious, with lots of cinnamon.

As I turned the Range Rover into the Lafayette House's parking lot, I remembered the other phone call I had received that morning, and I made a sloppy U-turn. It only took me a few minutes and I was back at Alice Crenshaw's house. The gate was open and the lights in the two-story Victorian were off, the windows darkened. I drove onto the gravel driveway and waited, the Range Rover's engine running, the lights illuminating the front porch and the empty wicker furniture. Alice's blue Volvo was parked in the open garage.

The wind was picking up and I waited, wondering about staying and seeing if she would eventually show up. She was probably on a bike ride or one of her walks, and I didn't think she'd be that late, since it was getting dark. I heard a banging noise. The front door to the house was open and was flapping free.

The door was open.

In a moment I was outside of the Range Rover, my unholstered Beretta in one hand and my flashlight in the other. I walked up to the porch and leaned in and called, "Alice?"

There was no reply.

Call the cops, I thought. Of course. And the nearest phone was inside the house. How convenient.

Broken glass was on the floor as I walked in. "Alice?"

With my flashlight I found a switch to the inside lights and I murmured, "Oh, shit, Alice," as the lights came on.

The living room was in pieces, the couch turned over, the chairs smashed, a mirror on one wall shattered, and glassware and dishes in broken pieces across the floor. Milk and food and what looked like motor oil had been dumped across the rugs.

"Alice?" There was no answer, and I didn't bother to ask again.

It took me some minutes to go through the empty house, my arms shaking, my clothes quickly becoming soaked with sweat as I went into the darkened cellar and then upstairs to the bedrooms and sitting room. Everywhere in the old Victorian house someone had gone on a rampage, turning over bureaus, breaking chairs and table lamps, swabbing oil and grease on the walls, stomping on framed photographs. In Alice's bedroom the person—or persons—had torn off the blankets and slashed away at the mattress. In her closets all of her dresses and clothes had been slashed and cut and tossed into multicolored piles of useless fabric.

There was no sign of Alice. I had a terrible need to urinate and I stank of sweat, and my arms were still trembling. I went back downstairs and into the kitchen. The refrigerator door was open and the tile floor was covered with a puddle of milk and flour and beer and wine and ketchup and flour, and in the puddle were smashed glassware and dishes.

The door to the rear porch was also open and I went outside. No one was there, and the sound of the waves didn't sound too loud at all. I rested my flashlight and Beretta on the porch railing and wiped my hands dry, and then picked them up again. The U.S. Navy spyglass that had once belonged to John Crenshaw had been torn off the railing and smashed against a porch pillar. On the porch were the wicker table and a wicker chair, and I remembered the last time I had been out here, just a few days ago, when we had talked and I had a glass of orange juice, and the June sun was quite warm on my back.

Just a few days ago. When there was a table and two chairs. And now there was only one chair.

I went off the porch and across the short back lawn, which ended at the bluff of land that marked the very point of Weymouth's Point. Below me was a tangle of boulders and rocks that fell for over fifty feet before reaching the waves of the cold Atlantic. I aimed my flashlight down and something tightened up in my throat, tightened so much that I almost forgot to breathe, because beneath me on the rocks were the crushed remnants of her chair, looking like the white bones of some animal.

9

WHEN THE HELICOPTERS CAME THAT MORNING
we all stood there, looking up at them
flying by, just as silent and as dumb as the sheep penned up
below us.

There were two of them, modified Hueys with some type of
metallic outrigging on the side of their hulls that made them
look like crop dusters. They were flying low and coming straight
at us, and as that was registering in my mind, Carl Socha looked
at me, tearing away the camouflage scarf from his black face.

"Lewis," he said, his voice urgent, and I never knew what
he intended to say next, since they struck us then.

The mist was fine and oily and fell upon us all about the
same time. I took a breath and my lungs seized up and refused
to work, and I fell to my knees, gagging. I looked up once and
saw Carl sitting down on the sand and rocks, a puzzled look
on his face, as blood started streaming from his nose and mouth.
He looked at me and then rolled over and collapsed. I jack-
knifed forward and tried to breath.

When I got up to look again, my eyes were tearing over and
my mouth was filling up with some sort of fluid, and the sound

of the helicopters was quite loud, drumming into my head, almost splitting my skull in two. The sheep were all still except for a couple piled up in one corner of the fenced-in area, kicking and trembling. All about me were the folded-over and now shrunken forms of the people in my section and the others in the desert that day, lying still in their camouflage gear. I tried to find Cissy. I tried to stand up, I tried to clear my mouth, and in everything I failed.

I was on the sandy ground and the sound of the helicopters would not go away, would not go away no matter how much and how long I yelled through the fluid in my mouth. And then someone turned me over and I looked up and saw two shapes there, wearing robes, with shrouds over their heads, with large eyes and noses, and labored breathing.

One spoke to another: "Here's one who's still kicking."

And that was that, for a while.

Some dreams are slippery when they deal with reality. You can dream that you're eating roast pork and potatoes with the Princess of Wales, both of you wearing bathing suits, and then you're up to your waist in snow while climbing K-2, fighting off flamingos.

Then there are the dreams that are too real, that are merely replays from some video recorder in your head. I had just had one of those dreams, about the helicopters in the desert, and I was outside on my second-floor deck, naked and leaning against the railing, airing out the smell of sweat and bad dreams from my bedroom. My telescope rested in one corner of my bedroom, where it would remain this night. It was about two in the morning and up on Weymouth's Point, the lights at Alice Crenshaw's house had now been darkened.

When I have a bad dream it can rest on my soul like a foul fog for the rest of the day, and I remembered what had gone on during the past few hours. Diane Woods and other officers of the Tyler Police Department had arrived after my phone call from Alice's home, and Diane had a tight-lipped yet puzzled look about her. She pulled me aside and said in a furious voice, "If you're doing something and you're not telling me, Cole, I'll have your ass in the county jail so fast you'll leave your goddamn socks in Tyler."

With that she went back to work and a couple of uniforms went down to the rocks and retrieved Alice's chair and searched in and out of the jagged boulders and found nothing, though one of the cops cut his hand fairly badly when he took a serious fall. The U.S. Coast Guard and N.H. Fish & Game were alerted that there might be someone in the water, and in a while a Boston whaler from the state came up to Weymouth's Point, stabbing at the night with a spotlight, and it was later joined by a 44-foot Coast Guard utility boat from Newburyport, but the waters were empty.

I answered some questions from Diane in the stinking and cluttered mess that had once been Alice's living room, and then she walked me to my Range Rover and said, "You believe in coincidences?"

"Depends on the type of coincidence," I said, hand on the Range Rover's door handle. "I can believe someone thinking about their favorite type of ice cream cone, and five minutes later an ice cream truck comes by. I find it hard to believe that Lynn Germano and Henry Desmond get killed in one week, and that Alice . . ." I wavered and my tongue felt thick, and I grabbed the door handle harder. "That something bad happened to Alice around the same time, and that's all just a coincidence."

She folded her arms and rubbed her wrists. "I get the same feeling, Lewis. Something awful is roaming through Tyler and I don't like it." She looked over at the house and said, "We'll be doing some print work and whatever. Some of our boys will be walking the beach tomorrow, seeing if . . . well, seeing if anything washes up, and I know the Coast Guard will stay out there for at least another day. Meanwhile, why don't you get home, Lewis, and for God's sake, stop calling me."

Being a good citizen, I did just exactly that. And now I was leaning over the railing, watching the lights of Tyler Beach and the stars overhead, and I was tossing things through my head, remembering my dream of a few minutes ago. I had lost a lot that day the helicopters came by, and I didn't like what was happening in Tyler. The feeling I was getting reminded me too much of what had gone on that morning in Nevada. I wondered about Alice, about what might have happened to her. I hope she had given a good account of herself.

Lynn Germano. Henry Desmond. Alice Crenshaw. And almost me. Someone was a busy person out there, with a lot of plans and dreams and a sharp edge that hadn't been dulled. And there had to be a thread there, some sort of connection. I knew Alice and had known Henry slightly. Alice knew practically everyone in Tyler, so I didn't doubt that she knew Henry Desmond. And Lynn Germano and Henry Desmond? Well, maybe. Though that wasn't certain yet. Though I remembered a dinner date I had with Alice, a few days ago at the Marshside Restaurant when she had told me that something was bothering her. And the tone of voice in that message on the answering machine. Something was there.

I knew I had a lot of work ahead for me. Still, I wasn't tired. So I waited there on my deck, waiting for sleep to call me back in.

On Friday morning I talked for a few moments with Diane Woods, who told me that nothing new had been found since I left her that morning at Alice Crenshaw's house, and that none of her quiet neighbors had seen a thing. In the afternoon I met Paula Quinn for lunch at Sam's Clam Box, just over the town line into North Tyler. Sam's place used to be a house, subdivided into four apartments, until Sam decided he would make more money by ripping out the apartments and making it into a restaurant. He was right, and five years later, after hard work and eating too much of his own product, he had died from a heart attack. Sam's Clam Box was on its third set of owners and they hadn't changed a thing Sam had been doing, so business was fine. The old house was on a rise of land, just above Samson's Point, where the state wildlife preserve is, and there are fine views of the ocean and the Isles of Shoals and the grass-covered hills that were once concrete gun emplacements.

We sat at a table with paper placemats that showed diagrams of how to eat a lobster for people who had never been face to face with a crustacean, and after we ordered, Paula took a drink from her water glass and said, "Tell me, why were you such a shit with me yesterday when I tried to find out what went on at the harbor?"

Today she had on tapered jeans and black shoes, and a black wrinkled polo shirt with the top three buttons undone. Her ears still stuck through her blond hair and I was too polite to mention it. Her large black leather purse with reporter's notebook sticking out of it was hanging off her chair.

"I had a lot on my mind," I said. "You were at your newspaper office, on your home turf, on deadline. Thing was, if I told you something that was off the record, you might have been tempted to put it in your story, in some way or shape. I didn't want that to happen."

"Didn't trust me?"

"Paula, I trust you. I don't trust your job." I scratched at my ankle. Underneath my own pair of jeans I was wearing an ankle holster, with my .32 Browning automatic. It was a warm day and wearing a jacket to cover a shoulder holster would not only raise a few eyebrows, it would make me sweat like a dolphin out of water.

"Hmmph." She took another sip of her water and said, "Some journalist you are, Lewis."

114

"Never claimed to be a journalist, Paula. I write for a magazine."

"But didn't you ever write for newspapers before you came to Tyler?"

"Years and years ago, in Indiana." Which was partly true, if one counted a college newspaper as a real newspaper, which most reporters don't.

"Speaking of which," I said, deftly trying to change the subject, "you did a good job on the Henry Desmond piece in this morning's paper. Didn't know you knew Henry that well."

She folded her hands and looked out the window. "I didn't. I did a couple of pieces about the fish co-op. Then I got to know him because, for a while, he was one to go to the Conservation Commission meetings every month. Sit in back by himself, stinking in his work clothes, and when the Conservation Commission was done with its meeting on buying tree saplings for the Boy Scouts or putting up salt marsh signs, Henry would get up and ask them when they were going to get off their ass and do something about the harbor."

Paula paused for a moment, still looking out of the window. "He wasn't original, Lewis, because he kept on saying, over and over again, that Tyler Harbor was the heart of Tyler, and if we kept on dumping sewage and chemicals in there it would kill the town. When the meeting was over he'd come to me and make sure that I had taken good notes about what he had said, and I nodded a lot and grunted in the right places, and the next morning I wouldn't write a goddamn thing about him for that day's paper. So that's how I knew Henry Desmond. By listening politely and not writing a word."

That particular reporting technique sounded familiar. "You got any pet theories, Miss Local Reporter, on why he was killed?"

She smiled at that. "Stop calling me that or I'll spank you. Who knows? Maybe he was running drugs. Maybe he was humping someone's wife. Maybe he pissed off some other lobsterman—they're very feudal out there on the ocean, Lewis. There are places where you set your traps and God help you if you set them somewhere else. Boats have been known to burn at dockside for stuff like that. So it could have been a number of things."

"Well, one person knows, Paula."

"Yeah. The mad bomber." She looked up at me and said, "What were you doing there, Lewis? Buying some select lobsters?"

I carefully decided what to say next. Paula's my friend, but she's also a newspaper reporter. "He had left me a note. Saying he had to see me about something important. I had done a column on him and the local co-op last summer. So I went and got there in time to see his boat blow up."

She shuddered. "Talk about luck."

"Yes," I agreed. "Talk about luck."

Paula unfolded her paper napkin in her lap and said, "Saw in the police log this morning that you had some excitement over in your neighborhood last night, up on Weymouth's Point. Someone trashed Alice Crenshaw's house—you know, the woman who's president of the historical society—and she's nowhere to be found. The police were out on all the beaches this morning, and some firefighters, too, and nothing came ashore. I even hear that the fishermen have been alerted in case something comes up in their nets. Jesus, what a place. What do you think happened to her, Lewis?"

"I don't know," and I was telling the truth.

"Hmm," she said, smiling and leaning back in her chair, with her hands across her slim stomach. "What a time these past couple of weeks have been, Lewis. When I was with the Dover newspaper I was covering a couple of towns in Maine, right across the border, and all I did were stories about town managers getting fired and apple festivals and Maine politics. Nothing really there for a portfolio. So when I came to the *Chronicle* I thought being here would give me more meat, with the beaches and the summer business and tourists. A nice mix with a lot of opportunities for stories."

"And what kind of meat would that be?" I asked.

"Stories with oomph, with impact, stuff that would make people sit up and take notice," she said, leaning back across the table, eyes alight. "I once read a story about Edna Buchanan, the Miami *Herald* crime reporter, and she said something about her stories only succeeding if they caused a guy to spit out his coffee at breakfast and grab his heart and say, 'My God, Martha! Did you read this?' "

I saw our waitress approaching and said, "I suppose you didn't find those kind of stories right off."

"Are you kidding?" she said. "Lewis, being a reporter's a business, just like anything else. When I was in J-school I thought it was a noble undertaking, and that kind of bullshit is fine, if noble undertakings could ever make a car payment. Nope. It's a business. You either move up or you get stagnant and end up your days rewriting press releases on school lunches and checking over your health plan. I want to get to Boston and do some real reporting, and this stuff over the past couple of weeks—the Body in the Marsh, the deaths of Lynn Germano and Henry Desmond, and this thing with Alice Crenshaw— that stuff will get me there. It's the first time since I've been at the *Chronicle* that something exciting's been going on in Tyler, and I intend to report the hell out of it."

As our waitress dropped off our lunches Paula smiled and said, "Like they say. These are stories a reporter would kill for."

About then I lost my appetite.

Since I was in North Tyler that Friday afternoon and for a few other reasons, I went up to Felix Tinios's home and found him in his small backyard, sunning himself. He had on a small pair of black running shorts, wraparound sunglasses, and the obligatory gold chain around his thick neck. His dark skin was covered with fine black hair, and in a few spots—on his stomach and shoulder—he had pink scars. I had a silly thought for a moment of pulling open some of my own clothes and comparing scars and notes, but it wouldn't work. His stories would probably be more interesting than mine, and I'm sure he wouldn't understand why I had let some people keep on breathing.

He was resting on a cushioned lounge chair, facing the house—understandable, since it would be difficult to climb up the rocks and the sands behind him—and at his elbow was a small table, with a glass filled with melting ice cubes. A copy of the *Globe* was folded over on the table, and by the awkward way it was folded, I knew it was hiding a metallic object of some sort.

Felix took his sunglasses off as I approached and tilted his head, giving me a quizzical look.

"Carrying?" he asked.

"Yep," I said, standing next to him. I caught a whiff of his cologne and made a guess about the shape of the bottle it came in. "Thirty-two. In an ankle holster."

He shook his head, smiling. "Either you're getting better, Lewis, or I'm losing my skills. And I don't know if I like either of those explanations."

"Let's just say I'm getting a bit lighter on my feet. Got a moment?"

"A moment. Yeah."

I sat down on the grass, resting my forearms on my knees. "Let's talk about what happened yesterday in Tyler Harbor. About the boat explosion and Henry Desmond's death."

His smile was still there, but I think it was only from courtesy. "You seem to think I know something about that."

"No, but I do know of the things you have interest in, and I'm sure you're up to speed on this one. Talk to me, Felix. How could it have been done?"

"Not interested in the 'why'?"

"I've got a lot of interest in a lot of things," I said. "Explosives, for one."

Felix put his sunglasses down on the table and for a horrible moment I thought he was going to reach for the folded-over newspaper, but instead he threw one large arm behind his head. Behind Felix were the bright waters of the Atlantic, churning and hammering against the beaches and rocks of North Tyler and its sister beach to the south. People were out on these beaches today, seeing if Alice would wash up ashore, and I felt like an altar boy who had stolen some sacramental wine: I should be out there, taking part in the search, instead of being with Felix. But being with Felix could mean some answers, and working the beach wouldn't get me too far, except for taking care of the guilt.

That would have to be taken care of later.

"Explosives," Felix finally said. "Two likely possibilities. Dynamite or C-Four. Care to hazard a guess?"

"I'd say C-Four. Easy to get, if you've got the connections. Easily concealed. And hard to trace. Dynamite is made with a company-specific chemical, so an analysis could tell you the manufacturer and lot number, and that makes for a good trace. No such luck with C-Four. And it's easy to use."

Felix nodded. "Very good, Lewis. But remember, too, that everything is now dumped in the ocean. Mixed with the fire from the boat and who knows what else, that doesn't leave much for any forensic types. Plus, law of supply and demand. Maybe C-Four is easy to get, maybe it isn't. Now, with that decided, how does the explosion occur? That leaves us with the option of a timer or a command switch."

I didn't like the answer but I said, "Command switch, Felix. Timer has too many faults. If someone is late or a boat engine doesn't work or the weather's bad, then you miss your target if you've set a timer. Command detonation. Someone was at the harbor that morning and set off the charge."

"Conveniently missing you in the process, Lewis."

I thought a cool breeze had stirred up, for my skin prickled. "Care to elaborate on that, Felix?"

He gave me a quick wink. "Sure. You were at the harbor that morning, waiting to see Henry Desmond about something, maybe something connected with the Lynn Germano case. While you were waving madly at Henry Desmond, who was putt-putting away in his boat, the killer—or killers—set off the charge. They couldn't risk having Henry find the charge later in the day, so they decided that morning to take care of fifty percent of their business. You were supposed to be on that boat, but you weren't. Congratulations, Lewis, for being that missing fifty percent. But your value or whatever for the killer hasn't changed, so I would guess he's still out there, sharpening his knives, waiting for another opportunity. Which makes me happy to see you carrying, Lewis. I would recommend you keep on doing that."

I was stunned at what Felix had said. Except for Paula Quinn, whom I had just left, the only ones who really knew of my presence at the harbor yesterday were Diane Woods, an assistant attorney general with the state, and an investigator with the state police. Which meant that Felix had a source with the Tyler Police Department, the attorney general's office, or the state police. This did not give me a good feeling, knowing that someone who got paid with my tax dollars was busily passing along information to Felix Tinios.

I said, "Maybe I should get volunteers to start up my Range Rover for me."

Felix laughed and shifted in his lounge chair. "It wouldn't hurt. How does it feel, Lewis? How does it feel to be among the hunted? It's a marvelous feeling, you know. Your senses are sharper, everything tastes better, and it's tremendously exciting not knowing what's going to happen next."

"I think it's a feeling I can do without," I said. "There are times that I'd rather like to be bored."

"Ah, but you might not have a choice," Felix said, sitting

up in the lounge chair. "You should be asking yourself, why did this fisherman die? Perhaps he was seeing another man's wife. Perhaps he was smuggling something into the harbor. Perhaps he was smuggling something *out*—you never know. Many questions, many theories. And then, Lewis, what connection did you have with Henry? Could it be something that would make someone so scared or angry that they tried to get you on that boat too?"

A good point. I had asked myself that question a lot. "I barely knew him, Felix. Did a little squib on him and the fishing co-op, back when they were starting. That's it. Would hardly recognize him if I saw him again."

"So the time you see him again is connected to the death of that waitress. So that's your connection. You weren't humping that girl by any chance, were you?"

I didn't even feel insulted, which I'm sure meant something. "Nope. And it doesn't look like Henry was either. There's another thing, too. A neighbor of mine, Alice Crenshaw. She's, uh, she's disappeared." To Felix right then, I didn't want to say the words.

I added, "Right after Henry Desmond's death, she's gone. I'm sure she knew Henry—they were about the same age and grew up together in Tyler—but they didn't exactly move in the same circles."

"But there's some sort of connection between all of these things, Lewis."

"Of course," I said. "And I'm going to find it."

Felix waved his sunglasses at me. "Be careful, my friend. I know you like to think of yourself as a simple little writer, just busily scurrying around, trying to uncover the truth. You might find in this one that you're uncovering something that's going to bite your hand off, and then your head, for good measure."

"Really?" I asked. "Do you have an interest in this matter, Felix?"

He put the sunglasses on his tanned belly, picked up the glass of ice water, and rubbed it across his face. "Let's say I've been getting a few phone calls. I've been asked a few questions. Some of the people I work for, they like to think of Tyler as a nice little haven. They don't like this place being in the news because it can mean the wrong type of publicity. The waitress, well, too bad. Your friend Alice, oh, who knows. But the lobsterman, well, the way he died was quite dramatic, quite loud. Something that some of my contractors have seen before in their lives. Something they don't particularly like seeing up here. So, I've been asked to look into some things."

"You have, have you? Well, Felix, maybe we'll run into each other."

Felix put on his sunglasses and smiled. "I doubt it, Lewis. I doubt it, and I don't think you'd want the two of us to run into each other. It might frighten you."

I said, "There are times I doubt that."

For a moment we said nothing, and then I tossed something out, just to check his reaction: "Tell me, Felix, you've probably had some experiences with explosives. Would you like to tell me where you were yesterday morning?"

His hand reached out and barely touched the folded-over copy of the *Globe*. "No," he said, and I hardly recognized his voice, it was so soft. "No, but I would like to tell you to leave. I'm getting bored all of a sudden."

I got the word. Standing up, I walked away from Felix, sitting there like an oiled animal in his lounge chair, and though I've known him for some years and can count on him as a friendly acquaintance, I didn't turn my back on him until I passed by his house, heading to the gravel driveway where my Range Rover was parked.

10

It had been a warm June evening so I was sleeping with the windows open and the screens down, which probably explained why I had woken up so quickly from the noise.

I checked the bright red numerals of the clock on my night-stand. It was a little past three on this Saturday morning. I paused, waiting. Then there was a muffled whisper and the sound of one rock striking another, and I was sitting up in bed, sheet around my waist, waiting, feeling the blood pound in my ears.

There was silence, but I was sure I hadn't imagined the sounds of a few seconds ago. The noise had been too loud, too distinct. I waited some more, but I didn't wait long. Only by going outside to see who or what was making the noises would I be able to go back to sleep. I wasn't about to go back to bed and pull a blanket over my head. That kind of stuff only worked in bad books about ghosts or UFO visitors.

I spun off my bed, slipped on a pair of shorts, and tugged on a pair of topsiders. Underneath my bed, covered by a white cloth and resting on a foam pad, was my Remington 12-gauge shotgun, loaded with eight shells of no. 4 pellets. I slid it out and into my hands. The metal was cold to the touch and I didn't bother to check to see if the shotgun was loaded. There are no children or other innocents in my house, so I keep all of my weapons loaded. Trying to load a weapon with shaking fingers as something is on the prowl and battering down your door is always a losing proposition. It usually results in newspapers writing cheerful obituaries about the people who made the attempt.

On my nightstand is a small flashlight, about the size of a roll of quarters, and I put that in the rear pocket of my shorts as I went downstairs, keeping to the wall so I wouldn't raise too much noise by stepping on the center of stairs and causing the old wood to creak. I waited at the bottom of the stairs, between the living room and the kitchen, listening and willing my heart to slow down. It didn't feel like anyone was in the house. Except, of course, my memories and the old sweats and scents of the people who had lived here before me, including vagrants and tourists and officers of the U.S. Coast Guard Artillery units stationed at Samson's Point. Nothing seemed disturbed. But there were those noises from outside. The shotgun felt as light as a balsa-wood model, and I slipped out the front door, making sure it was unlocked in case I had to make a quick reentry.

Outside the air was warm and the sound of the ocean waves was a low rumbling that I tried to ignore as I listened hard to whatever else was out there. I stepped away from the front steps and crouched down against the worn wood of my house. I paused for a while, waited for my eyes to adjust to the darkness of the night, and then I moved north, crouched down, the shotgun still incredibly light in my hands. I went around the corner of the house, waited, and moved on. The land slopes down some from the front of the house so I moved to the supports for the rear deck and stopped, looking at the short expanse of lawn and the tumbled boulders that marked the beginning of the oceanfront and my isolated cove. The flooring of the deck was just above my head, and I leaned against a wooden beam for support. Waiting. Breathing.

I moved my head back and forth for a few minutes, looking out of the corner of my eyes, and that's when I spotted the shape that didn't fit. I had lived some years here and I knew all of the rocks and the driftwood and the shape of my tiny lawn, and there was something there that didn't belong, something only about fifteen feet away and by the edge of my lawn.

So I did something about it.

I dug out my flashlight and jammed it in a corner of one of the support posts and the deck, making sure it was pointing in the general direction of the shape, and then I stood at arms' length away and switched it on and brought up the shotgun, taking a few more steps to the left, just in case someone wanted to take a potshot at the flashlight. The light glared out and someone said, ''Shit,'' quite loudly and stood and dropped something, and there was the sharp sound of breaking glass. Then the shape dropped down and I heard a scurrying noise across the rocks as the person ran away.

I yanked the flashlight out of the wood and ran to the rocks, holding the light out as far as I could with my arm, scanning the rocks below me with the light. It wasn't that powerful, so all I saw were the dark and cold rocks, the tiny beach, and the ocean's waves curling in. I played the light across the rocks and saw a broken quart bottle of Budweiser beer, and I felt silly for a moment, like an overeager Rambo homeowner coming out to protect his homestead from a kid or two drinking beer on the rocks and trying to see a shooting star.

Then I smartened up—I still must have been slightly sleepy—and I squatted down and looked closer at the shattered brown glass. There had been a rag in the bottle's neck, and the gasoline odor was now quite thick. I stood up and scanned the light across the empty rocks again, then switched the light off and shoved it into my back pocket. I raised the shotgun up to my shoulder in one motion and fired off a round in the general direction of the running person.

The noise was a hollow boom that tore at my ears, and the light from the blast was quite impressive, almost like a miniature torch. I dropped the shotgun down and with a *slick-slack* of the pump action, ejected the empty shell, then rubbed at my shoulder.

Wasn't worth much, I knew, except to make an impressive noise and make my ears ring. And also to tell my friend with the taste for Molotov cocktails that I knew he had been there, and I knew what he had intended to do, and if a few moments had changed here and there, I wouldn't have been aiming into the stars. I would have been aiming at him.

I walked back to the house. The empty shell and the broken glass could wait for a daylight cleaning. I went to the kitchen, and in the darkness—no point still in turning on lights and silhouetting myself as a target—poured myself a tall orange juice and threw in a jigger of Stolichnaya vodka ($12.75 at the state liquor store in North Tyler) for good measure. I unlocked the sliding glass door to the downstairs deck and went outside and sat there, with the shotgun across my lap, sipping at the orange juice and vodka. There would be no more sleeping tonight. My heart was still trip-tripping along, like a ten-gallon-a-minute pump facing a twenty-gallon-a-minute waterfall, and my hands were shaking, and my right shoulder and ears still hurt. I hoped my friend out there was just as uncomfortable.

I sipped at my juice and tilted my head back and looked at the stars. Vega was a bright hardness, and I made out the constellation of the winged horse Pegasus, racing endlessly across the night sky toward the swan Cygnus. The shotgun started to weigh heavy right about then and I rested it across the wooden sides of the fake redwood chair I was sitting in. The night air was still warm and yet I shivered here and there, as my heart began to race down and the adrenaline and other chemicals in me started to drift away. A lot of thoughts spun and flickered through my head, and most of them were dark fantasies and thoughts of me waking up to flames and clambering over the second-floor deck in terror, while someone below took their leisure at blowing me in two with a half-dozen rounds of whatever weapons they—or he—had been carrying.

Enough, though, and I tried to think of other things. I was still here. I was still breathing. And I would continue my work.

Alice. Did you meet this dark man, the man who tried to burn my home?

I stayed out on the rear deck for some while. Out on the dark ocean was the beacon from the White Island lighthouse, one of the tiny Isles of Shoals, where legend had it that pirates had buried treasure as they stopped to get fresh water for their ships. Maybe so, even though I knew that if all the legends were true, one could walk over buried treasure chests from Portland in Maine to Cape Ann in Massachusetts without missing a step. There were only a few other lights on the ocean, and they were probably stern draggers out from Tyler or Foss harbors, going out for an early run, or trawlers from Gloucester and Cape Ann, working their way north, or nuclear-powered submarines, gliding in or out of the Porter Naval Shipyard, going back out to the hunting and killing fields in the wide gray waters.

The ocean was a constant murmur and rush of water crashing against the shore. A few sea gulls cried out among the slow thermals, and there was the faint *hoot-hoot* of a whistle buoy farther north, marking the entrance to Foss Harbor. I was lucky where I lived, for I hardly heard any traffic from Atlantic Avenue, not more than a hundred or so yards from my house, and the only traffic that ever made any impression on me was the type that floated on the seas.

After a while I finished my orange juice and vodka and was feeling almost human. I tilted my head back again, looking for shooting stars, but Lewis Cole's Theory of Meteors took hold, which says the harder you look for shooting stars, the less likely you'll see them. The sky began to lighten toward the east, and in a while the stars began to wink out, except for the brighter ones and the shiny one that was a star in disguise, which marked Saturn. I looked to the horizon and I could start making out the lobster pots, bobbing out there in the waves, and on the horizon, there was a smudge of pink and red, growing wider and deeper, until finally the sun rose up. There was no great moment of demarcation, where it was night and then suddenly dawn. No, there was just a gradual state, a gradualness you could miss if you didn't look for it.

I blinked a few times and it seemed like the sea gulls' cries were louder and full of more emotion. I rubbed at my face and watched the rising sun for a few minutes, looking out to the great ocean and the waves from the safety of my home, and I remembered again why I had come here, and why I loved it so.

I am almost certain—and I knew it would eventually make a great column for *Shoreline*—that the Tyler Beach Chamber of Commerce was a front for a Satanic cult, a group that met each week to pray for good weather. These businessmen may pretend to be good Christians or Jews but I believe it's all a farce. Get them talking and mention the magic word *weather*, and you see their eyes narrow and their brows tighten. They will discuss weather and tropical depressions and cold fronts with the fervor of ones possessed, for it was weather that could make or break a season, and the short summer season of a handful of weeks, running from Memorial Day to Labor Day, was all that they lived for. Many still talked darkly about the famous Summer Without a Sun of 1985, when it rained almost every weekend and so many businesses had been hurt that the arson fires that fell among several motels and restaurants along North Tyler and Tyler lit up the cold October and November nights like pagan bonfires.

Maybe those arsons were their sacrifices. Maybe so. All I knew was that this Saturday morning, the Chamber's work must have been doing well, for the day was a good one, hot and slightly breezy, and by noon the beach sands were jammed with towels and umbrellas, coolers and radios, and Atlantic Avenue and Ashburn Avenue and the streets between were all jammed with slow-moving cars that never went above 10 mph, and most of those cars had license plates that didn't say "Live Free or Die."

One of the few benefits I had in writing for *Shoreline* was the parking pass I threw in my windshield that allowed me to park for free at the Tyler police station. I had gotten the pass in a good moment with Diane Woods one summer, but I didn't like to use it that often. But on this day I made an exception, and parked the Range Rover between two Ford pickup trucks in the private police station lot. One of these days I would have to get Diane Woods to explain to me why so many cops drove pickup trucks. In the meanwhile, the cops had been busy: The search along the beaches of Tyler and its neighboring towns had been empty—no sign of Alice Crenshaw, and the fishermen returning to the coast's harbors had captured only their normal catch of the day.

Alice, I thought, walking out of the police station lot, I hope I know what I'm doing.

I went up to the Tyler Beach Palace, passing families with Mom and Dad carrying coolers and lawn chairs, snapping at each other and dragging squealing and crying kids, all of them out for a good time. There were young men and women, some of them quite beautiful and handsome in their own ways, wearing skimpy pieces of nylon and Lycra bathing suits, but most of the youngsters were doughy and tough-looking, with cigarettes in hand and loud black T-shirts that looked like wearable graffiti. Although it was warm enough for shorts, the .32 Browning in my ankle holster had its own dress code demands, so I had on a pair of jeans and a blue T-shirt.

At the Palace Diner I looked at the waitresses, wearing their uniforms of white shorts and black T-shirts that said PALACE DINER in bright pink neon. I passed among the outer squares of booths and tables, and I couldn't see Sarah Lockwood working anywhere. I went up to the inner square of the diner, where the kitchen area and cash register were, and I asked the cashier where Sarah was.

The cashier was about seventeen, with heavy pink makeup over skin that was breaking out, she wore large hoop earrings, and her light brown hair had been moussed and teased and tortured into a tall mane.

She shook her head and said, "She don't work here anymore."

"Why's that?" I asked. "She was here last week."

She looked up briefly and then looked away and said, "Listen, okay? I gotta get back to work."

I turned to where she had looked and saw a familiar face. Derek Cooney, Oliver Mailloux's gofer and manager. This time he was wearing a better style of clothing: white chinos and his own Palace Diner T-shirt, though how they got one that size, I didn't know. His black hair was combed back from his puffy red face, and standing there in the diner with the waitresses moving about him, he looked like a pedophile at a Girl Scouts convention.

I called out, "Got a promotion, Derek, or is this a demotion?"

He answered with the one-finger salute for people with limited vocabulary. I didn't mind the salute that much. What I did mind was the bloody scrape around his right wrist. I wondered if he and I had been keeping the same hours this morning.

Falconer is the southernmost town on the New Hampshire seacoast, a town with a lot of contradictions and history, with elegant homes on large acres on the northeast end of the town, and with shacks and rusting trailers on sandwich-sized lots to the south, near the Massachusetts border. Some people in Falconer would literally stop at night to give you a jumpstart for your car, and then come back a week later and steal it. Many of Falconer's children go into the armed services upon graduation, and among the businesses in Falconer, I've been told that the workers there have the highest percentage of donations to the United Way. Contradictions. After the first English settlers arrived in Tyler back in 1638, poor Scotsmen landed in the marshlands to the south of Tyler, forming the town of Falconer. More than 300 years after it was first settled, most of the families in Falconer still have Scottish names, such as Magruder, Mackinnon, and Stewart, and they have an accent and a dialect all their own. Rumor has it that a high percentage of doctoral dissertations in New England colleges on anthropology and language had their basis in the marshes, shacks, and expensive homes of Falconer.

That poverty-related past and other things have helped to ensure there is still no love lost between the relatively well-off residents of Tyler and their poorer and prideful cousins in Falconer. While Tyler has its resort beach and its image as New Hampshire's oceanfront playground, Falconer has the state's only nuclear power plant and tattoo and gold jewelry parlors on Route 1. People in Falconer call Tyler residents beach bunnies, and people in Tyler call Falconer residents birdmen. Those words have sparked a lot of fights in the bars and American Legion halls in this part of Wentworth County.

After a few phone calls I learned that Sarah Lockwood was now working at MacGregor's Lobster Pound on Route 286 in Falconer, just across the border from Salisbury, Massachusetts. Route 286 cuts right through the marsh, almost parallel to Route 51—farther north in Tyler—and on the marshlands are the concrete dome and buildings of Falconer Station's Unit 1 and the rusted and not-to-be-finished-in-this-century dome of Falconer Unit 2. The nuclear power plant is in MacGregor's backyard, and Sarah was working at the order window when

I walked up to her after parking in the cracked asphalt parking lot.

Her curly black hair and pudgy face were smeared a bit with flour, and there were no cute white shorts and black polo shirts with the restaurant's name over the chest, like at the Palace Diner. Instead she was wearing a too-tight pink polyester waitress's uniform and the thick, sensible white sneakers that are easy on one's feet. Business was slow in the afternoon; I was the only one in line and she looked up at me and frowned as I came to the window.

She said through the screen, "You've got nothing else better to do, you want to get me fired from here, too?"

I halted, gave her a look. "I didn't know I had anything with getting you fired in the first place."

Sarah looked down at the long order pad before her. "Sure. Word came down from Mr. Mailloux himself. I was taking too many breaks, and was talking to troublemakers, especially troublemakers who were out to hurt his business. Since you seem to fit that description, I guess that's why I'm here, making about half of what I made at the Palace Diner."

The smell of the grease and other things began to make my stomach clench, and I said, "What else did he say?"

"Jesus." She looked behind her and said, "Will you please give me your goddamn order, all right? Then I'll bring it out to you."

I ordered and paid for a lobster stew with a glass of ice water, and I sat at a brown picnic table on an outside deck. Both table and deck were splattered with white sea gull droppings. A picnic table next to me was littered with trays and empty beer cans and greasy cardboard plates, and flies buzzed around for attention.

The deck overlooked a tidal stream and the tall grasses of the marshland. Beyond the stream was a wide sweep of salt-marsh hay and the saltwater creeks and low ditches cut by the farmers here two centuries ago when they harvested the saltmarsh hay for their cattle. When they cut the hay the farmers would place great haycocks on top of wooden stakes set in the ground, called staddles, and even now, more than fifty years after the farmers had stopped cutting the saltmarsh hay, the stakes are still out there along the marshes of Falconer, Tyler, and North Tyler. I started thinking of what it must have been like to have been out there with scythes or horse-drawn harvesters, fighting the heat and flies, not knowing that in a few years tens of thousands of tourists would start to stream through the roads in their new motorcars, changing everything and building motels and restaurants and homes on the cleared farmlands.

Changes. In another hundred years, this place would probably become a tourist attraction for rich Japanese or Brazilians, and they'd probably wonder why people were so hell-bent on eating fried food and throwing away plastic and metal trash that would last for centuries, and they'd line up to take pictures of the grass-covered park that once held a nuclear power plant.

Some thoughts. I also started thinking of my return to Tyler Beach tonight, and a visit I was going to make to the St. Lawrence Seaway. It was a hot afternoon and some sea gulls were circling overhead, and the rest of the deck was empty, save for a couple in their sixties, mechanically eating fried lumps of something and staring over each other's shoulders, and perhaps staying quiet because they had run out of things to say to each other. The ankle holster made my lower right leg sweat and I scratched at it.

Sarah came out after about fifteen minutes, carrying a tray with a Styrofoam bowl and a cardboard glass of ice water. As she started setting down the food I said to her, "Sarah, look. I'm sorry about what happened to you at the Palace Diner. We talked for a few minutes, on your break. Neither of us knew what Oliver Mailloux was going to do."

"Sure," she said, spilling some of the lobster stew on the picnic table and not bothering to clean it up. "Neither of us knew, and you're still writing at your fancy magazine and I get to work in Falconer and pray that I get twenty-five-cent tips from old people on Social Security. Nice arrangement."

"Something must be getting at Oliver Mailloux. Something that made him angry enough to fire you, Sarah. What was it? What's he up to?"

"And I should help you, just like that, right?"

I felt uneasy, and the look on her face was a sharp one. I could see her becoming a terrific prosecuting attorney before the century was out. I hoped my future legal battles wouldn't land me in her arena.

I said, "You should help because you feel right about it."

She looked over to the restaurant windows and went over to the picnic table next to me and started clearing the table, piling the trash together on one tray.

"Sure," she said. "The right thing. That's one of the many pieces of shit you folks push on us while we're in school, Mr. Cole. Keep your nose clean and be good and honest and work hard, and you'll get far. Fair enough. Those were the rules of the game, and I accepted them, Mr. Cole. Accepted them even when student loans got cut back so far I had to bike a couple of miles every day to a job that was going to help pay for college. Accepted them even when a shithead like Oliver Mailloux fired me, and now I have to work at this dump for my uncle, who makes me wear a tight outfit like this so he can see my tits."

She crumpled up the napkins with fury and tossed them into the center of the tray. "I even accepted those rules when I was busting my tail at the Palace Diner, and Lynn Germano worked half-shifts—whenever she worked at all—and she made more money than all of us put together and stayed in her own cottage and rubbed up against Oliver Mailloux every chance she could."

"What was going on?" I asked, feeling slightly lightheaded at the thought of Oliver with a seventeen-year-old girl like

Lynn Germano. "You're telling me that she had something going on with Oliver Mailloux?"

She tossed the trash into a waste container at the corner of the deck, banging the trays against the plastic rim. "No. I'm telling you that if you come here again to MacGregor's Lobster Pound, I'm going to tell my uncle and cousins that you tried to pick me up, that's what, and then you can talk to them."

Sarah went back into the restaurant, slamming the door behind her. I looked out again to Tyler and its beach, feeling quiet and subdued, and not particularly proud of what had happened.

I took a spoonful of the lobster stew and almost gagged. Someone had poured salt into the stew, making it inedible, and I choked again when I took a sip of the ice water. It was soapy.

Then I smiled. Sarah Lockwood. You sure as hell don't need any help from me.

I left a tip of forty dollars and as I got into my Range Rover, I saw her go out to the deck and pick up my tray. She looked at me with that dark look, and I saw the two twenty-dollar bills flutter into the trash, along with my uneaten lobster stew and glass of soapy ice water.

As I drove south on Route 286, heading to the beaches, I hoped that she was waiting until I was gone from sight before retrieving the money, but I wasn't betting on it.

I also wasn't betting on a quiet evening.

11

AFTER SOME DREAMLESS NIGHTS THOSE YEARS
ago, right after the helicopters came to us
in the desert, I woke up in a hospital room, my mouth dry and
my arms and legs feeling quite weak, as if my skeleton had
been taken out and replaced with dry and hollow sparrow
bones. The room was bare of any decorations and had no
windows, and there were no get-well cards or flowers along
the side counter. There were IV tubes running into both of my
hands, and by moving around a little, I could feel taped sensors
on my chest and elsewhere. There was a call button clipped to
my white pillow, so I pressed it.

A male nurse and a female nurse came in. I tried to speak
and managed to croak something, and the male nurse held a
cup of water with a straw, which I suckled at. The water was
sweet and cool and seemed to wash away a year's worth of
crust and dirt.

Dirt. Sand. Dead sand in my mouth. Helicopters overhead
and dust and grease falling across us . . .

"Where is this?" I whispered.

The male nurse started to say something and the female one

136

said, "You know the orders. He's to be summoned when this one wakes up, and that's it."

"But—" The male nurse started to protest, and the female one said, "Orders." They left, and in the next few seconds I learned two things. One was that when I lifted the sheet there was an incision along my left side, with ugly black stitchwork that almost made the sweet water come back up, foul and smelly this time around.

And the other was that neither of the nurses had been wearing a nametag.

Then I heard footsteps and a man whistling, and I sat up.

After my visit to MacGregor's Lobster Pound I took a nap that Saturday afternoon and didn't sleep well, which wasn't surprising. It's hard to sleep well with all of the doors and windows of your house locked, and with the weight of a 9-mm Beretta in your hands. When I got up the eastern sky was getting darker and a few bright stars were finally poking their way into the first few minutes of dusk. I got dressed, and under my navy blue blazer I wore a Bianchi shoulder holster and my Beretta. There are some who say you shouldn't go looking for trouble, and in a way, I wasn't. I was just presenting myself at trouble's door. I made a quick phone call to the St. Lawrence Seaway and asked for Oliver Mailloux, and when he answered the phone, I hung up, switched on the answering machine, and left.

My stomach growled as I got into my Range Rover and drove up the bumpy winding driveway, up to the parking lot of the Lafayette House. I hadn't eaten anything since the disastrous meal Sarah Lockwood had served me earlier, and in some way, I was going to see if I could at least get repaid for that.

As I went through the parking lot I looked over at the blazing lights of the Lafayette House and saw the well-dressed, well-mannered men and women climbing the short steps with ease, going into a warm and welcoming environment, where the drinks were cold and the credit was endless. In a sharp way I almost envied them, envied their good fortune and good times, but that sour tang of envy lasted for only a moment. I saw only the surface of their appearances and I fantasized about the rest—I didn't know what demons rested there in those pretty minds, resting on muscled legs and cloven hooves, breathing and waiting for their chances. I didn't know their demons and I didn't want to. I was busy enough with my own.

I headed south, down Atlantic Avenue, heading to Tyler Beach, and after a mile I made a turn and drove past the crowded and expensive homes of Weymouth's Point. I let the Range Rover halt in front of Alice Crenshaw's home. The front gate had been barred and sealed, and the windows were still dark. Her Volvo was parked in the gravel driveway. I remembered Thursday evening and the cold walk I had made through the debris of her house, calling out her name, and hearing nothing except for my own breathing and the crunching noise of my footsteps on broken glass. And then going out to her rear lawn and seeing the crushed wicker of her favorite chair, scattered among the sharp rocks and boulders.

Jesus, Alice. What kind of demon traipsed into your house and made off with you? And where the hell are you now? Dead and submerged in the ocean or buried in a shallow grave somewhere in the woods of Wentworth County? Or did you escape whoever was here and somehow get out? And if you did escape, why haven't you called?

The day's *Chronicle* had a story that said the search along the beaches would be over in another day, and then, well, it was up to nature and the waves or whatever to bring Alice Crenshaw back.

What a wait.

"Damn brooding," I announced, and I put the Range Rover into drive and went down the slight hill, trying without success not to look at the rearview mirror.

* * *

It was dark by the time I found a parking place near the St. Lawrence Seaway. The crowds along Atlantic Avenue and Ashburn Avenue and the side streets of Tyler Beach had changed since I had been there earlier. During the daylight hours the crowd was a good mixture of kids out looking for some good times, and parents with children, looking for something they could remember years from now and say was fun. But with sunset and the cooler air most of the families had retreated into the motels and cottages, to the heated indoor pools and HBO and Showtime cable channels, and it was a young and sharp crowd this Saturday night, as it was every Saturday night from May through September.

I didn't mind it that much, unlike some people I knew. I liked the play and the energy and the freeness of it all, as the teen-agers cruised in their cars or traveled in packs along the sand-dusted roads, laughing and shouting at each other, confident that every day would be like the one before it, and that they would live forever young, safe, and secure in the thought that the hardest decision they would ever face would be what brand of beer to buy, what kind of video game to play, and whom they should kiss.

What I did mind was the casual brutality of the loud drunks braying at every attractive woman who sauntered by, the furtive looks and gestures with folded cash being passed from one hand to another, the dirt and trash along the streets, the electronic spasm of the video game noises, the grumble of the car engines, and the pounding rhythms that roared from shoulder-carried radios.

The cry of the gull, the hiss of the waves, and the gentle whistle of the buoys were not only drowned out, they were trampled and buried and crushed under the weight of everything else at Tyler Beach. I remembered with a wistful smile last summer, walking along Atlantic Avenue with Alice Crenshaw, hand in hand because of the crowds, and her squeezing my hand tight and whispering into my ear: "These are the nights I wish for a hurricane to sweep through here and scour everything clean, Lewis, clean right down to the sands. Next time 'round, maybe we wouldn't foul this place so bad.''

Maybe so. But I doubted it.

At the corner of Atlantic Avenue and Baker I turned and walked to the St. Lawrence Seaway. The three-story building was still light gray and still looked the same, and I went into the lobby, past the yellow-and-green wallpaper with seashells and the rack with vacation folders. Instead of young Lucy from last week, this night a middle-aged woman was working behind the counter. She was smoking a cigarette and reading a paperback novel that had the front cover ripped off. By its pink back cover I deduced that she probably wasn't reading a physics text. I gave her a friendly half-wave and she grunted back as I bounded up the stairs to the second floor, to the door that marked Oliver Mailloux's office. It was closed and locked. I knocked and there was no answer.

Then I remembered our last conversation, about his complaints about his living conditions, and I went up to the next set of stairs. At the first right-hand door on the third floor, there was a sign that said PRIVATE. I knocked there, too, and there was no answer.

Damn. Some ambush. He had been here only a few minutes ago, when I had called from home. I looked up the corridor, at the rows of identical numbered doors, all painted a shade of yellow that somehow reminded me of an infant's drool. Halfway down the corridor was a fire alarm box, and at the corridor's end there was a fire exit, with its glowing red-and-white sign. Near the end of the corridor a door to one of the rooms opened and two young girls, about sixteen or seventeen, stumbled out, giggling and laughing. They looked like cousins, with light brown hair done up in hairspray and mousse, and wearing black stockings and dresses that ended at mid-thigh. I walked up to them and took out my wallet and flashed it before their eyes.

"I'm from the Tyler Health Department," I said, lying with the easy conviction that they wouldn't know there wasn't a health department in Tyler, only an animal control officer who was a health officer part time.

"Yes?" the one on the left asked cautiously, hand still on the doorknob. She had light blue makeup caked over her eyes, making me think for some reason of ancient Egypt. Her friend had rouged her cheeks so red it looked as if she had just come in from a February evening. They looked slightly silly, though I admit I'm not up on the current makeup rules.

I smiled. "Nothing to worry about. Just a random inspection. You two girls work for Mr. Mailloux?"

The one on the left nodded and the one on the right, with red cheeks, said, "We're both chambermaids here. Tammy works on the first floor, and I have the second."

"So you get a discount by staying here, right?"

They both nodded and Tammy, hand still on the doorknob, said, "Look at it this way. Corinne and I get to save a lot of money by staying here, and though we have to put in a lot of hours a day, our nights are free."

"Is he a good boss?" I asked.

They both looked at each other and shrugged and Tammy said, "Well, he pretty much leaves us alone."

Corinne added, "Though he does like to stare sometimes."

"Really?"

Corinne with the red cheeks giggled and I smiled again and said, "Well, all I need is to have a quick look in your room, make an inspection, and make sure everything is fine, and I'll let you get going. We do these types of inspections up and down the Strip, to be sure you're not being mistreated. You wouldn't believe some of the ways the hotel owners treat their help."

Tammy with the heavy eye makeup frowned and said, "Corinne, will you let Paul know I'll be a few minutes late?" and Corinne said yes, of course, and she strolled away, swinging a little purse with metal flakes on it, humming some tune I didn't recognize.

I went into the room and just did a quick spot check. I was doing this more to fill time than anything else, and because I also wanted to feel out what other people who worked for Oliver Mailloux thought of him. But I also wanted to be quick. My count was one waitress being fired. I didn't want to add a chambermaid to the score.

The room was tiny, with two single beds, and by the rumpled sheets and blankets and the smell and the pile of clothes dumped on the light green carpet, I guessed that Tammy and Corinne were saving their chambermaid skills for paying customers. The wall was cracked plaster, almost matching the color of the doors, and there were two framed prints of the White Mountains hanging on the near wall; I wondered if at mountain lodges upstate the rooms had framed prints of the sands of Tyler Beach. On the wall where the two beds butted up against the plaster, the girls had tacked up a long, wide poster for the New York Ballet, showing long legs and ballet shoes and nothing else.

On the opposite side of the room there was a low counter covered with coins, newspapers, hairbrushes, hairspray, mousse, and other makeup tools, and there were two mirrors, reflecting both single beds, set just above a color television set that was chained to the wall.

Tammy sat on the edge of the bed near the window and said, "You looking for anything in particular?"

"The usual," I said. "Illegal hotplates, rat droppings, lack of smoke detectors. You see any rat droppings?"

She shivered and for a moment she looked like a cat, with that mane of hair and the makeup over the eyes. "God, don't even mention rats to me."

As she sat there I went to the closets and opened them and saw the usual mishmash of jeans, blouses, sneakers, high-heeled shoes, and two yellow-and-white uniforms. Hanging from each uniform was a bundle of keys, and someone was smiling at me that night, for one key on each bundle was clearly marked with a white tag: Passkey.

I didn't bother to look behind me to see if I was being watched. That would be too suspicious. Instead, with one quick motion, I tugged one of the keys off and palmed it and said, "Things look fine, Tammy. Sorry I took your time."

She sat with a fearful look, arms folded. "Any rat droppings?"

"None. You're clean." Which was slightly true.

I let her go out first and she walked quickly down the hallway, no doubt hurrying to catch up with Corinne and her friend Paul, and as I took my time walking down the hallway, I heard a familiar voice, talking loudly to someone. I turned and pretended I was a guest, fiddling with the door to my room, when I heard Oliver Mailloux come to the top of the stairs. He was talking to someone, and when the door of his room opened, I turned and, in a few more steps, followed him in.

Oliver Mailloux looked at me, a brief moment of surprise etched on his face. He was carrying a large cardboard box with the word SONY on one side, and so was his companion, a boy of about eighteen, with heavy acne, wearing jeans and a black T-shirt with the face of Madonna silk-screened on. Unlike Tammy and Corinne's warren, this room was large, as big as an apartment. The three of us were in a living room with vinyl couches and chairs that looked like they had been salvaged from somewhere else in the hotel. Off to the right was a kitchen area with a fake oak dining room set and what looked like the door to a bathroom, and off to the left was an open door leading to a bedroom. I could make out some shelves in there and a big-screen television, one of those mammoth numbers that can easily cost several thousand dollars.

The room was quite clean, which seemed somewhat unusual, but then I suppose the chambermaids who came in here were extra careful. There was a moment and then Oliver surprised me. Before doing anything, making any sound, making any motion, he went to the bedroom, followed by the young boy, and they dropped both boxes and came back and he closed the bedroom door, and by then, a few seconds had passed and some color had returned to his face.

"What the hell do you want, Cole?" he demanded. "And who the fuck do you think you are, barging in here like this? This is my property, my apartment, and you can get your ass out of here."

Tonight he had on one of those lime green polo shirts with an alligator on one side and faded jeans, but he ruined the effect with the three gold chains around his neck. His skin was dark, and in the light, I saw that his face was more pockmarked than I had first remembered. His gray-black hair was parted on the same side and combed back, and his brown eyes had the warmth of sodden driftwood.

I said, "That's pretty foul language, especially for a potential customer, Oliver. Suppose I came by just to say that my magazine wanted to rent a suite of rooms for a conference here next month, complete with guest speakers and television coverage. The way you just treated me would have destroyed that deal."

"You're bullshitting me," he said, slightly troubled, looking at the boy next to him for a moment, as if seeking some sort of reassurance. I thought, who the hell is that kid, anyway?

"Very good," I said. "Here I was, just thinking that you were a flinty guy, only worried about counting columns of numbers or counting sheets, and you've just showed me that an occasional thought can stumble through your mind. No, I came by tonight to talk about your hiring and firing practices, Oliver Mailloux. Like the nonsense you pulled with Sarah Lockwood, when you fired her because she spent a few minutes talking to me. That doesn't tell me you're one caring soul."

Oliver turned and said something quickly in French to the young boy, and the only word I caught was "Derek," so I was certain of more company in a moment. The boy scurried past and Oliver smiled, showing off yellowed teeth that could have sent an orthodontist to Cancún for six months.

"First, I can fire any young bitch I want, because it's my business, not yours," Oliver said. "Second, if you don't get your ass out of here, I'm gonna have someone break it for you. So stay if you'd like—I'm sure I'll enjoy the show."

"I think I will," I said. "I'm finding the conversation charming. Tell me, Oliver, you ever buy lobster or fish from Henry Desmond, the lobsterman who got killed this week?"

Oliver kept up his grin. "Screw you, Jack."

"The name is Lewis," I said. "Or did you throw away the business card I gave you, Oliver? One other question—you're a pretty clumsy liar, you know, in saying you knew nothing about Lynn Germano, or where she lived, or what kind of person she was, when you put her up in one of your cottages—probably for free—and the two of you had something going on together. So what was going on between you two? I'm pretty curious—she must have kept her eyes closed through everything."

Oh, my, how that had an effect. He licked his lips, quickly, like a hyena looking up from his meal to see if he was being spotted, and his eyelids narrowed down, and he said, "Just you wait," and that's when the sound of heavy footsteps coming up the stairs made its way into the room.

I decided not to wait. I left. Oliver followed me out, still smiling and probably looking forward to what he thought was going to happen next. Coming up the stairs, thick legs chugging together, was Derek Cooney, wearing his white chinos and black Palace Diner T-shirt.

Behind me Oliver said, "You've got five minutes with this shit, Derek, and then I want what's left dumped out back with the rest of the trash."

Fairly inspiring words. Derek grinned, probably not knowing some basic laws of physics and balance, especially regarding stairways, and he kept on coming. I waited until he was a few steps from the top, having made up my mind in Oliver's office what I was going to do, and then I spun on one leg and kicked out with the other, catching him full in his chest. He said "Ooof" and spread his arms out, windmilling for a moment like a silent movie character, and then he fell on his back and slipped and tumbled down to the stairway's landing, his legs spread open, losing a Nike sneaker in the process.

Oliver said something sharp but I ignored him and followed Derek down to the landing and jumped on him, making sure one of my feet landed square in his crotch. He made a loud noise like a squeal and bellow, and as I got off him—this all happening about as quickly as it sounds—his hands went to his crotch and I grabbed his T-shirt with one hand and slapped him three times in the face with the other.

With Derek lying there, the wind knocked out of him, his back hurting and his crotch feeling like someone had been using it for batting practice, I could have punched him in the face. Or kicked him in the ribs. Or done any number of things. But by slapping him like that, I humiliated him, humiliated him before his boss, and that's what I wanted to do. I had no intention of waiting for Derek to arrive on the third floor and join me. I knew we were going to have a confrontation, and fighting "fair" or whatever the hell someone else was going to call fair was not an option this particular night. He was on his back and I was standing up, and that was just fine, thank you.

I also wanted Oliver to see the whole thing, to let him know that a certain writer for *Shoreline* could do more than just cancel his magazine subscription. I stood up and pulled back the blazer, so that he could see the shoulder holster, and I said, "I'm leaving now, Oliver. And I won't look too kindly on either you or your friend here following me out. Or doing anything else. Understand?"

Oliver said a long phrase, mixing both French and English, going into great detail about my sexual habits and how they involved animals and both of my parents, and then I walked downstairs and went out through the lobby, and the woman was still there at the counter, reading her paperback romance, completely insulated by the paper pages from what was going on around her. In a way, I almost envied her. The last things I heard as I left the hotel were Oliver's shouts, this time directed at Derek.

I made it a couple of blocks from the St. Lawrence Seaway before the shakes began and I started limping. My right foot and knee were aching from the kick I had given Derek in the chest, and both of my hands throbbed and felt greasy from the slaps to his face. I smelled awful, and I knew that I had sweated out my shirt. Just before the Tyler Beach Palace complex was Romulus Men's Store, which, like every store on Tyler Beach this Saturday night, was still open. In going through the displays of glowing orange and red shorts, and the streams of T-shirts and sweatpants, I managed to find a small display of men's underwear and dress shirts at the back of the store. By paying a ten-dollar tip to a young man with spiked hair who was clerking that night, I got to change in a back bathroom. I washed out my armpits and winced as I put on the clean shirt and underwear. A couple of muscles were probably pulled and they would scream at me tomorrow, but that was several hours away, and I had other work to perform that night. I trashed my old shirt and underwear in a wastebasket and left the store.

Feeling tingly and quite awake, I actually went into the Palace Diner and ordered a lemonade to go, spending a dollar-fifty for a plastic cup of ice, sugar, and a squeezed lemon, which tasted wonderful and which I finished in three swallows. Traffic along Atlantic Avenue was going slow, with cars and pickup trucks stopping and starting as young girls ran from vehicle to vehicle, searching for something I'm not too sure even they realized they were looking for. On E Street I took a right, to a bank of phones, and I made three phone calls. One was to

Felix Tinios, and I arranged to meet with him in thirty minutes, and the second was to my home. There was a message on my answering machine, from Diane Woods: "Lewis, this isn't urgent, but I need to see you as soon as you can get free."

Then, just for something to do, I suppose, I called Lynn Germano's home in Lawrence, and the woman who answered the phone hung up on me the moment I said two words.

I then hung up the phone myself and breathed deep, and when I listened closely, I could hear the ocean's waves coming in, reaching for all of us.

I drove to North Tyler, the ocean on my right all the way, and I pulled into the Lady Manor House, a large bed-and-breakfast inn set on the oceanfront, just before the town line to Wallis, and near enough so one could see Wallis Harbor from the windows on the north side. The Lady Manor House is a large white Victorian and reminded me of my neighbor from across the street, the Lafayette House, though it was just a bit smaller and didn't have the interesting history of having the Marquis de Lafayette stop by. Some burden, I guess. The inside lobby was carpeted with Oriental rugs and tall potted plants, and there was a lot of brass and wood among the walls and doors.

I went into the lounge, which had slowly twirling ceiling fans and elaborate French glass doors overlooking a patio. The furniture was white wicker, and the chairs had flowered cushions. By the long bar there was a redheaded woman wearing a black cocktail dress and playing a piano. It sounded like jazz and I liked the way she played: She looked at the keys and smiled to herself and ignored everyone in the room, and she didn't sing. On the piano's polished surface was a brandy goblet, and most of it was clear glass, empty save for a few dollar bills. I guess some of the customers were upset that she wasn't playing Barry Manilow.

Felix was sitting with his back to the wall, a drink in his

hand, smiling at me as I came in. Tonight he wore a thin, soft black jacket that looked like an Armani, pleated gray slacks, and a tight black T-shirt, and he didn't bother getting up as I approached. His hair was flawless and his skin was clear, and he smiled and said, "When you mentioned a business proposition, Lewis, you certainly intrigued me."

"Well, then, that's one for me," I said. "Never knew I could ever intrigue you."

Felix raised a hand and then the waiter appeared, wearing black slacks and a white shirt. With his black crewcut the waiter looked like a college football student trying to pick up a few bucks before spring training started. As I saw him go back to the bar with my order for a Molson Golden Ale, I felt a brief pang of regret for Sarah Lockwood, slapping down fried food and ignoring the touch of her uncle, there in Falconer, and I hoped she would eventually find some comfort in what was going to happen to Oliver Mailloux, because I knew something bad would happen to him eventually.

Felix sipped at his drink and we waited for my ale, and when it arrived I said, "So. Interested?"

"Very. I can't imagine what I have that you would want."

"Not what you have, Felix. What kind of services you offer." I took a swallow of the Molson and wondered what cold bright stream in Canada this brew had come from. "I'm in the middle of a situation now, one that's a bit more than I can handle."

His smile was positively cheery. "I never thought I'd see this day come, Lewis, that a man of your . . . well, honor, I guess . . . would be looking for my talents."

"Don't get your hopes up," I said. "All I want is something of mine to be protected."

"Your house," he said.

"Exactly. I'm in the middle of something involving Oliver Mailloux and Derek Cooney. Nothing that I can't handle, but while I'm out and about, I don't want them or some crazies hired by them to torch my house or go in and raise hell on my property. Simple as that."

He seemed to settle in his chair, bunch up his shoulders. "You looking for wet work, Lewis?"

"No." I took another long swallow of the ale, remembering I was still hungry and needed to get something to eat before the night was over. "No, I just want my house and land protected. Doesn't have to be by you, Felix. I'm sure that in your work you hire out some of your tasks to other people. All I ask is that they be reliable and discreet. I don't want a couple of bikers in leather and chains, hanging out in the parking lot of the Lafayette House, harassing people. Can it be done?"

He smiled again. "Suppose I say no?"

"Then I'll depart and leave you with the check, and think of something else."

Felix laughed and ran a hand through his hair and said, "Lewis, consider it taken care of, the moment I get to a phone."

I felt a little better. His earlier prediction, of someone torching my house, had almost come true this morning. I had no interest in seeing the prediction come true anytime soon, or anytime later, for that matter.

"Good," I said. "How much will it cost me?"

He shrugged. "Won't cost you a cent, Lewis. Consider it a favor."

I put down my beer. "No. No favors, Felix. This is a straight business deal, a service for cash. I'm not going to get roped into something where I have to owe you or anyone who works for you any type of favors, Felix. You've got a problem with that, then I'll pay the check and leave and we can forget about it. No favors. A strict business deal."

By then he wasn't smiling. "It'll be expensive, Lewis."

"I can afford it."

"On a magazine writer's salary?" he scoffed.

"You tell me what it'll cost and I'll pay you."

He did and though some of the Molson's wanted to crawl back up my throat, I just nodded. "Not a problem."

Felix shook his head slightly, picked up his drink, and swirled the ice. "Where do you get your money, Lewis? I've always wondered about that. I know magazine writers don't get paid shit, but you drive a Range Rover and seem to live pretty well."

"Doesn't matter," I said. "Let's say I have some conservative investments. You'll be getting your share soon enough."

Out through the French doors I could see the lights of some of the boats on Wallis Harbor, a much smaller harbor than Tyler to the south or Porter to the north. It seemed to be a peaceful place, and I doubted any boats had ever blown up and sank there, or that anyone had died violently on those waters. Henry Desmond. Alice Crenshaw. For just a moment something tugged at me as I thought of Alice and wondered what might have happened to her, if she had been in her chair as it was tossed down to the sharp rocks below her home . . .

Felix said, "All right. But payment when the job is complete. How does that sound?"

My turn to shrug at him. "If you say so."

He finished off his drink and said, "Why are you making Oliver Mailloux and Derek Cooney mad at you, Lewis? They cheat you out of towels some night you stayed at their hotel?"

"No," I said. "I don't like the way they operate, that's all, and I've been asking some questions and poking around, and I don't like what I see. There's something there with them and Lynn Germano, and maybe Henry Desmond. And they don't like me asking questions."

"Sound like a couple of reputable businessmen to me, Lewis. I'd tell you to go pound sand, myself."

"That's not saying much."

He grinned and said, "I do know that Oliver's said this is his last summer on the beach, so watch your back. You might find yourself tied in a guest room at his hotel while Derek torches the place, to get the insurance money for Oliver."

"I'll remember that."

There were some more negotiations, which resulted in both of us leaving money for the check, and as we walked out, I said, "One other thing, Felix."

"Which is?"

"Which is this: I'm putting a lot at stake, trusting in your abilities. The night I go back to Samson's Point and there's nothing there except burnt rubble, or someone's dumped toxic waste on my lawn, then I'll believe you had something to do with it. Remember that."

Felix almost giggled, as if I was joking, and I said, "Felix, just remember what the price of tires is nowadays."

"Oh, I do, I do," he said, still smiling.

"I'm sure. Felix, you didn't ask me if I was carrying tonight, did you?"

Felix said, "I already knew the answer for that one, so I didn't bother asking the question."

As we passed the piano player, Felix put a twenty-dollar bill into the brandy snifter. The woman smiled at Felix and he smiled back, and I felt better, as if I were watching a hungry Doberman allowing itself to be petted by an infant.

12

ON SUNDAY MORNING I WOKE UP FAIRLY early, feeling well rested, I guess, in knowing that a pair of friendly eyes was out there somewhere, making sure my house was fine and that I slept unmolested. Though I had slept well, I grimaced as I made the short walk from my bedroom to the bathroom. Certain muscles that I didn't exercise very often were tight and creaky after yesterday's meeting with Derek Cooney on a stairway at the St. Lawrence Seaway. I wondered how Derek was feeling that morning, as well as his boss, Oliver.

I took a shower and carefully examined my body in the mirror, checking the old scars and feeling the fabric of my skin. Except for the taut muscles, which felt slightly better after the hot shower, everything else seemed fine. After getting dressed, I ate a small breakfast of tea and toast, standing at the counter reading a copy of *Forest Notes*, which is put out by the Society for the Protection of New Hampshire Forests. It's an environmental organization that appeals to me. It doesn't lobby or fight in Congress or picket. It just buys land in the state, preserving it forever from developers or businesses. It doesn't seek much media attention, and it gets the job done.

As I ate my slight breakfast I knew I had three things to do that Sunday, and one of them involved seeing Diane Woods. Another was finishing my magazine column before I started getting threatening phone calls from Boston. The third was my usual Sunday ritual.

Before I left I called Diane's home. There was no answer, so I tried the dispatcher at the Tyler Police Department. Diane wasn't at the station that morning, and the dispatcher, still true to her vow of silence, refused to tell me if she was on duty or not. So. I had an idea of where Diane might be, but I decided to try her home first. For all I knew, she was out getting the Sunday newspapers.

As I drove up the bumpy driveway—and despite the bumps, I vowed once again never to pave it—I looked around, curious at who my friendly eyes were, so newly hired through Felix Tinios. There were a few empty cars parked in the Lafayette House parking lot, along with a van, and a young man standing there, breathing into his hands, one of the valet parkers for the Lafayette House, taking care of the early Sunday morning brunch business. Someone in the van, looking through darkened windows? Or in one of the upper floors of the Lafayette House, or hiding among the rocks and low shrub of Samson's Point?

Or maybe it was the valet parker. I gave him a half-wave as I drove by. This early on a Sunday morning the sea gulls outnumbered the people along the beach, and the only people out there were a few joggers, power walkers, and the state work crews in tan uniforms, picking up trash and debris from the beach. I tried not to think of a bloated Alice Crenshaw rolling ashore with a cold toss of the waves. Although sleeping on the beach is against the law, there were a few huddled shapes in blankets on the cold sands, looking like corpses from some battle, ready to be airlifted out. I'm sure they had disquieting dreams, having slept out in the open, with the cries of the gulls and the sounds of the waves in their ears.

It was an oddly empty Sunday morning at the beach, with a few empty beer cans rolling across the road, and I managed to get through all of Tyler Beach touching the brakes on my Range Rover only once.

The complex where Diane Woods lives is on the northern end of Tyler Harbor, where it narrows to meet the tidal flow of the Wonalancet River. The complex is called Tyler Harbor Meadows and is made up of about a dozen townhouses built near the water's edge in a horseshoe formation. There is a small dock off the parking lot where most of the condo residents have skiffs or rowboats tied up, and out on the harbor, at its mooring, was the yellow-and-black sailboat that was Diane's *Miranda*, named for the not-so-popular-among-cops police warning. It was a bit after 8 A.M. when I drove into the condo complex and saw that the guest parking spot for Diane's unit was occupied by a light blue Toyota with Massachusetts plates.

I found an empty spot near the condo's dumpster and walked to the center of the complex. All of the townhouses are narrow, with three floors, and all are painted ivory. There was an upstairs light on at Diane's unit, number twelve. Except for myself, no one else was wandering around the parking lot. Diane's Volkswagen Rabbit was parked next to the Toyota. I wondered who the Toyota belonged to. I rang the bell and waited a few minutes, then rang it again. On the glass of the door was a sticker for the Tyler Police Association. The sea gulls were crying out on the harbor and there was a faint puttering noise of a boat departing this Sunday morning, heading out to the Atlantic to do the Sabbath's work for some family.

I was conscious of the weight of the .32 in my ankle holster as I raised my hand again to the doorbell, when Diane threw open the door, whispering, "What the hell do you want?" through the screen.

I said, "Beats the hell out of me. *You* wanted to see *me*, Diane."

"Jesus Christ, not at this hour on a Sunday morning." She

was wearing a man's blue-striped shirt and not much else. Her brown hair was tousled. "Your timing sucks, Lewis. Why didn't you call?"

"I did. There was no answer. And when you called yesterday, you said as soon as possible. This is the best I could do. Should I go?"

She yawned and rubbed at her hair and said, "Shit, no. Come on up. I must've disconnected the phone last night. I warn you though, I've got an overnight guest here who's about to leave. Promise me you won't be shocked."

I opened the door and followed her in, heading up the carpeted stairs. Her legs were quite long and tanned. "Who you choose to spend the night with has surprised me just once, Diane, and I got over it a long time ago."

Diane giggled and I went with her to her kitchen. The stairs made a sharp turn and there was a kitchen to the left, overlooking the parking lot and the harbor, and to the right was a small living room, with a low wood counter holding up a television and stereo system, and a tan couch with two matching chairs. There was another set of stairs that started in the kitchen and led upstairs, to a bedroom and Diane's study.

The kitchen had a white tiled floor, a glass-topped table, and white tubular chairs, and sitting in one of the chairs, sipping a cup of coffee, was a young woman about twenty-five or so. She wore yellow sneakers and black slacks and a long-sleeved tan T-shirt, with the sleeves rolled up her thin white arms. She had short blond hair, cut sharp along the sides in a zigzag pattern, and in one ear she had four earrings. She looked up at me as I came in and then looked over at Diane, a curious but friendly look on her face.

"Kara Miles," Diane said, "this is Lewis Cole. A friend of mine. He's a writer. Lives up on Tyler Beach."

She put down her cup. "No kidding? What do you write?"

"For a magazine out of Boston," I said. "Called *Shoreline*." I leaned back against the kitchen counter and Diane walked behind her, touching her cheek for a moment as she leaned over and picked up her own cup of coffee.

Kara smiled and said, "You know, I've always wanted to write, but I never seemed to get the time. The work I do, writing up software, makes heading to the keyboard the last thing I want to do when I get home."

"Sounds familiar," I said.

"I'm sorry I've never heard of your magazine."

I smiled at her. "I'm sorry, too."

She put down her coffee cup and reached under the table, pulling up a light gray gym bag. "Jeez, look at the time, Diane. I gotta get going. Nice meeting you, Lewis."

Diane winked at me and followed Kara down the stairs, while I stayed behind at the kitchen counter. I heard the murmur of voices and then the soft, wet sound of a kiss; a door slammed and Diane came back upstairs. She made it to the kitchen just as I saw the blue Toyota head out of the parking lot. Out on the harbor the boats drifted at their moorings, rising up and down with the ocean swells.

"Coffee?" Diane asked. I declined and said, "She looks nice, Diane. Been seeing her long?"

She put her cup down and crossed her arms. "This is only our third get-together."

"Really? How soon before she gets a key to your place?"

She smiled at me, saying, "Pig," and then she laughed. "That's sort of an in joke, you know. A cliché, but like all clichés, it has some truth to it, about our search for commitment. The joke is that on the second date, one of the two shows up at the other woman's house with a U-Haul."

Diane laughed again and I smiled with her, and said, "It's good to see you happy, Diane. Didn't think you'd had many opportunities to laugh or smile about lately. Where did you meet her?"

She picked up her cup and Kara's and walked to the sink, her bare feet slapping on the tiled floor, the back of her neck red. She started washing the dishes and said, "Promise me you won't laugh. Or frown."

"It's a promise."

"Well, it's like this," she said, washing out a cup. "Think of where I live and what I do for work, and what kind of shit would be slung my way if details about my personal life ever got out. So I always have to keep that in mind, whatever I do. There's a fair-sized gay community in Porter, you know, or up in Maine, at Ogunquit, but both of those places are too open and too near to Tyler. Being that open is something I can't risk, not in this area and these times, though I do hate skulking around. So for a while, Lewis, I was going to Boston and other places in Massachusetts, and the bar scenes there are like any other bar scenes you'll find. Lots of drinking, lots of smoking, and a meat market."

She shut off the water and began drying the dishes, speaking to the wall, not looking at me. "I hate drunks, I don't smoke, and I'm not in the mood to be on display, so I went searching somewhere else."

"Personal ads?"

She turned and stuck out her tongue. "Smartass. Yeah, ads, and thanks for not laughing. There's a weekly newspaper for gays and lesbians out of Boston, called *Bay Windows*. I started looking in those ads and after a couple of minor disasters, hooked up with Kara. She works for Digital and lives in Newburyport, and we have good times, Lewis, the three times we've been together. We really have."

"Good for you, Diane," I said.

"Thanks." She opened up a cabinet door and put away the dishes. "You know, it was a funny thing, going through those ads. We always like to think we're different and special from the straights, but reading those ads, well, it showed me that in some places, there is no difference. The male ads in *Bay Windows*, most of them were pure raunch, men looking for other men for hard and quick sex, and not much else. The female ads were just the opposite. Looking for friendship, looking for commitments. Not looking for something temporary.''

"Battle of the sexes, only in different uniforms.''

"Yeah,'' she said. "Right.''

I said, "You looking for a commitment?''

She almost sighed and said, "No, right now I'm looking for a cuddly someone who can be with me and make me feel good. That's all for right now, Lewis. And we do have fun—even after only a couple of dates, she makes jokes about my handcuffs. Says she wants me to chain her to the bed.''

"Have you?''

She tossed a towel at me. "Thought you wrote for *Shoreline*, Lewis. Not *Penthouse*.''

"Man's gotta have some outside interests.''

I picked up the towel and handed it back to her and she said, her voice quiet, "So they do. So what are you looking for, Lewis? I don't think you've ever mentioned dating, the time I've known you. Don't you have the interest?''

I paused for a moment, then said, "I have the interest, Diane. Right now, I'm just looking for some peace. And you're looking for something, or you wouldn't have called me.''

She closed the cabinet door and turned and said, "I want to do a little talking, Lewis. But I have to be back at the station this afternoon, and I want to do a few hours of sailing. Game?''

"Just show me which end of the boat you want me to sit at.''

An hour later, after rowing out to the *Miranda*, we were heading out of Tyler Harbor. The *Miranda* has an open cockpit and a tiny forward cabin where two people would have been breathing on each other's necks if they were in there at the same time. Diane had a five-horsepower Datsun outboard motor, and with the jib and mainsails furled, she held onto the tiller and set us out toward the Atlantic, the motor making a hell of a lot of noise for its size. The *Miranda* is a Holder fiberglass sailboat, just 20 feet long, and was purchased after the inheritance of some dead relative's financial legacy, or so Diane has told me. I've never pressed her for more details. As we approached the Felch Memorial Bridge, spanning Tyler Harbor, Diane held up an air horn and triggered two quick blasts.

Up on the bridge a man in the window of the tiny square structure in its center waved at us and we waved back. Traffic gates at both ends of the bridge came down and traffic on Atlantic Avenue came to a stop as the two sides of the bridge began to slowly rise up, as if sweating slaves inside the bridge were quietly spinning the cables under some overseer's whip.

The wind was beginning to rise up, tossing hair across Diane's face. She had on a pair of white corduroy pants and a faded pink polo shirt, and no jewelry, though I did notice that in her leather kit bag, with the charts, air horn, and marine radio, she had tossed in her service revolver and badge. Even out here, she was still on duty, and I don't think there was a time she ever considered herself off duty.

"You know," she said, as we motored through the open bridge, "one of these days, there's going to be a tidal wave warning, that a fifty-foot wave is heading to Tyler Beach. The sirens will sound and people will be racing away in their cars. And on that day, this bridge'll get stuck open again."

"It'll be a hell of a story, though," I said.

"Some story," she said. "You won't be able to write it, if you're home that day."

"Maybe I'll be lucky. Maybe I'll be at your place."

She kicked me. "Fat chance."

I looked back at the harbor and the other moored boats as we went through the bridge's opening, thinking for a moment of a pall of a smoke and a burning hull. I wondered if the eyes that had been watching Henry Desmond and me that Thursday morning were still out there.

I said, "You ever search *Miranda* for bombs?"

She waited for a moment, and said quietly, "Don't even joke about stuff like that."

"Who said I was joking?"

Diane didn't reply, and I kept quiet.

When we had cleared the breakwater we raised the sails, setting up the mainsail first and then the jib, the sails billowing and then snapping out as the wind caught them. I don't know that much about sailing but I'm good enough crew to take direction and do what has to be done and I know port from starboard, though I tend to get confused about the difference between a sheet and a line. Diane maneuvered the *Miranda* around and the wind caught us, heeling us over, and we headed southeast, to the distant shape of Cape Ann in Massachusetts, though we would never reach it in the time we had that morning. The water was gray and cold and wide, and I tried not to think about Alice Crenshaw, maybe still floating out here, her body swelling up and decomposing, the fish and birds picking away at the flesh . . .

I sat against the starboard gunwale, my feet braced on the other side, and Diane kept a hand on the tiller and another hand on the rope controlling the mainsail. Some salt spray was being tossed up by the boat's motion and was splashing into the cockpit. By now Diane had put on her sunglasses so I couldn't see her eyes, but I guess it was even, because I also had my sunglasses on. That way, too, I couldn't see her eyes when my pants leg rode up, exposing my ankle holster, but she did nod slightly, so I knew she had noticed it.

"Anything new about Alice?"

She tightened up the rope some, and the muscles in her tanned arm clenched up and then released. "No news, Lewis. We're still keeping an eye on the sands and the fishermen know what to look for, but nothing's washed up. Forensics showed no blood spilled in her house, which may be a good sign. Or not. I just keep remembering how Lynn died—strangulation."

Talking about Alice made me feel uncomfortable so I said, "What's going on that's so sensitive you don't want to talk about it at work or at your condo?"

Her jaw clenched and I knew I had hit home, and she said, "The usual sensitive stuff, Lewis. Look. Conversations you and I sometimes have can be used against me. I know what you do when you say you're writing one of your columns, and I don't like it, but I accept it, because I know what has to be done with what I have. And what I have this summer is me and two patrol officers on loan some days as part-time detectives, who have a lot of enthusiasm and not much else."

"I know that, Diane. And I know the ground rules. Always have." I folded my arms and looked at the thin ribbon of sand and marsh off to our right, slowly shrinking away with every passing minute.

Diane said, "Glad to hear that, Lewis. You know, one of the two deputy chiefs at the station has double duty, besides supervising the patrol staff and me. He also does Internal Affairs stuff, and I know that he's not averse to using technological means and anything else to gain information. Which is why we're here, and not at my condo or the station."

"You don't think the *Miranda* is bugged?"

"Oh, Christ, anything can be bugged, with enough time and effort. But I check the *Miranda* here and there and haven't found anything yet, and out on the harbor, it's hard to get aboard and slip something on. Even now, with the wind blowing us by, it would be hard to record a single word. And a shotgun mike is next to useless unless a fishing boat pulls up next to us."

"So that way, nobody can listen in when I tell you what I've learned," I said.

"Exactly. I'll tell you this, Lewis, I'm getting tired of getting phone calls from the AG's office in Concord every morning, asking me about Lynn Germano or Henry Desmond. On Henry Desmond, the only thing we've learned is that it looks like dynamite was used in his fishing boat, though we can't find the detonating device. Probably pieces of it are on the bottom of Tyler Harbor, and there's no money or gumption to start dredging the harbor to look for it. And we've done interviews with everyone connected with either Henry Desmond or Lynn Germano, and there's no connection, no connection between them at all."

I thought for a moment and remembered a wasted trip to Lawrence and a couple of equally wasted phone calls. Each time I had called, the woman on the other end had hung up on me. "You talked to her parents, back there in Lawrence?"

The *Miranda* heaved a bit, as a large swell went by, and Diane moved the tiller a bit, adjusting. "We did. Not me, personally, but one of our patrolmen. Nothing substantial or earth-shattering. Just a high school kid, up to Tyler Beach for the summer, making some money. Why do you ask?"

Out near the horizon I could make out the low red-and-black form of a freighter, heading north, to Porter and its harbor. "Back after her death, I went to Lawrence and tried to talk to the parents and I wasn't too successful. Not surprising, considering what they'd gone through and what I do for a living."

Diane nodded and waited a few moments, then said quietly, "What have you got for me, Lewis?"

Though it took only a second or two for me to reply, I confess that I had made up my answer an hour before, when I was going from Diane's skiff to the moored *Miranda*. There are times when I don't reveal all to Diane, because that little piece of metal she carries with her also carries a certain obligation to make a response. If there was going to be a response to anything I had learned, I wanted to be behind it, and know what type of response it was going to be. Not that I don't trust the criminal justice system—it's just that I sometimes trust my own instincts more.

So I said, "I've been poking around, asking questions. I've talked to her boss, the guy who owns the Palace Diner, and he hasn't been particularly friendly to me. Not looking for bad publicity, I guess. But I wonder if there's a connection between the diner and Henry Desmond, if he ever sold some of his catch there, or if he ate at the diner on a regular basis and got to know Lynn Germano. I've also been trying to track down if there was anything to connect them with Alice Crenshaw, Diane, and I've come up empty."

She nodded and hauled in the rope a bit more. "We have, too, Lewis. Someone trashed her house and even without any blood traces, it looks like she went up in the clouds. But you know, a little voice tells me that she's out here, floating somewhere, and that she's been killed. I'm glad to see you're carrying, Lewis. I still think someone wanted you on Henry Desmond's boat last week. And I have a guess on who, if you'd like to hear it."

For a moment the only sounds were of *Miranda* skimming through the waves and the thrumming of the wind against the sails. I rubbed at my arms, wishing for a sweater.

I said, "Do go on."

She braced a foot against the fiberglass. "You and I both know there's a guy in this town who has the resources, and the capability, to pull this shit off."

"Felix Tinios," I said, not liking what I was hearing.

"You got it, Lewis. Felix Tinios. Now, I know you got this odd friendship with him, and that you and he talk. Hell, nothing wrong with that. There's been a couple of times when he and I've had a couple of words, about a couple of cases I've worked on. But you watch yourself with him, Lewis. I get the feeling you enjoy being around him, maybe 'cause of the way he dresses and holds himself, but I've had traces done on him down in Massachusetts. He's a bad one, rotten in the soul, and if he decides to crack you one, I might not be around to save your ass."

I said, "Thanks for the warning, I think. But I'm fairly sure that Felix is clean on this one, Diane."

"Maybe. I'd like to know more about what he's involved with but there's a limit, Lewis."

"Resources getting stretched, right?"

She looked grim as she maneuvered the tiller again. "We're getting stretched so thin, Lewis, that I'll probably have to work 'til two A.M. tonight to make up for this sail, and you can thank our local government for that. Sometimes I don't know why I put up with this shit. I could get a good job in Porter, Boston, or someplace worthwhile in between, get paid better with less hassle, and have less worry with my personal life."

I said, "But you wouldn't be in Tyler. Look around. That's why you stay here, right?"

She did as I told her; she looked around, the wind tossing her short brown hair about, and she took in the swells of the ocean, the white sands of Tyler, and the tiny buildings, the gulls flying overhead, the other sailboats out there, and the fishing trawlers, the low hills of Cape Ann off in the distance.

The smells were of saltwater and the sound was that of a boat quietly tracing through water and nothing else, and Diane said, "You're one spooky son of a bitch, Lewis. Sometimes you know exactly what I'm thinking, and you did right. Yeah, I love this place, I love it in spite of itself. Not because of the shops and diners and all the punks that come here every summer, but because of the stuff that gives the potential for Tyler to be someplace special, you know? The beaches, the history, the real people here. How did you guess that, Lewis?"

"Just lucky," I said, glad and somewhat ashamed in that she was no longer pressing me about what I was working on. Or about my relationship with Felix Tinios. But I wanted Oliver Mailloux and Derek Cooney for myself.

"Fine," she almost snorted. "Get ready to come about."

She swung *Miranda* about and I ducked my head, as the boom swung past, and I leapt to the other side of the boat and hauled in the jib, and we sailed back to Tyler not saying much the entire way, and Diane surprised me by holding my hand as we came back into Tyler Harbor.

Before I headed back to my home and to work on my *Shoreline* column, I pulled into the parking lot of St. Joseph's Church, the Catholic parish for Tyler. It's a simple brick building with a white steeple, set near the center of town. Although I was baptized Catholic I've never stayed for a full service during the Masses I've attended ever since Nevada.

I slipped in at the right time—just before collection—and watched the service. I sat in a rear pew and waited, feeling tired, my skin hot and prickly with the familiar sensation of a sunburn. My muscles were still sore, though not as bad as when I woke up that morning. I didn't know the priest's name but he was a young fellow, maybe only a few years older than me, with light brown hair that seemed awfully long. His voice was strong but peaceful, and he didn't try to batter the congregation into submission. It was a Sunday afternoon and I was surprised at how many people were there.

As the Mass continued, I remembered how different it was when I was a child. I can still remember the foreignness and majesty of the Latin ritual, and how the priest would dress differently. This one today wore a simple white shift over his black shirt and collar, and I remembered the elaborate vestments that were worn back then, with different colors signifying different seasons and times of the year. And the music—none of this folk-music revival with guitars, tambourines, and flutes. It was real church music, with powerful organ notes that seemed to reach in through your ears and tug at your throat.

Something was lost when all of that was changed. There was a yearning and a sense of nostalgia in me and other Catholics for the old rites, but in a way I knew it was just a fantasy. Even if those rites and the music returned, it was different now, and nothing could change that. I would still stay away, save for those Sundays when I felt the need to make some form of penance.

When the collection basket came around I gave every single bill from my wallet, and, thinking of Nevada and Carl Socha, Trent Baker, Cissy Manning, and the others, the forgotten others, I left to go home.

I had a column to write.

13

On Monday night I was in the Tyler town
hall, sitting next to Paula Quinn and feeling
the sweat work its way down my shirt, knowing that if I stayed
another hour or so, the shirt would be ruined, depleting my
meager wardrobe once again. Tonight was the weekly meeting
of the Tyler selectmen, and I was sitting in the first row of
folded wooden chairs, on the left, the space traditionally reserved for members of the news media. I wasn't too sure if
being a magazine writer qualified me as being a member of the
media, but I was there to see Paula Quinn and no one asked
me to leave my seat, so I figured I was fine.

The meeting hall is an addition to the town hall, connected
by a short hallway to the rest of the town offices. There are
eight rows of chairs, set before the low wooden table where
the three selectmen and the town manager sit. As in most towns
in this state, the town manager works for the selectmen and
is hired—and fired—at their pleasure.

The walls were white plaster and on the walls were certificates of when Tyler was named a Bicentennial Community in
1976, a number of proclamations written in old English script

and covered with gold foil seals, and black-and-white photographs of prior selectmen, some of them going back to the 1920s. The chairs were full of residents and some people were actually standing at the rear of the small hall, which surprised me, since I am a supporter—but hardly a participant—in local town government, and Paula has told me that attendance at the selectmen's meetings was always spotty.

The only reason I was there was to talk to Paula, and she had told me earlier that day that the selectmen's meeting was the only free time she had for me. That seemed to be a bit of a contradiction, since Paula was there to cover the meeting for the Tuesday edition of the Tyler *Chronicle,* but I think she was still punishing me for being so short with her the morning Henry Desmond died. That was all right. For most of the day I had tramped along the beaches in Tyler, ignoring the legions of suntanned bodies around me, peering at the sands and rocks, thinking sad thoughts of Alice Crenshaw.

Before us was the selectmen's table, and sitting there, from the left, were Bruce Gerrity, town manager, with his polished bald head and taste for blue polka-dot bow ties, who had once told Diane Woods that he would do almost anything to keep his job, even if it meant siding on the selectmen's side during a dispute with the police or fire departments; Gage Duffy, a forty-year-old lawyer in town and the youngest selectman, who had a thick red moustache and often rolled his eyes in disbelief at what was going on during a meeting; Jack Fowler, owner of the Fowler Motel and new president of the Chamber of Commerce, who was also the selectmen chairman, dressed tonight in a white polo shirt that seemed stretched over his stomach like a drumskin; and Betsy Tyler, seventy years old and a descendant of the Reverend Bonus Tyler of Dover, England, one of the original settlers of Tyler in 1638, whose family ended up naming the town.

Betsy Tyler knew her age and didn't care who else knew it either; she wore her gray hair pulled back in a bun, smoked unfiltered Camels, and wore blue jeans most of the time. She was serving her third three-year term as a selectman—God help any reporter who called her a selectwoman—and she had a disconcerting habit of spreading out a jigsaw puzzle on the polished black wood of the table and putting the pieces together during a meeting. Betsy always looked like someone's grandmother sitting up there, getting ready for the return ride to the nursing home, but she listened carefully and could quote minutes practically verbatim from meetings a decade earlier, and God and His Mother help any visiting lawyer who criticized her jigsaw puzzles at a session.

Like I said, the town hall was packed, and as the building inspector was giving his report of how many building permits were issued that month and Paula doodled in her notepad, I leaned over to her and whispered, "What's the deal tonight, with all the people? Selectmen giving out free beer?"

She gave me a dirty look and whispered back, "I can tell you haven't been reading the *Chronicle* that much the past few days, Lewis. There's a proposed ordinance that's been submitted to the selectmen, asking them to ban pornography within the town limits."

"Define pornography," I asked.

She turned around at the crowd and nodded to a well-dressed group sitting on the opposite side. "Forget my definition. See them? Local citizen and church group. They define it as *Playboy, Penthouse,* and the swimsuit issue of *Sports Illustrated.* Naturally, the businesses in town—the supermarkets, the convenience stores, and so forth—they don't particularly appreciate it."

I said, "For once, I'm on the side of business."

There were no fans or air-conditioning in the town hall— no money in the budget, and besides, it's only hot a few months out of the year anyway, went the conventional wisdom. Even with the open windows, I was sweating. Some of the more earthy attendees were waving folded-up copies of the agenda before their red and sweating faces. Sitting in the front row was the tax assessor, Clyde Meeker, who had so thoughtfully helped me find out the extent of Oliver Mailloux's real estate holdings last week. His fake hair still looked fake, and he was wearing a two-piece gray suit and jiggling his right leg up and down. I tried to nod in his direction but he was staring straight ahead, looking at the windows behind the town manager and the selectmen. I wondered what his business was tonight.

With the heat, my own clothes would be fit for the wash by the time this was over. Paula's blond hair was folded back in a style that made her look like a 1941 starlet, and she wore brown sandals, tan shorts that showed a lot of leg, and a frilly short-sleeved white blouse. Every time she bent over to take notes, I noticed the white lace cups of her bra, and it seemed like she was bending over a lot.

After the building inspector's report, next on the agenda was a visit from the planning board chairman, a dumpy man wearing a plaid jacket; he was complaining about the lack of selectmen support for the planning board's work. There were murmurs and whispers behind me, and the door at the rear of the town hall opened and closed a lot, as people went out to get some air. The talking went on and on and then a representative from the local Boy Scout troop showed up, asking permission to hold a car wash at the fire station to raise money for their fall camporee up in the White Mountains. At about 9 P.M. Betsy Tyler looked up from her jigsaw puzzle and said, "Move to recess for ten minutes. Cigarette break."

There were groans from the crowd and someone said, "How about the ordinance?" and Betsy grimaced and stood up and said, "If I don't get a cigarette here in about a minute or so, I'm gonna make a motion to adjourn this meeting, so give us ten minutes. Besides, most of you've been shuttling back and forth from your seats all night long. Give us a break, too. My butt's ready to fall asleep."

Jack Fowler picked up his chairman's gavel, put on his businessman's smile, and said, "Don't worry, folks, we'll be back as soon as we can and we'll discuss the ordinance thoroughly, even if it takes another night. I know of some of your concerns and believe me, I respect them. I think all of us know firsthand how this culture of ours is getting polluted, and it's going to be up to townspeople like you folks to make a change. Whatever happens tonight, at least that's a good start."

Jack Fowler slapped the gavel down and Betsy Tyler started rummaging through her purse, while Gage Duffy rolled his eyes and Bruce Gerrity tugged at his tie and gave up an embarrassed smile. At that Paula whispered to me, "Oh, Jesus, give me a break, Jack. The way he talks, you'd think he was running for selectman again."

"Is he?"

"Not for another two years. In the meantime, I gotta make a bathroom visit, Lewis. My bladder's about ready to burst."

I went outside with most of the crowd and stood by myself in the town hall parking lot, which was adjacent to the uptown fire station, where the Boy Scout troop leader had been successful in arranging his car wash. I then saw Clyde Meeker ride away on his Fuji bicycle, looking slightly ridiculous in his proper suit. Odd that he would come to the meeting and leave before it was through. I was running through some of the items I wanted to talk about with Paula after the meeting when Betsy Tyler came up to me, a self-satisfied smile on her face as she inhaled her Camel cigarette.

"You're that Cole fellow, right? The one that writes for *Shoreline?*"

"That I am."

She nodded, cigarette between her fingers. "Not a bad magazine. Your column's okay, but you know, you ought to tell your publisher, if he wants to boost circulation, he should put pictures of girls on the cover. You know, like those swimsuit magazines. Big tits and swimsuits. That'll increase your sales."

I smiled and said, "That may be so, but that's not what *Shoreline*'s all about."

"Yeah," she said. "Too bad. Friend of yours called me over the weekend. Asked me to give you a message."

I looked over Betsy's head, to see if Paula Quinn was coming out to join me. "Oh? Who was that?"

Another puff on her cigarette. "Alice Crenshaw. From up on Weymouth's Point."

It seemed like everything about me shrank and all that was before me was the wrinkled face of Betsy Tyler, smoking a cigarette. The town hall, the fire station, the parking lot, and the forty or so people milling around had simply vanished.

I managed to say, "What did she say?"

She checked her wristwatch. "Shit. Meeting's about ready to start and I've not even finished this one butt. She called me yesterday. Said she was fine and wasn't sure when she'd be back. That was that, and she hung up."

I half-noticed some people going back into the town hall, and someone laughed at something. "Anything else? Did she say where she is? And why she left town? And did she say what happened to her house?"

Betsy Tyler cocked her head. "You don't listen so well, Cole? I said, that was that. She said she was fine and couldn't come back for a while, and that was it. Nothing else."

"Did you tell the police?"

She dropped her cigarette butt on the ground and ground it out with her heel. "Sonny, I didn't become a third-term selectman in this town—especially this town, the politics the way they are—by being a dummy. Sure I called 'em. Talked this morning to Detective Diane Woods. Told her just what I told you. And she asked the same questions, too, and got the same answers."

Diane Woods. She knew this morning that Alice Crenshaw was fine and didn't even bother to tell me. Damn it, Diane, I thought. What the hell is going on with you? And Alice. Jesus. Why didn't you call *me*? Why did you call Betsy Tyler?

Then I noticed I was standing by myself in the parking lot. I thought for a moment about getting in my Range Rover and confronting Diane this instant, but no, Paula was waiting for me. Diane could wait. I went back into the town hall where most of the people were taking seats. As I was going to the front row Jack Fowler came up to me and slapped me on the back.

"How's it going there, Lewis?" he said, his face pink and fleshy. His white hair was oily looking and there were small sweat stains on his white polo shirt. His black slacks had little paper crumbs on them and he wore what I guess was his standard summer uniform of white belt and white shoes.

"It's going all right," I said, thinking, Alice is alive. She's all right. But where the hell is she? And I wondered what was going on with Diane Woods that she wouldn't tell me. Maybe tomorrow. I'd see her tomorrow.

"That's good," Jack continued, breathing in my ear. "Just a friendly reminder, now, about me being named president of the Chamber of Commerce. Don't want you to forget to put that in your magazine."

I said, "It's never left my mind," and then he bustled up front, slapping Gage Duffy and Bruce Gerrity on the back, and only Bruce looked like he didn't mind being touched, which made sense, since Jack signed his town manager's paycheck every month.

Paula whispered, "Jack Fowler in *Shoreline* magazine, Lewis? That's something I'd pay money to see."

"Hush," I said. "Meeting's about to start."

After a while the main item on the agenda came up and, briefcase in hand, an earnest young man in a spiffy suit began to speak; he used a lot of fancy words about culture and trust and moral fiber. His hair seemed to be made of some foreign blond fiber that was stuck to his head, and as he droned on, Paula took a lot of notes and I remembered another spiffy man with a briefcase I had met once.

He had come into my hospital room in Nevada soon after I had awakened, his shoes tap-tapping on the tile, whistling what seemed to be a Sousa tune. He nodded as he came in and sat down in the sole chair in the room, balancing the briefcase on his knees. The suit was dark charcoal and he wore a white shirt and blue silk tie and his shoes were brightly polished. His face was slightly pockmarked along his jawline, and even lying there, groggy and dopey and wondering why there was a scar on my side and where I was and what had happened, I thought he might have been male-model handsome without those faint marks.

He had no jewelry on his fingers and no watch, and there were a few faint gray strands along both temples that highlighted the blackness of his hair. He moved some folders around and then closed the briefcase and opened the folders and looked up at me; he tried to smile and failed. I don't know if he had ever smiled at anything in his life. His eyes seemed dry, like they were tan rocks of some sort, and I felt the queasiness of fear resting in my stomach. He took out a pair of half-glasses from an inside coat pocket and put them on and started going through the folders.

"The name is Donovan," he said. "An old Irish name. That's all you'll have to know, Mr. Cole."

I whispered, "Where am I?"

"A hospital, of course, but that's not really the answer you're looking for, correct, Mr. Cole? Well, I can tell you that this is a federal facility, affiliated with the Department of Defense, used for, umm . . . unique cases, you might say. Like yourself. Cases that need special treatment. Cases that need to be isolated."

He flipped through the papers some more and said, "Your section wasn't supposed to be in that part of the desert, you know. Incredible how lost you were, and incredible how you managed to get all the way into that particular testing range without being detected. Unbelievable. This is beginning to rank with one of the great foul-ups of all time, Mr. Cole. Do you realize the expense, the ruined careers, and the possible security breaches you incurred that morning, because you were so lost?"

"Take it up with George Walker," I whispered.

"Can't," Donovan said. "He's dead. Along with everyone else in your section and in that group who were fumbling around there that morning. Except for you, Mr. Cole. Our lucky Mr. Cole. You've probably realized what happened up there at that range, correct?"

I moved my tongue around some, not wanting to ask the questions I knew needed to be asked. Dead. All of them. Their faces and their lives—and oh, God, Cissy—they all wanted to seize my mind, but I knew I had to talk to this man, talk to him with some sort of sense. If I started blubbering he would probably leave and I didn't want that to happen, not yet.

"Testing of some sort," I managed to say. "Some sort of gas. On the sheep pen. And we were exposed. . . . Right?"

"You do your job title justice, Mr. Cole. Research analyst indeed. Very good. Almost as bad as that sheep anthrax item back in the 1960s. That was a foul-up for the history books, but this one isn't going to make it to the history books if I can help it."

He took a deep breath, as if sighing, and said, "My Lord. Think of it. A bunch of mid-level research analysts—fancy names for readers and thinkers—are out trooping around in their yearly qualification that shows they can put on a uniform and play soldier with the best of them, if there were ever a national emergency so dire that it would come to that. Because they are skilled in reading Farsi and Russian and Pathan and God knows what else, they don't have the God-given skill to read a map, even if it probably came from a Mobil service station. So they merrily climb up the hill and down the hill, just as the airborne test commences. A half-hour earlier and you would have been spotted. A half-hour later, well, most of you would have survived."

I tried to move against my pillow. "Chemical testing was banned with that treaty some time back."

"Correct again," Donovan said, tapping one finger against a file folder. "You must have read that somewhere, right? Hah, hah. Well, this hospital stay must be fogging your mind, Mr. Cole. Chemical testing was indeed banned. But this wasn't a chemical test. It was an airborne biological agent of some sort—I won't get into the background of how it got created out here—and that was the test you folks took part in. Unwillingly, of course. Peace may be breaking out hither and yon in the First World, but there's still some nasty Third World types out there who wouldn't mind giving us a few on the chin. So, the research and testing continue, budgets are fulfilled, tests are conducted. I'm sure you understand."

I decided that I wanted to see Donovan weep sometime, that seeing tears run down those cheeks would make me a very happy person. But that was far away, if at all. I wasn't sure if I would ever feel the need to smile again.

I said, "Why am I stitched up? I don't remember falling on something after . . . after the helicopters came by."

Donovan peered over his glasses at me. "I'm sure you've read the expression somewhere that some good comes out of everything. Well, the very fact of your survival has thrown some of the medical types here into a frenzy. That biological agent previously had a one hundred percent lethality factor in the laboratory. One hundred percent, Mr. Cole. But you survived, and now they are busily holding meetings and looking back at previous test results and running tissue and blood sample checks on you, Mr. Cole. Some medical careers here may be ruined if that lethality factor is reduced to ninety-nine point nine percent, you realize."

"Of course," he added, waving a hand slightly, "you didn't come through the experience unscathed. Soon after you were hospitalized, a soft-tissue tumor of some type started growing on one of your kidneys, no doubt triggered—the doctors believe—by your exposure to this, um, unique agent. A very fast-moving tumor, something they tell me they've never quite encountered before. So they took it out, only a few days after you arrived here. You should consider yourself lucky, Mr. Cole. It was benign and your kidney is fine. Now the medical types are all wondering if additional tumors will return, and I think some are quite hopeful that one will so they can run further tests on it."

Lucky. My lips couldn't form the word. Lucky. I looked around the bare room and said, "What now?"

Donovan stood up, started returning folders to his briefcase. "Well. You get better, I suppose. And other meetings will soon begin, Mr. Cole, about what to do with you. You can't really expect to go back to your old job, considering, um, well, the fate of your entire section. And just discharging you and giving you a new suit isn't really an option. We will have to talk again."

As he left, Donovan said, "It would have been easier for all of us if you had just joined the rest of your section out there, Mr. Cole."

That Monday night, democracy, freedom of speech, and the business community at Tyler Beach won a tiny victory, as the censorship ordinance was defeated by the selectmen by a two-to-one vote, Jack Fowler voting yes with a determined look on his face. I whispered to Paula, "Why did Fowler vote for the ordinance? Doesn't he realize it'll make him look like a fool?"

Paula whispered back, "He knew it was a loser from the word go. So he casts a vote for it, and maybe he gets some joking and shit from the other businesspeople in the Chamber of Commerce, but he scores points with these lunkheads who want just *Good Housekeeping* on store shelves. Scoring points, Lewis. Just politics."

A few minutes after the vote was taken Paula folded up her notebook, nudged me in the side, and said, "I'm bailing out, Lewis. You still want to talk to me?"

I said, "The meeting's not over, Paula. Where's your journalistic integrity?"

She suggested that I do something rude with her journalistic integrity and added, "I have a little rule when it comes to government meetings. They start running past ten thirty at night, my brain starts to shut down, and my efficiency level drops to zero. So I leave and make phone calls tomorrow to those dedicated government officials, to find out what stuff they slipped by the town when no one was around."

"So what do you do if they get over before ten thirty?" I asked.

She slipped her notebook into her black leather purse. "Sometimes these clowns go out for a bite to eat and a drink, and sometimes I go with them. Gage Duffy's got the hots for me, I think, since he's usually the one who invites me. So I go. It can be a pain, Lewis, but sometimes you learn some great stuff off the record, especially if they had a few drinks."

"But there's no drinking tonight."

"If there is, I'm not going with them."

"Then let's get out of here," I said.

The town manager, Bruce Gerrity, was droning on about some new health regulations. Gage Duffy and Betsy Tyler gave us half-smirks, as if they were secretly wishing they could join us, but Jack Fowler glowered, like he was upset that we would no longer be watching them, since only a couple of die-hards were still in the wooden seats following the vote.

Outside the night air was still fairly warm. With the light from the streetlights and the fire station I could make out only

Vega and Arcturus, and not much else. "Where do you want to go?" Paula asked.

And as I thought to myself about possibly telling her what I had learned of Alice Crenshaw, I found myself saying, "Why don't you come to my house?"

Paula's eyes brightened. "Fine, I'll follow you," and she quickly walked off to her light blue Ford Escort.

I drove out of the parking lot in my Range Rover and started down Marshwood Avenue, heading to the beach, not knowing what I was heading into, only knowing that I wanted to get there. And a set of headlights followed me every foot of the way.

14

AT MY HOUSE I STRIPPED OFF MY SWEATY clothes and tossed on a black T-shirt and a pair of army green trousers I had picked up a couple of years ago from an army-navy store at the beach. I still had on my ankle holster and .32 and I decided to keep it there. It made me feel safe, which was a particularly good feeling. When I came downstairs Paula was standing on the first-floor deck, overlooking my tiny beach and the jumble of rocks where a visitor the other night had tried to toss a Molotov cocktail my way. She had a large glass of white wine in her hand and handed me another that had been placed on the deck's railing. She looked out at the ocean, at the slow swelling of the waves and the lights from the Isles of Shoals. There were the low running lights of a freighter heading into Porter Harbor, farther north, and I wondered what cargo they were carrying.

She sighed, saying, "I never get tired of this view, Lewis. Not once. Of course, the few times you've invited me here, I've never really gotten the chance to get tired of the view." She arched an eyebrow and took a sip from her glass.

I held up my glass in salute and said, "Just a precaution on my part, to make sure you didn't get bored."

"Hah. Fat chance of that happening." She put the glass down on the railing and placed her hands on the worn wood, tossing her blond hair in the slight breeze. She yawned and then giggled, covering her face.

"Tired, or is it the company?" I asked.

"Oh, definitely not the company. It's those selectmen meetings, Lewis. Trying to keep a straight face and take good notes while they blabber on can be exhausting. I was up early today, covering some damn breakfast business meeting for the Chamber, and that meant I had to listen to Jack Fowler prattle on, and when I get to the selectmen's meeting, I had to listen to him all over again. Jack Fowler in the morning and evening is sometimes more than I can handle."

"Democracy isn't always pretty," I said.

"I guess. Tell me something, Lewis," she said, "do you know the guy back up there at the parking lot, the valet guy from the Lafayette House?"

"No, I don't think so."

"Odd," she said. "I had the strangest feeling, after we left my car up in the lot and came down here in your Range Rover, that he was looking at you."

So maybe the valet parker was in Felix Tinios's pay. It could be.

"Just a friendly face, that's all. He's probably never seen me come down here before with a woman."

She punched me slightly in the ribs. "Hah. I find that hard to believe, Lewis Cole."

"You do?"

Paula turned and wiggled her nose at me, like a rabbit. It's one of her many skills. "Yes, I do. What is it with you, Lewis? You got something against me or against women in general? I know I've been sending you the signals, and I know you've been receiving them. What's the story?"

She had been smiling while saying that but it was an uneasy smile, one that wasn't held up by much. I took a sip of the cool wine and let it rest against my tongue for a moment, while I eyed her, standing there on the deck in shorts and sandals, her blond hair tossing a bit in the breeze, the outline of her lace bra clear through the soft white fabric of her blouse. The wind blew some more and her ears poked through her hair, which she hated, and it made me smile.

I cleared my throat and said, "Another woman's got a hold on me a bit, Paula. Not as recent as a year ago, or two years ago. But the grip is still there. It's still something I'm dealing with. It's not something I'm happy with, but it's there."

She seemed to shrink a bit and hunched her shoulders forward. "Oh. Should have figured as much. Another woman. You seeing her?"

"No, I'm not," I said. I looked out at the wide ocean, wondering how it would be to lose oneself in all that water. "I'm afraid she's dead, Paula."

Out near the horizon were the lights of an aircraft, heading to the northwest. A KC-135 refueling tanker, going to land at McIntosh Air Force Base near Porter. The lights were followed by another, and I could make out the faint whisper of the jet engines. Paula put a hand through her hair and said, "It seems like it's been a while, Lewis." She tried to stifle another yawn and failed.

"It has."

"And she's still a got a hold on you? She must've been a hell of a woman, Lewis."

I rested my elbows on the railing and said, "In her own way she was, but it's not like she walked on water, Paula. It's just that I knew, in seeing her and being with her, I just knew that she was the one. You always hear about people joining together and they make adjustments and compromises, and they hope for the best, hoping that they're making the right choice. That didn't happen to me, Paula. I knew, right from the start, that this one was right, that she was the one, and that she felt the same way about me. Then she died, before we got married, before we got to do much of anything. Since she died it's like a part of me's still wounded and I have to keep the memory of her, well, alive, I guess. Sounds stupid, right?"

She shrugged. "It sounds like it's something right for you, Lewis. But what are you saying? You're going to stay celibate the rest of your life?"

I half-smiled, took another sip from my wineglass. "Hardly, Paula. Hardly. No, I know that one of these days I'll be able to close my eyes and not see her face anymore, not remember any of her features, and then it'll be the right time. One of these days."

Paula moved closer. "What did she die of, Lewis? Cancer? A car accident?"

I remembered promises I had made, years ago. "I'd rather not say, Paula. I hope you understand."

She looked over, frowning. "You know, you can be one close-mouthed son of a bitch, Lewis Cole. You tell me almost nothing about your background. All I know is that you grew up in Bloomington and that you went to school in Indiana and did some newspaper work and then worked for a few years in Washington. You grin at me and tell me that you were a spy. Who for? You won't tell me, and you won't tell me what you did. And that's it. And then you got the gumption to look at me and ask me questions about things I run into and I empty my life to you, and for what? What do I get out of it?"

I raised up my wineglass. "My charming company. And interesting conversation on occasion. Tell me, you must have some ghosts in your past, a man who's got a hold on your heart."

I had unexpectedly said something that struck her, since for a moment it looked like she was fifteen, biting her lip as if not wanting to cry, and she said, "Guy I went to college with, name of Carl Miller, he was a journalism major with me. Wanted to write great stories and make a difference. Just like me. So we planned on going to work in the same area, maybe even work on competing newspapers, and after our journalism work we'd write great fiction and poetry on the weekends in our luxurious apartment, watch no television, go to great intellectual parties and drink white wine, and we'd be deliriously happy."

"So what happened?" I asked.

She held onto her wineglass with both hands. "A few months after graduation, he got some job at a chemical company, writing news releases about how life would be impossible without our friend toxic waste, and now he's probably making three times as much as me, and in one breath I can still love him and hate him. Love him for what he was, hate him for what he's become."

I said, "Sounds like the heart of a poet to me, Paula."

"Yeah, right." She finished the wine and seemed to weave a bit, probably from a combination of the wine and the hour. "It's your home, Lewis. Your request. What did you want to talk to me about?"

I said, "What you've heard, if anything, on what's new with the deaths of Lynn Germano and Henry Desmond."

She held the empty wineglass in her hands. "You're asking me stuff about those two cases, Lewis? Rumor has it that you're banging the police detective in town, so you should be getting the inside story."

With that I almost said, Screw it, let me take you back to your car. I didn't feel like playing sparring games with Paula. But she looked tired and instead I said, "That rumor's not true, and you know it. What I do get from Diane is official. You've got other connections here in Tyler. What are you hearing?"

She rubbed at her face. "I do hear some things, Lewis. And it beats the shit out of me why I'm telling you. But it's just little whispers, of connections between Henry Desmond and that waitress from Massachusetts. Stuff I've tried to track down, but so far I've come up with squat. I haven't found anything between the two to connect them. Even with Alice Crenshaw,

I was thinking that there was something there with the three of them, but while I'm sure Alice and Henry knew each other a bit, I don't think they were lovers or had some connection. I mean, there's Alice, living in one of the most expensive neighborhoods in Tyler, and ol' Henry, living in a shack that butts up against a hotel and other cottages. Not what you'd call a breeding ground for romance. So there's no string to the three of them so far. That's what the whispers have been telling me."

Alice Crenshaw. I thought of telling Paula what I had heard from Betsy Tyler but I had other things planned. "Who's been telling you these little whispers?"

She smiled. "Well, I guess that's none of your goddamn business, right?"

I smiled back. "Am I in for another lecture on the First Amendment?"

"Nope." She yawned again and said, "Excuse me," and added, "You know, my family up in Dover, they're so proud of me, their daughter who got to be a newspaper reporter. They think it's so glamorous and they ask me if I'm ever going into television, like I want to become a meat puppet on the tube."

"You don't see yourself reporting for Channel Nine?"

"Please," she said in a mocking tone. "I'd have to take a pay cut to do that. No, I want to get to the *Globe*, and then New York or Washington. That's where the real stories are. Then, maybe then, I'll agree with my parents about reporting being so glamorous. Watching small-town officials with equally small minds debate the merits of the *Sports Illustrated* swimsuit issue isn't my idea of glamour. Covering car accidents or school festivals doesn't do it either. You know, I even went down to Lawrence to try to talk to Lynn Germano's parents."

"That so?" I said, trying to hide my interest. "What did you find out?"

She shrugged. "The woman wouldn't let me in the front yard. Chased me away. Said she was still grieving and had nothing to tell me. I drove away a block and stopped and I was so tense I threw up on the side of the road. Scared the pants off a couple of little kids on bicycles. That sound glamorous?''

"Not particularly," I said. "But it probably beats covering the selectmen, right?"

"Right, though right now they're probably boozing it up and eating, thankful that another night's passed without the townspeople coming in and lynching them for gross incompetence."

Another Air Force jet passed nearby, its landing lights on, sending cones of light that looked like the headlamps of a passing car up there in the sky. "Any favorite place they go to?"

"Oh, the usual places," she said. "The Harpoon, the Palace Diner, the Gray Neck Inn. Depends on the mood and who's buying."

I took her wineglass and said, "This night's mine, so let me get you a refill."

As I went into the house she followed me in, sliding shut the glass doors to the deck. She stayed in the living room as I went to the spotless kitchen, spotless not because of any extra effort, but because I hardly ever got anything dirty in there. I rinsed out her wineglass and opened the refrigerator and saw the bottle I had poured from was empty. I reached in back and pulled out another bottle—Robert Mondavi, the only white wine I buy—and I undid the cork and poured out two more glasses. My head was feeling fuzzy and I was wondering about the options ahead for me, about what I was going to do this night, for I had some ideas, and Paula was going to take part in only a couple of them.

I walked into the living room, the two glasses of wine in my hands. On the couch, below the framed photograph of the White Fleet of 1907, Paula Quinn was stretched out, a hand fallen to the hardwood floor, sleeping soundly, her chest slowly rising up and down. I stood and watched her, seeing the blond hair across one of the blue pillows, the slim waist and legs, and I thought about Cissy Manning and that look of hers that could seize and pierce me with one blow. Ah, Cissy. I wondered what it would be like to kneel down and just touch that hair with my face and hands. I went back to the kitchen and poured the wine into the sink and washed my face, hands, and back of my neck with cold water.

From an upstairs closet I got a red-and-black wool blanket and I went into my study for a moment to retrieve a few items, and when I came back downstairs Paula had turned and was snuggled into the back of the couch. I draped the blanket over her and then touched her hair for a moment. On the back of a junk mail envelope I wrote her a note and propped it against a lamp on the endtable next to the couch. I locked the sliding deck doors and slid in the wooden rod to the runners, and then I went outside, to the night air. It was well past midnight. I felt refreshed. I locked the door to the house and went to my Range Rover, ready for some night work.

15

IN THE EARLY HOURS OF TUESDAY—AS ON
most predawn summer mornings—the
traffic along Tyler Beach peaked just a bit after 1 A.M., when
the bars along the Strip and the many side streets closed. That's
the busiest time for the Tyler police, and the regular and sum-
mertime officers have to watch carefully and shepherd along
the tourists and the residents as they stumble or try to walk in
a straight line from all of the drinking establishments on the
beach. Most of them crawl back into their bedrooms at the
cottages or hotels with no problems, but the cops' blood pressures and tempers rise from those drunks who like to toss
bottles at police cruisers, drive home with a bottle of beer
between their legs, or stand on street corners, chanting, "Show
us your tits" at passing women.

With so many people leaving it was easy to find a parking
place, and I walked quickly to the St. Lawrence Seaway, running through my mind what was going to happen, who I might
see, and what I would do. I was running through a little patter
in my mind, a little scam as I went into the lobby, and I almost
laughed as the door closed behind me. It was too easy. There

was no one there. Just a pot of coffee on the counter staying warm and a handwritten sign next to a bell that said, "Ring For Assistance," and out back I could hear a television set playing. I leaned over the counter and looked at the room assignments and keys; I looked for a special room on the third floor.

I quickly went up the carpeted stairs to the third floor, heart thumping, wondering what would happen if Derek Cooney or Oliver Mailloux were to pop out. If that were to happen, a scam or a patter wouldn't help much, and I knew I wouldn't do anything much except turn and run the hell away.

Up on the third floor I passed the room that was Oliver Mailloux's, and I kept on going, to the room I had picked: 305. I stood by the door and, just to make sure the room-assignment sheet downstairs was correct, I knocked on the door. There was no answer. Using the passkey I had so unashamedly stolen the other day from the two chambermaids, I let myself in. The room was dark and I felt for a switch on the side and turned on the lights. I closed the door behind me and went into the room. It was almost identical to the room that Corinne and Tammy—the two chambermaids—were living in, except that this one was empty and clean. There were two single beds and a low counter with a chained television set, and just on the left was a bathroom and to the right an empty closet. When I was sure of what the room layout was, I shut off the lights and locked and chained the door. I didn't want someone coming by and seeing a light on in a supposedly empty room. I kept the television off for the same reason.

I went to the window and opened the curtain a bit and looked down at Baker Street. The streetlights were quite bright and it was easy to see almost everything. Cars were parked up and down both sides of the street and people were walking along the sidewalk and in the roadway. There were some shouts, and a dark red car drove by, its rear hatchback propped open and two large stereo speakers booming rock music. A man wearing only blue jeans, with a tattoo on his back, leaned with both hands against a green Dumpster in an alley almost beyond my view and started vomiting, moving his bare feet back to avoid the fluids. A woman stumbled by, holding the hand of a young boy probably ten or fifteen years younger than she. He pushed her into the doorway of a darkened cottage and started kissing her, putting his hand up her T-shirt, and she started bumping her hips against him.

I let the curtain fall and looked at the red numerals of the digital clock on the nightstand. It was almost two in the morning. I lay on one of the beds, not pulling down the blankets or the sheets, and waited. I leaned forward and took off the ankle holster and placed it on the nightstand. Just a few feet down from me was Oliver Mailloux's room, his home, his nest. It wouldn't be a long wait.

A week or so after Donovan—the man in the fine suit with the taste in Sousa music—had left, my condition had improved so much that I could get out of bed and walk the corridors of the hospital ward, using one of those frame walkers to support my body. I didn't walk far or fast, but it was good to be moving. By then the bandage had come off my left side and the angry pink-and-red scar was quite visible; a doctor who didn't want to give me his name told me to examine myself every morning in the shower.

"From what we know," he said, "the tumor is a fast-growing one, extremely fast. Based on what happened to you and what we're, uh, learning, there's a good chance you may get a recurrence. But we can't tell when or how often. The easiest way to detect a new one is for you to check yourself, every morning after taking a shower, when your skin is warm and supple. Tell us if you feel anything out of the ordinary, a lump or a bump or a swelling. It can be anywhere on your skin."

"And what do I do when I get out of here?" I asked, trying to keep a quaver out of my voice. "Keep on doing that every morning for the rest of my life? Play touchy games in the shower? And what do I tell my local doctor?"

He turned away, seemingly embarrassed to look at me. "That's for someone else to tell you."

And I knew what Donovan had planned for me.

So I did as I was told each morning when I showered by myself in a shower room set in the ward, and that was when I allowed myself to cry and pound the tile walls of the shower and scream at the unfairness of it all. That's the only time I would allow myself to think of Cissy and Carl and Trent, the only time I allowed myself to grieve, for I would not do it in public, would not allow it to be recorded somewhere. And when I was done I would check my skin and shuffle back to my room, where I could watch television and read magazines and not much else, and where my quiet requests for visitors or a telephone were smiled away.

The hospital ward was shaped like a T, with a nurse's station set at the juncture of the two tiled hallways. The base of the T had a pneumatically sealed door that opened only with a key card that each doctor and nurse wore around the neck. One morning, wandering along the corridor, getting my exercise, I saw what lay beyond the door: a short corridor and another door, and a man in a shirt and tie sitting at a table, reading a paperback novel and wearing a shoulder holster.

That took care of my plans of overpowering a doctor, stealing his key card, and then shuffling off to freedom.

Most of the patients' rooms were empty, and those five rooms that did contain people contained patients who weren't able to join me in my daily exercises. I think there were three men and two women. They were hooked up with tubes and wires and beeping machines, and one or two would wake me every night with his screaming and shouting in a language I didn't understand. I knew what horror had placed me here—I had no interest in knowing what horror had caused the others to be in the same place.

There was one telephone, at the nurse's station, and someone sat by that phone every minute of the day. The doctors and nurses were friendly enough, but they had been well trained. They would talk sports and politics and my general health, but questions about where I was and where I was going were always cautiously deflected, like a self-confident hockey goalie playing against an eight-year-old who was just learning how to skate. After the first couple of days, I stopped complaining, and in a while I could sense their change in attitude toward me. I could wash and feed myself, and I seemed content to inch around, getting my exercise, and so I was left alone, left alone so I could watch and think and figure, and I noticed some things, including the way the mail left the ward every afternoon.

Over the period of a week I stole a pen, some envelopes, and a pad of paper, and I then wrote a dozen letters while sitting on the toilet in my room's small bathroom. I guessed that my room was monitored, but I had not found a camera lens in the bathroom. A microphone, maybe, but no camera. And every time I wrote a letter and addressed an envelope, I tore it up and flushed it down the toilet.

Then one day Donovan came back.

He was dressed in the same dark charcoal suit and he had his briefcase on his knees, and then he started talking and I raised up my hand and said, "Donovan, shut up. I have something to tell you."

He looked up from his open briefcase, looking at me in disbelief over the half-glasses he was wearing. "What did you say?"

"I said, shut up. I have something to tell you. The last time you came here, you and I didn't have much of a conversation. You lectured. I listened. And then you left. Well, it's my turn now, Donovan, and I'm here to tell you that I'm leaving."

He allowed himself a small smile. "You are, are you?"

"Yes, I am. I have a fairly good idea of what you and your folks have planned for me, Donovan. Keeping me here until your medical buddies figure out why I'm still breathing after I was exposed to your marvelous biowarfare experiment. And when you're done with that, well, I'm sure I'll die of heart failure along the way. At least, that's what it'll probably say on the death certificate."

Donovan said, smiling slightly, "I think paranoia has begun to seize you, Mr. Cole."

"Really?" I said, enjoying knowing that his smile would shortly disappear. "Then try this paranoid fantasy on for size. A patient being held against his will in a government facility smuggles out letters, letters addressed to a number of newspapers and law firms across the country. They all say the same thing: Please open the enclosed envelope if you do not hear from Lewis Cole in person within two weeks. And inside the enclosed envelope is a wonderful short story about a research analyst in a black-budget section of the Pentagon, who is almost killed in a bio-warfare accident on a government reservation. There are names, dates, and places, Donovan. And if I'm not out of here soon, that's the paranoid fantasy you're going to have to deal with."

His face now looked like it was made out of the same material as his briefcase. "This is a sealed facility. There is no way you were able to smuggle letters out."

I smiled at him sweetly, trying desperately to keep my voice calm and level. "At the nurse's station is a wire basket, marked *Outgoing Mail*. Every day a courier comes in and dumps the mail in his sack. Suppose there's an interoffice envelope marked 'Mail Room' in that wire basket and inside that envelope are a number of envelopes, properly addressed and stamped. Where would they go? I'd guess in the U.S. mail system, Donovan. After all, paper, pens, and envelopes were easy to come by in this ward, and the women nurses and doctors stash their purses in their lounge. Easy enough to rummage through since everyone's so busy, and you'd be surprised how many of them carry stamps in their wallets or change purses. Check it out, Donovan. See if anyone's missing stamps or office supplies."

He looked at me for a long while, like he was trying to psych me out with his gaze, and then he snapped his briefcase shut and left the room, and in the distance, I heard some shouting.

A while later two nurses came in and in a barely polite tone asked me to leave the room while they "cleaned up." I stood outside, leaning against my walker, feeling cold and exposed in my powder blue hospital johnnie, and they left my room, carrying the pens, extra envelopes, and the pad of paper I had stashed between the mattresses of my bed. I smiled at them as they walked by, and I knew that any future patients here, no matter how quiet and good-natured, wouldn't get the same polite and disinterested treatment I had received.

My meal that night was late and cold, and in the morning, Donovan returned. He didn't bother opening his briefcase.

He said, "We did chemical analysis on the paper pad, and it confirms that you wrote some letters, Mr. Cole. A couple of the nurses here also admitted that they thought stamps were missing from their purses, and the same is true of other supplies. But our mail service is adamant that nothing could have slipped by them."

Which is why every letter and envelope I wrote—and stamp I had stolen—I had flushed down the toilet. "You feel confident in that, Donovan?" I asked. "To stake your career and whatever stupid games you people play, you plan to rely on the competence of your mail room? I don't think so. You could even try to intercept the mail I sent out but it's been a few days. And all it will take is just one letter to get through, one letter to be opened and read. And then some phone calls are going to be made."

"We could wait you out."

I nodded. "You could. But are you that confident, to bet it all?"

He kept both of his hands on the briefcase and for a moment tapped his fingers, and then cocked his head. "What do you want, then?"

I took a deep breath, remembering what I had planned and what I had rehearsed. "I want out of here, safe and sound. I don't work for you or anyone else, but in the meantime you guys set me up. You owe me. I want one hundred thousand dollars in cash and a monthly stipend. You move me anywhere in the world and supply me with a job that I like that will serve as my cover, and you supply me with the best medical care anytime I need it. And then I'll grow old and fat and pretend I never worked for you guys."

Donovan crossed his legs. "And what do we get in return?"

"My silence. Absolute and complete. I don't say one word to anyone."

"How can we trust you?"

"You can't," I said. "You can have me sign some National Security Act affidavit if that'll make you happy, but remember those letters out there. If I'm ornery enough, I might follow those up with additional ones, just in case an 'accident' happens to me in a year or two, like a car running me down or a flowerpot falling on my head. But that's what I want, Donovan, and it's not negotiable."

Donovan said, "We could still wait you out. See if those letters really do appear."

"But the other course is safer, isn't it?" I pointed out. "After all, in the end, all you're looking for is my silence."

He looked at me again, with those cold and unmoving eyes, and after a moment said, "It's a deal. You'll be out of here in an hour."

He stood up and made to leave, and said, half-smiling, "But you didn't have to bother. You were going to leave anyway, Mr. Cole. We're not quite up to killing off our own people for our own survival and position."

I looked up at him, hoping the expression in my face matched the tone in my voice. "Why, I never had any doubt."

I sat up against the headboard with a start and looked at the clock. It was five past three in the morning. Time to get to work. I swung my legs off the bed and put the ankle holster back on, the Velcro strips binding tightly against my skin. I went to the door.

After opening it a crack I could look down the hallway. Oliver

Mailloux's door was shut. There was the faint sound of a television set coming from another room. I stepped into the hallway and took a few steps, stopping at the red-and-white fire alarm station.

I wrapped my hand in a handkerchief, and remembering faintly the state laws concerning what I was going to do ("Any person who knowingly gives or aids or abets in giving any false alarm of fire, by any means, is guilty of a misdemeanor") I pulled it down. No use in leaving fingerprints.

The alarm sounded like a bass steam whistle from a boat, repeating every three or four seconds. I went back to the room and closed the door, leaving it open just a crack. In seconds the hallway was full of people, in various stages of dress and undress, and a couple of the younger ones were crying and screaming. One of the two chambermaids I had met earlier—Tammy or Corinne, I couldn't tell—was running down the hallway, a sheet wrapped around her body and nothing else. I waited.

At the end of the corridor Oliver Mailloux stepped out, rubbing at his hair, shaking his head in disgust. He had on a short blue bathrobe and he tried to smile at his paying customers as they left, and he wasn't succeeding much. Poor Oliver. He'd have to spend the next hour or so apologizing to his guests for a false alarm, and maybe even give some of them discounts on their rooms. I wish I could have felt sorry for him.

When the hallway was finally clear and the fire alarm still hooting, I sprinted down toward Oliver's room, the passkey firm in my hand. It went in with no problem and in seconds, I was in Oliver Mailloux's room. It was certainly sweet.

The room was just as I remembered it, and Oliver had been thoughtful enough to leave the lights on. The living room was carpeted with that pale green covering that can withstand having M-1A tanks roll across it and still keep its shape. The two vinyl couches and chairs still looked like they had been salvaged from somewhere else in the hotel, and I was half-expecting to see velvet wall paintings of clowns or Elvis. Off to the right was a kitchen area with a fake oak dining room set and what looked like the door to a bathroom. Dishes were piled in the sink and there were a couple of newspapers on the table.

Off to the left was an open door to the bedroom. My mouth was dry and my hands were starting to tremble. I don't think it was fear so much as the primal messages my brain was sending to me, with the fire alarm still hooting and the far-off sound of approaching fire trucks. Part of my brain was busily telling me to get the hell out. I went into the bedroom, wrinkling my nose at the faintly foul odors. It seemed it had been a long time since Oliver Mailloux had taken a bath. There was a double bed pressed tight against a wall, the sheets and covers piled at one end. Set in the corner of the bedroom was a big-screen television, one of those huge pieces of equipment that make you feel like a football game is being played right in your living room, which some people—for the life of me I don't know why—think is wonderful.

But it was the shelves I had seen earlier that had caught my interest, that had brought me back. One whole wall of the bedroom was covered with shelves, but there was not a single book there. Only rows and rows of plastic black cartons holding videocassette tapes. There were three boxes of blank Sony tapes on the floor, and in a corner of the bedroom, which I couldn't have seen earlier because of its angle, was another door. I opened it and saw what looked to be very expensive, very high-tech, floor-to-ceiling video editing equipment.

I was trying to see what Oliver was working on when he walked back into his apartment.

His voice: "Goddamn it, Stacy, did you see any kids come in here, pull that freaking alarm? There's no fire here—do you smell any smoke?"

A woman's voice: "No, I don't, Mr. Mailloux. And I was at the counter the whole night. Everyone who came in was a guest."

Without hesitating I walked into the small editing room and closed the door behind me. There wasn't much room to move around in. It might have been a closet once and it was quite dark. I knew there had to be a light somewhere but I didn't dare turn it on. My .32 was still in my ankle holster, and I had no plans to remove it. Then the sounds of Oliver walking as he came into his bedroom.

"Damn it, I wish that alarm would stop blaring."

Stacy said something in return and I couldn't hear it. Either her voice was too low or the sound of my heart pounding was echoing and re-echoing in the tiny room.

Oliver: "Here. I knew I forgot to lock this. No way I'm leaving this stuff unlocked."

There was a clicking sound as he locked the editing room. I thought, Jesus, to spend the night here, and there was another voice, and Oliver said, "Derek, can you get that fucking alarm shut off? It's driving me batty."

Derek said something I couldn't make out and then added, "The fire lieutenant wants to see you now, Mr. Mailloux. He said none of us should be up here."

More curses, more mutters, and then they all left, leaving me locked and alone in the editing room.

I turned the doorknob and it spun easily in my hand, and I stepped into the bedroom. Like most doors everywhere, thank the gods, it locked on only one side. But that didn't matter. I was going through that door, no matter what, because I wasn't going to spend the night in Oliver Mailloux's hotel, either in his editing room or in a regular room.

The fire alarm stopped its hooting. The sudden quiet was quite scary. I went through Oliver's bedroom and took down three tapes from three different shelves, then shuffled through the remainder so the missing ones wouldn't be noticed. I walked quickly through the apartment to the door and went out, slamming it behind me.

Voices on the stairs, coming up. Oliver saying, "Damn it, I know the fire chief personally, and . . ."

I ran down the hallway to the other end, to the lit sign that said FIRE EXIT, which almost made me giggle, and I nearly leaped down three flights of concrete steps. In a minute or so I was outside, breathing the fresh salt air, moving through the crowds past the parked fire trucks with their flashing and revolving red lights, the sound of their radios quite loud, echoing off the buildings. The three tapes were snug and secure under my arm, and suddenly tired, I made my way to my Rover.

I drove back home and saw that Paula Quinn's Ford Escort was still at the Lafayette House parking lot, and I hoped that she wasn't up, waiting for me. It would be awkward, trying to tell her what I had been doing for the past couple of hours. I didn't notice the parking valet in the lot, and at that time of the morning I didn't particularly want to.

After parking the Range Rover in the garage I stashed the tapes under the front seat and then walked the short distance to the front door, listening to the waves, their constant motion, slipping in and out, nibbling every time at the shoreline. In some years distant, this old frame house would fall into the ocean and the timbers would be carried away to far-off lands, and by then, I hoped, my bones would be dust.

I froze as I went into the house. Something was wrong.

Most of the lights were off, except for a small one in the kitchen, and in the few moments it took for my eyes to adjust, I saw that the couch was empty.

"Paula?" I bent down and took out the Browning .32, holding it in both hands, walking slowly through my house. It didn't seem right, it didn't seem right at all, and part of me wondered—as I looked at the empty kitchen and the empty living room and the locked glass doors leading outside—if my agreement with Felix Tinios didn't cover guests, if it only covered myself.

"Paula?" I repeated, my voice a bit louder.

On the kitchen counter was the note I had written on the back of a subscription envelope from *Smithsonian:* "Paula—Off to run some errands. Will be back. Stay if you'd like. Lewis."

The envelope was resting against an empty wineglass. I went to it, the .32 in my hand, and picked it up. Another line had been added below my handwriting:

> Lewis—
> I would like.
> —Paula.

I holstered the .32 and went upstairs, feeling my heart ease some when I stepped into my bedroom and heard the slow, measured breathing of Paula Quinn in my bed. I turned and was heading back to the stairs to go back to the living room and open up my couch to sleep there for the rest of the night, when I stopped.

There was a soft scent to the air in my bedroom, something that had never happened before in the few years I had lived here. I closed my eyes and listened to the breathing and the faint rustle as she moved, and I tried to think of other faces and shapes, and all I saw for that moment was Paula Quinn, her blond hair and fair skin and upturned nose, and the funny way her ears poked through her hair.

I opened my eyes and in the faint darkness and the light from the stars outside, I went to the edge of the bed and undressed, taking off the ankle holster and .32 and putting it on the floor, tossing my T-shirt on top of it. I stripped down to my underwear—I usually sleep sans pajamas or underwear but tonight I was making an exception—and slipped under the covers. I lay still for a moment. It was quite warm. I reached out with my leg and rubbed it against her thigh. The skin was soft, and I thought of touching it with my hands, but didn't. I lay there awhile, listening to Paula breathe, just thinking.

16

SOMETIME IN THE NIGHT I WAS AWAKE. PAULA was against my shoulder, and I reached over and touched her and felt that she was wearing a T-shirt. She murmured and moved closer to me.

"It's your shirt," she whispered. "I hope you don't mind."

"Not at all," I whispered back. There were only the two of us in my house and there was certainly no real need to whisper, but I felt an obligation not to disturb the moment, not to disturb a thing, so I kept my voice low.

She yawned and snuggled against my shoulder again. God, how long it had been since a woman had done that. "You run your errands okay?"

"That I did."

"What were you doing out there, Lewis?"

I thought for a moment and said, "Something I'll tell you. Not tomorrow or the day after that, but something I will tell you eventually, I promise you."

Even in the darkness I thought I could sense her smile. "What a news flash. Lewis Cole admits to something and tells me. Tell me another thing."

"Yes?"

"Did you take advantage of me, Lewis, anytime in the past couple of hours?"

"No."

"Good." She touched my face and said, still in a soft and sweet whisper, "When and if it does happen, Lewis, I want it to happen because you want it. Not because I crawled into your bed and forced you. I want it to happen because of what you want. Nothing else."

After a while I said, "That sounds fine," but by then, I think she was asleep, for she said not one word in reply.

Even though I didn't get much sleep, I woke up at about 7 A.M. that Tuesday and slipped out of bed, leaving Paula Quinn behind, still dozing. I went into the bathroom and took a quick shower, and as I stepped out from the stall I looked at myself in the steamy mirror. I ran my fresh-wet hands across my skin, across the raised scar tissue on my left side, on my knee, and on my back. Everything seemed fine. I ran a comb through my hair and wrapped a towel around myself and went out into the bedroom. The morning light was quite strong and Paula Quinn was sitting up in my bed, rubbing at one eye, her blond hair a tangled mess. She wore my 1986 Red Sox American League Champion T-shirt—which I privately called my eternal second-place T-shirt—and in the early morning breeze that came through the open windows, I could tell that she wasn't wearing a bra.

She yawned and said, "Jesus, I only got an hour to go home and change and then get to work."

"You need to change?" I asked, smiling.

She grinned, straightening out her hair with a hand. "Lewis, I go to the *Chronicle*'s offices today, wearing what I was wearing yesterday, and that'll cause about a month's worth of gossip. No thanks."

I still had on the towel and she got up and said, "You look

pretty good in a towel, Lewis. Nice scars. You get in a fight or something?"

I resisted an urge to look down at myself, partly in shame or embarrassment, and I also didn't give my usual line, about fights won or lost.

Instead I shrugged and said, "I've been unlucky a couple of times, Paula. Sometimes I've needed surgery. Nothing life-threatening, but something very inconvenient."

A small lie, but necessary. I didn't want to discuss it anymore. Instead, I asked, "Breakfast?"

"Unless you have an ice-cold Coke and a bran muffin, forget it. That's all I feel like right now. But I will use your shower, if you don't mind."

I held out a free hand. "It's all yours."

She winked and walked out of my bedroom, to the bathroom, and as she walked by, I saw some skin that wasn't tanned, and I learned that she also wasn't wearing any panties.

I got dressed and went downstairs, listening to her sing something in the shower, feeling kind of warm, like the sun was at my back all that morning.

Less than an hour later, I was in Diane Woods's cramped office at the Tyler police station. I had called earlier, wanting to see her, and she had said, "I've got a few minutes before nine o'clock, if you hurry. I've got to get over to the county courthouse in Exonia for an appearance this morning."

It might have been the court appearance or maybe an urge to do something new, but Diane Woods was wearing a skirt that morning, a tan number that reached a couple of inches below her knees. She wore black shoes with only a slight heel, a white ruffled blouse, and a clip holster with her .357 Ruger at the side of the skirt. The matching tan jacket was on a coat rack in the small office.

She was at her desk, the other desk still empty. It seemed like there were more cardboard filing cartons in the office this morning, jammed against the faint green cinderblocks and next to the dented black filing cabinets. But the wall chart from the DEA, listing drugs and their side effects, was still there, as well as the blonde-and-string-bikini poster advertising Charter Arms handguns and gun control. Not much light was getting through the two barred windows but the office's marijuana plant on the sill looked fairly healthy.

As I sat down at her desk Diane picked up a tape recorder and said, "Here, listen to this."

She pressed a button and there was a hissing noise, then a loud beep, and then a woman's voice: "Tyler police, your call is being recorded."

Another voice: "There's a body at Twelve Dogleg Avenue."

There was the click of a phone being disconnected, and then the dispatcher: "Hello? Hello?"

A pause, and her voice changed, then, "Tyler D-one?"

"Tyler D-one, go ahead."

"Tyler D-one, report to Twelve Dogleg, possible Ten-fifty-four."

A 10-54 was an untimely death. Fair enough. There are no ten-codes for anonymous phone calls, promising a body at a house. Then Diane's voice, replying, "Tyler D-one, responding."

"Ten-four, Tyler D-one."

And then, a minute or two later, "Tyler D-one, at the scene."

There were a few more minutes of the radio calls, and Diane came back over the airwaves, asking for backup and an ambulance, and a few moments later there was also a call for the Wentworth County medical examiner. It all came back to me by listening to the tape, the night air and the crowd around the parked cars, and that awful thick smell in the cottage, and seeing Lynn Germano hanging there from a rope, her strangled body making occasional, slight side-to-side motions. Diane rewound the tape and then replayed the call with the voice announcing the body at 12 Dogleg Avenue.

"Hear that voice?" she asked. "What do you think, male or female?"

I looked at the black Sony tape recorder. "I don't know. Play it again."

She did. I looked up and said, "I'm not sure, Diane. It could be a man, disguising his voice to sound feminine, or a woman, trying to sound like a man. Hard to tell."

"Yeah," she said. "That's what I think, too. Had a couple of tape dupes made of the dispatch recording that night, and I've been listening to them here and there and at home on my off hours. You know, I get the craziest feeling that somehow I've heard that voice before."

"Really?" I replayed the tape a third time, listened to the pitch of the voice. Someone trying to disguise something. But a man or a woman? I wasn't too sure. And if it wasn't the killer, then it was someone who knew something about Lynn Germano and how she had died.

I remembered the way the cottage looked that warm summer night. Everything was locked and the shades had been drawn. It hadn't been a tourist or a drunk stumbling along Dogleg Avenue who had phoned in to the Tyler police dispatch after seeing Lynn's body through an open window or door. No, it had been someone who had left the cottage, either after helping hang the strangled body, or who had come into the cottage soon afterward and had left in a panic.

So why the police call? Feeling guilty? Or wanting to flaunt what had happened?

I said, "You know, there is something odd about that tape. Or the voice. You said you had dupes made. How about letting me have one? I'd like to listen to it again later."

Diane passed a cassette tape over to me without a word and I slipped it into my shirt pocket, took a deep breath and said quietly, "You know, I've been thinking about you the past couple of days."

"Oh?" she asked, lifting up the skull paperweight to remove

some file folders from the top of her metal desk. "What have you been thinking about?"

"I've been thinking about all of the times we've had and we've shared, and I've been wondering why you wouldn't tell me that Alice Crenshaw is still alive, that she's made contact with someone in town."

She didn't look at me. She piled one folder on top of another. I wondered if her friend from Newburyport, Kara Miles, had spent the night in her bed last night, cuddling in her arms, whispering to her that it would be all right.

"We don't know that, Lewis," she said. "All we know is that a call was made to someone. Didn't have to be from Alice Crenshaw. We have no proof of that. Could be a crank."

I said, "You and I both know Betsy Tyler. God Himself could come down to speak to her and she'd demand to see a driver's license or a passport before she believed it was Him. If Betsy said Alice Crenshaw had talked to her, then it was Alice. And why didn't you tell me, Diane?"

She picked up the folders and stood them on end on her desk, as if she was placing a shield of some sort between the two of us, then looked away at the far wall, apparently composing her thoughts.

When Diane finally looked at me, her voice was as quiet as a sharpened razor as she said, "Lewis Cole, I don't have to tell you shit, but I will tell you three things. First, I'm so goddamned tired that there's a good chance I'm going to fall asleep and run my Crown Vic off of Route Fifty-one as I go into court today. Second, questions are being raised by the state police and the attorney general's office over your relationship with Alice Crenshaw. They're looking into your background and they don't like what they see. They don't like the blank spots in your record. They—and I include myself in this—don't like your relationship with Felix Tinios. Being a suspicious lot, they also don't like the odd coincidence of you witnessing Henry Desmond's death and then being at Alice Crenshaw's house when she disappears within the same twenty-four-hour time span. You might just reflect on that in your travels over the next few days, and check out the name of a good lawyer in your Rolodex."

Diane stood up and grabbed her tan jacket, saying, "And third, Lewis, right now I'll make a deal with you. I don't tell you how to conjugate verbs or adjectives or whatever the hell for your magazine, and you don't tell me how I should do my job. Deal?"

Her eyes didn't seem to blink and the skin across her face seemed stretched and the scar on her chin was much whiter, and these were all warning signals I had seen before. No argument with her would be worth it, and the winning of such an argument would be a worthless victory, as useful as an Allied parachute drop into Nazi Berlin in 1942.

I said, "Deal," and walked with her in silence as we both left the Tyler police station, and she headed west on Route 51 in her Crown Vic and I headed back to my empty home.

With my business with Diane over for the day, I got home and retrieved the three videotapes I had stolen the night before from Oliver Mailloux and took them into my house. I put the first tape into my VCR and turned on my television, and then opened up the sliding glass doors, listening to the cry of a few gulls circling around out in my tiny cove. I stepped out on the deck and looked at the ocean and the jumbled rocks and my homemade No Trespassing signs, and looked up to Weymouth's Point, at the silent and empty house of Alice Crenshaw, and I thought about where she might be on this bright and sunny Tuesday morning.

To my left were the low wooded hills of Samson's Point and the state wildlife preserve. Hidden in those trees and brush were underground concrete chambers and gun emplacements, built to repel the Spanish in 1898, and then widened and deepened for the Germans in 1918 and in the 1940s. In the

1950s the great guns had been torn out and carted away, and for a few brief years the station had a radar installation on its grounds, looking for low-flying Soviet bombers coming in to hit McIntosh Air Force Base, farther up the coast, but that station had shut down in 1960.

Not once had any of the guns for the Samson Point Coast Artillery Station been fired in anger, or even in distemper. Not once. I wondered if the hundreds of sailors and artillerymen who had come in and out of the station over the years had ever felt that their work and their lives had been wasted, had been useless, had been for absolutely nothing. That would have been a sour feeling, one I was familiar with.

As I went back inside I checked the answering machine. A steady green light. No calls. Yet Alice had called Betsy Tyler. Why her and not me? Scared of what was going on? Scared of what I might ask? I sat on my couch, underneath the old framed photograph of the White Fleet, steaming into history and oblivion, and I looked over at the photograph of *Discovery*, hoping it would be spared a similar fate.

I had the remote control unit in my hand and played the first tape. The television—which had been set on an all-music station—clicked into static as the VCR unit came on. I sat back on the couch and watched. And watched. And watched. A full three hours of nothing but static. What fun. I used the fast-forward button as much as possible but it looked like one-third of my stolen booty from the other night was a blank tape.

The second tape wasn't much better. It was a film taped off one of those movie channels that you get on cable television and which bill you for the privilege. I've never been one to trust those movie channels. They reel you in by advertising two or three big-name films and you sign on each month to pay good money for those films and others. Once you get aboard and start getting the movie guide every month, you find out that the "others" are made-for-television nonsense and films that came and went at the movie theaters with the frequency of an Italian government. This particular movie was about a mail pilot in the 1920s who crashed his plane in the wilderness with a young female brat, and for about an hour or so, they bleed and yell at each other as they stumble back to civilization.

When that charmer was over, my back hurt and I was hungry, and it was now Tuesday afternoon. I thought of how many sunny Tuesdays in June one got in one's life, and how I had wasted most of this particular one in viewing static—both machine and man-made—and I was in a grumpy mood. I got up and rummaged through the near-empty refrigerator and found an apple in good condition. After I ate the apple and tossed the core off my rear deck for the seagulls' benefit, I washed my face and hands and was practically yawning as I played the third tape.

More static. Great. I settled back into the couch and flipped on the fast forward. More static.

Then a picture jumped into focus. I switched the VCR to regular play. The picture was slightly grainy but showed a room. It looked like a hotel room, and it seemed quite familiar. The room was tiny, with two single beds, and on the wall where the two beds butted up against the plaster, someone had put up a poster for the New York Ballet, showing long legs and ballet shoes and nothing else.

"Oliver Mailloux," I nearly whispered. "You sorry son of a bitch."

I watched the tape for the next hour and fast forwarded it some, and then I made a phone call. Before I left my house I took another shower. I felt greasy, like I had visited a landfill where bad things smoldered and burned day and night.

Felix Tinios answered the door and gave me an odd look as I came into his house, carrying the videotape. He had on a pair of faded plaid Bermuda shorts and a light yellow tank top. He hadn't shaved that day and his face was covered with a blue-black stubble. We went into his living room, which was next to the large kitchen that was almost the size of my own living room at home. The kitchen was clean and on the marble counter was a small cup of coffee, which Felix carried with him as we went to the living room.

The room had shaded windows that would probably look out over the ocean if someone other than Felix lived here. The chairs and couches were airy, wooden structures that reminded me of Scandinavian design, and there was an ivory wall-to-wall carpet. On the glass coffee table in front of the couch were copies of *Boston* and *Gourmet* magazines, and folded-over copies of the day's *Wall Street Journal* and *New York Times*. On the walls were old prints of peasants working fields, their backs hunched over from the weight of the wheat and tools on their backs.

Felix had once told me, "During those few times when I feel cranky about my life, Lewis, I just look up at those pictures. They show me my ancestors, and they also tell me several stories. One is that I never liked outdoor labor. And another is that my ancestors would have killed their own mothers to be where I am today."

Today, as we went into the room, Felix said, "This is a first, you know. I don't think you've ever told me that you had something for me that might impact my business, impact what I do for work."

Which was no doubt true. I said, "I'm not doing this because of any great respect for what you do, Felix. I'm doing it because I knew this would get your attention. And I'm doing it because there may be something here of mutual interest."

He waved an arm at me as he held his other hand open for the videotape. "Don't talk to me about respect, Lewis. Makes me feel like I'm back at the North End. Let's see the tape."

I sat on his couch and instantly felt uncomfortable; my back tightened up and felt strained, and I wondered if the furniture had been designed by Scandinavian socialists who decided to get their revenge on a capitalist society. Felix finished off the coffee and placed the cup on top of a wooden cabinet, which he opened to reveal a large Mitsubishi television set. How a Japanese company that made bombers that killed our sailors and marines in World War II got to make large-screen television sets that were currently killing our economy was something that I could never understand. It seemed like a bad joke. The set had its own built-in VCR unit and Felix came back with the remote control.

"This better be interesting, Lewis," he said, sitting down next to me and switching on the television. It was set to a sports channel. "I had someone coming over this evening."

"Someone of equal interest?" I asked.

He smiled. "Make that plural. Two people, two females, young and with much interest."

The tape came on, and there was no long wait for something to occur, for I had queued it up to when the action started. There was the hotel room with the two single beds and the New York Ballet poster. Two girls came into the picture, from the left, wearing bathing suits and towels over their shoulders. They dropped the towels down and sat and talked and although the sound wasn't that great, their voices came through on the tape. The talk was of the hot sun and the work ahead for the night, and though no names were mentioned, I knew who they were. Tammy and Corinne. The two chambermaids I had run into the night I had my somewhat physical meeting with Oliver Mailloux and Derek Cooney at the St. Lawrence Seaway.

"Young," Felix observed.

"Still in high school," I said. "Both of them."

One of the girls got up and left the screen. The other—who I believed was Tammy—started combing her hair and then stood up and deftly removed her light green one-piece suit. Her body was white and pink and soft with baby fat, and she came to the mirror and the camera zoomed in on her as she walked. She then left the screen and the videotape went blank.

"Not very extraordinary," Felix said.

"No, not yet," I said. "Keep on watching."

The picture of the room came back on. It was night, for the lamps in the room were on, and they made ghost-like reflections on the mirrored glass. The other girl—Corinne?—came in, giggling, holding the hand of a boy who seemed to be about her age. She had on white shorts and a pink top, and he wore jeans and a Tyler Beach sweatshirt, and his hair was almost as long as hers. They both fell on the bed, laughing, and though the sound was rotten, it was obvious that they had been drinking. Clothes came off and there were some muffled gasps and sighs, and then the boy was on top for a while, and then they reversed positions, and the girl was on top. While she was on top the boy spanked her buttocks. Occasionally the camera would zoom in and out for a close-up of their faces or their pelvises.

We watched for a few minutes and I felt awkward watching something so intimate in the company of Felix Tinios. He sighed and picked up the control and switched everything off.

"The rest of the tape the same?" he asked.

"Pretty much. There's another section later on, with the same couple."

"Where was the tape made, Lewis?"

"St. Lawrence Seaway, owned and operated by Oliver Mailloux," I said. "Those two high school girls work as chambermaids there. I would guess that Oliver has that room and others set up with one-way mirrors, to film waitresses and chambermaids during the summer as they work for him. That's one thing I learned about him, Felix; he likes putting his young female employees up at his hotel or cottages."

Felix rubbed at his face with a hand, almost smiling. "Fairly imaginative of Oliver, though the risks are somewhat high. Suppose you pass the tape along and somebody recognizes their daughter or sister. Easy enough to trace back and then Oliver has to try to manage his businesses with broken kneecaps."

"Not easy to trace if the tapes go to Canada," I said. "You suggested something like that before, Felix, that he's involved in a cross-border business. Not guns or drugs, though. Home-made pornography. Connections up in Montreal or Quebec who come down for a week or two, and then smuggle the tapes back across when they leave New Hampshire."

The smile on Felix's face widened a bit. "Yeah, I can see that happening. So this is what he's been up to. He's boasted before that this would be his last summer at Tyler Beach, Lewis. These tapes could be his ticket out."

I said, "Not that I'm a connoisseur of stuff like this, but what could the market be, Felix? It's amateurish and there's not much in production values. The sound's awful and as explicit as it is, there's just the one static shot, coming through the mirror. Most of the time you can't even see their faces."

Felix slapped his hands on his thighs and stood up and walked over to the television, closing the cabinet doors. "True enough, Lewis, but there's something about these tapes that could make them very pricey indeed, to the right collector with the right kink in him. Easy enough to sell with the right mar-keting, Lewis. Think of it. Real people, not actors. Shot secretly, without their knowledge. And the participants are minors, so legally, this stuff is child pornography. Put those three factors together and you could charge a hefty price for each tape, even with the currency rates this summer. So. Very interesting, Lewis. Oliver's probably making a ton of money. But what's my connection? Why did you show it to me?"

"I can't exactly bring this to the police, Felix."

"And why not?"

I stood up and we went into the polished kitchen, and with-out asking, he drew me a glass of ice water. The small television set on the counter was off, and the three tall stools were empty. I said, "You can put your mind to it, Felix. I stole that tape, and by stealing it, I make it useless for evidence. Besides, my stock with the Tyler Police Department isn't particularly high this week."

"A spat with the attractive Diane Woods?" he asked, leering only slightly.

"More of a disconnect. Which is why I brought the tape to you, Felix. I'm sure that you have some weight with Oliver."

He opened up a bottle of mineral water and poured it in a crystal goblet, and then opened the refrigerator and pulled out a lime, which he deftly sliced with a tiny knife that seemed like a toy in his huge hands.

"Let's assume that I do. Go on."

I said, "Isn't what he's doing here, with the taping, something that he should have cleared with you first? Pornography being the industry that it is, and especially this type of pornography."

"Lewis . . ." he said, still working with the knife.

I rested my hands on the back of a wooden stool. "No, not that I think you would have been interested in getting a percentage of whatever Oliver was making. No, I was thinking of his asking for your permission, as a symbol of respect, before he started all of this. Shouldn't you have known of this taping beforehand?"

He crushed a piece of lime between his fingers, squirting it into his mineral water. "You've been seeing too many movies, Lewis. That talk about respect goes with the spaghetti-eaters. Not with me."

"I haven't seen a movie in over a month, and if you're not going to answer me, fine. But wouldn't Oliver be thinking the same way as me? Don't you think he'd be a bit nervous about your finding out what was going on?"

Felix drank some of his water and then put the goblet down, leaning on the counter with his elbows. "Okay. You've got my interest. Go on."

"Give Oliver a call. Tell him you're angered by what's going on, and what's been happening. You want to talk to him, and when he does arrive, I'm there with you. Then we start asking questions."

He smiled at me, as if amused by everything I was saying. "Questions about what?"

"Questions about these tapes. And questions about Lynn Germano, Felix. She lived in a cottage that was owned by Oliver Mailloux. I want to know if he filmed her, and if he filmed her on the night she was murdered."

Standing up, he scratched at his unshaved face, and the sound was that of a credit card being scraped over sandpaper. "Good questions, Lewis. But why would you be there, at a meet between me and Oliver?"

I shrugged. "Pretend I'm your distinguished counsel or something. But Oliver's the man, Felix. He's got some interesting information I want."

Felix was grinning again. "Suppose I say no? As interesting as this proposal is, this type of stuff is skirting close to being free-lance, and my employers frown on most free-lancing, Lewis."

"If you're not there, I'll ask him the questions myself," I said. "And since he no doubt doesn't have the same respect for me as he does for you, it would probably get bloody."

Felix laughed and finished off his mineral water, then chewed on the lime. "That's a sight I'd like to see, Lewis Cole drawing blood. Yeah, I'll do it, Lewis. Why the hell not."

"And this isn't a favor, Felix. Remember, I'm not one for owing you favors."

He tossed the ice in the sink. "Thought never entered my mind, Lewis. Let's just say I'm bored and this sounds like fun."

"Okay," I said. "Let's leave it at that. Fun."

Some fun.

17

THAT TUESDAY AFTERNOON I LEFT FELIX Tinios's home in North Tyler with a promise
that he would call me the moment he had set up a meet with
Oliver Mailloux, and he had said, "It could be five minutes or
five days, Lewis. This is about as delicate as an arms agreement,
without the benefit of news coverage. Just wait for the call,
and we'll go from there."

On my way home I headed west through North Tyler and
got onto Route 1, and spent some time shopping at a Shop &
Save and picked up some essentials, including the day's copies
of the *Boston Globe* and the Tyler *Chronicle*. After I left the supermarket I hit the North Tyler Fish Co-op and bought myself
a pound-and-a-quarter lobster. Always buy your lobsters at the
smaller stores or from the dirty-looking guys in jeans and tall
rubber boots selling them from the back of their pickup trucks:
they're fresher and they're cheaper.

Since I was in a cranky mood to kill something and eat it,
lobster sounded just perfect.

At home I put the groceries away and checked the answering
machine. No calls. No answer from Felix, and no messages

from Alice. It was nearly four o'clock. The house was spotless and though there was always yard work, I went upstairs to my study, with the floor-to-ceiling bookshelves containing everything from Spanish textbooks to the complete works of Tom Williams, New Hampshire's greatest writer. I sat at my desk and powered up my Apple computer and began to work on something that was for real, a column for the December issue of *Shoreline* magazine, which went under my name and was called "Granite Shores."

That went on for about an hour, and my total output for those sixty minutes was about a paragraph and a half. Not a very good day, and it was easy to see why. It was hard to put my mind into a piece about the snow-covered homes of the New Hampshire seacoast and the cold ocean waves and the frozen salt brine, when so much was going on and the sun was streaming through my windows. So I turned the computer off and went through my bookshelves, pulled down a book about the last years of the Roman Empire, and began to read. I believe I had read this book before, maybe five or six years ago, and returning to it was like seeing an old friend in a crowd. There are some who read books and throw them away or give them to their friends or families, and that's one thing I've never understood. Giving away books would be like giving away your children, a part of yourself. It simply cannot be done.

As I went through the half-remembered pages of the book, other memories came back to me, of the warm and sunny days back in Indiana when my parents would try different ways of getting me out of the house and onto a pond or a basketball court. They used bribes, they used threats, and they used bitter silence. They never understood how a printed page could be more interesting than what they thought were the normal pursuits of a boy, and they always said that reading and books were going to ruin my life, for there was no money in it, no future.

To me, though, the printed page was a mysterious machine

that could place me in the future or in the past, flying past the rings of Saturn or breaking bread with Oliver Cromwell, and it was hard to see how basketball could beat that.

When I graduated from college with a journalism major in English I was half-considering getting a job at a local newspaper before sending out the résumés. I did like to write, though I disliked talking to perfect strangers and trying to form their thoughts and experiences into something intelligible. But before I took the newspaper job I took a government test in an empty basketball gymnasium with about twenty or so other students, and after a few more tests and an all-expenses-paid trip to a military reservation in Maryland, I was offered a job, doing nothing except reading and writing an occasional document.

At the time, it seemed like a wonderful opportunity, and like most wonderful opportunities, it was too good to be true.

After a few chapters of the book, leaning back in my chair in my study, listening to the ocean and half-listening for the ring of the telephone, I went back to the computer. I had a column to write, and though the deadlines were flexible, it was still a responsibility. So back to the keyboard.

After getting out of the hospital in Nevada I drove east, knowing more of where I wouldn't go than where I would, and after waking up from a dream in a Pennsylvania motel and thinking that I could smell saltwater, I remembered some happy times as a youngster, when my mother and father would take me to Tyler Beach. And that's how I ended up here, and how a little cottage on a secluded part of the New Hampshire seacoast had its title transferred from the U.S. Department of the Interior to one Lewis Cole. All because of a dream and some warm memories.

At the cottage, the day I moved in, the business card of a doctor was taped to the empty and warm refrigerator. Prior to this day I had gone to small clinics to have two growths removed: one from my knee and one from the small of my back. Both growths were tiny and were done under local anesthetic, and I left the area before any of the doctors asked for a follow-up. In an odd way, I suppose I had been lucky. I knew this luck would probably not hold, and I was glad to see the business card.

I drove the next day to see him and even without an appointment, I had an hour of his time in his office, in a teaching hospital in Cambridge, Massachusetts. His name was Dr. Jay Ludlow and he was about ten years older than I, with tan skin and dark curly hair. He examined me thoroughly and leafed through my file and gave me another card, and said, "That has my day and evening numbers. Anytime you need anything, no matter how minor, call me. And I do hope, Mr. Cole, that I never do see you again."

Then he closed my thick file and said, his brown eyes suddenly looking quite tired, "Still, all I ask is one thing. That you never ask me what I did, what happened, for me to receive your case."

I said that was a deal and I left.

With that out of the way, when a month or so had passed, it was time for a job, and I made a phone call. A week later a list arrived in a plain brown envelope, along with a phone number next to each job position. I couldn't teach and didn't want to fish or manage a store, but the *Shoreline* job sounded interesting. I made the call and mentioned my name, and then made the hour drive down to Boston, near the South End train terminal, where tall brick factories and warehouses had been subdivided into offices and storage areas. In one building, looking over the murky liquid of what was called Boston Harbor, I met the editor and publisher of *Shoreline* magazine.

His name was Seamus Anthony Holbrook, and he was a retired rear admiral from the U.S. Navy. His office had large windows and there was a brass telescope—refractor, which slightly disappointed me—overlooking the harbor. Photographs of every ship he had ever served on hung on the brick walls of the office, and there was a framed black piece of cloth that had his medals and service ribbons. His hair was gray and white and cut short, and his brown face was lined and wrinkled. He shook my hand and we sat down, to a very brief and to-the-point interview.

"*Shoreline* covers the New England coast, from Eastport in Maine to Greenwich Point in Connecticut," he said, leaning back in his officer's chair, hands behind his head. "We run stories about the fishing and boating industry, about the U.S. Navy in New England, and the history of the region. You ever read it?"

"Nope."

He shrugged his shoulders. "That's fine. When you leave, the receptionist will give you a couple years' worth of back issues to look over. I've been told you can write. Is that true?"

"True enough, though it's been a while since I've written for an audience," I said. "Everything I've been writing the past few years has been black work, with a very limited circulation. Not much chance for recognition."

"So I know," he said. He lowered his arms and leaned forward in the chair and said, "After I retired I still kept my contacts going, both in the navy and in the department. Budgets for defense and intelligence can be raised and cut depending on the year and the mood of the nitwits serving in Congress, but there's always a voluntary network out there that the navy and the department and other services can count on. Sometimes that means favors, in doing research or running errands. Sometimes," he said, looking at me with emphasis, "sometimes the favor means putting someone on your payroll."

I said, "The job sounds interesting, Admiral. I'll do what it takes."

He smiled and I wondered if the teeth were really his. "We need a columnist for the New Hampshire coast. You supply a column each month, subject of your choosing. If it's crap, we either don't run it or we rewrite it and run it under your name. Still sound interesting?"

"It does."

"Then it's yours."

We shook hands again and I filled out a little paperwork, and when I left the building, as promised, I had a stack of *Shorelines* under my arm. And that was the last time I have ever been in their offices, and it was also the last time I ever spoke with Rear Admiral Seamus Anthony Holbrook, U.S. Navy (Ret.).

After finishing off the column work I came back downstairs and started boiling water in two large black pots. In the pot on the right I added some salt and as I waited for the water to boil, I went through the papers. The front page of the *Chronicle* had a story by Paula Quinn about last night's selectmen's meeting, and the defeat by the selectmen in a two-to-one vote on the pornography ordinance. There was a picture of Jack Fowler, the selectmen chairman, along with a sidebar piece on why he voted yes. Jack used the words *family values* a lot.

I quickly went through the rest of the paper and then picked up the *Globe*. The *Globe* took a bit longer, since it carries more international news, and I smiled a few times at the *Globe*'s preachiness and at the number of letter writers with hyphenated last names in the editorial pages who were "concerned" about something or other and who always lived in Brookline or Cambridge.

When the water was boiling I went to the refrigerator and took out the lobster and said, "Sorry about that, sport," as I tossed him into the pot on the right. I held down the pot's lid as he thrashed around a bit and when that stopped, I went back to the counter and the *Globe*. In its arts section, I read a review about a performance artist who sat naked on a lawn chair in an auditorium and daintily tore the skins off hot dogs with his teeth. The art reviewer prattled on about the phallic imagery and the symbolism of the processed meat industry, and how it reflected unfavorably on the American capitalist system of living. From those words, I deduced that the *Globe* reviewer had enjoyed the show.

When five minutes had passed I took out two ears of Florida corn I had gotten at the supermarket and shucked them, and then tossed them into the other pot of boiling water. I also began melting some butter in another pan, and by the time I reached the sports section on the *Globe* and read depressing news about the Red Sox, ten minutes had passed and dinner was ready.

It took two trips but everything went on a small table on my rear deck, and with a glass of Robert Mondavi white wine at my elbow, I started cracking apart the lobster and dipping its meat in the melted butter. I didn't wear a lobster bib. A lobster bib is for wimps or tourists. I ate the lobster and the ears of corn and watched the waves coming in, each swoop of water as graceful as the last, and in a while the sky began to darken as the sun started sinking to the west. I brought the dishes in and washed them and stacked them back on the shelves, and with the single glass of wine—I only allowed myself one glass that night—I went back outside and sat on the rear deck and propped my legs up, sipping slowly, a pair of binoculars in my lap.

I brought the binoculars up and looked at the buildings on the Isles of Shoals, which were divided among a church group, the U.S. Coast Guard, the University of New Hampshire's Shoals Marine Laboratory, and a couple of private citizens. The nine islands of the Isles of Shoals have a long and romantic history, from pirates burying treasure to a grand hotel to murder and incest, and the tourists driving up and down Route 1-A never tire of stopping and taking pictures of them. Among the famous people who had once lived there was the poet Celia Thaxter, the daughter of a lighthouse keeper, who had lived on White Island in the 1840s.

The light at White Island is still there, and visitors still go to the Shoals. I had a friend who once spent a night on the Isles of Shoals, and he said the sea gulls cried so loudly that he got about one hour of sleep, and his hair was soiled by the gulls as he waited for a boat to take him back to the mainland.

I was wondering if that sea gull incident would make a potential column for *Shoreline*, when the phone rang. Felix? I carefully put down the glass of wine on the wood table and went back inside. I recognized Paula Quinn's voice. "Nice story on the selectmen's meeting," I said. "But why did you give Jack Fowler more play than he deserved on his yes vote for the pornography ordinance? Trying to keep him in office for another three years?"

She laughed. "No, Lewis, that's not it. My editor thinks Jack's a fool, and by giving him the publicity, he's letting Jack hang himself on his own words."

"I think your editor'd better look in a mirror the next time he thinks about what constitutes a fool."

Paula laughed again and said, "I called to thank you for last night. It was special, Lewis, even if it didn't get sweaty or bothered."

Out on the horizon, I saw the lights of a fishing boat, beating its way back to Tyler Harbor. "Not sure if that's a compliment or an insult, Paula. Tell me, what are you working on nowadays?"

"Oh, the usual," she said, sighing. "Doing an update on the Body in the Marsh case. North Tyler cops say they're getting some possible leads, but they're more closemouthed than your detective friend. I want to do a follow-up on the Henry Desmond and Lynn Germano cases. I think I might have something worth tracking down. And then there's always the Alice Crenshaw disappearance."

I stepped out on the deck, carrying the phone and the receiver with me. I thought for a moment about what I was doing and what was going on, and I said, "I have some information on that, if you'd like."

Her voice perked up, and I knew I had pressed the right button. "On what? Alice Crenshaw?"

"Yeah," I said, not wanting to look up at Weymouth's Point and the darkened house on the point of land. "You don't know where you heard this, but give Betsy Tyler a call. She has some information and I'll tell you, it looks like Alice Crenshaw is alive."

"Jesus," Paula said. "How do you know this? And what's Betsy's connection? Is she—"

"Paula," I interrupted. "That's all I know."

We talked for a few minutes more and then she said she owed me lunch, and by the time I hung up the phone it was dark outside. I put the binoculars away and went upstairs to my bedroom and opened the door to the side deck. I hauled out my 4½-inch reflecting telescope, built on a black tripod, and I got my flashlight with red lens and went to work. To the west were three bright stars, hanging almost in a row; it was a rare conjunction of three planets: Venus, Mars, and Jupiter. Jupiter was the highest and I focused in on it with a low-power lens and made out the four Galilean satellites, named because they were discovered by the real first astronomer, Galileo Galilei. There are about fourteen or so satellites of Jupiter, but the four largest moons are the first ones you see with a telescope of the size of mine, or even a good pair of binoculars.

With the help of a chart from that month's *Astronomy* magazine and using the red-lensed flashlight (which saves your night vision), I noted the positions of the little four dots of light around the striped sphere of Jupiter, and noting the time and the date, I knew which dot of light represented Europa, Io, Ganymede, and Callisto. Knowing that gave me a little warm feeling at the base of my skull. In the long run, it was probably useless knowledge, for by looking at Jupiter and its four Galilean moons I couldn't possibly contribute anything to my own learning or to astronomy. But still, I felt good about it. Nobody else would probably care, but on this Tuesday evening in June, I knew I could look up at Jupiter with binoculars or a telescope and correctly name the four dots of light around the solar system's largest planet.

Not much of a victory, but it was one that made me feel confident for some reason.

The phone rang.

I left the second-floor deck and got downstairs in time to pick up on the fourth ring. "Hello?" I said.

"It's on," Felix Tinios said. "In an hour. Why don't you meet me at ten?"

"I don't see why not."

Felix told me where to go and after I hung up I grabbed some items and threw on a jacket before I left. I tried not to dwell on what was ahead or if I was nervous about what might happen, but I was halfway to North Tyler in my Range Rover before remembering that I had left my telescope outside.

I didn't bother to turn around.

18

THE MEETING WAS SET FOR 11 P.M. BUT FELIX insisted that we get there a half-hour earlier. We were at a parking lot on a tiny point of land that jutted out from Route 1-A in Wallis, the next town up from North Tyler and the community one has to pass through before getting to Foss Island and Porter, the northernmost towns on the New Hampshire seacoast. The lot was across the street from a drive-in restaurant, Benny's Beach Bonanza, and there were about a dozen or so cars in the parking lot, and people were lined up at the windows. There were no pretty waitresses in short skirts and roller skates. I don't think there's ever been a restaurant with pretty waitresses in short skirts and roller skates in the entire history of New Hampshire.

There was another car in the parking lot at the south end, a Chrysler Le Baron, and it was a good distance away from my Range Rover and Felix's Mercedes. When I got to the parking lot Felix was already there, leaning against the hood of his car, all in black with a dark brown leather jacket. Under my tweed jacket was my Bianchi shoulder holster and my 9-mm Beretta. I didn't insult Felix by asking him if he was carrying.

"I wish we could have gotten here earlier," he said. The lights from Benny's Beach Bonanza were bright enough so I could see the scowl on Felix's face.

"Ambush?"

He looked around. "No, I don't think so. Oliver's not very happy with me but I don't think he has a gripe that would cause him to whack us one. But I always want to have enough time to check things out, see who's where and what the roads out look like. It makes me feel better, makes me feel confident. Hold on a sec while I check this car out."

Felix walked away from his Mercedes, heading to the parked Le Baron. I looked around at the jagged rocks and boulders. There was no beach on this part of Wallis, just rocks and debris and the waves. Out on the wide ocean were the lights from the Isles of Shoals and a couple of dim ones that belonged either to container ships or fishing vessels. The stars were fairly bright, even allowing for the light pollution from Benny's, and I saw Jupiter, a bit lower in the night sky than when I had last seen it. I hoped the salt air wouldn't condense much on my exposed telescope, back at home. The hazards of living near the beach.

At the Le Baron, Felix pulled something out from his jacket, and I felt my shoulders tense up, but there was just the small beam of a light, and I watched as Felix played the flashlight through the windows of the car. The driver's side window came down and Felix leaned over. There were some voices but I couldn't make them out at this distance.

At Benny's cars were pulling in and leaving after a while, and the people there—young kids, tourists, and families— seemed to be having a good time. There was a couple sitting on the trunk of their red Lumina, licking ice cream cones. The man's dark hair looked like it had been caressed by $30-an-hour beauticians. He was laughing a lot, and the woman was leaning against his shoulder. Though it was cool, she was wearing shorts and a black bikini top, and her smile was quite wide and even, her long black hair tied back by a little red bow.

The Le Baron's engine came on and its headlights flicked into life, then it sped out onto Atlantic Avenue, its tires spitting up gravel. Felix came back smiling.

"Friends of yours?" I asked.

"Not particularly," he said, resuming his place at the Mercedes's fender, folding his arms again. "You know, I gave that boy a piece of advice, something I learned a long time ago and still follow. There are certain sexual practices that are dangerous when your lady partner has braces on her teeth. But somehow, he didn't appreciate the advice."

"I can't see why." For some reason I rubbed my hands together and then I said, "Felix, do me a favor when Oliver shows up. Play along with whatever I say."

I could sense the humor in his voice when he said, "Like you, Lewis, I don't like owing you favors."

"Then add it onto my bill for my house-sitter."

Felix laughed. "It's done."

A car came up Atlantic Avenue, slowed, and then pulled into the parking lot, about fifteen feet from us. It was a black Trans Am with green-and-white New Hampshire vanity plates that said PALACE. From the Trans Am stepped Oliver Mailloux, dressed in white slacks and black dress shoes, with a long, thin suede jacket. He must've left Derek Cooney at home. He slammed the door hard and strode across the lot, and then looked at me. I crossed my arms and nodded in his direction.

"What the hell is this, Tinios?" he said, jerking a thumb in my direction. "I thought this was just a meet between the two of us. What's he doing here? Is he gonna write a story on this or what?"

I said, "You can be quiet, Oliver. In this little matter, Felix and I are partners."

"Really?" He reached into his coat pocket and Felix was standing straight up, like a spark of fire, and I could not believe how fast he had moved.

Oliver stopped, hand inside his coat, and then withdrew his hand slowly, showing a pack of Marlboros and a gold lighter. He smiled and his teeth were as crooked and yellow as ever. "Don't fret yourself, Tinios," he said.

"I'm not fretting at all, Oliver," Felix replied. "Sometimes my reactions just get the best of me. Like right now. I thought you were going into your coat for a piece and the only thing I was deciding on was how hard to hit you."

"Oooh," Oliver said. "Very scary."

He lit the cigarette and shut the lighter off with a satisfied click and placed the pack and lighter back into his coat, then said, "This clown telling the truth, Tinios? You two together? Story I've heard, you always work alone, even when you're on contract."

Felix slowly leaned back against his Mercedes and said, "Lewis is right. We're both in on this one. Tell us about your business, Oliver, and I don't mean your hotel, your cottages, or the Palace Diner."

Oliver took a drag on his cigarette, smiled, and said, "I have other businesses?"

I said, "What you have is a movie-making arrangement, Oliver. Pretty sleazy but probably a money-maker. You've got your hotel and your cottages wired for video, and you're filming the high school girls who are working for you this summer. Most of the time you just get shots of them getting dressed or undressed but sometimes you get quite lucky and you have some tapes of them with their boyfriends. Or girlfriends, for all I know. You're smuggling the tapes into Canada and I would guess you're doing fairly well, Oliver, and that you're not supplying any tax information to the IRS. How am I doing so far?"

Oliver's jaw was clenched and he looked at Felix and back at me and said, "If Tinios wasn't here, boy-o, I'd take this cigarette and shove it into your eyeball. See how you'd like that, then. You know, I had the feeling someone was rooting around my place the night of that false alarm. You were there, weren't you? What's the matter, you need some cheap thrills, you're gonna jack off while watching my movies?"

"No, I didn't plan to," I said back, "but you sound like an authority on this, Oliver. Tell us what it's like."

He murmured something and came forward and Felix held up his hand and said quietly, "Bickering isn't doing anything constructive, Oliver. What I want to know is why you didn't come to me first. What you're doing is something that should've been cleared with other people in Boston."

Oliver took another drag on his cigarette and said, his voice almost shaking with anger, "Why? Why should I've done that? So some shithead guinea from the North End can get a five or ten percent cut from my gross? As a tribute? Fuck that shit. They wouldn't've done anything for me."

His voice still quiet, Felix said, "It would have been the logical thing to do, Oliver. And they could have done a lot for you. Think about that."

"Hey, Tinios," he retorted. "Think of this name, all right? Lawrence Lambert. From Montreal. His organization's the one I'm dealing with."

I said, "Montreal's a long way from here, Oliver."

"Spare me the geography lesson, writerman," Oliver said. "Last year some people from Lambert's group came down here. I gave them a good time, spared their asses from the local jail, and I showed 'em my hobby. It's a fun hobby and it's never hurt anyone, not ever. Well, they liked what they saw and we made a deal. The tapes get edited and spliced down here, and every couple of weeks, one of Lambert's boys comes here for a few days off and heads back north. They dupe it and run ads in some papers and magazines, and it's doing real well."

Felix said, "Did Lambert clear it with Boston?" Two cars passed by and the tourists were still lining up at Benny's Beach Bonanza. I wondered if any one of them could imagine what was going on in this little parking lot on the Atlantic Ocean.

Another puff from the cigarette. "I don't know and I couldn't give a shit. Boston's some distance away, too, Tinios. This part of the state is sort of neutral territory, right? I'm making money and I'm not running into anything you deal with, so I can't see the beef."

I scratched at my side, to show him my shoulder holster, and I said, "Can you see a deal, though, Oliver?"

He opened his mouth, as if he planned to say something insulting and had reconsidered it. "Go ahead."

I nodded to Felix. "There's no beef, no gripe, Oliver. Just a chance to increase your profit. Felix and I have an arrangement, all set to go. All we need is you. This time, instead of north, the tapes go south and from there they get shipped out to the West Coast. Better markets out there, Oliver. Plus you don't have to worry about Customs checks or the exchange rate for the Canadian dollar. You can also get a more sophisticated customer, one who can appreciate what you're producing."

"Why should I change?" Oliver said, eyes flicking at both Felix and me. "I'm doing just fine."

Felix—and I could have almost kissed him for reacting so well—smiled at him and said, "Because this means money for everyone, Oliver. Even with the cut from Boston, you'd be making ten or fifteen percent more with each tape. With that type of money, I'm sure the people in Boston could work out something with Lambert, so he wouldn't be too upset. But—"

And with that little word, Felix's look and tone seemed to darken, as he said, "But . . . so far, the Boston people I work with don't know squat about what you're doing here in Tyler, and while you might think this is neutral territory, they would love to teach you a geography lesson, Oliver. Tell us no and a lot of things happen. First, calls get made to Boston and whatever they decide, happens. Maybe you have some surgery on your knees or something. Then maybe the IRS gets a call about your cash flow, and you have problems getting food and supplies for your businesses in Tyler. Think you'd like that?"

He glared at us, and the light from the nearby streetlights

made the pockmarks on his face look fresh and raw. He said, "What a pair. You two fags? Is that why you're here?"

"That's very sweet," I said. "But is there a deal?"

"I gotta think about it," he said, his tone defiant. "I'm not going to toss everything overboard in one night."

"Fair enough," I said. "But tell us about Lynn Germano, the girl who was killed a couple of weeks ago in one of your cottages. Do you have tapes of her?"

"Yeah," he said, almost sneering. "I got tapes of her. Good ones, too. And you know why? She was a natural, that's why. She hardly ever said no, from what I heard. I even managed to get a couple of pieces from her myself, and man, I wish I had tapes of that action. She left scratch marks on my back, that's how good she was."

Seventeen, I thought, feeling queasy, seventeen years old and learning of affection and sex from something like Oliver Mailloux. My stomach felt like I had eaten a half-pound of undercooked bacon and my voice was quiet as I said, "You have anything to do with her death, Oliver? Or any idea who did it?"

"Nope," he said, smirking. "Not a thing."

Felix said, "That'd better be the straight and narrow, Oliver. We start a business arrangement, we don't want that girl's murder clogging up the works a month or two down the road."

Oliver held out his hands to us and said, "Guys, like I told boy-o here a week ago. She was one hot ticket, even for her age, and chances are, she ran into the wrong guy. That's all. Happens all the time. You read about it, these type of chicks get unlucky and get picked up at a bar or hitchhiking, and they get their jollies and so does the guy, but instead of stopping as usual, the guy decides to get extra jollies and kills 'em. So what. Read the newspapers or watch the news. That's what happened to her."

My mouth felt like it was drying out from the salt air. "You have a tape, then, of her getting strangled?"

He almost looked wistful. "No, I don't, and I wish I did. It could've been the first legitimate snuff film ever made. The number of dupes and the money I could make off of that one tape . . ."

Felix said quietly, "Worth a lot of money, Oliver."

"Yeah, worth a lot of money," he said, taking a final drag from his cigarette. "Yeah, enough money so I can get off this scummy beach this year, and I don't have to worry about having enough clean towels or getting enough frozen french fries or paying whatever the tax rates might be this year, and I can stop kissing everyone's ass, from the health officer to the building inspector to the Chamber of Commerce. Getting off this beach is what I want, and this tape money is how I'm gonna do that."

I said, "Then here's your chance. Felix and I, we want to look at your finished product. See exactly what we're getting into, what we can recommend to the people down in Boston. How about another meet, tomorrow, at your place?"

Oliver flipped the cigarette butt at me and it fell at my feet; I moved not one inch. "All right. Tomorrow night. Seven o'clock. And bring something along to show your good interest."

Felix said quietly, "Could be arranged, if you tell us what you mean by good interest."

He grinned and started walking back to his Trans Am. "Ten grand, boy-os," he called to us over his shoulder. "Show me ten grand tomorrow and you can take any one of my tapes home and play it over and over again. No ten grand, you can rent your own fuck films."

He got into his car, slammed the door, and sped south, the red taillights blinking at us as he rounded a curve in Atlantic Avenue. I looked over at Felix and said, "Nice job."

"Thanks. And what do you plan to do tomorrow when we get to Oliver Mailloux's place?"

I said, "Just what I told him. We're going to look at his tape collection, and we're especially going to look at the Lynn Germano tapes.''

Felix clasped his hands together and shrugged. ''The man said he didn't have anything that showed her getting killed. If he did, Oliver Mailloux's the type of guy who would've bragged to us that he had an honest-to-God snuff tape. Believe me, there's been claims made here and there, but there's never been any real proof of snuff tapes being out and about. A real one would be worth a lot of money.''

''I know that,'' I said. ''But that's not what I'm looking for.''

Felix looked over at me. ''Oh? You have another agenda, Lewis?''

''Yep,'' I said, putting my hands into the pockets of my jacket. ''I want to see the tapes and see who she was with this past month. Someone might have been with Lynn Germano and then learned later about the filming, and that might have made him angry, angry enough to come back and chat with her about it.''

Felix gave a sharp laugh. ''I hope you're not trusting that guy Oliver with telling the truth.''

''No, not all of the truth. But I do believe he has tapes of Lynn Germano sleeping with some men, and I want to see who those men were. Might prove to be something interesting. By the way, you wouldn't be on that tape, would you, Felix?''

He grinned. ''Gave up teen-agers last year for Lent, and found out later I had lost my taste for 'em. Another thing, Lewis, you have any idea where you're going to get the ten grand that Oliver wants to see?''

''Sure I do,'' I said. ''From you. You seem to be a man who's doing well, Felix. Couldn't you come up with the money?''

For a moment it seemed like Felix was trying to decide whether to say something in anger or laugh in disbelief, and after a moment he chose the middle road and almost giggled, saying, ''Sure, I'll bring the money. We'll keep the bargain,

Lewis. I'll bring ten grand, but I'm sure as hell going to walk out of the place with it, too."

I shrugged and started over to my Range Rover. "Sure," I said. "Oliver said he wanted us to bring ten grand. Didn't say anything about us handing it over to him."

Felix said, "Now you're talking."

At home I retrieved my telescope from the second-floor deck and I wiped down the red metal tube with a towel from my bathroom. After putting away the lenses and putting the black plastic lens caps back on the telescope, I took a long shower, trying not to think of Oliver Mailloux and the satisfied smile he had shown us with his memories of Lynn Germano. I stood under the shower head for a long time, feeling the hot water pound at the base of my skull.

After drying myself off and checking my skin and finding nothing unusual, I put on a terrycloth robe and went downstairs. It was near midnight and I was tired but not sleepy. From my refrigerator I took out a Molson Golden Ale and after popping the top off, I unlocked the first-floor deck and went outside.

The summer night air felt nice on my wet hair; beads of water were still running down my neck and trickling across my shoulders. The deck's wood was smooth and cool against my bare feet, and I leaned against the railing and looked out to the west. Jupiter was still out there, though much lower, and at this time Andromeda was just rising over the eastern horizon, and I could make out the bright star of Pegasus in its constellation.

Every night there is something different in the sky: the constellations rising up and the different phases of the moon, along with the sudden streaks of light from meteors and the steady passage of bright dots of light, marking satellites or spent boosters or other space debris. Each night is different, each night is special, each night has something to offer you. Try explaining this to almost anyone and you will usually receive an odd look in return. The night sky is nothing to them. The night means dinner and sleep and parties, and the night sky is nothing to look up at.

On this night, Oliver Mailloux was probably back at his hotel apartment, looking over his tapes, thinking about the lies that Felix and I had just passed to him, and Felix was no doubt at his home, maybe even starting the job of securing the money that we would use tomorrow afternoon. To both of them, Jupiter and Pegasus and Andromeda probably meant nothing, nothing at all, except as character names used in bad science fiction films.

And Lynn Germano? I wondered what she had thought about the night sky, if it had meant anything to her. Maybe she had looked up at the stars or the moon and had wondered a bit, in walking from the Palace Diner to her cottage on Dogleg Avenue, wondered about what was up there. Or maybe the night just meant a brief moment to her, a time of spending sharp minutes with the men or boys in her life, men like Oliver Mailloux. Maybe the night was something that wasn't special, was something that filled her with dread. Or maybe not. Oliver Mailloux. That thought almost made me shudder—Lynn being with Oliver Mailloux—yet there was also a sense of anticipation for what was planned for the next day, knowing that I would see tapes of a live Lynn Germano. I knew almost nothing about her, and I hoped that that would change by this time tomorrow. I would see her talk and act and see who she had been with, and I hoped it would help.

I sipped from my beer and looked over at Weymouth's Point and the still blackness that marked the empty house of Alice Crenshaw, thinking of what she might be doing this evening, and then I watched the slow progression of Andromeda into the eastern sky, not even moving when I had finished my beer.

19

ON WEDNESDAY MORNING I SLEPT LATE, THE consequences of a late bottle of Molson Golden Ale and a stubborn determination in wanting to see all of Andromeda rise in the eastern sky before going to bed.

I showered and dressed and called Felix about our meeting that day with Oliver Mailloux, and he said, "We'll do the same thing today we did last night. So meet me early."

"Six, then?"

"Sounds good. Any particular place strike you?"

I said, "Maid of the Seas statue, just across from the Palace on Atlantic Avenue. Fairly public and open."

Felix laughed over the phone. "You're doing pretty well there, Lewis. Always remember to get to places early. Gives you a chance to scout things out and maybe trip off some traps or alarms."

"You're a suspicious person, Felix," I replied. "I've read in *The New York Times* that this is supposed to be a new age of commitment and cooperation."

He laughed again before hanging up. "Yeah. Write to me when they decide that one's over."

There seemed to be an endless stretch of hours before 7 P.M., the official time when we were to meet with Oliver Mailloux, so I decided to be mobile for a while. After arming myself with my .32 Browning in my ankle holster, I left for the day, locking all doors behind me. On the way out of my house I looked again for my housekeeper among the grass and the rocks by the ocean but I saw not a soul, and if someone was out there, they were earning every penny and nickel that they would soon be making from me, once I paid Felix.

I got into my Range Rover and decided to go into the town of Tyler proper, inland about three miles from the ocean. I went up through the parking lot and by the parked foreign cars, and then past the quiet elegance of the Lafayette House. It was a sunny day, with that edge of humid warmth that hinted at what was ahead during the steambath days of July and early August. As I drove into town I listened to the cassette tape over and over again, trying to decipher the messages that both voices were telling me:

"Tyler police, your call is being recorded."

The strange voice: "There's a body at Twelve Dogleg Avenue."

There was the familiar click of a phone being disconnected, and then the dispatcher: "Hello? Hello?"

A pause, and her voice deepened, "Tyler D-one?"

"Tyler D-one, go ahead."

"Tyler D-one, report to Twelve Dogleg, possible Ten-fifty-four."

I played the tape back three times as I got into town, and I knew Diane Woods was right. There was something familiar about that voice. Besides listening to the voices of the dispatcher and the mysterious caller, I also paid heed to Diane's voice. Even in a moment of tension like that, when we had come across Lynn Germano's body, her voice had not failed her by being strained or high-pitched. In asking for a medical examiner and a fire department ambulance and for the state police, her voice was even and relaxed, almost bored. The voice on the tape was nothing like the voice I had experienced the other day in her office, and I wondered about the duration of her anger toward me.

Traffic in town was light, and I had no problem picking up my mail at the post office, which was located on Route 1 at the south end of town. There were two supermarket fliers and a mailing from the Planetary Society, looking for more money for their Mars Rover project, which I was glad to accommodate.

I trashed the fliers and put the society's mailing on my front seat, and then I went north on Route 1 for about a half mile, passing the town common on my left. I found an empty parking spot by a Welby's drugstore and made the short walk across the common, heading to the small brick-and-white-clapboard building—called, for some strange reason, the Tyler Building —that contained a dentist's office, the local cable television station, a legal firm, and the offices of the Tyler *Chronicle*.

In many communities in New Hampshire and other parts of New England, the towns still center their life around the common, where early colonial settlers had shared the area as a "common" place to graze their livestock. It was also used back then as an open space for fairs or for drilling the town militia, and around the green grass of the common the towns in this area slowly grew, from the rough-hewn garrison houses to the statelier homes, and then the shops and churches. The cliché of New England is the small town with the green common, and the stores and the white spires of the Congregational or Episcopalian churches.

In many towns, this cliché still exists. In Tyler, alas, it doesn't. The original common was nibbled at and built over, until only about one-third of the original green was left. There is a small road—almost like a circular driveway—that bounds it against Route 1 and this area of Tyler is called Common Square. Besides the Tyler Building there's a gift shop, an automotive parts store, the Common Grill & Grill, and a barbershop. No more animals feed on this small piece of pasture, and the town militia exists only in the history books.

The *Chronicle*'s offices are on the ground floor of the Tyler Building. I walked in and waved at the receptionist, whom I didn't know, and went to the editorial offices in the rear. I've found that you can go practically anywhere if you act like you belong and know where you're going, and if you're polite to the receptionist. The *Chronicle*'s a small, struggling daily—I know things are bad when Paula tells me that the accountant urges them to cash their paychecks quickly every Friday—and it can afford only three other reporters besides Paula to cover this part of the entire county. The newsroom is small and carpeted with a worn pale green carpet, and the desks are battered gray metal exhibits bought from company auctions up and down the seacoast. The only concession to the late twentieth century are the Digital computers and the wires that run up from them and into the false ceilings.

Paula looked up at me from her cluttered desk as I came in, her blond hair framing her face. She had on a denim miniskirt, low black shoes with no stockings, and a white short-sleeved blouse that had tiny flowers embroidered along the shoulders. Before her was a copy of the *Union Leader*, New Hampshire's only statewide paper. She ran a hand through her hair and nodded at me, smiling, and said, "Your subscription run out?"

"Hardly," I said. "I don't have a subscription to the *Chronicle*. I just pick it up on the newsstand when I see your byline."

"Hah. Thanks for your support. Newsstand sales like that can't keep us alive, Lewis. You should get a subscription."

"I don't want little paperboys or papergirls visiting me every day, Paula," I said. "Sorry."

At one of the other desks a woman about the age of Alice Crenshaw was laboriously typing on her DEC computer, looking over her glasses at the glowing green letters on the screen. For someone like myself, who types pretty fast, it was painful to watch, like seeing her juggle chain saws with her eyes closed.

I said, "You've got a few moments to kill? I was thinking about buying you a late breakfast."

She looked beyond me, at a larger desk near the wall that was swamped with newspapers and photographs and overflowing In and Out boxes, and an almost obscured nameplate that said ROLAND GRANDMAISON. The desk was empty and Paula frowned and said, "Well, it looks like Rollie's still recovering from last night's bender, so why the hell not."

On the way out she picked up a copy of the day's *Chronicle* without paying for it—"One of my very few fringe benefits," she said—and we walked across the well-groomed grass of the common, past flower banks that had little wooden signs planted in front of them, saying DONATED BY THE TYLER FLORAL SOCIETY. She stuck the folded-over copy of the newspaper in her black leather bag and slung her arm through mine as we headed to the Common Grill & Grill.

"Not a bad day, Lewis Cole," she said, looking over at me, a sly smile on her face.

"Not bad at all," I said. "So why are you smiling?"

With her free hand she punched me in the ribs. "You'll see."

At the Grill & Grill we sat at a card table with folding metal chairs at the rear, which is fairly typical for the Grill & Grill, one of the smallest restaurants on Route 1. There are a half-dozen red vinyl booths that have been repaired with gray duct tape, and a mishmash of tables and chairs that looked like they had been salvaged from a flood. The Common Grill & Grill is in a small brick building that near the end of the last century had actually been Tyler's post office, and then became a storehouse and eventually the Common Bar & Grill, until the then owner lost his liquor license in the late 1970s.

The place was eventually bought and is now owned by John Thiakapolous, a permanently sweating hulk of a white-mustached man who always wears white diner clothes and a sweatband around his head, and serves as the only cook for the place. He didn't feel like spending too much money to change the name of the place, so he took out the word *bar* and replaced it with an extra *grill* he found in a back room, and for some reason tourists from Massachusetts find that adorable. High school girls of all ages drift in and out as waitresses, and while the service is always shaky, the food is simple and is served hot. In New Hampshire, most pizza places, sub shops, and Italian restaurants are run by Greek immigrants. I'm not too sure if it makes sense, but I'm not one to complain.

Even though it was mid-morning the Grill & Grill was doing well, with retirees stretching a long morning over a cup of coffee, lawyers from Tyler going over briefs and papers before making the ten-minute drive to the county courthouse in Exonia, and a couple of well-dressed folks from our sister state to the south, giggling over the prices on the handprinted menu. I had an English muffin with tea while Paula dug into three scrambled eggs with ketchup, home fried potatoes, and four links of sausage.

"Here," she murmured between bites. "Check this out."

She handed over a copy of that day's *Chronicle* and on the front page, below the fold, was a story headlined "Missing Local Woman Believed Alive." Under the headline was her byline, Paula Quinn, *Chronicle* Writer, and the story's lead said: "There are now indications that a prominent local woman, missing for several days and thought to be possibly dead, is alive and in the area, according to local officials."

"What officials?" I asked.

Paula chewed, swallowed, and said, "Read on." There was a smidgen of ketchup on her chin, and I read on.

The story quoted Betsy Tyler and another long-time resident, Grace Mackinnon. Both of them said that they had received calls from Alice Crenshaw, who had told them that she was fine. Neither of the women said that Alice had given them any additional information, and both said they had received only one call.

Diane Woods was quoted, but only as saying, "The matter

of Alice Crenshaw's departure from her home is under investigation. We know of the phone calls, and we have no further comment."

I folded the paper and handed it back to Paula. I said, "In your story you say officials told you that Alice Crenshaw was alive. Who were the officials?"

She winked. "Betsy Tyler, for one. She's a selectman, and as a selectman not only are you a town official but you're also considered a police officer. Honest to God. You can check the state laws."

I finished my tea. "All right, I'll give you that one. And Grace Mackinnon?"

She wiped up the last bits of ketchup-drowned scrambled egg with a piece of toast. "Grace is on the town historical society, same as Alice Crenshaw. She gets reimbursed for expenses and that's compensation, and under the law, that makes her a town official, too. I may stretch things out of recognition, Lewis, but I never lie in my stories. Never."

"How did you get Grace Mackinnon's name?"

"Thanks to you, of course," Paula said. "When I talked to Betsy Tyler after you gave me her name, she told me that she had talked to Grace the other night and that Grace had also gotten the same phone call from Alice. There you go. Then I called Diane Woods and she gave me the usual runaround— except this time she seemed more pissed than usual—and bingo, page-one story, thank you very much."

She wiped her face with a napkin, her eyes shiny, and I was thinking some of Alice Crenshaw. Another phone call, another sign that she was all right, but no word, no mention to me. Was she hiding something? Or was it really Alice Crenshaw who was making those calls? I could probably make out Alice's voice all right and could tell if someone was imitating her. But if I were the ages of Betsy Tyler and Grace Mackinnon, then maybe I wouldn't be so discriminating. I could be fooled. Which would explain the lack of calls to my home.

Questions, more questions, and damn few answers.

I noticed Paula's expression and I said, "You're looking particularly gleeful today. Getting a page-one story making you look so happy?"

She folded her arms on the table and the beaming look on her face hadn't changed. "In a way, it does, Lewis. But not in the way you think. You see, most of the time, the stories I get are predictable. From week to week, I can tell you the type of stories I do. Every Monday morning, there's a roundup of the police news from Tyler and Tyler Beach. Every Tuesday morning, I have two or three selectmen stories. The week before the Memorial Day weekend, I do a summer preview, and the week after Labor Day, I do a summer review. Fall means back-to-school stories and winter means Christmas stories. Pretty routine, except for the occasional fire or traffic accident."

By then a waitress had taken away our plates and dropped a grease-stained receipt on the table, which was our bill. Paula leaned back, her arms wide open, and said, "But the stuff I've been working on the past couple of weeks, Lewis—I'm going to sound awful and cold-hearted and cynical—but it's been wonderful. Body in the Marsh. Strangled high school girl. Missing woman. Lobsterman blown up in own boat. Those are the type of stories you don't get that much, and this month has been a hell of a good one for me, Lewis."

"Not a particularly good one for Lynn Germano or Henry Desmond," I said. "Or maybe even Alice Crenshaw." I picked up the check and left a ten-dollar bill on top of it. Behind the counter John was cursing to himself and working at the grill.

She shrugged. "Not my worry, Lewis. I'm an observer. Not a critic, not a defender, not an investigator. An observer. I see what happens and I report it, and what's happening in Tyler will get me somewhere far from here, Lewis. I'm not going to wait around for five or ten years until Rollie Grandmaison's liver croaks him and I move into his job. I want someplace different, and I want someplace where people recognize me when I walk down the street."

"And this is going to do it?"

She drummed her fingers on the table. "Yeah," she said, her voice soft. "This just might do it. Can't you feel it, Lewis? There's something in the air, a bite, a tension. I feel like something new is going to break, and going to break soon. This story's far from over, Lewis, and I'm going to be right there, pushing it and printing everything I find."

"You working on anything new?"

She winked at me. "Many've been the times when you've been secretive with me, Lewis, and now's my chance for a payback. Yeah, I'm working on something new, but nothing I'm going to tell you now." She turned and looked up at a clock on the wall and said, "Well, Rollie's probably back now, eating breath mints and wondering where the hell I am. Here, might as well leave this for the next customer."

With that, she pulled out the *Chronicle* and left it on the table. When she did that, the black leather purse opened a bit and for a brief moment I saw something in her purse, something that kept me quiet as I walked her back to the *Chronicle*'s offices. I never knew Paula Quinn had been one for arming herself.

By 7:15 P.M. I had eaten one box of popcorn and had drunk two Cokes, and there was still no sign of Felix Tinios.

The Maid of the Seas statue was still here, the reclining stone woman looking out to the ocean with a wreath in her hand. I looked again at the low concrete wall with each of the dead men's names carved into it, sailors and marines from New Hampshire who had died out there in the gray vastness. I wondered if their spirits were eased a bit by this monument, this memorial to their short lives, or if there was nothing that anyone could do to ease their disquiet. There must have been some rage out there, in dying in a warm or cold ocean, far away, knowing you would never return to the tall pines and mountains of this state, or to your family. Some rage. And all that was left was this stone statue with its blank eyes.

In my time at the beach I had made two phone calls to Felix Tinios's home and there had been no answer. Felix was supposed to be here at least an hour earlier, along with the ten thousand dollars in cash that would allow us the opportunity to see the tapes of Lynn Germano. I looked around at the midweek visitors who were drifting in along the sidewalks, and the two rows of cars and pickup trucks, making their slow journey north along Atlantic Avenue. No sign of Felix. No sign of anyone. I remembered Felix's warnings about traps and I started walking north, going almost as fast as the bumper-to-bumper traffic by my side.

After my late breakfast that morning with Paula Quinn I had spent the afternoon in the Gilliam Memorial Town Library, reading through magazines I don't subscribe to, knowing that if I did subscribe to them, my post office box would be full every day and I would never get any work done, or anything else for that matter.

In the library's lobby is a plaque mentioning the day the library was dedicated, nearly a decade ago, and there is a large framed black-and-white photograph of a balding old man, wearing wire-rimmed round glasses and a black bow tie and suit. Dr. Gilliam, for whom the library was named, and who had also been Alice Crenshaw's father. I spared the photograph only a glance as I came in, and tried not to think what might have happened to the good doctor's daughter.

Alice once told me that the day the library was dedicated was one of the happiest of her life, and I had no reason to doubt her. Still, being in the library and seeing Alice's name on the plaque—she was on the library building committee— had given me a brief shiver.

With that I spent the afternoon thinking about what was ahead for me, and what I might find on those tapes, as I read through *Archaeology* and *The Nation* and *Aviation Week & Space*

Technology and *Paris Match* and a dozen others. Reading has always been an escape, almost a drug for me. I do love the printed page, reading arguments and opinions and counter-arguments, learning something new and connecting it to something I had learned before. Some years ago I thought I had been lucky to work at a place where they paid me to read, and that thought stayed with me until a cool morning in Nevada.

I had lost much since that day, but I've always been grateful that I've never lost my love for words on paper.

After the library I had made my way through the traffic to the beach and had even gotten to the Maid of the Seas statue earlier than six o'clock, because I wanted to see Felix's expression as he came upon me there, already waiting for him, but of course, he had never shown up.

After about ten minutes of walking I half-jogged across Atlantic Avenue, nimbly passing across two lanes of traffic, going to Baker Street and the St. Lawrence Seaway. As I got to the entrance I started to head into the lobby and then suddenly veered out again and kept on walking down the street.

Too obvious. Too open. And, no doubt, too stupid. As Felix said, I didn't know what little traps were there, or if Oliver Mailloux had set up a greeting committee for me.

I'm sure Derek Cooney wouldn't be as dumb the second time around.

I reversed direction and went down a trash-strewn side alley and came to the fire door that I had slipped through the last time I had been at the St. Lawrence Seaway and gone into Oliver's apartment. No one was in the little alleyway as I took out my key ring. On the key ring was the passkey I had stolen, what now seemed so many days ago. I wondered if the key would work on the fire door.

It did.

I went quickly upstairs, two steps at a time, and came out on the third-floor hallway. It was empty. I walked along the hallway, past the room of Corinne and Tammy, the two high school chambermaids and unwitting film stars, and as I was about to knock on Oliver Mailloux's door, I stopped.

The door was open.

I stepped back. It wasn't open wide, but it was open, about a couple of inches. With the tip of a finger I pushed the door back. The apartment's lights were on, and there was a loud hissing noise.

"Oliver?"

The living room was slightly messy, with newspapers and magazines on the floor. The kitchen was empty and clean. There was a thick odor in the room. I bent down and in a few moments, the Browning was in my hands.

"Oliver?" And then I decided to shut up. If someone was in this apartment, they would have heard me by now. So about the only other person who would hear me would be someone passing by in the hallway, and about then, I didn't want to be disturbed. So yakking wasn't going to do anything constructive.

The door to Oliver's bedroom was open, and the hissing sound came from the large-screen television, which was on, busily broadcasting nothing but static. I went into the bedroom, .32 firm in both hands, and found Oliver, lying facedown on his bed. He had on jeans and polished black shoes, and what looked to be a red-and-white silk shirt, and his face was in his pillow. He wasn't moving, which wasn't much of a surprise.

The top of his head had been blown off.

20

I DUCKED BACK INTO THE LIVING ROOM AND dropped my arms down, because by then my hands were shaking and it took a lot of effort to hold onto the .32 Browning. I also started breathing quickly through my mouth, bringing a lot of oxygen into my bloodstream, as my stomach began a very sharp debate on whether or not to vomit. As the debate continued I blinked my eyes a few times and looked around the living room and the kitchen again. Nothing out of place. Nothing disturbed. No cigarettes in an ashtray with some butts stained with lipstick, no two empty glasses or two empty plates, and no anonymous notes from the killer or killers. Nothing. Oliver might have had one visitor, or two, or a dozen. That wasn't sure. But what was sure was the cold object now staining his bed.

My Browning looked very silly in my hands and I reholstered it, bringing my leg up to do it, because I was afraid that by bending over I might faint. I took a couple more deep breaths and stepped back into the bedroom. Another quick glance at Oliver showed a wide spray of brown and gray stains on the wall, the awful mess of what had been his head, and then I looked at the shelves against the wall.

On each shelf, a number of tapes were missing.

Easy enough then to see what had happened. Oliver had received a visit from someone who didn't want his—or maybe even her—performance to be advertised or sold.

The television kept on hissing as I left the apartment, sliding my way back down the fire stairs to the alleyway, filled with an urge to burn my clothes and never come this way again. I got into my Range Rover and started driving with no destination in mind—just a voice telling me to get the hell away from Baker Street and the St. Lawrence Seaway and the sands of Tyler Beach.

A couple of hours later I made it home, having spent the time driving up and down the interstate, hoping that by being in heavy traffic, I would concentrate on driving and the cars and trucks about me, and forget the sight of the flesh and blood splattered on Oliver Mailloux's bedroom wall.

It hadn't worked.

When I got inside I locked the doors and saw that the green light on the answering machine was blinking, meaning someone had called. I played back the tape and found there had been three calls, and each time, the caller had hung up without leaving a message. I made a short and loud reference to that caller's parentage, and then I went upstairs. I put the .32 on the sink and stripped and took a shower. My hands were still shaking, and I dropped the soap a few times in the spray of the hot water. I kept my eyes open in the shower, even when the soap started to sting them, for every time I closed them, I kept seeing that decaying hunk of meat and bone on the bed in Oliver Mailloux's apartment.

When I got out of the shower I quickly wiped myself down, not bothering to check my skin. I wasn't in the mood. I went downstairs, taking my soiled clothes with me, and holding the Browning in my right hand. I tossed the clothes into a green garbage bag and twisted the bag shut. I unlocked the front door long enough to throw the bag out into the yard. It would stay there until I took it to the town dump. Those clothes were no longer going to be in my house, no matter if I could have cleaned them.

As I went across the living room, still naked except for a few drops of water running down my back, the phone rang. My voice was sharp and to the point, and on the other end was Felix Tinios.

"Is that you, Lewis?"

The receiver felt cold in my hand. "What do you think, Felix?" I quickly asked. "You dialed my number, who did you think would be here? The Flying Dutchman?"

There was silence and I said, "You call earlier?"

"Yeah."

I swore at him and said, "Don't you keep up with Miss Manners? It's considered rude not to leave a message on an answering machine. You got a problem with that?"

Felix didn't reply, saying instead, "You hear the news about Oliver Mailloux?"

I was going to say something about just how much I knew about Oliver Mailloux, when I said, "No. You tell me."

"He's dead. Shot."

I shifted the receiver to the other hand. It still felt cold. "Oh. So that's where you were this afternoon, Felix. You kept me waiting for a couple of hours and instead of getting to the statue early enough to see what kind of traps might be there, you decided to cut out the middleman and go right to the inn. Is that right, Felix? Did you shoot Oliver? Or whack him, as you folks are so fond of saying?"

"Not funny, Lewis."

I said, "Why not? Sounds perfectly amusing to me."

"It's not funny because your cop friend thinks it's true. I'm at the Tyler police station. I was arrested an hour ago."

By then I wished I was dressed, and I said, "You've been arrested for Oliver's murder?"

"No, I've been arrested for assault."

I tried to take a deep breath. "Who the hell did you assault, Felix? You're not making too much sense."

Felix said, "Listen, Lewis. Give me a minute or two, all right? This afternoon, I'm at the Blue Whale Restaurant in Tyler, working on some other business, having a drink, when Oliver's best buddy comes in for a visit. Derek Cooney. He wanted to chat about how I was making Oliver nervous, and how the whole deal about the movies should be put aside. And if I had a problem with that, we could talk about it. Well, I did and we did. We went behind the restaurant, back behind some Dumpsters. The discussion lasted a bit and then he managed to stumble out, and I went back home, my ribs aching and not ready to move anywhere. So I called you, to tell you that the meet was off. But you weren't home."

Over the phone, I made out a slight cough. "An hour or so later, the cops come and they put me down for assault. Seems Derek found Oliver's body back at the hotel, panicked, called the cops, and your detective lady friend saw all his bruises and started asking him questions. He decided to answer them. So. She made a connection with our little disagreement and Oliver's murder. An arrest warrant for assault was drawn up and the friendly North Tyler cops executed it, and here I am, standing in my shoes with no laces and no belt on my pants at the Tyler police station, and I need five thousand dollars for the cash bail to get me out."

I said, "And why are you calling me, Felix? Why not a lawyer, or one of your business associates? Don't you have comrades on the payroll who can come rescue you?"

I think for the first time ever I heard Felix sigh and seem overwhelmed at what was happening to him. He said slowly, "That wouldn't be a good idea for me, Lewis. Word would get around that I couldn't keep my own house in order, that the cops were giving me hassles, affecting my job performance. I don't need a reputation like that to get passed on down."

"So you called me."

"So I called you, Lewis. Listen, I'm not going to beg here, Lewis. I just need to know, are you going to come bail me out?"

I wondered if he could sense what was going through my mind, if his ear could somehow pick up the way my hand was shaking on the receiver, shaking a bit from the coolness of the air and the thoughts that were racing through my mind. The killing of Oliver Mailloux looked very professional, a shot or two right to the back of the head, and in that type of business, Felix Tinios was the most professional person I knew.

"Lewis?" In the background I could make out the murmured sounds of a police radio.

I said, "Fifteen minutes," and then I hung up and finally got dressed.

It actually was twenty because it took longer than I expected to get the money. It was in a secure place within walking distance of my house—no need to get into any extra details—because I've always felt I should have cash on hand in case old ghosts with sharp teeth decided to pay me a visit, and I needed to move quickly. Five thousand made a dent in my cache, but not a serious one, and I was soon on my way.

When I got to the Tyler police station it was early evening, about nine o'clock, and Diane Woods met me in the waiting area near the station's dispatch center, where the sole female dispatcher was on duty this night. Diane had on gray slacks and a thick red-and-green rugby shirt, the sleeves rolled back. Her holstered revolver was exposed at her side, snug on a belt, and next to it was her detective's shield. Her brown hair was shiny with dirt and grease and her eyes seemed thick with exhaustion, and she was not smiling when she came out.

"Tinios told us that you were coming down to bail him out," she said, her arms folded, leaning against the cinder-block wall.

"Since you're here, I can see he's at least telling us the truth on that."

"You have doubts about anything else he's said?" I asked, knowing full well that I had my own doubts about what he was saying, and what he had done.

"Come here, Lewis, will you?"

I followed her into the station and she took me to a small kitchen near the chief's and deputy chief's offices, where during the day some of the administrative staff ate their lunches. She closed the door and sat down at a round wooden table, scarred with cigarette burns. Hanging on three of the four walls were cork bulletin boards, and tacked to the boards were police patches from all across the country and Canada and Mexico. I noticed one from Ontario as I sat across from her.

There was a telephone on one wall and before Diane sat down its intercom buzzed. She muttered something and picked up the phone and said, "Woods," and there was a pause, and I noticed both her jaw and hand tighten, and then she said, "Tell her I'll call her back."

Another pause, a louder muttering, and then she said, "Okay," and in one breath, said, "Listen, I told you never to call me at work, and never means just that."

Then she hung up the phone with enough force that I was sure the cell block's inmates heard the slam; she sat down in her chair, glaring.

"Problems with Kara?" I asked.

She refused to answer. She just stared at me and said in a low, firm voice, "You have any idea what the hell you're doing, Lewis?"

I decided not to pursue the matter. I said, "What I'm doing is helping an acquaintance of mine exercise his constitutional rights, by getting him bailed out."

Diane tapped on the kitchen table. "Bullshit, Lewis. What gives? What do you owe Felix Tinios that made you come down here and bail out his ass?"

There was also a shoulder patch from British Columbia up on the bulletin board. For a moment I started counting the patches, for I had a hard time looking at her.

"Nothing is owed, Diane," I said. "I might have a little responsibility to repay him for some things he's done to help me in the past, but he doesn't have me in a bind, if that's what you mean."

She shook her head and pressed her hands against her temples. "What I mean is that a couple of hours ago, Lewis, I had the distinct pleasure of seeing Oliver Mailloux get pulled out of his bed and placed in a rubber bag, and seeing his blood and brains drying on his bedroom wall. You know, when the firefighters picked him up, the bed's sheet stuck to what's left of his head? That's what I've been doing. So in a span of three weeks, I have three bodies, Lewis. I'm not sleeping and my phone is ringing and the chief and selectmen and the state want to know what's going on, and what my progress is. And for the first time during this miserable month, I have something to hold onto. Felix Tinios. I get him here and someplace where I can see him, and you patter in and want to set him free."

I said, "He's in for an assault charge, Diane. If you're so sure that Felix was involved with Oliver's death, why don't you charge him with murder?"

"Because we don't have everything yet!" she nearly shouted.

I sat up straighter and she seemed slightly embarrassed at the outburst and shook her head and said with urgency, "We're working on it, Lewis, but we don't have everything in just a few hours. We're working it hard."

"What do you have, then?"

She said, "When we got to Oliver's apartment at the hotel, we found evidence that Oliver was involved with something illegal, something that Felix might have had an interest in. We need time to track that down. At least a day or two. And you're not helping things by being so eager to bail him out."

"So what was Oliver involved with that had Felix as a con-

nection?" I asked, lying in my best manner. "Was Oliver involved with drugs, or something like that? Did he cheat Felix
out of something?"

She shook her head again, pursed her lips. "Not telling,
Lewis. But there's something there that we're looking at, and
we plan to charge Felix with the murder, quick as can be, once
we get all the evidence in. Hell, the clerk at the front desk said
she saw someone leave in a hurry, just about the time of Oliver's
death, and she thinks it might have been your Felix. And it'd
be a hell of a lot easier for us if he's here or at the county jail,
where we can keep an eye on him. So. Again I ask you, Lewis,
why the hell are you bailing him out?"

The kitchen seemed stuffy and slightly ridiculous. A kitchen,
in the middle of a police station. I said, "I'm bailing him out
on the assault charge, Diane. I don't think Felix killed Oliver
Mailloux. If I had the slightest thought that he did, then I
wouldn't be here."

"You got an alibi for Felix, then?"

Not yet. "No."

She sighed, rapped her fingers on the scarred table. "I wish
I could say I was disappointed in you, Lewis, because right
now you're acting like a class-one fool. But being disappointed
in someone indicates some sort of relationship, Lewis, and I
don't think I know you or our relationship anymore."

I said nothing. She stood up. "Is that all, Mr. Cole?"

I said, "I'd like to see Felix now, Detective."

In a small room just outside of the booking area, Felix Tinios
sat in a folding metal chair, his belongings in a paper bag,
staring at a wall and not looking at me. The bail bondsman
was Ralph Potter, a huge man who always smoked cigars and
was nearing three hundred pounds, and who liked to wear
large white T-shirts, bright yellow shorts, black knee-high
stockings, and black shoes in the summer. He was a retired
Tyler cop and boasted that he spent more time at the station

in his retirement than he had in his previous thirty years in the department, and was making more money to boot. I passed over the $5,000 in cash and he wrote up the receipt with his thick fingers, cigar ash dribbling onto the table.

He passed over the receipt and winked. "He's all yours, Lewis."

"Thanks. I can hardly think of what to do with him."

Felix was quiet as we went outside, and he held his bag to his chest as we made the short walk to my Range Rover, although I noticed his shoulders seemed to ease some. His self-confidence and the swagger of his pace seemed to have diminished. I started up the Range Rover and in a minute or two we were heading north on Atlantic Avenue, back to where we both lived.

As I drove, Felix opened up the paper bag and took out two sets of black shoelaces. He kicked off his shoes and put them in his lap, and began carefully relacing his shoes, his fingers looking quite delicate. As he did this, he said, "For what it's worth, Lewis, I'll say out front that I didn't do Oliver Mailloux."

"I'm not the one you're going to have to convince on that, Felix. It's going to be Diane Woods and the state police."

"Well, that might take some doing," he said. He finished one shoe and started on the other. "But I had nothing to do with it."

Traffic was light on Atlantic Avenue, and in just a few minutes I was passing Weymouth's Point and Alice Crenshaw's quiet and empty house. To my right the waning moon was over the Atlantic, making a shiny, wavy path on the rolling water. Atlantic Avenue dipped and swerved and Felix finished his second shoe as we went by the lit and too-perfect splendor of the Lafayette House. I saw no towering cloud of smoke or sparks flying up beyond the Lafayette House's parking lot, where my house lay hidden, and I thought for just a moment about asking Felix about my watcher.

Instead I said, "I don't put too much together regarding

coincidences, Felix. So you tell me. The two of us meet Oliver Mailloux about viewing some of his tapes. Less than a day later, he's dead and some of the tapes are missing. And chances are, those are the ones with Lynn Germano on them. Two other people knew about Lynn Germano and the tapes. You've always told me that I didn't have the temperament for your type of work, so that leaves you as a pretty good suspect, don't you think?"

He looked over at me, leaning forward a bit in the seat so he could thread his belt through his pants. For Felix it was an odd position, and I thought about what type of humiliation he must be going through, to be here at this moment.

Felix snapped the belt shut and said, "But for what benefit, Lewis? I'm doing just fine right now, away from the craziness of Boston and the North Shore. There's not much going on but I'm still connected enough for a fine living. For a bug like Oliver Mailloux, I would threaten all of that?"

I turned into Rosemount Lane and pulled into his driveway, next to his Mercedes. The tires on his car still looked fine.

"Maybe you were on those tapes, Felix."

He shook his head. "Not my taste."

Felix opened the door and stepped out onto his driveway, and then leaned back in. "But think of this, Lewis. Maybe Oliver was lying to us. Maybe he did have that chick's death on the tape, and he was trying to work a side deal with the killer. That would explain a lot. Would explain Derek Cooney's visit to me earlier today. If Oliver had something sweet going, he wouldn't want to involve us."

"Maybe, at that," I said. "One of a few possibilities."

He leaned back out. "A damn good possibility, Lewis, and you know it." He gently tapped the roof of my Range Rover. "I hate to say thank you to anyone, and I think you know that. But I owe you one, Lewis."

"No," I said. "You owe me five thousand."

He laughed. "That I do. And you'll get it tomorrow, after I sweat it out of someone."

"Derek Cooney?"

Felix said, "The same, Lewis. The very same. I want to know why he turned me in so quickly."

I shifted the Range Rover into reverse. "Well, don't leave any bruises, Felix. You damn near wiped out my bank account tonight, and I can't afford to bail you out again."

As I backed out of the driveway, I saw his stride return to that of the Felix Tinios I had known. I wasn't too sure if that was a comforting thought, so I drove home.

I stopped at a Kwik-Mart in North Tyler for some frozen lemonade and other shopping, and it was just after ten when I resumed heading south, back to the bright lights of the Lafayette House and its quiet parking lot. My Range Rover did the usual bumpy ride down the driveway, past the No Trespassing signs, to my garage. My house was still standing well, unburnt and undamaged, and when this was over, I intended to make sure that the watcher Felix had hired got a bonus.

When this was over. Good suggestion, good wish. I switched off the lights and the engine, and got out on the packed dirt floor of the garage, carrying my grocery bag in one hand.

With the moon's rising, the land about my house was well lit, almost like a streetlight had been built in the backyard, which explains how I recognized Derek Cooney the moment he walked in front of the open garage.

And how I saw the gun in his hand.

21

IN SITUATIONS LIKE THE ONE I WAS FACING, A lot goes through your mind, and your senses seem to expand and sharpen. I could smell the richness of the packed earth, feel the rough touch of the grocery bag in my hands, see the moonlight making the finish of my Range Rover look like it had just been waxed. I also thought about other things, about Paula Quinn and Cissy Manning, and how much protection the grocery bag would offer me when and if Derek started pulling the trigger on his pistol, which looked a 9-mm of some sort and which was only a couple of yards away. My own .32 Browning was with me, of course, but since it was in my ankle holster, it could have been in Spokane for all it was worth at that moment.

Derek's face was bruised and scratched, so Felix had been telling the truth about their little visit. He had on a short leather jacket, red T-shirt, blue jeans, and white, scuffed sneakers, and his belly was a large, round object pressing against his jeans. His black hair was slicked back and shiny, as if he had just combed it in saltwater, and he had a small, quiet smile on his face, as if enjoying something slightly amusing.

He said, "Looks like I've got you at a disadvantage, writer-man."

I didn't move. "Looks like it to me, too."

His grin grew wider. "'Course, my dad was one to put that in a bit coarser terms, like I got you by your short hairs. That make sense to you?"

"About as much as anything does."

He nodded. "Good." He pulled aside his short leather jacket and stuck the 9-mm in his rear waistband, and everything seemed to sigh and decompress, and no longer could I smell the earth in my garage. I shifted my own weight.

"Proving a point?" I asked.

"Exactly," he said. "Wanted to prove that you weren't so special, that if I wanted to, I could have blown off your head as easy as steppin' on a flopping fish. Wanted to show you that I didn't forget that little number, few days back, when you tossed me down the stairs at the inn in front of my boss."

"That probably made Oliver pretty mad at you," I said.

He nodded again. "That it did. He told me that I'd embarrassed him as much as it had embarrassed me. But with what I just did, I'll consider what's between us even, if that's all right with you."

Who was I to argue? "That'd be fine, Derek. You and I are even."

"Good." He looked behind him and then looked back at me, and he was no longer smiling. His face was troubled, and he said, "I need to talk to you. You got a beer or two in that bag?"

Some switch in attitude. "No, but I've got a couple in the house. Hold on out here, and, Derek, I hope you understand, I'm not going to invite you in."

He shrugged. "That's all right. I'm lookin' to be flexible myself. I'll wait out here."

I went past him and unlocked the door and went inside, switching on only a small table lamp. The answering machine light glowed at a steady green. There was a smell about me, the rich stink of sweat and fear, and I didn't like it, not one bit. I put the groceries away and grabbed one Molson, and then two and an opener, and went back outside. I left the door open and the small lamp made a little light in my small front yard. I opened both Molsons and handed one over to Derek. He took a long swallow, sighed, and then wiped his face on a sleeve of his leather jacket. He sat down on my stone steps and I sat on the rough ground before him, conscious that in crossing my legs, he could make out the ankle holster.

He did. He nodded in my direction and said, "We're even, so don't even worry about that type of crap."

"All right." I swallowed some of my own beer and tasted not a thing. "Felix Tinios is looking for you, and he's not in a very happy mood."

Derek scratched at an ear. "Yeah, I can see why the little shit wouldn't be."

"From the way your face is looking, I'd say he's big enough."

He grinned at that. "Maybe not big enough, but Jesus, yeah, he's quick enough. Real quick. I met him out behind the Blue Whale and just as I was thinking, where should I pop him one, he was comin' after me. Now I know why he carries so much weight around here. The bastard's good. You know, I didn't have much of a choice this afternoon after I called the cops when I saw Mr. Mailloux, spread out like that. If I'd been thinking better, I would have just closed the door and gone home and forgot about it, but it's like when I saw him lyin' like that, I had to talk to someone, to tell somebody what had happened. So I called the cops."

Derek took another swallow and I said, "And when they started pressing you, about what Oliver was up to and why your face was so marked up, you gave them Felix's name?"

He looked shy, almost embarrassed. "Didn't have much of a choice. They knew I worked for Mr. Mailloux and when they started going through his tapes and stuff, they started asking me hard questions. I couldn't really shag 'em off, 'specially when they said they might charge me with some of the taping stuff. Corruption of minors, child abuse, child porn—shit like that, I don't need."

I said, "What do you need, then, Derek?"

Far overhead an airplane passed, and I thought of the curious bravery of those who would take small airplanes over the ocean in the dark. So many random violences out there, from dying because of a wrong road taken, a wrong sidewalk walked upon, the wrong neighborhood lived in, and some people seemed to revel in temptations like flying at night in a small plane over the wide and unforgiving Atlantic.

Derek took a deep breath. "I need you to contact your friend Felix. Ask him to pull back and call off the hounds. Man, I know he must be pissed, but I had to give him up this afternoon. There's no way that Mr. Mailloux's project is going to get me sent to Concord."

"Why did you see him at the Blue Whale this afternoon? I heard you were sent to discourage him. What did Oliver have in mind?"

Derek balanced the beer bottle in his hands and hunched forward. "Mr. Mailloux made some phone calls, the morning after he met up with the two of you. He said a better deal was goin' to come through, one that he had been workin' on for some time and that was better than the two of you could have put together. So he told me that I should go talk to Felix, tell 'im that the deal was off, and then go see you."

I felt almost like smiling, which I thought was unusual, considering who was sitting across from me. "And did you come by to see me earlier?"

He shook his head ruefully. "No. I was hurtin' so much, I wanted to go back and tell Mr. Mailloux that it was going to be tougher than he expected. And that's when I found him . . ."

"Who did he call that morning, before he sent you out?" I asked. "Was it his friends in Montreal?"

He slowly shook his head. "No, I think it was local. You

know why? 'Cause he spoke in English. Every time he called up north, he'd speak in French. I couldn't make out the words, but I'm sure it was English. I think maybe it was his partner.''

"And who's his partner?''

Derek opened up one hand to me. "Don't know that. Honest. Mr. Mailloux, sometimes he'd say that he had a shadow guy behind him, helpin' him get things going. I think it was the guy who fronted him the money for all those tapes and that editing equipment. That was pretty expensive shit, you know, nothing that Oliver could afford. But he'd never tell me the name. Just his shadow guy, that's all. On some stuff, Mr. Mailloux was dead quiet.''

"Tell me more about the tapes, Derek. When did they start, and why?''

"Jesus, I don't know . . .''

"Derek,'' I said, the tone in my voice enough for him to look up at me. "If you want me to talk to Felix Tinios about you, start answering me. What I tell Felix will depend on what you tell me.''

He rubbed his beer bottle, rotating it a bit, as if trying to start a fire in the concrete at his feet. "Mr. Mailloux, he said it just started out as a hobby to get him through the week. You know? Running cottages and working in a hotel and a restaurant like the Palace Diner, Jesus Christ, you don't know the hours you put in. Every freakin' minute, it seems, there's complaints or problems, from dirty dishes to missing towels. You're on call every day of the week, and for what? Money and time off in the winter, when you can't enjoy what you've earned. So he did what he did with the videos, give 'im some kicks at the end of the day. You think you meet many chicks the kinda work he was in?''

The ground was cool against my butt. "It seemed like he met a special chick, like you said. Lynn Germano.''

He gave a short laugh, looked down again at his beer bottle. "Yeah, Lynn Germano. She was wild, that one. Didn't mind her job at all. Think she enjoyed it, enjoyed it a lot.''

Something tasted sour in my mouth. "I suppose you're not talking about her waitressing job.''

"You suppose correct, writerman. Story, the way Mr. Mailloux told it, I guess he kinda liked the way she filled out her waitress uniform and he went out a bit too much in the deep, and he set up the video stuff in her cottage, hoping to catch some hot stuff in action. Which was pretty stupid; I mean, it's hard to find the video gear in the inn, but it was easy to notice it at her cottage."

Of course it was, and I remembered that electrical cord, snaking out from that storage area in her bedroom, the night I visited her cottage after her body had been taken away. Real easy to find, and I should have known better.

"Go on."

Derek took another swallow, finished his beer. "Not much to tell about it. He set up the video gear and sure enough, she found it. The way he told me, she came in screaming and he screamed back at her, and then he offered her some money to forget about it—a hell of a lot more money than waitressing, I'll tell you—and that smell of green settled her down. Then they got to talkin'. Pretty soon the two of 'em worked out a deal. I mean, the tapes in the inn were nice, but those chicks didn't know they were being filmed so sometimes the quality of the tapes sucked. But with Lynn, Jesus, I think it kinda turned her on, knowin' there was a camera takin' pictures of her, and she'd put on a hell of a performance. You wouldn't believe those tapes. So hot you'd think they'd melt."

"She have any regulars you know of?" I asked, the cold ale roiling in my stomach, and somehow there was a stench of decay in the air, as if a ton of month-old seaweed had washed up on my tiny beach.

"Nope. Just guys she'd pick up at work, or at the beach. Occasionally Mr. Mailloux, and I'm sure he let his partner have a piece." He smirked. "Once I went over to her place and got her drunk, and I had a piece, and it was pretty good, someone as young as that. Not bad at all."

I tried to smile but probably failed, and I said, "Who was her last one, Derek? Was it you?"

He smiled back at me. "Good try, but the cops already questioned me and I was workin' that night, and there's about a half-dozen people who never saw me once leave the Palace Diner. No, I don't know who it was, but it wasn't me, and it wasn't Mr. Mailloux. But there is one guy . . ." And with that, his face darkened.

I decided the night was coming to a close and I stood up, brushing the sand and grass from my pants. "Oh? And who'd that be?"

Derek followed my cue and also got up from the steps. "Your buddy there, Felix Tinios. I tell you, writerman, if you live in a neighborhood and your cat gets torn to shreds, you don't start asking questions about the pet hamsters and rabbits people are keepin'. You look for the pit bull or the German shepherd, and Felix Tinios is this town's pit bull. I don't know what he might be up to and at this point, I really don't care, but he's the only one that comes to mind. With Lynn and that fisherman and Mr. Mailloux, well, someone's either got some serious problems or a serious agenda, and I think Felix fits the bill."

He handed over his empty bottle and said plaintively, "You will talk to him, won't you?"

I nodded. "Yeah, I'll give it a shot. But one more thing."

He zipped up his coat a bit, and the zipper and fabric strained against the swelling of his stomach. "Yeah?"

Thinking of Felix and promises that were made, I said, "Did you have any problems coming here to my house? Anyone talk to you?"

He smiled and wiped his hands back against his oily hair. "Yeah, someone did, at that. My cousin Clarence. He's on the state road crew for this section of the beach. He came over a while ago and asked me what was up, and I said I wanted to talk to you. He asked me if it was going to be peaceful and I said, yeah, no problem, and he said, okay, see you later. Why? Does Clarence work for you?"

My stomach still felt queasy. "No, thank God." I looked him

over and he was slightly pathetic, standing there at my steps because I didn't want him or his scent in my house, and I said, "Where do you go from here, Derek?"

He had stuffed his hands in his coat and started walking up my driveway, but he turned and said, "Good question, writerman. You know, I come from Falconer, and I've never lived more than three miles from home. I'm not that good with numbers or words or writing, but I am good with my hands and in starin' people down and gettin' things done. I've worked as a bouncer and a repo man and for Mr. Mailloux, and that last one was the best so far. Not much hand-to-hand work and I could scarf as many free meals as I could and look at some pretty babes. Now I gotta look somewhere else, and it's rough, writerman. The type of jobs I'm good for aren't the type of jobs that are advertised in the newspapers."

Then he looked over at the far lights of Tyler and the beach, and before he started walking again, he said, "Thing is, too, I might move away from the seacoast for a while. Until I read in the newspaper somewhere that the cops got whoever is raisin' hell around here. I don't need to stick around and have some loony like Felix Tinios decide that I should be swimmin' with the fishes with an anchor chain wrapped around my neck, if you know what I mean."

I said I did and I watched him trudge up my driveway until he was out of view. Then I went into my house and tossed the two bottles into my recycling bin and after getting another beer, I went out on my deck to watch the stars rise.

There was a time before Nevada where I remembered sharing a late Sunday morning breakfast with Cissy Manning, sitting on the porch of her condominium in what was a relatively quiet part of Alexandria, Virginia. The furniture was metal and white and the round table had a clear glass top, and she had cooked us eggs Benedict and toast and there was a special-blend coffee and croissants from a shop down the street, and we were sharing that morning's editions of the *Washington Post* and *The New York Times* over the collection of dirty dishes. She was a marvelous cook and I was an equally marvelous dish washer, and both of us thought we were getting great deals.

Her red hair was freshly washed and tied behind in a pony-tail, and she was wearing a white terrycloth robe that was fairly open at the top, and I determined that fairly open meant I could make out the faint spread of freckles down her fine cleavage. She had the *Post* and I had *The Times*, and that morning I was wearing her other terrycloth robe, the blue one, and she sighed and turned the pages with an effort and looked up at me with her green eyes that seemed to have the power always to seize my attention. It worked this morning and I put down *The Times* and said, "Something on your mind?"

She said, "No, not really, Lewis. Just the general angst of the times, I guess. Reading about all that's going on in the world, and especially in our part of it, in D.C. I can remember being a kid at my school and getting dressed in my best uniform to visit D.C., and getting goose bumps at actually seeing the monuments and the Capitol building and the White House. There was so much history there, it almost made me faint."

"Then I envy you," I said. "My big school trip highlight was a bus ride to Indianapolis to see the governor. Then we went to see the racetrack, and I think most of us enjoyed the racetrack better."

She laughed and said, "You Midwest boy. You know, Lewis, I go through D.C. now and I wonder about the kids getting shot because they were in the way of rival drug gangs or wearing the wrong baseball caps, and I look at the monuments and think of them as relics from an earlier and better time, and I wonder about the well-bought fools who work in the Capitol building and live in the White House."

I turned the pages of *The Times*, wondering what possible ideology test the reporters were following, and said, "Ben Franklin once said our government was a democracy, if we could keep it, but I don't think he ever figured out how dreary it was going to get. I'm not too sure that a government that puts up with open-air drug markets, senators that are bought out by oil companies and bankers, and an incumbency rate that makes the Soviet Politburo proud is a government worth keeping."

"Maybe so," she said, crossing her legs, and there was a lot of leg. "Maybe, but what do we do about it, Lewis? We work for the government. Don't you think we're part of the problem? And what do we produce? All we do is read and write reports that get a circulation of about ten or twenty. That's it. Not much of a contribution."

I looked around and half-seriously said, "Hush, my sweet one, or the I.I. unit will be coming by, wondering why you're spilling secrets over Sunday brunch."

She made what she called her Phyllis Diller face, scrunching it up and sticking her tongue out, and she said, "Internal Investigations can go pound sand and you know it. Don't you feel you should do more, Lewis? What about our responsibility to our fellow man?"

I folded up *The Times* and passed it over to her, and said, "What you and I do is to fulfill our responsibilities to our government. We read, Cissy. We read newspapers, magazines, intercepted messages and documents, novels, screenplays, and whatnot. We're not poorly paid, and we write reports and make predictions about defense and military matters, and if we're right sometimes, then we get commendation letters that no one reads. We help people who get paid a lot more than us to make decisions. When we don't work, we let the world go by and pay our taxes and donate to charities, and that's it, Cissy. Just you and me and friends and family, that's it. Those people who have agendas they need fulfilled, they can go do that. Fine. All power to them. I have other things on my mind."

She crossed her arms. "What about participating in humanity, Lewis?"

I lifted up my coffee cup and saluted her. "A noble goal, that one. But right now, my goal is to participate in you, Miss Cissy Manning, and get sweaty and comfortable while doing it."

Cissy responded by tossing the Style section at my head, but she was laughing as she did it, and eventually we slid back into bed.

At my fingertips, resting on the wood floor of my deck, were two additional empty bottles of Molson Golden Ale; I tried to remember how many of those funny Molson man-woman radio commercials I could recall, and lost count after six.

The stars had come out even brighter as the moon had set, and I drew my knees up to my chest and hugged myself for a while, just thinking. It was a quiet night, and even the waves didn't seem that loud. The ocean was empty of lights, save for the standard ones at the Isles of Shoals. But the seaways and harbor traffic lanes were still this night, and the fish and lobsters and other life out there were swimming unmolested in the cold saltwater.

So much change. I thought again of that breakfast morning, and the words I said then seemed as cold as ashes in my mouth.

A meteor streaked by, a faint flash that was gone by the time I recognized what it was. It was Wednesday evening and shortly it would become Thursday morning. Almost time for bed and some welcome sleep. I thought again about Cissy Manning and Trent Baker and Carl Socha and all the rest, and I began thinking of what I would do this Sunday, what form of penance I would perform for them. And as I thought of what I could do, another thought came to me, of what I would be doing tomorrow and the next day. I thought back to what Derek Cooney had told me, and then I decided what I would do on Sunday.

And I knew that before Sunday came, I would visit the person I believed was responsible for the deaths of Lynn Germano, Henry Desmond, and Oliver Mailloux.

22

SOME YEARS AGO I HAD ATTENDED A TRAINING session for my job with the DoD. A group of us were sitting in one of those classrooms that has raised auditorium seating for the students. Our ages ranged from late teens to mid-fifties—at least—and one would be hard-pressed to try to categorize us. We were tall and short and thin and fat, and black, yellow, white, brown, and red. About the only thing we had in common were the plastic badges with our photos that said TRAINEE, which we had to hang around our necks. None of us knew each other by name, so there were a lot of polite smiles and nods during class every morning, but all of us knew our instructor, a Colonel Webb, and he knew all of us.

Though he wasn't retired military, he wore civilian clothes and carried a cane as he walked across the floor of the class-room, lecturing to us without notes. He was about forty-five and tall and fit, with a tanned face and short gray-black hair. His right leg was a prosthetic, and he had a disconcerting habit of rapping on his fake leg with the cane when making a point during his lectures.

This winter morning he was talking about connections, about history and the past, and he talked about the disastrous Marine barracks explosion in Beirut in 1983. I sat in the rear, listening intently. I didn't take notes, for notebooks were not allowed. Since the government thought we were so smart, we were expected to remember everything we heard.

The government in this occasion must have been right, for it worked.

He stood in the center of the room, staring at everyone and anyone, and, with his voice dripping contempt, said, "There were a lot of contributing factors to that screwup, some of which got fixed immediately, some of which we're still experiencing a serious deficiency in. The standard things were pretty easy to fix: a lousy chain of command structure, which made it hard to pin down who exactly ordered what, and who had what responsibility. The utter stupidity of the orders placing marines in harm's way and not allowing them to load their weapons. And the lack of a definite mission. Those poor bastards weren't sent into Beirut to seize ground or to kill someone—and that's the mission of the Marines. They were sent into Beirut as part of something called an international peace-keeping force, and the only peace some of them ever accomplished was the peace of the grave."

Then he strode across the room and stopped in front of his lectern and used his cane for emphasis again on his leg. *Tap-tap*.

"But one major factor contributing to that disaster was something that couldn't be easily fixed or addressed, for it wasn't as tangible as a stupid order or a fouled-up chain of command. It was a lack of sense, a lack of understanding of what had occurred there in the past."

He looked up at us again. Colonel Webb had the unerring ability to make you feel like you were the only student in the classroom. He said, "If you asked any of the White House weasels, the DoD planners, and even the commanders in the field for a basic history lesson of what had occurred in Lebanon for the previous fifty years, you would have gotten a blank look. None of them knew anything about what had gone on before. They didn't care, and in not caring, they didn't realize that their ignorance of the different sects, militias, and religions and their tangled history in that region would kill damn near three hundred of their fellow countrymen."

Colonel Webb went back to his lectern and then turned quickly. "Mr. Hagopian?"

"Sir?" came the reply, from a young, dark-skinned man sitting near the front row.

Tap-tap went the cane. "You have a smile on your face. You seem to be enjoying a portion of my talk, or perhaps you disagree with me. Do let us know what you're thinking."

Hagopian was still smiling as he said, "I just don't agree with your premise, about the past playing such an important part. I think that current tensions, current rivalries play a much more vital role."

Colonel Webb nodded. He and Hagopian had sparred before on other issues. I, on the other hand, had been content to stay quiet in an upper row. I was trying to keep what snipers called a low profile.

"So," the colonel said. "You would be one for letting the past bury the past. Don't worry about previous events."

Hagopian shrugged. "In some cases, yes. The past is dead, is gone. It can't reach you."

Colonel Webb arched an eyebrow. "Then do me the favor of standing up, if you will."

Hagopian paused and I felt the back of my neck tingle. Colonel Webb had such a look about him that if he told us not to come to class the next morning wearing pants, I was certain that there would be a lot of naked legs that day. I supposed Hagopian wasn't immune to the effect, for he stood up slowly. Unlike any other class I had ever been in, no one dared laugh.

The colonel said, "I'm going to begin a children's poem. You will complete it. Understand? Here we go: *Ring around the rosy.*''

Hagopian's face seemed to redden. "What do you mean by this?''

Tap-tap. "I mean that if you do not finish this rhyme, you will be out of this building in exactly one hour. Now. Complete the phrase: *Ring around the rosy.*''

Again, no laughter, even as Hagopian cleared his throat and said, "*Pocket full of posies, ashes, ashes, we all fall down.*''

Colonel Webb nodded and said, "Quite good. You may return to your seat. Does anyone recognize the significance of this little demonstration?''

For some reason I raised my hand and announced, "Black Death.''

"Exactly,'' Colonel Webb said, and he looked up at me and I knew he was remembering my name and my answer. "The bubonic plague, which destroyed about two-thirds of Europe in the fourteenth century. Listen again to the words: *Ring around the rosy.* A reference to the red, boil-like marks that appeared on the skin of the plague victims. *Pocket full of posies.* In those times it was thought that 'vapors' were a cause of the plague, and some thought carrying certain flowers would ward off the vapors. *Ashes, ashes.* A reference either to the blackened skin of those nearing death or to the ashes of the bodies that were burned. *We all fall down.* Fairly self-explanatory, don't you think?''

He leaned against the lectern, one hand still grasping his cane. "The Black Death was an event that wiped out entire villages and families and caused such death and terror that it is remembered even to this day by humanity, through the four lines of a simple children's nursery rhyme, passed on from generation to generation.''

Someone in the room coughed and Colonel Webb glared at Hagopian. "You just repeated a message over five hundred years old that had been given to you as a child, Mr. Hagopian. Don't you ever think that the past means nothing.''

* * *

Though it had been some time since I had last been there, I remembered the drive fairly well and got to my destination easily enough. All the time I was driving, I was chastising myself for wrong decisions and wrong choices. I had let events maneuver, overwhelm, and control me, and with that lack of control, I had let some things slide. That hadn't been particularly bright of me, and I didn't like it. In my former job at the five-sided palace, it would have been enough to have gotten me fired.

I made the correct turns this Thursday morning and went down Rye Lane in Lawrence, Massachusetts, and this time the small homes with smaller yards looked almost fake, as if they were part of some large amusement park, being more at home in the flat swamps of Florida than in the overbuilt and slightly wooded hills of northern Massachusetts. As I went down the road I checked the gas gauge of the Range Rover. Almost on empty. I would have to gas up soon.

I parked in front of number sixteen, the light yellow house where Lynn Germano had once lived, and a place I should have come to again before now. The late-model blue Buick was parked in the cement driveway. I got out of my Range Rover and looked at the windows of the house. They seemed empty.

I went up the short walk to the front door. I felt clean but slightly anxious, as if I knew I would be soiled this day. The last time I was here I had left my card, covering the name *Germano* in its little slot on the side of the door. My card was gone and the name was still there, covered with clear tape.

I rang the doorbell and waited, seeing my faint reflection in the plastic of the storm door. No screens. I wondered if Mr. Germano had been remiss in putting the screens up, or if he had been too busy during the past few weeks. The latter was my guess. I now believed that he had been quite busy. I heard footsteps coming down a hallway, heading to the door, and I felt myself stand straighter. I was armed with two weapons that morning, my .32 Browning in my ankle holster and my business card from *Shoreline*, which was in my fingers.

The same woman from last time answered, opening the door with a quizzical look, which changed to sullen resignation when she recognized me. Mrs. Germano's face was still puffy and pale, but her curly gray hair was freshly combed. She had on light green polyester slacks, open-toe gardening shoes, and a yellow pullover blouse. A pair of eyeglasses was suspended from a thin chain around her neck, joining another chain that held a silver crucifix.

"I thought I told you that we didn't want to talk to you," she said, her voice soft but harsh, and she started to close the door. "Go away before I call the police."

I wasn't fond of myself but I said, "Mrs. Germano, in one week's time my magazine will be on the newsstands, and it's going to have a story about Lynn's involvement with prostitution at Tyler Beach, unless you can convince me otherwise."

That and a few other words and lies got me into the house, and by the time that had happened, my feelings had come true. I felt grimy. The things I do.

The living room looked like it had been part of a federal dust-control experiment, for not one throw cushion, not one couch doily, and not one Hummel sculpture on the mantelpiece above the closed-off fireplace was out of place. The floor was hardwood and brightly polished.

I sat on a light green couch that had a pebbly fabric that feels awful if you're wearing shorts, and she sat across from me in a matching chair. There were two other matching chairs and a stereo system that looked like it was top of the line when a Georgia peanut farmer was president, and there was a dusty GE television set in one corner. There were some framed photographs on the wall, on the television set, and on the mantelpiece. Some showed a much younger Mrs. Germano with a man I guessed was her husband. There were two or three photographs of a gangly and youthful Lynn Germano, and a framed one that looked like a high school photograph, Lynn's blond hair and skin flawless. On the television set was a faded photograph of a couple holding a baby. There was a built-in bookshelf on the far wall, and from most of the dust jackets it looked like the books came either from *Reader's Digest* or a book-of-the-month club.

Besides the hallway I had come through, there was another door in the living room, which led off to the kitchen, and from there, I could make out the sound of a television.

From the kitchen area, a male voice: "Who is it, dear?"

Mrs. Germano called back, "Just a magazine man, Tom. He'll be gone shortly." She turned to me and her eyes were tearing up, and in a form of alchemy I think all middle-aged women share, a wad of blue tissue had appeared in her fist.

She said, "He'll be out here in a minute or two, but let's see what we can get out of the way before that happens. What do you know about Lynn?"

I said, "The basics, Mrs. Germano. That she was involved in some criminal activities involving prostitution, and those activities resulted in her death."

She brought the tissue up to her mouth and gave a deep sigh, and murmured, "God, the things that Tom and I did for her, and nothing worked, Mr. Cole. Nothing worked. She was a wild one right from the start. Fights with the neighborhood kids, stealing things from stores, lying and cheating at school." She looked up at me and it was like she didn't know if she could smile or not. "Do you know, in fourth grade, she was sent home because she damn near bit the ear off another fourth grader?"

"It sounds like it must have been difficult," I said, and I knew I had said the wrong thing, for she gave me a scornful look.

"I know what you're thinking, big-shot magazine writer,"

she said fiercely. "You're thinking that Tom and I were ignorant mill workers from Lawrence, that all we did was beat Lynn up and didn't do things right by her. Maybe we were religious freaks, right? Or drunks? And she rebelled against us because we were so strict. Right? That's what you're thinking. Well, it didn't happen that way. We worked with her, we watched over her homework, and we took her to doctors and psychiatrists and counselors. We spent thousands of dollars, Mr. Cole, thousands! And for what? She became a cheap whore."

The tissue came back to her face and she seemed to have clenched her teeth. I could still make out the sounds of the television set from another room. I crossed my legs and rested one hand on my thigh, rehearsing in my mind the few steps I would have to take to get at the Browning if the need arose.

I said, "Did you know what she was doing before her death?"

She nodded fiercely. "We had suspicions, Tom and me. She had too much money for a girl her age, and too many nice clothes. We both knew she couldn't make that much money working as a waitress. One night we were talking about it with her, one day that she came back to visit. Tom accused her of dealing drugs. She denied it. He accused her again and they started yelling, and then she ran out that door there and turned and slapped her behind, and she said, 'You want to know, that's where I got my money. Okay? From my ass. You happy now?'"

Mrs. Germano bent over and wiped at her eyes with the tissue. Her voice sounded hollow. "That was the last time we saw her."

"How angry was your husband, Mrs. Germano? Did he know who she worked for?"

She shook her head. "I don't think he knew, though he always swore he'd find out. He couldn't sleep for nights, you know. He'd be laying there, just shaking with anger, and that's all he could talk about. That Lynn was selling herself to older men, and that neither of us could do anything about it."

I cleared my throat and said gently, "Mrs. Germano, has your husband been up to Tyler Beach at all this past month?"

She looked slightly surprised. "No, of course not."

"Are you sure?" I said. "It wouldn't take that long to go to Tyler Beach and then come back to Lawrence. You might not have noticed he had done that, if you were busy doing something else."

With that, Tom Germano came into the living room, and Mrs. Germano turned to me and said, her eyes still shiny with tears, "Mr. Cole, I know what you're thinking, and I'm positive. He's never gone up there."

I nodded. She was right. Tom Germano came in almost silently, for he was in a wheelchair.

23

TOM GERMANO LOOKED A FEW YEARS OLDER
than his wife. He had on a checked flannel
shirt and a light orange blanket tucked about his waist. Both
of his legs seemed to end just above the knees. His shirtsleeves
were rolled up his thick wrists, and his upper chest looked
muscular. His face was flushed and he had the beginnings of
wattles underneath his chin; his gray-black hair was slicked
back and parted to one side. His pale blue eyes were rheumy
but focused on me quickly enough. Balanced in his lap was a
cocktail glass; an ice cube and an olive floated in the glass.
When he stopped the wheelchair he picked up his drink and
took a sip.

He said, "My first of the day, even if it is in the morning.
My own rules, you know. One in the morning, one in the
afternoon, and one after dinner. Not much to do around here
except read and watch the goddamn television, and all I've
been watching right now is one of those talk shows for fat
housewives whose husbands don't ball 'em enough. You ever
watch those programs?"

"No, I can't say that I have," I said.

He nodded. "They suck, most of 'em. But you gotta have something to get you through the day. I'd offer you a drink, 'cept you might be offended, and right about now, I think you're a son of a bitch, and I don't drink with sons of bitches."

I shrugged. "That sounds fair enough."

He had a small, sly smile. "Not much seems to get you riled."

"But some things do."

"I imagine," he said, replacing the glass in his lap. "I've been listening some to what's going on, Mr. Lewis Cole. Why the hell are you here?"

"Like I told your wife, I'm working on a story for my magazine," I said, not bothering to repeat the lie that it was a story ready for publication—lead time for any magazine article is several months. "It involves Lynn and what happened to her up in Tyler. I'm just trying to find out what went on, find out from you two what I can."

He hunched his shoulders forward a bit. "Magazine writer. Bah. Almost as bad as newspaper writers. You're all the same. Just the other day Sarah made the mistake of talking to a newspaper writer and when I found out about it, I tossed the little witch out. I may not have any legs but I believe I can still cause you harm, Mr. Cole."

Sarah Germano was scrunched up on the couch, not saying a word, just holding the blue ball of tissue to her face.

I said, "I believe that you can probably attempt just that, Mr. Germano. Tell me. That newspaper writer you tossed out, was she from the Tyler *Chronicle?*"

He nodded. "Yep. Said we had to talk to her and I told her, miss, I don't even have to subscribe to your goddamn newspaper."

Paula Quinn. She had said she had been working on something she didn't want to tell me about. Had it been her visit to the Germanos? Had she learned something she wouldn't tell me? Or was it something else?

Tom Germano went on. "Let me tell you a little story about

newspapers, Mr. Cole. You ever hear about the great Labor Day miracle, about ten or so years ago, happened near here on I-four-ninety-five?''

"Tom," Sarah admonished, and I said, "No, I haven't."

"Well," he said, a delighted look on his face. "You're pretty fortunate, being here and talking to one of the actual participants in this great Labor Day miracle, for that's what the newspapers called it. It was a Labor Day weekend and I was hauling freight to Worcester, heading along Four-ninety-five when some drunk bastard cuts me off. Well, I nearly have to stand on my brakes to stop and the load starts swinging out of control, and I slam right into a Volkswagen some young momma was driving with her infant daughter.''

He nodded and picked up his drink from his lap and took a satisfied sip. "Well. We fuse together and go screaming off the roadway, all crumpled up and tumbling. When the firefighters and state police showed up, momma was pretty bung up, with a broken arm and some broken ribs, and the usual cuts and scrapes. Me, well, I'm so twisted up that by the time they squeeze me out of the cab, the butchers up at Lawrence Memorial take off my legs, right above the knees.''

"Tom," came the quiet sound from the couch. It was so quiet then that I could hear flies, buzzing around outside, and the sound of a small airplane.

"But that wasn't the miracle," Tom said. "The miracle was when they ripped that Volkswagen apart and found that momma's little girl, sittin' in her car seat, still holding onto her doll, and without a cut or a scratch. My, how the newspapers loved that story. The miracle of Labor Day. They took photos of me, bandaged and doped up in my hospital bed, with the baby sittin' on my chest. A local bank even started a fund drive for me, 'cause my driving days were over, and they managed to raise me one thousand and fourteen dollars. Remember that, Sarah? One thousand and fourteen dollars. I could still show you the check stub.''

Another nod. Another sip of the drink. "Then the newspapers went onto something else and that girl's momma decided miracles weren't enough, so she sued me and the insurance company, and soon we're on welfare and food stamps, and well, your newspapers weren't so interested in that story anymore. So you can fairly tell, Mr. Cole, that I'm not too fond of newspapers, magazines, or your goddamn Tyler, New Hampshire. Hate the place. Wish I never heard of it. Tyler and whatever's come out of Tyler has caused me and Sarah grief and cost us money."

I looked over at Sarah and she was nodding her head, her jaw set grimly, and she looked at me and said, "Tom's right. Oh, he's still torn up about what happened back then and what happened to Lynn, but he's right. Nothing good's ever come out of Tyler for us."

"Damn right," Tom said, raising up his glass. "Especially that little terror Lynn. Everything we did for her . . . It was bad blood in her, Sarah, that's what I've always said."

I looked at the two of them and said, "What do you mean by that?"

Tom grumbled as he drank from his glass and Sarah dabbed at her eyes and said, "Well, you know, Lynn was originally from Tyler, before she came here."

"She was?"

In the same instant I'm asking the question I'm looking again at the photograph on the television set, of a couple holding an infant. The woman looks vaguely like Sarah, but the man looks nothing like Tom Germano.

Sarah nodded. "Lynn wasn't our daughter, Mr. Cole. She was our niece."

Tom swallowed and finished off his drink. "She was just a babe when her real parents got killed, back in 1975. Lynn was with her grandmother on New Year's Eve that year, while her parents—Mike and Beth Dumont—they was killed in a house fire at a party in Porter. They were partying and drinking so they spent the night, and them and another woman died in the fire, and a couple of others damn near got killed, too."

Sarah nodded in remembrance and said, "Beth was my sister, you know, and after she and Mike died, well, there wasn't any place for little Lynn to go. So she came here."

She got up from the couch and said, "See? There's their picture over there. And let's see . . ." She started tracing the spines of the books on the shelf near the television set, standing up on her toes, and then she took down a slim volume, light green and slightly dusty, with a gold-embossed cover that said *The Tyler Warrior: 1953.* She opened the book up and handed it over to me and said, "See? Class sweethearts, and that they were. They got married only two years after this picture was taken."

The picture was on a page with familiar captions, from a long-ago time. Class clowns. Class brains. Most likely to succeed. And class couple was Mike Dumont and Beth Lajoie, parents of Lynn Germano, who would die in that town more than thirty years later. Even at that young age, when the photo was taken, there was evidence of the facial structure and smile of Lynn Germano in the photo of her mother. Mike was thick and stolid looking, with his black hair greased back, his arm around Beth's shoulders, almost pulling her too close to him.

Sarah sighed and sat back on the couch and said, "Beth was my older sister, but only by a year. She and Mike had worked so hard to get a child, and they were so happy when Lynn was born. And what a tragedy, to have your parents taken away at such an early age. That's probably why Lynn was such a hell-raiser, you know. She never really thought of Tom and me as her real parents, even though we had adopted her and she had our name."

"Bad blood," Tom Germano grumbled. "It was all in the blood. Your sister Beth was a good sort but that Mike was a sour one. Always getting himself in trouble."

I flipped through the yearbook and got to the senior high

school photos. There were Beth Lajoie and Mike Dumont, looking almost the same as they did in their class sweethearts photo. Beth had been active in home-ec and the Future Club, and her goal was to see the world and have a family. Mike had played football and his goal was to make a lot of money. I rubbed at the slick pages, thinking about where all of these children were now. In 1953 black-and-white television was still the rage and a war was being ended in a far-off country called Korea, and cars were beginning to have fins, and America's rich place in the world was secure and safe. My God, the years they had lived through.

I touched the book again, and then looked at the cover, running my fingers across the embossed gold letters. For some reason the book seemed familiar to me, and with a sudden chill seizing my spine, I knew why. I had seen one like it, only about a week ago, in a quiet, deserted house on Clipper Lane on Tyler Beach. I returned to the seniors' photos, and there he was. One Henry Desmond.

"Sweet Jesus," I breathed.

And I looked again, and after a minute or so, I found the photo of one Alice Gilliam, who was later to marry a Navy man named Crenshaw, and who would live in a big old house at the end of Weymouth's Point in Tyler Beach, New Hampshire.

24

ON THE DRIVE NORTH ALONG I-495 BACK TO
New Hampshire, I managed to keep my
speed at 55 miles per hour, conscious of the fact that I wanted
to get back to Tyler as fast as possible without being stopped
for speeding by a Massachusetts State Police trooper. I was also
conscious of the fact that not only was I in a state where first-
degree murderers sentenced to life in prison regularly got weekend paroles but also that I of all people would be considered
a dangerous criminal, since I was carrying an unregistered
handgun in my ankle holster, and the law in this state calls for
a mandatory year sentence for carrying an unregistered firearm.

And I think the excuse I would give to any state police trooper
who stopped me wouldn't quite make it: that I had suspected
that a legless man in a wheelchair was involved in the deaths
of his daughter and two other people in Tyler, New Hampshire,
and that I had carried the weapon for self-protection.

Hell, even I wouldn't believe it.

So though I was keeping the speed legal and feeling quite
stupid at the same time, I also felt a tingle of anticipation along
my arms and my back. I had gotten a connection, tenuous and

unusual as it might be. Henry Desmond and Alice Crenshaw and the parents of Lynn Germano all knew each other. So the killer—or killers—were following some sort of agenda, some sort of guideline. Unfortunately for that particular thought, Oliver Mailloux had not been a student at Tyler—he had told me earlier that he had moved to Tyler from Massachusetts to own and operate the Palace Diner and the St. Lawrence Seaway.

Still, there was something there, a lot more than what I had started out with that morning, or last week, even. Since I had first seen the swollen corpse of Lynn Germano, gently swaying from the end of a rope in her cottage on Dogleg Avenue, the whole matter had been a case study in frustration. It was like I had been traveling down a country road at night in a fog and had come to a brick wall. I couldn't see over and around the brick wall, so there I had sat, counting the bricks and examining their surfaces, until the morning had come and the fog had burned away, and I had found a path around the wall and there before me was an intersection, with many paths and roads leading away into the distance.

So I had a lot of work to do this late morning, a lot of roads to examine, and many people to see.

Interstate 495 intersects with I-95 north, and a moment or two after passing back into New Hampshire (and thereby also being safe from any weapons charge), I increased my speed and inserted a cassette tape into the Range Rover's tape deck, listening again to the radio traffic from that night:

"Tyler police, your call is being recorded."

"There's a body at Twelve Dogleg Avenue."

The click of a phone being disconnected, and then: "Hello? Hello?"

A pause, and the dispatcher's voice deepened, then, "Tyler D-one?"

"Tyler D-one, go ahead."

"Tyler D-one, report to twelve Dogleg, possible ten-fifty-four."

Damn. Still something familiar about that voice.

I took the first exit off I-95, which brought me to the two-lane Route 1 in Falconer. I made a left turn at the exit and headed north, passing by the gates to the Falconer Station nuclear power plant and a number of shops in the process. Along the two short miles of Route 1 in Falconer, there are a number of stores and outlets, and you can rent an adult movie, pawn your gold jewelry, do your grocery shopping, get a tattoo, buy takeout Chinese food, or purchase a gun.

Since I was interested in none of these particular activities, I kept going north, passing through Tyler Falls in the process and going by a carefully groomed town common bordered on its four sides by large black cannon. Again I listened to the tape, and again it seemed I knew who it was, even though I couldn't tell if it was male or female.

Beyond Tyler Falls Route 1 levels out, passing through the wide expanse of the salt marsh, which surrounds it on both sides. It was just past noon and it seemed to be mid-tide, and the traffic was fairly light. To the east were the power lines coming out of the Falconer nuclear power plant, and about two miles away from the power lines were the low buildings of Tyler Beach, where I would soon be going.

But first I was heading into the center of Tyler. There were some things that needed checking. Oliver Mailloux had a business partner, Derek Cooney had told me, someone who had fronted him money for his editing equipment, someone who had even sampled what Lynn Germano had to offer. At the Tyler Town Hall I would talk to Clyde Meeker, the assessor who had helped me the first time I was hunting for information on Oliver Mailloux, and a man who knew who was doing business with whom in Tyler. Then a quick check with Betsy Tyler, selectman and friend of Alice Crenshaw, to see what she might know about the 1953 senior class at Tyler High School, to see who was still in the area, still active, and who might know something, something about a connection between the bodies and a missing person from the past few weeks at Tyler Beach.

Then to Diane Woods with what I had learned. No matter her feelings toward me this week, I'm sure she would welcome the information. Hell, maybe she would even rummage through the police department archives for me to look at the file on the house fire that killed Lynn Germano's parents in 1975 in Porter. Was it an accident, or had there been a suspicion of arson back then?

I passed over the town line, going into Tyler, heading toward the town hall and Clyde Meeker and the town records. But then I saw a street sign to the left and quickly made the turn, going onto Hillside Road, part of the Towler Hill section of Tyler.

For living on Hillside Road was one Jack Fowler, chairman of the board of the selectmen.

And president of the Tyler Beach Chamber of Commerce. He could probably tell me who had been working with Oliver Mailloux.

The road ahead seemed fairly open.

Jack Fowler lives about a half-mile down Hillside Road in a light brown split-level garrison that is on the left-hand side, on a fairly good-sized lot of land. His light blue Lincoln Town Car was in the driveway and I pulled in behind it. The lawn was ringed by shrubs and I went up the gray flagstone path to a set of concrete steps that were sided by black decorative ironwork. I rang the doorbell three times and Jack came to the door, his face reddened, breathing a bit heavily. He had on cream-colored slacks, a tan belt, a bright yellow polo shirt with the obligatory little alligator, and black tasseled loafers.

"Sorry for being out of breath," he said, letting me in. "You caught me downstairs, in the basement, and I don't get much exercise nowadays. What can I do for you? Need something more for that piece about me and the Chamber?''

He laughed as he brought me into the living room, which was just off a small entryway. To the right of the entryway was what looked like a study of some sort; the living room was large, with a kitchen visible through an open arch, then another hallway leading farther into the house. There was a glass-covered coffee table and two black vinyl couches facing each other, and another set of bookshelves. On the coffee table was an open copy of that day's *Chronicle*. Right at my elbow as I came into the living room was a metal-and-glass bookcase that had some ceramic bowls and figures. The walls were white plaster and had two paintings of sailing ships, looking like antique treasures from New England but most likely made in a paint shop in Hong Kong or Tijuana.

I said, ''That's not far off, Jack. I'm looking for some information about someone who was active in the Chamber. Oliver Mailloux.''

Jack sprawled out on one couch and grimaced, running a hand across his slicked-back white hair and crossing his legs. I sat across from him on the other couch, listening to the squeak my pants made against the vinyl and wondering why anyone still bought vinyl couches.

''Oliver Mailloux,'' Jack said. ''Yuck. Bad business, Lewis. Very bad business, what happened to him yesterday. That and the other nonsense we've put up with these past couple of weeks can only hurt everybody down at the beach. Hell, some of the families in my cottages call me up, worried and wanting better locks for their doors. And do you think new locks are cheap to come by? Jesus. Anyway, what do you want to know? Is this for an article in your magazine?''

''It just might be,'' I said. ''How well did you know Oliver?''

He stroked his fleshy chin and said, ''There's scores of people in the Chamber, Lewis, do you know that? Everyone, from the owner of the Lafayette House—probably the most prestigious hotel in this area—to the guy who owns Ted's Fried Dough Stand down on A Street. It's hard to keep track of them all, but yeah, I knew Oliver somewhat. More of a nodding acquaintance than anything else."

"Did you know who his business partner was?" I asked.

Jack's eyes lit up and he said, "Business partner? Oliver Mailloux? That's the funniest thing I've heard this morning, Lewis."

"Why's that?"

He shifted on the couch and then got up, brushing at his shirt. " 'Cause Oliver Mailloux was the type of guy who'd charge his own grandmother double for a hotel room, that's why. I don't know of anyone who'd have wanted to sit next to him at a Chamber meeting, never mind going into business with him. He was one shifty character. You know, there were rumors that he was involved with some not-so-legal deals with some guys in Montreal, and that's what got him killed. You ever hear of that?"

"A bit," I said. So much for Derek Cooney's story about a partner for Oliver Mailloux. I thought for a moment of how to track down Derek, and I decided it would be almost impossible. He was on the run, sure that Felix Tinios was chasing him, and he had probably gone to ground somewhere miles away.

"Yeah. A bit." He smiled and said, "Excuse me for a moment, will you? I was having lunch downstairs when you called and I want to bring up the dirty dishes. It's much cooler down there and I hate leaving stuff just sitting around."

When he left he went down the hallway, and I heard the *tromp-tromp* of his feet as he went down to the basement. I picked up the *Chronicle* and looked at it for a moment. Paula Quinn had a story there about Oliver Mailloux's murder, and I scanned it, finding nothing new. But something tickled at my mind, and I thought: Paula.

Alice Crenshaw. Henry Desmond. Lynn Germano and the

Palace Diner. Oliver Mailloux. Paula Quinn knew all of them. Had known all of them before anything had happened to them.

Paula Quinn. Writing stories to get out of this town . . .

I put the paper down and stood up, wondering if I should leave right then, but I decided not to. I still wanted to talk to Jack about Oliver, and then I wanted to ask him a couple of questions about Paula. About the dinners after the selectmen's meetings, which she would often attend. To area restaurants, including the Palace Diner. Good God. My hands were almost shaking at the thought.

To keep occupied I walked around the room, looking at the ceramics and the awful paintings on the walls. I went through the entryway and into the study and saw a lot of business files, a desk covered with papers and folders, an adding machine with a long looping tape of paper in one corner. Jack Fowler's office, no doubt. On the walls were certificates of business achievement, another bad painting, this time of a lighthouse, and an old photo showing a much younger and thinner Jack Fowler standing between an older and a younger man, in front of a Ford dump truck. On the door of the dump truck was painted "Fowler & Sons, Construction." Jack Fowler's secret previous life, before he started buying and selling properties?

The sound of feet on stairs came back and I returned to the living room, just as Jack came back carrying an empty plate, silverware, and a glass.

"I like having lunch here, you know?" he said. "People who work for me, when I go out to eat they think I'm shmoozing at some restaurant, having expense account lunches, but instead I relax here and watch some television, and I decompress and unwind and get ready for the afternoon. Listen, can I get you a drink?"

I said, "How about a lemonade?"

"Two lemonades it is." He went into the kitchen, and I looked down at the *Chronicle* and tried not to think about what was going on. Paula. I examined the bookshelf and got past the usual paperbacks and the dusty and unread encyclopedia, and I saw a familiar thin green volume. Jack came out of the kitchen as I held it in my hands, and the dust from the book seemed to settle in my mouth. *The Tyler Warrior: 1953.* I flipped through the senior pages and the underclass photos, and my tightened chest relaxed when I didn't see Jack's photo.

"Your wife's?" I asked, holding it up to him.

He shook his head, putting the lemonade glasses on the coffee table. "No. It belonged to my older sister, Karen."

I flipped through the pages again, puzzled, for I was sure I hadn't seen a Fowler in any of the photos, and Jack picked up both glasses and said, "Jesus, sorry about that, Lewis. I forgot the ice."

He went down the hallway. I went to the front of the year-book and just beyond the title page was a large photo of a young girl, bordered in black. Above the photo was a line: "Dedicated to Our Classmate," and beneath, KAREN FOWLER in large black letters. There was also an insipid poem about being among one's friends for only a short while and leaving memories for a lifetime, and suddenly I wondered why the hell Jack Fowler hadn't gone into the kitchen. I took a few steps and looked down the hallway and said, "Jack?"

He came out of a bedroom at the end of the hallway, closing the door behind him. He was no longer carrying two lemonade glasses. He was carrying a large black handgun.

I turned and ran.

He shouted something. I didn't care what he said and as I went through the entryway, I pulled down the metal-and-glass shelf of ceramic figures behind me, hoping it would slow him down by a few seconds.

My feet didn't even hit the concrete as I leapt to the front lawn and ran to the Range Rover, willing myself not to look behind me, knowing that to spare a look backward would cost a few seconds, and I knew those were seconds I couldn't spare.

I clambered into the Range Rover and didn't even close the door behind me, just concentrated on starting the engine, and as the engine roared to life, I had already shifted into reverse and was backing out of the driveway.

He made it out of the house, the gun still in his hand, as I got the Range Rover into drive and headed up the street, to Route 1.

I got the door shut just a few feet before the intersection.

At the intersection I stopped, breathing hard, the whole Range Rover filled with a stench, and I felt something curdle inside me as I glanced in my rearview mirror.

A Lincoln Town Car, coming barrel-ass up the road behind me.

I swore and made a right turn, barely missing a light red van that swerved and honked at me and stayed at my side as I missed the turnoff that would have brought me back in a loop to Tyler and Route 51 and Tyler Beach and Diane Woods.

The Range Rover quickly got up to 50 miles an hour, and then I had to slow down, as traffic stretched out before me on Route 1. Another glance in the rearview mirror. The Lincoln Town Car with Jack Fowler and his handgun was three cars back; another van and a pickup truck were between the two of us. In a matter of moments I was back in Tyler Falls, still heading south, and I thought: Make a U-turn, head back into Tyler and to the Tyler police station?

But a U-turn meant slowing down in a store or business parking lot. It meant having to stop in traffic. And it could mean Jack Fowler pulling up next to me and spraying the Range Rover with rounds from his handgun, and as good as the Range Rover is, the body's not built for warding off lumps of jacketed lead coming in at 800 feet per second.

I kept on going south, looking up every moment or so at the rearview mirror. He was still back there, along with the van and the pickup truck.

In the tape deck of the Range Rover, the damn dispatch tape was still running, and then it all made terrible sense.

The traffic lights at Tyler Falls were green and I raced through the intersection. Next stop was Falconer, and I tried to remember where the police station was in Falconer. Two side streets off Route 1, just past the power plant's gates. I could roll up to the Falconer police station, but it was in a residential neighborhood, with narrow side streets and kids playing and people on bicycles. Just a few seconds to stop for a kid running across the street and Jack Fowler would be on me in a moment.

Then there was the weight on my ankle. A shoot-out, in a residential neighborhood? And how accurate would my aim be, knowing there was a man gunning for my head, my body? Damn. I'd be lucky to hit the ground.

Another green light in Falconer. The restaurants, the tattoo parlors, the adult bookstore, the pawnshops, and the shopping plaza went by in a blur, as if they were cardboard cutouts.

There was the interstate exit off Falconer. Of course. Get on I-95 and start heading north or south, and slam the accelerator down, pressing it with both feet if necessary. At speeds in excess of a hundred miles an hour, there was bound to be a state trooper or three in each state whose radar would start screaming, and if that happened, I would gladly slow down and surrender myself to their custody, no matter how illegal they thought my handgun might be.

The traffic light near the south gate of the Falconer Station nuclear power plant turned red and I stopped, about ten cars away from the lights. The exit to the interstate was just ahead. My hands were shaking on the steering wheel and I kept my eyes on the Lincoln Town Car. It was still there, three cars back.

I could open the window and shout that the man in the car back there had a gun, was dangerous, and trying to kill me.

And no doubt the good people of Falconer walking or driving by would nod and say to their companion, Jesus, look at that drunk in that four-wheeler, and it's not even two o'clock yet.

I looked ahead. The light turned green. And I looked down to the dashboard.

The needle on the gas gauge was resting on empty.

I kept on going south, passing by the interstate's exits. I couldn't chance trying to race either north or south on the highway, and then sputter to a stop as the Range Rover ran out of gas. Jack Fowler would be right behind me, smiling all the while, I'm sure. I spared another glance. The pickup truck had made a turn into a Getty gas station and now there was just the van between me and Jack Fowler. Gas. Obviously there wasn't enough time for a fuel-up, and I made a vow then to never let the Range Rover's tank drop below half full.

If the van turned off, would Jack try for a shot at me while driving? Trying not to think too much about it, I sat lower in my seat, trying to shrink my profile, half-expecting to hear the sound of the rear window shattering.

I passed by other stores and restaurants. People were walking in and out of the stores this fine June day, having some worries, no doubt, about family matters and work and money, but I would gladly trade my worries for theirs at any price. I suppose I could drive up among them and say a madman is after me, but that might not stop Jack Fowler. I'm not sure what would. He could start shooting away and to hell with any innocents. And if he hit me, well, it would be the word of a respected businessman and selectman against an out-of-towner who supported himself by strange means and lived alone on the beach.

Probably rate a story or three in the *Chronicle*, and that would be it. Besides the obituary, Paula might do a nice feature about me, and Jack Fowler would probably come in for tough questioning and spin a fantastic tale of how I had threatened his life in some way, and by this time next year, I would be forgotten.

And who knew who'd be living in my house by then.

I came within view of a set of traffic lights that marked the intersection of Route 1 and Route 286, and which was also the state line between New Hampshire and Massachusetts. Salisbury, the most northern community in Massachusetts, was just a few feet away. And where was their police station?

Another rearview glance. Lincoln Town Car still there.

I couldn't remember.

At the lights I turned left, heading east, to the beaches.

Some of Route 286 is in Massachusetts, and the two-lane road cuts right through the marshes, just like Route 51 farther north. I sped along, the needle hovering just above fifty miles per hour, as I nearly hugged the bumper of a light gray Buick Regal ahead of me. On both sides of Route 286 were side roads that led either into Salisbury or back into New Hampshire and Falconer, but I focused on the road ahead. Route 286 ended at an intersection with Route 1-A at Salisbury. A quick turn to the left and I would be heading north, and within a few seconds or less, I would pass over the state line back into New Hampshire and could be pulling into the front lot of the Tyler police station within minutes.

With some quick steps on my part, I'd be inside the station and yelling at someone in uniform by the time Jack Fowler brought his Town Car to a stop, and I doubt if even he would have enough of the whispering creatures inside him necessary to shoot at me inside a police station.

After a half-mile Route 286 was clear in the marsh, and far off to the left was the dull gray of the concrete dome and buildings of Falconer Unit 1 and the red rusted dome of Falconer Unit 2. I'm sure some of the people within speaking range were terrified of having a nuclear power plant in their backyards but probably wouldn't even bat an eye at thinking of a vehicle chase with two armed men in their neighborhood. Something typical, no doubt. Just another day in Falconer.

I passed by MacGregor's Lobster Pound, where a proud Sarah

Lockwood had thrown away my help. Not a bad choice on her part, considering how mistaken I had been.

At the intersection of Route 1-A and Route 286, the light was just changing to yellow as I flashed through, and I looked up to the mirror again and saw that two more cars were now between me and Jack Fowler. God bless the driving terror that was the Massachusetts driver. Two of them had just put themselves between me and a man who was following me with a gun, and I took back every single joke I had ever made about Massachusetts motorists and their driving.

The road ahead to Tyler Beach was clear. I pressed down on the accelerator even more.

And then I had to hit the brakes. Traffic in front of me was slowing down, the taillights mocking me.

Jesus.

I came to a stop, as did the cars in front of me and to the rear. I checked the mirror. The shape of Jack Fowler was still there in the Town Car. I bent over and touched the ankle holster. What was going on?

Up ahead was the Felch Memorial Bridge, and then I made out the span as it was being raised. Drawbridge time. And I could make out the bobbing mast of a sailboat heading out to the Atlantic Ocean.

Great timing.

Mirror check: Jack Fowler was still there.

The mast went out to the channel leading to the ocean; it belonged to a fair-sized sailboat, several feet longer than Diane Woods's *Miranda*. Diane. My, oh my, I certainly hope you're working today, Dianne. To the right were some houses and an ice cream stand and farther out toward the ocean, the dunes and tiny Falconer Beach. To my left were some condo units, a seafood restaurant, a bar, and the wide and open expanse of the marshes, ending a couple of miles west at a line of trees near the nuclear power plant.

The span was still up. The Town Car was still occupied.

Hell of a long time for the bridge to be up. No other boats were in view. Nothing was approaching, either from the harbor or the channel.

Horns started blaring. People started stepping out of their cars. Then I knew.

The bridge was stuck open. Again.

Damn.

I checked the mirror.

The Town Car was empty.

I swung around and saw Jack Fowler walking up the line of cars, on the passenger's side, holding something close to his leg, everybody ignoring him, and I threw the Range Rover in park, opened the door, and started running, not daring to look behind me.

Across the street was a guardrail, which I sprinted over, and an embankment leading down to a small series of dunes. I tumbled a bit down the embankment, jamming my legs into the soft dirt. I ran and dodged, trying to get some of the rolling mounds of sand and beach grass behind me. Before me was the open marsh, as far as I could see, as far as I could run.

25

To the north was the expanse of water
and coves that marked both Falconer and
Tyler harbors, and if I kept on going in that direction to the
tidal beaches by those harbors, I would be as exposed as a lead
soldier on a tabletop. Before me and to the west was a good
square mile or two of tidal marshland, scoured out by glaciers
tens of thousands of years ago and now interconnected with
gullies, ditches, streams, and canals that were dug here in the
1920s in an ill-fated attempt to drain the area for farmland or
some damn thing.

I crouched low in an open ditch, in the green-gray stinking
mud of the marsh, and waited for a moment, knowing that
my Range Rover and Jack Fowler's Town Car were in the
middle of traffic on Route 1-A, and that eventually traffic would
get moving and someone would call the cops about the two
idiots who had abandoned their cars in the middle of the road
in the middle of the afternoon and had run into the marsh.

That's what I was hoping for, but in the meantime, I wasn't
going to wait for the cops or cavalry to come to my rescue. I
meant to keep moving. I raised my head a few inches, and

between the grass blades I saw the shape of Jack Fowler, about a hundred yards away, coming in my direction. I crouched down and started moving, heading to the treeline so far away to the west, moving past debris in the gully that came from years of neglect and trash dumping from people who didn't know and couldn't spell the word *environmentalist*. There were broken lobster traps and old bottles, bits and pieces of rope, and a dull orange lobster buoy, and as the gully widened into a streambed, there was even the rotting hulk of a rowboat, left there to be swamped twice a day with the salt tide that came through these marshes.

I stopped and raised my head again. Jack was still there, a bit closer, panting, looking slightly ridiculous standing in the soggy soil and the marsh grasses in his cream-colored slacks and bright yellow polo shirt, with his black tasseled loafers. Dressed more for a day at the store than a day on the marshes. Ridiculous, yes, but the ridiculous factor was quite over-whelmed by the gun in his hand.

After ducking down again I headed along the muddy banks of the streambed, my shoes squishing in the mud. Off from the beach area I heard the sound of sirens, but I tried not to let the sound cheer me up. Could be a fire truck or an ambulance, or a cruiser from Tyler or Falconer, responding to a traffic accident. Nothing more.

Yeah? Then what about the two abandoned vehicles out there on Route 1-A? Surely there'd be cops going there, to find out what the hell was going on.

Sure. Two cars, blocking traffic, as tourists try to get to the lovely sights and sounds of Tyler Beach. I had an idea of what was probably going on, as Jack and I floundered around this 10,000-year-old marsh. A bunch of college students, confident that nothing would get in the way of their beer and broads, were probably pushing both vehicles off to the side of the road. Later on during the day, they'd be ticketed and towed, and end up in a storage garage in Falconer, next to cars that had been parked in handicapped spaces by athletic drivers.

I didn't want to think which one of us would be paying tow and storage fees later on this day.

I halted. The stream bed was curving around, bringing me closer to Jack Fowler. Damn. I raised my head again and there he was.

"Cole?" he called out. "You're out there, Cole. I know it. You shouldn't have started running like that."

I sat back against the mud, the wet stickiness going through my shoulder blades. Mud and water had been splattered all along my tan chinos and my loafers looked gray now, instead of light brown. Not very good footwear to go running through a muddy marsh. I took a series of deep breaths, trying to un-squeeze the knot that was in my stomach. Mosquitoes and flies buzzed around my head and arms and legs, and the stench of hundreds of years of decay and mud and the saltwater seemed as thick as fog.

"Cole," he said, his voice fair and strong. "I had to do it. Had to do it, because they killed my sister Karen. Killed her and rolled up her body in a tarp and dumped her in the marsh like she was trash or something. But she wasn't trash, Cole. She was my sister, and they took her away from me."

The Body in the Marsh, I thought. And Jack's voice sounded like he was still getting closer. I thought about moving in either direction along the streambed, hugging close to the embankment, and trying to outflank the fool. Great idea, except that the banks of the tidal stream were not more than three or four feet high. All he had to do was to stand at the edge and look down and he'd see me, fair enough and easy to hit.

With the streambed looping back to where Jack was, the only thing left was the embankment in front of me. The marsh was crisscrossed with canals and gullies and other streambeds. Up and over and some running, and then I'd duck down again.

Unless this was one of the sections of the marsh that was

flat and grassy and unscarred by streams or drainage ditches.
Right.

I got up in a crouch, sloshed across the low water and mud
of the stream, then ran up the other embankment and I was
on the marshland, back in the bright sunlight. I ran across the
knee-high grass, moving zigzag, feeling the air across the wet
mud on my back, seeing a Coors beer can in the grass and the
lines of wooden stakes—the staddles, where saltmarsh hay had
once been left to dry—and there was a shout of "Cole!" and
a very large boom, and as I dove for the open streambed before
me, something stung my leg.

I rolled and collapsed, breathing harshly, the stench of mud
and something stronger tugging at my nostrils. This streambed
was narrower and was filled with more trash. I sat up, looking
at my lower leg. Something had struck there, either a bullet or
a sharp object, and it hurt. It felt like I was bleeding, for my
leg was warm and something was trickling down its side. The
chino was torn down there and I couldn't tell the damage to
my leg, and right about then, I wasn't much for looking into
it. Winston Churchill had once said that there was nothing
more invigorating than being shot at with no effect, but I was
thinking that sorting my socks would be higher on my own
personal invigoration list, if he didn't mind.

Jack kept on yelling out to me. Prominent businessman and
head selectman and president of the Chamber and killer. Not
what one would call an ordinary mix. What the hell was going
on in that head of his?

"Cole? You might as well stop running, Cole. I'm right behind you, and you know it, don't you?"

Sorry, Jack. No time for replies. Littered along the mud and
water were some soggy lengths of rope and the broken wood
of a lobster trap and a couple of lengths of driftwood. I moved
forward and muttered something dark and foul. This streambed
looped sharply around to the right, and the marsh and grass-
land at the loop came to a sharp point, almost like a peninsula.

If I started following this streambed, it would bring me almost right back to where I started. Right before the gunsights of one Jack Fowler.

I sat back against the mud. No more time for running. I felt dirt under my fingers. Sand. Dead sand. A picture, of the Falconer and Tyler cops, pulling my body from this streambed, my mouth full of dead sand . . .

Sure. Whatever you say. The streambed was running about north to south, and I was sure that Jack was back there, maybe not more than a couple of hundred feet away. Time to get things ready. It was like I was packing up my soul in a trunk and putting it in storage for the winter, for I had been shot at once, and I did not intend to be shot at again. And I was going to do what I had to do.

I tried not to sigh, and I pulled up my right pants leg and reached down to my holster and my .32 Browning, and my fingers clasped around the empty leather.

I closed my eyes and sat back against the stinking mud. Lost. Practically anywhere from here to when I first jumped down the embankment off Route 1-A, my revolver had tumbled out into the grass and soil of the marshes.

Where were those damn cops?

And who had made this damn holster? He or she would be getting a hell of a nasty letter from me.

Right. Let's just work on one thing at a time.

"Cole?"

Damn, that voice seemed closer.

"Cole? Tell me where that crusty witch Crenshaw is hiding out, and I might let you go. Everyone knew that the two of you had something going on. You tell me where she is and I won't hurt you."

My left hand was resting on something wet and rough. I picked it up. Rope. A good length. I started working at it with both hands, untangling it and running it out. A hell of a good length. I took one end of the rope and tied it firmly around a two-foot piece of scrap wood, and then I turned and jammed the wood into the wet soil of the embankment, pushing it in deep with another piece of wood that I used as a brace. I tugged at the rope. The scrap of wood stayed, and the rope remained anchored. I got up, hunched over, trailing the rope behind me, and I sloshed the few short yards along the streambed, where this piece of marshland came to a point. I raised up the rope and then went around the point of land, and back down the opposite streambed, looping the rope behind me, heading in Jack Fowler's direction.

This piece of marshland was only about twenty feet wide from streambed to streambed, and the rope was just barely long enough to stretch across it. I hoped that as the rope moved across the grass, Jack wouldn't see it. I walked a few more feet and stopped. The rope was fairly straight, stretching across the marsh grass. In the mud were the tangled wet feathers and the carcass of a sea gull, and greenhead flies buzzed around the decay.

I let the rope drop and went back to the point of land, popped up my head and yelled, "Jack! Come here if you want to talk!"

He fired again as I dropped down. So much for promises. I went back to the rope, slipping and sliding in the mud. I grabbed its end and looked up and saw a shape running by, and I wrapped the rope around my fist and pulled it taut and up, and in a few seconds, the rope damn near tore off my hands and I heard a gasp and a muffled groan as Jack tripped on the rope and fell.

I clambered over the embankment and only glanced for a moment at Jack, sprawled out on his face on the grass and mud. His cream-colored slacks were spattered with mud, as was his polo shirt. His bare arms looked fleshy and his hands were empty. Where in hell was his gun?

Then I spotted the revolver, about a yard away from his trembling hands, and I picked it up, holding it in both of my hands, conscious that it was quivering in my grasp as if it weighed a ton.

"C'mon, Jack," I managed to gasp out. "Get up."

He didn't. I moved around and saw the blood near his head. My stomach clenched up.

Jack Fowler's throat was impaled on one of the wooden stakes.

Then he groaned and moved, and I stepped back, realizing just then that I was wearing only one shoe. There was an awful sucking sound as he pulled himself up, his face bloody and wet with mud, and he sat up, wheezing and gurgling, both of his hands clasped around his neck. Blood started trickling down his muddy forearms.

He wheezed and coughed and started talking, and I only made out a few words, and most of them were obscene.

"Sorry about that, Jack," I said, backing away from him, weaving and feeling off-balance because of wearing only one shoe and the weight of the gun in my hands. "My mother and I were close but all we did was kiss each other on the cheek. If she were still alive, she'd probably take great offense."

Jack's face was beginning to go pale and he said, "Oh, God, I'm gonna need an ambulance, Cole. I'm cut. I'm cut real bad."

I coughed and tried to ease my breathing, the gun seeming to grow even heavier in my hands. "Give me some answers, and some quick ones, and I'll get you some help. But don't waste your breath, Jack. Tell me about Lynn Germano."

"Cole, please, an ambulance . . ."

"Talk first, and then I'll take care of you, Jack. Now. Lynn Germano."

Even with his whitened face and the blood seeping through his fingers, there was a faint hint of a smile as he talked to me. "Lynn. What a trampy little girl. It's hard working around all that young meat, and not being able to touch 'em. But not Lynn. She let me do anything I wanted." He wheezed some more. "And later, when I found out she was the daughter of Mike and Beth Dumont, well, that gave it an even better tingle, you know? Banging someone young enough to be my daughter . . . and the kid of someone I knew . . ."

"What happened?" I asked. "What made you string her up like that?"

Jack shook his head, moving stiffly because of his hands against his bleeding throat. "I'll deny saying this, you know," he said. "I'm just tellin' you this because I need an ambulance."

"Whatever you say, Jack."

He closed his eyes, talked some more. "That day, I found out the real news about Karen. She hadn't run away. She wasn't living somewhere else. She hadn't drowned. No, she had been dead all those years, rotting away in the marsh. Later I was with Lynn and I started to get angry, Cole. Angry because I knew her parents had been with my sister in high school and they had hurt her. Angry because Lynn was Karen's age, and Lynn would get to live longer and have a happy life. It was all I could think about. Then Lynn started teasing me because I couldn't get it up, and I was so mad, so angry when she laughed at me, and it wasn't fair, not fair at all, that Mike and Beth Dumont's daughter got to live . . ."

He blinked, hands clasped around his neck, and said, "I always knew Karen would come back, that my sister would come back to me, Cole. Last time I saw her, back in 1953, she came up to my bedroom and said she was in trouble, that she was going to get the trouble taken care of and then she'd come back. But she never did." He looked up at me plaintively. "She never came back. My parents and some of her friends thought she had run away, or had even died, but I knew better. I was sure she was alive, and I knew one day, she'd come back to Tyler."

I took another step back. I wanted to close my eyes and just walk away from it all, but I forced myself to stay, to keep him talking. "She was the Body in the Marsh."

Jack only nodded. "I got a friend on the North Tyler police department. When he told me about the ring they found on the body and told me what that ring looked like, then I knew it was Karen. I had given her that ring. So after all those years, she had come back. And let me tell you, Cole, after all those years, I remembered. I knew who she had spent time with. I knew it must have been Henry who got her into trouble. I knew who must've buried her in the marsh. And after taking care of that little tramp, well, it was easy. It was fun. So I kept on going. That damn fisherman was next. Almost got you on his boat, and then at your house. You were sniffing around too much."

I said, "Tell me about Oliver Mailloux, Jack. You were his money man, weren't you? You helped set him up with the video gear."

He blinked and nodded and said clearly, "The bastard tried to blackmail me after I helped set him up. We had a good deal going, both of us making money, and then he got greedy. He said he saw me leave her cottage that night and he said he had a tape of me and that little bitch I strangled. I didn't believe he had any tape, but I strung him along and told him I'd get the money, enough money for him to retire on."

Jack wheezed and coughed out a wad of spit and blood, his hands still firm against his throat. "Hah. Greedy fool. When I showed up, he was expecting cash, and I gave him what he deserved, right to the back of his head."

"Not exactly the way you should treat your voters," I said.

He blinked again. "That was just business, nothing else. The other stuff, that was personal."

"Why Alice Crenshaw?" I said. "Why were you after her?"

He closed his eyes and his eyelids wavered as he opened them again. "I'm in a world of hurt, Cole," he said, his voice getting slow and soggy. "My throat's cut pretty bad. You gotta get help."

I thought of all that had gone on before, from Lynn Germano

to Henry Desmond to even Oliver Mailloux and to this afternoon, and I said, "Sure, Jack. I'll get you some help. You sit
right there."

I walked back across the top of the marshes, carrying his
handgun in my shaking and sweaty hands, and taking my time
as I did so. I think I heard him shout once again, back where
he was sitting with his weakening hands against his throat, but
I may have been mistaken. I didn't change my stride one step,
didn't quicken one bit. Among other things, I had on only a
single shoe.

It hurt to walk.

26

THAT EVENING I HAD A SMALL BANDAGE ON my lower leg that made my shin itch, making me think there might be some marsh fleas stuck in there, but even then, I was feeling fairly comfortable, having dinner aboard the *Miranda*, firmly and safely anchored in Tyler Harbor. The night air was warm, and even though it was past 7 P.M., it was still fairly light out. It was Friday evening, two days since I had left Jack Fowler alone on the open marshes of Tyler and Falconer, New Hampshire.

Diane and I were sitting in the rear cockpit, the small rowboat attached to the stern by a length of line. My legs were stretched out and next to me was a blue EMS knapsack, and inside the knapsack I had a sweater in case it got cooler and some other things. The sails of the *Miranda* were furled and we were in the open cockpit, along with the gas-fired grill that had been set up an hour beforehand. The two of us had dined on barbecued steaks and corn on the cob, and we had eaten by ourselves in the harbor.

The only other boats in the harbor were also moored. To the near east were the lights of Tyler and Falconer beaches, and to the south were the strong lights of the Falconer nuclear power plant. Beyond the shoreline was the marshland where I had run and fallen so many times that Wednesday, and where Jack Fowler was eventually carried out on a Stokes litter, tied in and secure, his face covered by a red blanket.

I sipped at a glass of red wine and raised it in a salute to Diane Woods, and she nodded, smiled, and returned the salute.

"A marvelous meal, Diane. Marvelous."

She laughed, a glass of wine in her own hand. The boat swayed gently in the evening breeze. "Nothing so marvelous about it, Lewis. Just your basic New England summer meal. Anyone could have made it."

"Ah, but there was something about this one that made it very special."

"Which is?"

"Which is that it was made with a smile. Anything else, and in dealing with you, Diane, I might have been concerned about poison."

That made her laugh again, and my sense of contentment grew. It was good to be with her and see that comfortable look. It had been a while.

She said, "When it's all said and done, you did good, Lewis Cole. You did good. But you'll never hear me say that in public."

I drank some more of the wine. I didn't know what kind of bottle it came from or from what country and I didn't particularly care. It tasted fine. That was enough.

I said, "Paperwork pretty much wrapped up on this one, Diane?"

"Hell, no," she said. "Just the preliminary stuff, and I'm still meeting with the state police and the attorney general's office. But I only wish the newspapers and the TV stations would get themselves wrapped up and go somewhere else."

"I know, I've had my own calls." I looked at the wine in my glass and said, "I talked to Betsy Tyler yesterday, about what was going on at Tyler High School back in 1953. She was fuzzy on some of the details but she remembered Karen Fowler. Betsy said she was slightly slow, and was one for doing almost anything to become part of the 'in' crowd. Betsy remembers that the 'in' crowd at Tyler High School that year was particularly rough, and in Karen's quest to become popular, rumor had it that she became pregnant. Soon after that rumor, though, was when she disappeared. Some people thought she moved out to have her baby, and others thought she killed herself. Maybe even drowned. Either way, she was gone. Yearbook committee that year even dedicated the book to her."

Diane held up her glass, holding it delicately between two fingers. "So something bad happened to her, back then in 1953. Maybe the guy who fathered the child was mad at her and beat Karen up, and lost it until she was killed. Or maybe she tried a self-abortion, and that went wrong."

"Maybe so," I said. "Question is, who was the father? Henry Desmond? Maybe Mike Dumont? Or somebody else?"

Diane said, "Whoever it was, he or his friends probably freaked when she was dead, so she ended up in the marsh." She shook her head. "Think about it, Lewis. None of this would have happened except for that greedy developer who was digging where he shouldn't have been. And after her body was found, North Tyler cops said it was hard to figure out what had happened with what was left, except that she was a woman and was wearing a ring."

"With Jack Fowler being the only one around who could identify the ring, since it was his gift," I said.

She shuddered and brought the glass down. "In a way, I hope she was murdered. Imagine, trying to do something to yourself like that, a self-abortion, and then bleeding to death. Talk about horrors. It's like another age, when they used leeches and vapors."

"Hard to believe," I said. A lot of things were hard to believe. A thought came to me, of the plaintive shouts of Jack Fowler as I slowly trudged across the marshes back to my Range Rover, and then I remembered another sight, of a young woman, strung up by her neck, and I felt a little better.

She shifted against the side of the boat. "Yeah, hard to believe. With Jack gone and Lynn Germano's parents dead and Henry Desmond's ghost floating in this harbor, I don't think we'll ever know what happened back here in 1953."

I nodded and said nothing. Earlier this day, I had made another phone call to Betsy Tyler and she had confirmed something for me, something I would not talk about this evening but that would wait until tomorrow.

Diane looked at me strangely, then gazed over my shoulder, as if scared to look at me directly, and said quietly, "What was it like, out there on the marsh?"

"With a half-mad Jack Fowler chasing after me with a gun?" I tried to smile and said, "It was smelly, wet, and quick. That's it. Everything moved very fast. And when I got back to the road, I think I threw up. Nothing thrilling or adventurous, Diane."

"I didn't think so."

"Then you thought right."

We sat quietly in the cockpit of the *Miranda* for a while, and I looked up at the darkening sky, waiting for the first star to appear. Not because I wanted to make a wish or anything, but because it was an event that was predictable, that would happen every night, and I wanted to see it. I needed some predictability right around then.

"We found the dynamite Jack used in blowing up Henry's boat," Diane said.

"Left over from his construction days, right?"

She nodded. "I'm also sure it'll come as no surprise to you that the bullet we took from Oliver Mailloux's skull matched test cartridges fired from Jack Fowler's revolver."

The story had come out yesterday in the *Chronicle* from Paula Quinn about Oliver's "hobby," and I knew that none of the tapes found at the hotel showed Lynn Germano, and that no tapes had been located at Jack Fowler's house. So they had been destroyed by Jack before he and I had that little race out on the marshes. I felt like staying quiet for a while and not raising the interest of Diane and her friends from the state. If the records about Jack and Oliver's financial dealings eventually showed up, so be it. Both of them were far beyond going to trial.

With that in mind I shrugged and said, "Lynn Germano was living in one of Oliver's cottages. Maybe Oliver knew something about the way she died, and that Jack was involved. Blackmail's always a possibility. But I tell you, Diane, we should have known from the very beginning that there was something rotten about Jack Fowler."

She held her glass with both hands. "Oh?"

"Certainly," I said, opening up the knapsack at my side and taking out a Sony cassette player. "Listen to this."

I punched the "play" button and the sounds of the dispatch tape from the night we found a dead Lynn Germano came out from the tiny speaker. Diane rolled her eyes and raised a hand and said, "Please, Lewis, stop playing that crap, will you? I listened to that dispatch tape over and over so much that I've been dreaming about it."

"Sorry," I said. "You've got to listen to it. It won't take long."

So we did, past the time when Diane's voice came across, looking for an ambulance and backup units. When I clicked it off, I said, "Bring back any memories?"

She crossed her legs and said, "Yeah, and none of them are too pleasant. What's the point, Lewis?"

I leaned forward and said, "The night we found the body, Jack Fowler showed up, remember? And what did he say?"

Diane thought for a moment and said, "I think he said something about her ID, if we knew who she was."

"Pretty close. He asked you, did you know anything about the poor girl?"

She smiled. "You were right. I was close."

"Diane," I said, as softly as I could, "Jack got there only a few minutes after we did, right after the ambulance arrived. Listen to the dispatch tape. Not once did you or anybody else mention over the radio that there was a female victim at twelve Dogleg Avenue. Not once. The call into the dispatch only said there was a body at twelve Dogleg. Nothing about whether it was male or female. So how could Jack have known what was in that cottage? Only by having been in there earlier and having done it."

She leaned back and looked up at the darkening sky and whispered, "That son of a bitch." She shook her head. "Lewis, if I had picked up on that any earlier—"

"Diane," I said, scratching at an itch on my left side, "you can't dwell on it. It's done. Everything's done. If Kennedy had gone in a different car in Dallas in November 1963, he'd still be alive today, wondering what the hell happened to the Democratic party. If Humphrey had another week to campaign, he would've been president in 1968, and Nixon would be a retired Disney executive. You can't play that type of game with yourself, Diane. It will only drive you to drink, or to depression, or to getting a job as a meter maid at the state park."

"Hmmph," she said, finishing her wine, looking off at the Felch Memorial Bridge and the channel that led to the Atlantic. "What could have it been, Lewis, that kept Jack Fowler burning so long that he responded so quickly when he found out about his sister? You would have thought he might have waited a few weeks to find out more, but it was only a matter of days before he started getting his revenge."

"Don't know," I said. "It's not often that we control events, control the past. A lot of times they control us. I'm not sure what was going on inside the mind of Jack Fowler, and how he did what he did, considering the type of guy he was, selectman and all. I'd leave it up to the psychiatrists and inmate advocates. They love to explain why men kill women because their mommies made them eat their peas when they were younger.''

She twirled the empty wineglass in one hand and gave me a sly smile. ''What drives you, Lewis?''

I finished off my own wine. ''What drives everyone? To do good things, and try not to pass on any hurt along the way. Though I'm not sure what the political establishment of Tyler might think, me having indirectly killed one of their selectmen. It might be pretty damn awkward for me the next few years. Lucky I don't write for a newspaper.''

Diane laughed and said, ''I talked to Betsy Tyler myself, Lewis, and about the only thing she's worried about is that the misguided voters of Tyler somehow end up electing a liberal during the special election this summer to fill Jack's seat. On the board, she doesn't like the idea of being a minority.''

''Who would?''

That brought another laugh and she said, ''Will there be a column in *Shoreline* about this one, Lewis?''

I stood up and stretched my legs and said, ''You know, there just might be. I wasn't sure about doing a column about this when I started, but there's a lot of good stuff here, though it'd be hard to keep it short enough for the magazine.''

''I'm sure you'll do fine.'' She got up and we packed away some of the dishes and I zipped up my knapsack and Diane looked at me one more time and said, ''There's many a time that I don't know who you are, Lewis Cole. I know damn little of where you came from and how you ended up here.''

I said, ''I'm still trying to find that out myself.''

In a while we motored back to the dock and as we were walking to her condo unit, she said, ''I hate to be a bitch hostess, but I have someone coming by and . . .''

''And you don't particularly want a threesome.''

She smiled, swinging a light pink duffel bag in her hand. ''Not this time, Lewis.''

''Let me guess. One Kara Miles coming by?''

"Good guess." Diane took a breath and said, "She wants to try something a little less demanding. Not as much time or commitment on my part. Less stifling. So I'm open to that. We'll see. A lot of times, you just have to do the best you can with the chances you get."

"Not a bad line, Diane. That sounds nice, and don't worry about being a bad hostess. I also have to see someone else tonight."

We stood in the lights of her condo's parking lot. She had a shy, hesitant smile. I leaned forward and kissed her for a moment, and she returned it with a slight pressure of her own and broke away and said quietly, "I usually hate to kiss men, but in your case, I'll make an exception."

"Thanks," I said.

"Thanks for the kiss?" she asked.

"No. Thanks for making the exception."

An hour later I met Felix Tinios in the lounge of the Lady Manor House in North Tyler, near the harbor for the town of Wallis. As before, he was sitting in the lounge in one of the white wicker chairs, his back to a wall. The French doors were open and the overhead fans were slowly twirling, and as I walked past the piano player, she smiled at me and then turned her eyes away. There were three single-dollar bills in the brandy glass and a fifty, so I guessed Felix had been busy for the past few minutes. Her red hair was done in a French braid that fell across the light tan of her back, which was sprinkled with a few freckles.

I sat down in one of the floral-cushioned chairs and Felix handed over a Molson's to me and said, "You're walking pretty good for a man who took a round in his leg."

"Thanks," I said, picking up the Molson's and taking a long swallow. "You can thank Exonia Hospital for that—they do good work. Besides, I didn't really take a round, Felix. Looks more like I caught a piece of scrap wood or metal as I was running through the marshes. Sorry. No romantic story for later on."

He winked as if he believed my lie and picked up a glass with ice cubes and clear liquid. "A pity. There's something invigorating about going ahead with things after a bullet wound's been healed. Everything's a challenge, to see if you can enjoy things and do your job, right after someone did his damndest to hurt you or put you away."

"Cheerful thoughts, Felix." I turned and glanced at the piano player and saw that she was looking our way, and I said, "Speaking of invigorating, have you been taking piano lessons these past few days?"

He chuckled. "Maybe I have. Her name is Fiona, and she's a high school music teacher who plays piano here in the summer. You know, there's something decadent and special about doing it with a schoolteacher."

I took another swallow of ale. "I wouldn't know."

Felix laughed again and crossed his legs and said, "You should get the opportunity to learn. But in the meantime, let's talk about debts, Lewis."

"Why the hell not."

He hunched forward on the table and said, "I still owe you five grand for when you bailed me out this week, Lewis. And I appreciate the heat you took and the quiet way you went around the business. Near as I could tell, no one I've done work for ever found out."

"So far, sounds pretty good, Felix," I said, scratching at my left side.

"So." Still hunched over, he glanced both ways, looking for a moment like a football player in a crouch, holding a football in his arms, ready to blast through a line of players. "There's the other matter, too, you know, between the two of us."

I rubbed a thumb across the top of my bottle of ale. "About the protection for my house."

He nodded, smiling. "Right. That was both expensive and

extensive work, Lewis, and it all played out for the best. Right? House is still standing. Range Rover is still running. Now, normally, the cost of such day and night security's pretty high, Lewis, but what you did for me, well, here's the deal. When my assault rap goes to court, you'll be getting your bail money back. When that happens, just send the money over to me, and we'll be even. It'll just be like a swap, a——"

I raised my Molson to him, winked. "No deal, Felix."

He looked like he was beginning to choke. "What do you mean, no deal?"

It was my turn to shrug. "No deal, and I owe you squat. In fact, you owe me, for misrepresentation. You were supposed to have someone there, watching my house, protecting me and my property. A couple of nights ago I came home and had a nice face-to-face with Derek Cooney. Now, if a Girl Scout had shown up with some cookies, that I could understand. But I don't understand how Derek Cooney could've slipped by. Luckily, for all of us, all we did was chat and tell stories to each other."

Felix's eyes looked like they were contracting, like a couple of neutron stars, and he murmured, "That little——"

"That little whatever happens to be a cousin of Derek Cooney's, which is why he let him on my property. Remember that the next time, Felix. Check your references. Right now I think you owe me something, and I think by amazing coincidence it's about equal to that bail amount. Five grand."

The ale was nice and cold and the piano music seemed to reach right through my ears and strum at something that was dear to me, and I had a contented smile on my face as Felix Tinios reached into his coat pocket, took out a checkbook and fountain pen, and wrote me a check drawn on the First National Bank of Porter, not once expressing any mood or emotion. But right about then, I would have hated to be Derek Cooney's cousin for the next forty-eight hours.

I folded the check and shoved it in a pants pocket and said, "You're not mad, are you, Felix?"

"Hmmph." He swirled the ice in his drink and said, "I still feel like I'm getting cheated, and I don't like it."

"Just look at it as having the good guys winning one this time," I said. "Both here and out on the marshes."

"Hah," he said, scowling and looking out the open doors, where the lights of the harbor seemed to sway in the breeze. "Read your newspapers, Lewis. There's an awful shortage of good guys out there. It's mostly guys with different shades of gray and different ways of dealing with things. Just like you and me. And one word of congratulations, Lewis. I have a pretty good sense of what you did out there on the marsh. I know the cops want to believe that ol' Jack Fowler merely tripped and fell and impaled himself while you were huddling in the marshwater, but I got a good feeling that you had something to do with it."

"You do, do you? Any evidence of this? Any photographs?"

He smirked. "Nope. Just knowing you and the way you do things. With your gun at the bottom of the harbor and with that idiot chasing you, I'm sure you came up with something creative. Just a feeling of mine, Lewis, but I'm sure I'm right."

"All this talk about feelings, Felix, I'm beginning to believe you're from Southern California, and not the North End."

He smiled. "How do you like being in my world now, Lewis? Working and running in the shadows, just over the line, sometimes stepping over, sometimes stepping back?"

I finished my beer. "Felix, give it a rest. I'm not in your world."

He shrugged, picked up his drink. "Like it or not, you're here. Might as well get used to it."

I turned my back on him and looked at Fiona. "I'd rather listen to the music."

27

WHEN I WAS SURE SHE WAS SLEEPING I SOFTLY got out of my bed, and I stood there, nude in the starlight, just listening to her gentle breathing, imagining that I could hear the sounds of dust motes striking the hardwood floor around us. Though it was night there was enough light from the stars and the waning moon to illuminate my bedroom, and her shape was quite visible, huddled under a single sheet on my old bed. The room and the house were quiet, and save for the sounds of her breathing and the ocean waves outside, there was nothing there that should have disturbed me.

In the pale light I made out our clothes in a pile on the floor next to my antique four-poster. On the far nightstand were the glowing red numerals of a clock radio, two empty wineglasses, and a puddle of wax where a candle used to be. Underneath the bed was my 12-gauge Remington, but I was sure I wouldn't need it this night. No, not tonight. But still, having it there made me feel comfortable, and comfort has been something I've prized these past few years.

I walked over to the sliding door that led to the small second-floor deck and slid it open, conscious of not making much noise, leaving the screen door shut. Near the door was my reflecting telescope, squatting on its black tripod, but I left it there. I moved forward against the screen and looked out at the stars and the thin crescent moon and the rolling, curving waves of the Atlantic, and to the south, the lights and homes of Weymouth's Point. Through the mesh of the screen I felt a faint breeze over my skin. I looked over at her, to make sure she was still sleeping, and then I looked back out at Weymouth's Point, remembering where I had been that morning.

That Saturday morning I had taken my bicycle up to Weymouth's Point and eventually made it to the front porch of Alice Crenshaw's house, and Alice was there on the porch, sitting stiffly in a white wicker rocking chair with a drink in one hand and a cigarette in another. She had on white sneakers and a baggy pair of pressed jeans, and a red-and-blue striped shirt that looked two sizes too large for her. The sleeves were rolled up and her wrists were thin, looking like they were covered with scaly parchment. As expected, she had on her makeup this morning, but the lipstick was slightly smeared, as if her hand had slipped earlier in the day, and there were a couple of strands of light blond hair floating free from her usual careful coif.

I leaned the bicycle against the house and came up to the porch and stood on the stone steps, not bothering and not wanting to go any farther. She lifted her drink and took a sip, her hands trembling, and she gave me a firm nod.

"Figured you'd be up here eventually," she said. "To answer your very first question, I was at a second cousin's, up in Portland. I was fine, and I'm still fine."

I crossed my arms and leaned against a white pillar on the porch. "Nice answer, Alice, but that wasn't going to be my first question."

"Oh?" she said, a demanding tone to her voice. "I thought

that's what everybody wanted to know. Why crazy Alice was gone from her home without leaving a note or a message, and where'd she been these past days.''

A sea gull swooped over her large house, and then flew away, not making a sound. I said, ''No, not really, Alice. I knew you were all right. I just wanted to know why you ran, and why you didn't tell anybody what you knew about Jack Fowler.''

She turned away from me, her jaw set. ''What I knew was my own damn business. I might have been wrong about what I thought was going on, and that would have caused a mess. So I did what I wanted to do. I got the hell away from here and figured it would settle itself soon enough without me being in Tyler.''

''Sorting it out cost a couple of people their lives and a lot of heartbreak,'' I said. ''Damn near cost me mine.''

''Pah.'' This time she took a puff from her cigarette. ''From what I heard and read, none of them were very innocent. And you look like you came through pretty well. It doesn't matter to me what happened here, Lewis. Not one damn bit.''

She still wasn't looking at me and she moved only slightly when I said, ''Tell me what it was like here in Tyler, in 1953, when you were at Tyler High School, Alice. What happened to Jack Fowler's sister, and why would Jack have been angry at you, Alice? From what Betsy Tyler told me, you weren't part of the clique that Jack Fowler's sister belonged to, but still, he was furious. He tore this place apart and destroyed almost everything, looking for you.''

Alice slowly smiled and turned a bit and said, ''Looks like that's my secret, and the secret of whoever else is alive in my senior class. Looks like your magazine will have to do without old Alice Crenshaw's insight.''

I rubbed at my arms and said, ''Still protecting your dad the doctor, Alice, after all these years?''

Alice sat stock still and even though she wasn't moving, it looked like she was shrinking in upon herself. The stern set of her chin wavered and she looked at me and said, "Leave my father out of this."

"Can't do that, Alice," I said, thinking of the confirming phone call I had made to Betsy Tyler yesterday. "I remember what you said about your father, that he wouldn't turn anyone away, not a single family in Tyler, no matter what their problem. Well. Suppose those problems were unwanted pregnancies. Did your father perform abortions back then, Alice, when they were illegal? Was that the case? And is that what happened to Karen Fowler? Your dad make a mistake and, like all good doctors, he just buried this one? Any other mistakes buried out there in the marsh?"

"Lewis . . ." she breathed, crossing her arms, still holding her glass and her cigarette.

"So that's why Jack was going after you. He couldn't get back at the person he wanted, so he went after the next best thing. The daughter of Dr. Henry Gilliam."

Alice closed her eyes and leaned back in the chair and neither of us said anything for a while, and then she started talking, in a low whisper that got louder with each passing minute.

"Father was one for knowing right and wrong, or so he said," she began, rocking slowly in her chair. "I remember him telling me years later that it was only the luck of God and His angels that he hadn't been arrested during those years. Isn't it funny and tragic that a difference of a decade or two could mean a ruined career and a jail sentence? What he did back then is so common today that young girls don't even think twice about it. He performed abortions, Lewis, because he was a good man and a good doctor. He did them mostly for the poor women of Tyler and North Tyler and Falconer and other towns, who couldn't afford to go to other states or find some back-alley butcher to take care of them. He was a hero, Lewis. And can you believe we lived in such a time, Lewis? And that there are so many righteous people who want to return us to that time?"

She shuddered and opened her eyes. "So you had Karen

Fowler, in 1953, wanting to be popular and well liked. And for whatever reason, she hooked up with a foul group—Mike Dumont and Beth Lajoie, Henry Desmond, and a fella named Doug Ballard, who joined the army and later got himself killed in Vietnam. So in her simple quest, this simple girl got herself pregnant—I don't think she even knew who the father was. And one night she came to this house right here and asked to see Father. He saw her later in the week and that was that. I don't think Father ever knew what happened to Karen later on. Me, I think there was some complication and she panicked and something awful happened, and whoever was with her, they panicked, too, and put her into the marsh. That's all I can think of what happened, Lewis. I know my father. He wouldn't have done something bad to Karen Fowler."

I shifted my stance, still not wanting to join her on the porch. "Why didn't you say something when you figured it was Jack Fowler out there?"

She grimaced and said, "You have to keep true to your history, Lewis. I had to keep true to my father and the memories of what he did for this town. Think of the scandal, Lewis, if his name had been brought up in all of this mess. Think of what had been involved—my God, his name is on the Little League ballpark, the library, and the town flagpole. And there's my reputation, Lewis, and all the organizations I belong to. . . . So I kept true. Oh, I knew what was going on with Jack Fowler, but I knew he was so stupid that he'd eventually get caught. And whatever he did, well, I wasn't very popular in my class, Lewis. I really didn't like my classmates, and they returned the favor. Even now, I don't really care for them that much. If Jack went after them, that was fine. They probably deserved it."

I felt something awful in the air, and I knew I would be going very soon. "Keep true to your history, Alice? Was that it? It sounds pretty pathetic. It sounds like you were letting history control you, just like Jack Fowler did. Living and dreaming about the past, and nothing else. Ignoring or not caring what's next to you. Hard for me to tell the difference between the two of you, Alice."

She sputtered and tossed her glass at me. It missed, even the liquor, and the glass rolled harmlessly on the lawn. "You can go to hell," she said, her eyes blazing.

"No thanks," I said. "But I will just go."

I went back across the lawn and picked up my bicycle and in a few moments I was heading off Weymouth's Point, leaving Alice and her big house and her memories of her father behind me. She had tossed her drink at me. Not very original. But in a way, I wish she hadn't missed. It might have made her feel better, if only for a moment, and that was about the only thing I could have offered her.

I breathed in the salt air, looking out to the lights. A captive of one's past. Some accusation. I turned and spoke to the dark form sleeping in my bed. "Paula?" I whispered. "Paula? Are you awake?"

No reply. I crossed my arms, wondering why I was doing this, and I thought again of the faded memories that had driven Alice Crenshaw and Jack Fowler so far.

I whispered, "My name's Lewis Cole, Paula. You want to know my secrets? When I left Indiana University I worked for the Department of Defense in an intelligence group, working as a research analyst. I was there for a few years. I read. That's all I did. I read a lot and wrote reports, and I loved it. I avoided people, controversies, and causes, and I lived and wrote and started to love a woman named Cissy Manning. And then she and some friends and even an enemy of mine died in an accident, Paula. We were exposed to something awful in the Nevada desert. I came here, Paula, and now I wait. There's always a chance I might get sick again, that I may not come back. And in the meantime I want to do things. I want to make a difference. I want to protect this little turf of mine. Those are my secrets.''

Her breathing continued. I remembered that day when we had breakfast, and how odd it had been, to see a knife in Paula's purse. I had asked her about it today and she had laughed, saying, ''With all those bodies around, Lewis, I was beginning to get paranoid. So I decided a knife would make me feel better.''

Maybe so. I thought for a moment more and said, ''And Paula, I am so very sorry, but for about ten minutes this week, I thought you might have killed Lynn Germano and Henry Desmond and Oliver Mailloux. All for a story.''

I slid open the screen and walked outside onto the deck. It was a few hours past midnight and I could not understand why I was so awake. The stars were very bright and I made out the early summer constellations of Pegasus and Cygnus and Andromeda, and about me the night seemed peaceful, with the waves tossing themselves again on the sands and rocks below me. To the south were the lights of Tyler Beach and Weymouth's Point, and I looked again at the fine homes of Weymouth's Point, and the shape of Alice Crenshaw's house was darkened. I wondered what sounds and whispers were going on at that home tonight.

I took a couple of deep breaths. It seemed right, in a way, though I had gone down some odd roads and lanes these past few days. Though I knew Felix Tinios would disagree with me, in this case, at least, the good guys did manage to win, though it wasn't much of a victory. There was a family in Lawrence that was grieving and a couple more families in Tyler that were doing the same, and there were other lives that had been disrupted or moved or changed, and all for the sake of one June evening, when a man went to a summer cottage and found himself taking out his revenge on a seventeen-year-old-girl for something that had happened a lifetime ago.

Good going, good guys.

Not much of a victory, but I would take it. Tomorrow was Sunday, and as I always did, I would make penance for being alive when so many others were dead.

I turned to go into my house and back to the warm sleeping form of Paula Quinn, and as I did so, I scratched at my side again, and there was a sudden taste of defeat, sour and noxious.

For on my side, just above my old scar, I felt a lump.

The good guys had just taken a hit.